Praise for the Troy Pearce Novels

Drone Command

"A worthy military thriller series."

—*Publishers Weekly*

Blue Warrior

"A multifaceted political thriller that will delight tech junkies." —*Kirkus Reviews*

"Adrenaline junkies will be thrilled to know that Troy Pearce and his drone technology team are back in action. . . . Suspense lovers will find their hearts racing because of the abundant and creative detail. The plot is rich, and the villains are . . . everywhere."

—*Suspense Magazine*

Drone

"A brilliant read with astounding plot twists . . . Maden's trail of intrigue will captivate you from page one."
  —Clive Cussler, #1 *New York Times*–bestselling author

"Mike Maden understands that sometimes the most lethal warriors are those just out of sight. *Drone* is action-packed with cutting-edge technology and an unforgettable cast of characters."

—W.E.B. Griffin, #1 *Wall Street Journal* and
New York Times–bestselling author

ALSO BY MIKE MADEN

Blue Warrior
Drone

DRONE COMMAND

MIKE MADEN

G. P. PUTNAM'S SONS
NEW YORK

G. P. PUTNAM'S SONS
Publishers Since 1838
An imprint of Penguin Random House LLC
375 Hudson Street
New York, New York 10014

Copyright © 2015 by Mike Maden
Excerpt from *Drone Threat* copyright © 2016 by Mike Maden
Penguin supports copyright. Copyright fuels creativity, encourages diverse voices, promotes free speech, and creates a vibrant culture. Thank you for buying an authorized edition of this book and for complying with copyright laws by not reproducing, scanning, or distributing any part of it in any form without permission. You are supporting writers and allowing Penguin to continue to publish books for every reader.

The Library of Congress has catalogued the G. P. Putnam's Sons hardcover edition of this book as follows:

Maden, Mike.
Drone command / Mike Maden.
p.   cm.
ISBN 978-0-399-17398-1
I. Title.
PS3613.A284327D77   2015   2015017116
813'.6—dc23

First G. P. Putnam's Sons hardcover edition / October 2015
First G. P. Putnam's Sons premium edition / October 2016
G. P. Putnam's Sons premium edition ISBN: 9781101983324

Printed in the United States of America
1   3   5   7   9   10   8   6   4   2

Book design by Gretchen Achilles
Cover design by Eric Fuentecilla
Cover photograph © Mark Fearon/Arcangel Images
Photograph of the author © Jun Kang

For all the brave sons,
mine most of all

CHARACTER LIST

JAPAN

SANJI HARA	Vice Admiral, JMSDF
DR. NITOBE IKEDA	Director, NEDO
HIROSHI ITO	Prime Minister of Japan
KOBAYASHI	Yakuza boss
HIROSHI ONIZUKA	Captain of the submarine *Sword Dragon*
OSHIRO	Yakuza underboss
KATSU TANAKA	Parliamentary Senior Vice Minister of Foreign Affairs, LDP member of the House of Representatives (Nagasaki Prefecture)

PEOPLE'S REPUBLIC OF CHINA

GENERAL CHEN ZULIN	Vice Chairman, Central Military Commission
ADMIRAL DENG ZILONG	Fleet Commander, PLAN South Sea Fleet
FENG YONGBO	Vice Chairman, Central Military Commission
FENG JIANLI	Son of Feng Yongbo
ADMIRAL JI DONGSHENG	Fleet Commander, PLAN East Sea Fleet
HUANG YONG	Minister of State Security
PANG BO	Ambassador to Japan

| SUN QUAN | General Secretary of the Communist Party of China, President of the People's Republic of China, Chairman of the Central Military Commission |
| DR. WENG LITONG | Head, GAD Expert Working Group (robotic weapon systems) |

UNITED STATES OF AMERICA

DR. T. J. ASHLEY	Pearce Systems associate
HENRY DAVIS	Ambassador to Japan
DR. WILLIAM (WILL) ELLIOTT	National Security Research Fellow, the Hoover Institution, Stanford University. Ex-CIA, friend of Troy's dad
JIM GARZA	National Security Advisor
STELLA KANG	Pearce Systems associate
DAVID LANE	President of the United States
IAN MCTAVISH	Pearce Systems associate
MARGARET MYERS	Former President of the United States
GENERAL GORDON ONSTOT	Chairman, Joint Chiefs of Staff
TROY PEARCE	CEO, Pearce Systems
MIKE PIA	Director of National Intelligence
BREN SHAFER	Secretary of Defense
GABY WHEELER	Secretary of State

DR. KENJI YAMADA   University of Hawaii
                                 faculty, Pearce
                                 Systems associate

OTHER NOTABLES

AUGUST MANN   Pearce Systems director
                                 of nuclear facility
                                 deconstruction (Germany)

DR. LINH PHAM   VAST drone researcher
                                 (Vietnam)

TAMAR STERN   Former Pearce Systems
                                 security associate,
                                 Mossad agent (Israel)

ABBREVIATIONS AND ACRONYMS

4GW	Fourth-Generation Warfare
A2AD	Anti-Access/Area Denial
AAV	Autonomous Aerial Vehicle
ACTUV	Antisubmarine Warfare Continuous Trail Unmanned Vessel
ADPS	Automated Dynamic Positioning System
ASAT	Antisatellite
ASV	Autonomous Surface Vehicle
ASW	Antisubmarine Warfare
AUV	Autonomous Underwater Vehicle
AWACS	Airborne Warning and Control System
CAP	Combat Air Patrol
CIC	Combat Information Center
CMC	Central Military Commission
DARPA	Defense Advanced Research Projects Agency
DNI	Director of National Intelligence
EMP	Electromagnetic Pulse
FIC	First Island Chain
GAD	General Armament Department (A PRC/PLA version of DARPA)
GWOT	Global War on Terrorism
HGV	Hypersonic Glide Vehicle
HPM	High-Powered Microwave
HUMINT	Human Intelligence (spies)
ICBM	Intercontinental Ballistic Missile

JPALS	Joint Precision Approach and Landing System
LDP	Liberal Democratic Party of Japan
LRAD	Long-Range Acoustic Device
MAD	Mutual Assured Destruction
MIRV	Multiple Independently Targetable Reentry Vehicle
MOD	Minister of Defense (Japan)
MSS	Ministry of State Security (PRC)
NEDO	New Energy and Industrial Technology Development Organization
NKP	New Komeito Party (Japan)
SAC	Second Artillery Corps (PRC)
SLBM	Sub-Launched Ballistic Missile
STEM	Science, Technology, Engineering, and Math
TAD	Threat Assessment Display
TEPCO	Tokyo Electric Power Company
TNF	Technical Nuclear Forensics
TTO	Tactical Technology Office (DARPA, USA)
UCAV	Unmanned Combat Aerial Vehicle
UCLASS	Unmanned Carrier-Launched Surveillance and Strike Vehicle
UFP	Upward Falling Payload
USV	Unmanned Surface Vehicle
UUV	Unmanned Underwater Vehicle
VAST	Vietnam Academy of Science and Technology
VPA	Vietnam People's Army
VTC	Video Teleconference

AUTHOR'S NOTE

While many of the drone and related systems described in this novel are currently deployed, others are based on patent filings, prototypes, and research proposals. In some cases I modified or simplified their performance characteristics for the sake of the story. However, I'm confident that some variants of what I've imagined could soon be a reality.

Being unconquerable lies with yourself;
being conquerable lies with your enemy.

—SUN TZU, The Art of War

DRONE COMMAND

ONE

The bloodred flag with the five golden stars snapped in the crisp morning breeze. The national flag of the People's Republic of China was one of three held high by the naval honor guard, along with the flags of the People's Liberation Army Navy (PLAN) and the East Sea Fleet commander, Admiral Ji Dongsheng.

Two hundred Chinese PLAN officers and sailors stood at rigid attention on the fantail of the seventy-five-hundred-ton guided-missile destroyer *Kunming*, its ASW helicopter stowed away in the hangar for the occasion. The ship's skilled helmsman fought to stay in place as the vessel rose and fell in the long swells.

Admiral Ji's commanding voice cut through the buffeting wind. The handpicked crew stood proudly before him at rigid attention in their starched white uniforms and broad Soviet-style caps. The admiral's thick neck, powerful jaw, and broad nose had earned him the nickname Bulldog behind his muscular back. A shrouded object stood just behind him.

"A thousand years ago our ancestors crossed the

oceans of the world. We are not becoming a new navy, as the Westerners believe; we are the world's oldest and greatest navy, reclaiming our lost heritage, reclaiming our lost territories, reclaiming the vast resources of our waters from the thieving hands that stole it. We are the guardians of the blue soil of our homeland and will defend it with our blood and our honor.

"Today is a great day. Today we lay claim to that which was always rightfully ours. Someday you will tell your grandchildren and your great-grandchildren that you were here this day, on this ship beneath our glorious flag, taking another step in the long march toward our rightful destiny, our rightful place under heaven."

The admiral paused for effect, surveying the proud young faces before him. He twisted around and whipped off the linen shroud behind him. An engraved white-marble stele gleamed in the bright sun, thick and rectangular like a giant headstone. Admiral Ji nodded to four muscled sailors. They marched forward in lockstep and lifted the heavy stone off the fantail and heaved it into the rolling blue water in a geysering splash.

The admiral shouted out the words from the national anthem, "Arise! All who refuse to be slaves! Let our flesh and blood become our new Great Wall!"

The officers and crew shouted and cheered as they pushed forward to the end of the fantail, but the marble stele had already sunk beneath the waves.

Ji's weathered eyes caught a speck of gray in the faultless blue sky far above. A drone.

He smiled.

And so it begins.

TWO

I can even see the admiral's gleaming brass buttons."

Commander Hiroshi Onizuka had his eyes glued to the crystal-clear HD flat-panel display. A Sandia Multimodal Volant drone fed its images directly into his control console. Pearce Systems had just developed the integrated drone and sensor system, and installed it on the *Sword Dragon* for testing. Onizuka preferred his beloved periscope, but he was impressed with the expanded capabilities of the new electro-optical sensors in the retrofitted photonics mast married to the far-ranging surveillance drone. "But that's not what worries me."

Troy Pearce stood beside him, watching the same images. The former CIA SOG operative's black hair was flecked with gray—one for every bullet ever shot at him over the years, he joked—and the laugh lines in the corners of his world-weary blue eyes were anything but. As the CEO of the world's premier drone security company, he'd seen plenty of surveillance video before, but never while standing in a submerged submarine. "Looks like some kind of ceremony. A burial at sea?"

Onizuka pulled off his ball cap and ran a hand through his thick hair. At thirty-six, the handsome naval officer was the youngest sub captain in the Japan Maritime Self-Defense Force (JMSDF) and commanded one of its newest vessels. The diesel-powered *Soryu*-class submarines were the largest and most advanced Japan had built since the war, but the stealthy *Sword Dragon* carried only short-range conventional torpedoes and antiship missiles as befitting the JMSDF's mission limitations.

"The way he was flapping his arms? I don't think so. Definitely a ceremony of some kind, but not a burial." Onizuka's English was slightly accented, but perfect—one of the reasons Pearce was assigned to his boat. "Too bad we don't have audio."

"The Volant is too high up."

"Yes, of course."

"But we can get a closer look at the object they threw overboard."

This was a perfect real-world scenario for Pearce to demonstrate the extreme value of drones to the skeptical Japanese captain and, by extension, the JMSDF establishment. Pearce's covert assignment was to privately reassure the Japanese that the United States was willing and able to help the beleaguered nation find another way to defend itself against recent Chinese aggression without a massive conventional naval rearmament program. The prospect of Japan rebuilding another blue-water navy was too problematic for its Asian neighbors, especially the Chinese.

But tensions between China and Japan in the East China Sea had risen dramatically over the last few years, focused symbolically on what the Japanese called the Senkaku Islands, a collection of five small islands and three uninhabitable rocks situated in an area of vast new oil and gas reserves recently estimated at triple the original forecast. Both China and Japan claimed them as sovereign territory, partly to control the incredible resource wealth buried beneath the ocean floor. But Pearce was quickly learning that symbolism and history were just about as important as oil and gas on this side of the planet.

Onizuka nodded to the ensign at the Volant's control station. "Engage."

A thousand meters above the Chinese missile destroyer, the modified Sandia Volant slowed as it began a programmed descent. Within minutes, the delta-winged aircraft dove effortlessly into the water, the ailerons on its wings' trailing edges now serving as dive planes. It traveled much more slowly beneath the surface than above it, but the Volant proved highly maneuverable underwater.

Thanks to a partnership with MIT and the Pearce Systems research team led by Dr. Kirin Rao, the new, highly reliable spread-spectrum signaling technology deployed today made long-distance underwater wireless communications possible. Rao did her best to explain the physics behind it all, but underwater acoustics was beyond Pearce's reach. That's why he let her run his research division with a free hand. Rao's breakthrough was significant. UUVs could now be deployed beyond the limited reach of tethered communication lines and manipulated more adroitly than automated underwater navigational software, which was still in its relative infancy.

Automated sensors onboard the Sandia Multimodal prevented collisions with large underwater objects, but the Japanese ensign could manually direct it with a joystick, steering it via the first-person video perspective from one of the drone's onboard cameras, illuminating the dark waters by a powerful LED cluster. For the moment, the Volant steered itself, homing in on the *Kunming*'s location that it had fixed with its laser range finder before it dived.

It wasn't long before the multimodal drone came within a hundred feet of the engraved marble stone, nestled on the slope of a five-hundred-foot-tall seamount looming like a dark pyramid in the dim waters.

Pearce and Onizuka watched the ensign's video feed. The air was cool in the cramped but gleaming high-tech control room. Pearce tried to ignore his creeping claustrophobia. He wiped away a bead of sweat on his face with the tip of his thumb.

Onizuka barked an order in Japanese to his navigation officer on the other side of the control room. The navigator tapped on a computer screen, called back to his captain.

"Our Chinese friends apparently have found an uncharted seamount," Onizuka translated. "Now, let's see if we can get a closer look at that stele they tossed overboard."

The ensign eased the drone into the current closer to the stone. Electric-powered thrusters held it in place. The video camera zoomed in. The image was a little wobbly, but clear.

"My Chinese isn't so good," Pearce said.

"Nor is mine. But we use the same kanji. I believe it says, 'Mao Island. China. 1 May 2017.' It includes longitude and latitude coordinates."

"'Mao Island'?" Pearce frowned with confusion. "What does that mean?"

Onizuka laid a hand on the young ensign's shoulder. "Well done, Kenzo. Please forward that video to fleet HQ."

"Yes, sir."

Pearce had done his homework on the Senkaku Islands controversy before arriving. "I don't remember any Mao Island around here."

Onizuka's affable face hardened. "Apparently there is now. At least that's what the Chinese believe, according to that territorial stele." He didn't bother to add that the Chinese had scattered such steles over its vast empires as border markers for centuries.

Onizuka ordered the ensign to return the multimodal drone to the *Sword Dragon* for recovery. A portable launch/recovery module was installed in one of the forward torpedo tubes.

Pearce sensed the young captain's unease. He had every reason to be concerned. If Japan and China were going to start a shooting war, it would most likely start right here, and thanks to defense and alliance treaties with Japan, the United States would be dragged into the fighting quickly—an outcome the Pentagon wanted to avoid at all costs.

Pearce had signed on with President Lane before he was even elected on the strength of Margaret Myers's personal recommendation, and Pearce was eager to serve again. It was easy enough to agree to a private consultation with the Japanese navy. His company was the best in the world at drone research and operations, both civilian and military. It was a smart play by Lane to send him. This way, the American government didn't appear to be publicly bolstering Japan, but Lane could send a strong personal message through Pearce. He didn't mind being an envoy. The idea of not being shot at for once was fine by him, even if he felt like the submarine hull was closing in on him.

"So what good does it do for the Chinese to invent an underwater island? What can they do with it?"

"In their minds, they can now make new territorial claims—up to twelve miles, according to international law, besides the two-hundred-mile exclusive economic zone. But it means much more than that."

"Like what?"

"Your Global War on Terrorism didn't begin on 9/11."

"No, it didn't. It really began the day Osama bin

Laden declared war on us in his 1996 fatwa. He claimed we invaded the Muslim holy land and that we needed to be pushed back out. We just weren't paying attention to him at the time."

Onizuka pointed at the display monitor. "With that stele, it's exactly the same thing. The Chinese are making their own declaration about their sacred territory."

Pearce noticed that the control room had become eerily silent. The young crew was hanging on Onizuka's every word.

"So you believe it's a declaration of war?"

"It means, at the very least, that China is prepared to fight a war." Onizuka's eyes narrowed. The Japanese captain was six feet tall and broad shouldered, just a few inches shorter than the former CIA special ops warrior. "The question is, are you?"

Pearce felt the heat rise up in his face. It was an accusation, not a question. Anywhere else, he'd be tempted to punch the guy's lights out. He stuffed the anger back down into its hole. His mission was to smooth things over, not mix it up with the locals, insults or not. Besides, if he were Japanese, he'd have the same worry about America's commitment to its allies.

"I'm just a private citizen, Captain, not a government official. But I know President Lane well and, unofficially, I can assure you that my country will not abandon the Japanese people in a time of crisis."

Onizuka's eyes searched Pearce's. He nodded. "I want to believe you but this provocation tells me that China thinks otherwise."

A sonar ping smashed into the sub's hull like a sledgehammer. Pearce flinched.

"Splashes, Captain." The bespectacled sonar operator couldn't have been more than twenty years old. The crew scrambled back to stations.

Onizuka was unfazed. He smiled at his American guest, enjoying his obvious discomfort. "Waiting for the depth charges to blow?"

"Something like that."

Onizuka laughed. "You've watched too many submarine movies. That sonar ping was just the Chinese letting us know that they know we're here. The splashes my sonar operator just heard are only more sonar buoys breaking the surface of the water."

The radar operator called out, cool and professional. It seemed to Pearce that all the faces of the fighting men he met lately were getting younger.

"Aircraft. Speed, six-five-two kph. Distance, twenty kilometers. Heading, two-seven-zero."

"Chinese antisubmarine patrol. Nothing to worry about." Onizuka flashed a mischievous grin. "Unless, of course, they decide to fire their weapons." He gave his XO the order to dive a hundred meters down and deploy electronic countermeasures.

"I thought the Chinese weren't very good at ASW," Pearce said.

"They're not, but they're getting better, thanks to French sonar technology and the German diesel engines powering that guided-missile destroyer we just saw."

A light flashed on a nearby console. The captain frowned. "Excuse me, Mr. Pearce."

Onizuka picked up the phone. The *Sword Dragon* was still tethered to its communication buoy on the surface. He listened. His body stiffened and he bowed slightly. Obviously someone in authority on the other end. His eyes widened. Onizuka handed the phone to Pearce. "It's for you. The president of the United States wants to speak with you."

Pearce took the phone, confused. A series of clicks, then a woman's voice. "Mr. Pearce? The president is on the line. He'd like to speak with you, if it's not too much trouble."

"Of course."

"Troy, David here. How's everything on your end?"

Troy felt the deck diving beneath his feet. "In the middle of something, sir." Lane was technically calling him from last night. A thirteen-hour time difference. Must be urgent.

"Then I'll cut to the chase."

Lane filled him in. Pearce handed Onizuka the phone. "I've got to get back to shore. Now."

The captain hung up the phone then squared up in Pearce's face. "Is that an order?"

"It's an urgent . . . request."

Onizuka nodded, smirking. "Yes, of course. Urgent." He turned away and ordered his men to prepare to surface.

Another ping slammed into the submarine's hull.

Pearce swore under his breath.

So much for not abandoning friends.

THREE

Vice Chairman Feng was arguably the second most powerful man in China after President Sun, and he was thinking about Hawaiian shaved ice.

Feng was thinking about Hawaiian shaved ice because he was staring at the Wu-14 hanging in its gimbals in the giant test facility at Base 51. The hypersonic glide vehicle (HGV) was shaped like a nearly flattened shaved-ice paper cone. He'd like to go back to Honolulu someday, he thought, and get another shaved ice.

"It's magnificent, isn't it?" General Chen said. He was a missile man who rose through the ranks of the Second Artillery Corps, China's strategic rocket command. Feng and Chen were the two vice chairmen of the Central Military Commission (CMC). The CMC was primarily a Party instrument, a political device to maintain control of the generals and admirals, long seen as the main competitors to the Party's rule.

"Yes, it is," Feng agreed. The Wu-14 was the stuff of science fiction—push-button warfare in its purest form. And Feng had climbed the ladder of his ambition by shepherding the HGV through years of bureaucratic entanglements, engineering crises, and interservice turf wars. Unlike General Chen, Vice Chairman Feng had no prior military experience. He was the only civilian in the governing ranks of the CMC. (This wasn't unprecedented. Former president Hu Jintao was also a civilian vice chairman and used his post to catapult to the top of the Party hierarchy, a career trajectory Feng himself hoped to emulate.)

The two men stood alone in the cavernous test hangar. All of the technicians had been dismissed earlier to give them some privacy. Feng was the shorter of the two, though trim and athletic. Today the well-groomed vice chairman was impeccably dressed in a custom-fitted dark green Mao jacket and slacks, an anachronistic but potent symbol of proletarian power. The long tunic with its high buttoned collar and large cargo pockets looked like a soldier's uniform, which was why it had been largely abandoned by China's ruling elites in favor of Western-style business suits over the last decade. But Feng found the Mao suit useful when dealing with uniformed military officers like Chen, especially the older ones who had suffered under Mao's regime.

The Wu-14 was China's most advanced missile warhead and a true "carrier killer." Launched on top of the DF-21 medium-range mobile-missile platform, the maneuverable Wu-14 warhead could fly at ten times the speed of sound, nearly eight thousand miles per hour. No nation in the world, including the boastful Americans, possessed a missile defense system that could stop the highly maneuverable vehicle at those speeds. One Wu-14 launched from a DF-21 or, for that matter, a submarine launch tube or some other platform could take out an entire American aircraft carrier, the strategic center of America's power-projection capabilities.

Vice Chairman Feng understood that the Wu-14

wasn't just another missile capable of taking out a large target. It was what the Americans called a "revolution in military affairs." The United States dominated the globe and fought its far-flung wars primarily through its power-projection capabilities, which were entirely dependent upon its navy, and the heart of the United States Navy was its aircraft carrier battle groups. Before World War II, the battleship was seen as the predominant naval weapon, and few admirals anywhere in the world saw the potential of the aircraft carrier, in part because they couldn't appreciate the strategic value of aircraft operations. From Pearl Harbor forward, it would be aircraft carriers that would dominate the ocean battle space.

Until now.

The Wu-14 would make the twelve-billion-dollar *Gerald R. Ford*–class aircraft carrier, and all those like her, obsolete. That meant the Americans could be stopped cold virtually anywhere in the Pacific, opening up the South and East China seas to Chinese dominance. It meant the end of Taiwanese independence, too. The end of all Western meddling in Chinese affairs.

The end of the aircraft carrier also meant the beginning of China's rebirth as a great-power nation. Perhaps the greatest, given America's precarious economic and political condition. Ironically, China was now hell-bent on building four aircraft carrier groups of her own, beginning with the refurbishment of an abandoned Soviet aircraft carrier, the *Riga*, which the PLAN named the *Liaoning*. It was now fully operational after nearly a decade of work and training. At least the PLAN was smart enough to know that such carrier groups would only be effective against weaker naval powers like the Philippines.

"The Americans will withdraw from our waters the first time we threaten to take out one of their aircraft carriers. The East China Sea will be completely ours again, and rightfully so," the old missile general said. His green digital camouflage battle-dress uniform didn't accommodate the fistfuls of medals he'd earned over the years, though none in wars, of course. His last general's star was earned the new way—with cold, hard cash transferred to one of Feng's offshore accounts.

"The new gas and oil reserves we've found there will be ours as well," Feng said.

"Yes, those too. Most necessary," the general said. "For the future of our country, of course. There's untold wealth in those waters, is there not?"

Feng saw the hope washing over the old general's rheumy eyes. He'd seen it many times before.

"Yes. Untold wealth."

Vice Chairman Feng had risen through the ranks of the state oil ministry before joining the state-owned company, China National Petroleum Corporation, the largest energy company in China. Many of his relatives worked for CNPC as well and had amassed great fortunes from their endeavors. Feng had left CNPC several years ago to fulfill his political ambitions, but he kept his hand in the family business and an eye on all things gas and oil related.

"Of course," Feng added, "that wealth will be shared among the people in the most equitable means possible."

General Chen's eyes gleamed. "Yes, of course." Feng couldn't have said it any plainer. The general was already calculating the potential amount of his share.

Feng understood that the general and his cronies were as greedy as the capitalists they derided, and leveraged it to his advantage. Admiral Ji, on the other hand, was a notable exception—utterly incorruptible. And like most true patriots, Ji was deeply resented by pragmatists like General Chen. No matter. Today's deal cemented the uncomfortable alliance between the three of them, the last piece of Feng's elaborate puzzle.

The general laughed. "Those American bastards will run like scalded dogs when the Wu-14 smashes one of their carriers!"

Feng nodded outwardly, but he didn't share the general's enthusiasm for war. Wars were inherently unpredictable, and unpredictability was bad for business. Better never to fight them, if possible.

"I thought the supreme art of war was to subdue the enemy without fighting," Feng said, quoting China's most famous military strategist, Sun Tzu.

"The Americans don't believe the Wu-14 is fully operational. We may have to use it against them to prove it works." The general sneered. "It would serve them right."

"They don't believe the Wu-14 works because their hypersonic program is a failure." Feng resented the arrogant Americans as much as General Chen did.

"They forget that we invented the rocket!" Chen's eyes bulged. "Maybe it's time we showed them we know how to use them, too."

"I hope it never comes to that," Feng said. An actual shooting war with the Americans would be a disaster. Everything Feng hoped to accomplish wouldn't require one. Just the threat of a fully operational Wu-14 would be enough to knock the Americans back on their heels.

"Merely a conjecture," Chen said.

"Admiral Ji is waiting for my phone call. Is there any reason I shouldn't make it?"

The old general smiled, but not from happiness. His obsequious grin was a practiced defense against apex predators like Feng, spots on a lizard hiding in the shadow of a falcon.

"The transfer of the Wu-14 to Admiral Ji and the PLAN has caused great concern among many of my colleagues in the Second Artillery Corps. They fear President Sun may transfer all of our missiles to PLAN control.

But then again, they fear many other things about President Sun, as you well know."

"As well they should," Feng said. He was sympathetic to the military's plight and was, in fact, their staunch defender. President Sun's New Direction policy had embarked on a program to slash China's defense budget and cut its conventional forces in half, all in the name of economic development. In reality, President Sun and the Party feared a military coup, and rightly so. Having abandoned Communist ideology in favor of capitalist development, the Party resorted to jingoistic nationalism and expansive military budgets to bolster its credibility, but in so doing created a dangerous new political force among the nationalistic officer corps, Admiral Ji chief among them.

The Party also feared a popular uprising from below, fueled by decades of corrosive political corruption and gross income inequality. The New Direction promised sweeping anticorruption reforms to restore legitimacy in the eyes of the people.

But Sun's New Direction created enormous anxieties among the corrupt political elites who stood to lose under his anticorruption reforms, and seething resentments within the military ranks who viewed the impending defense cuts as treasonous. Vice Chairman Feng exploited those same anxieties and resentments to build a powerful coalition he believed would soon push Sun aside and win him the presidency. China was dancing on the knife's edge, and Feng was planning on picking up the pieces whichever way they fell.

"My colleagues in the Second Artillery Corps are fully prepared to cooperate with our comrades in the navy," General Chen said. But there was hesitation in his voice.

Feng checked his watch, annoyed. "It's time." He motioned to the massive doors of the oversize hangar. The two men began the long walk toward them. "Is there something else that concerns you?"

The general cleared his throat. "This so-called New Direction is naive, and dangerous for the army and the country. I'm a patriot. I support Admiral Ji's plan to secure the East China Sea and all that that entails. I trust that my support is seen as worthwhile."

Over the years, Feng found that the only thing his Communist comrades hated more than Western imperialism was personal poverty. The higher their party rank, the greater their greed. Or was it the other way around?

"There is no limit I put on the value of patriotism," Feng said. "Or loyalty."

General Chen smiled broadly. "Thank you."

The massive hangar doors slid open. Eight-wheeled troop carriers slowed to a stop next to a DF-21 missile carrier rig painted in green camouflage. The DF-21 was already in its tube, and the tube was secured flat against the trailer that was somewhat longer than an American eighteen-wheeler, which it resembled slightly. Dozens of sailors dressed in blue digital camouflage leaped out of the troop carriers, greeted by green digital SAC soldiers still securing the missile carrier and its support vehicles.

"You see? Interservice cooperation. The future of China is assured," Feng said, smiling. "The Wu-14 must be secured in its container for immediate transport." Once both were located at Ningbo, the Wu-14 warhead would be attached to the DF-21 missile.

"It shall be done immediately." General Chen shouted orders. SAC officers and troops thundered into the hangar toward the Wu-14.

"And the launch codes?" Feng asked. The last piece of the puzzle. Everything Feng had planned hinged on the launch codes.

"Yes. The codes."

General Chen reached into his shirt pocket for a thumb drive, but hesitated. The Wu-14 was an object of great power, and in the general's mind, that should mean great reward. Greater than even what Feng was promising.

But Feng's narrowing eyes bore into him. General Chen knew of other powerful men who'd crossed Feng and mysteriously disappeared. The vice chairman was a generous friend, but an even more dangerous enemy. And he could well be the next president of China. The old general fished the thumb drive out his pocket and handed it to Feng.

"Thank you, general. Your cooperation is essential to our success and the future of China. Your service won't be forgotten."

General Chen nodded. "I'm grateful."

Both men stared at the missile launcher, the other half of the combat system Feng hoped would never be used.

"You're certain DF-21 is perfectly reliable?" Feng asked. He'd read all of the reports and seen the test results. But if the missile failed to launch, the Wu-14 was useless. He wanted one last assurance.

The general nodded vigorously. "I'd bet my life on it."

You already have, you fool, Feng thought.

And the lives of millions more, too.

FOUR

The tee box on the fifteenth hole was a golfer's dream. Hugging Japan's rugged Pacific coast along the Izu Peninsula, the Kawana's Fuji course was long known as the Japanese version of Pebble Beach, but the fifteenth hole held a particular allure for avid, well-heeled golfers. It was postcard perfect in its beauty, perhaps the most picturesque hole of its kind in the world, and one of the most treacherous.

The tee box stood high on a hill overlooking the untamed Pacific Ocean crashing into the rocks below on the left. A lush manicured fairway nestled between majestic twisted pines beckoned like the Sirens, while a steep, unforgiving precipice stood a short distance away between the tee and the fairway below.

The course designer, Charles H. Alison, knew his business. The least hesitation or distraction in the tee shot here inevitably led to disaster. The serenity of the surrounding landscape demanded equal poise within. More than any other hole on the course, the fifteenth required both intense concentration and uninhibited flow. Golf was Zen, a game not so much of skill as self-mastery.

Many Asians believed that Tiger Woods's successes were due to his mastery of Buddhism and the lack thereof his undoing. The Japanese who could still afford to play the game on courses like this one—corporate executives, movie stars, yakuza bosses, and senior politicians—were crazy about it.

The titanium driver rang like a gunshot. The white Titleist golf ball lofted high and true toward the cliff edge, then arced effortlessly in a right-hand fade, landing finally in the center of the fairway.

Prime Minister Hiroshi Ito laughed. The gusting Pacific breeze tousled his famously wild silver hair, which complemented his sky-blue shirt and black slacks. He was sixty years old but still rakishly handsome. He was often compared to the Hollywood actor Richard Gere, but his avid passion for golf earned him the nickname the Obama of Japan.

"That kind of drive puts a lot of pressure on me, Margaret. My gender and my nation demand I rise to the occasion."

Former American president Margaret Myers snatched up her tee with a satisfied smile. She hit from the same tee box as the men. "What pressure? Just don't think about the wide blue Pacific on your left or the cavernous gully in front of you or the impossibly tall pines and you'll be fine."

It was a cool day in the high sixties, no rain. Perfect golf weather save for the coastal winds. Mt. Fuji, a prominent feature of the course, loomed in the distance, but unfortunately it was shrouded in cloud cover today. Myers wore a black Nike long-sleeve polo shirt and a matching golf skort and shoes, very subdued. She still had the toned arms and shapely runner's legs to carry off the ensemble smartly. She was more than fifty but looked a decade younger. Heads turned when she entered a

room—men and women both. Having been a public figure for several years, she was never sure if she drew attention because of her fame or her good looks. Modest to a
fault, she always assumed it was the former.

The one thing she didn't want to do today, however,
was draw attention to herself, another reason to wear
black. To help keep this meeting secret, Prime Minister
Ito's security team also stayed two holes ahead and behind them, clearing away the other players on the course
at all times. President Lane asked Myers to pay her old
friend a visit off the record and, as far as she knew, neither
the American nor the local press had gotten wind of their
private tête-à-tête.

"Seems to me, Hiroshi, that you were always the
better . . . putter."

Ito laughed.

Myers and Ito first met in Colorado. They discovered
a mutual passion for Kentucky bourbon and golf, which
her late husband had also shared. The future prime minister was serving as a trade representative at the Japanese
consulate in Denver when he helped arrange Myers's first
business deal in Japan, just a year before her husband was
killed by a drunk driver. Her husband's needless death at
the hands of a repeat offender thrust Myers into state
politics with a personal mission to stiffen the lax DUI
laws. But even after she was elected governor, she and Ito
played together as often as her schedule allowed until Ito
returned to Japan and ran for office himself. They managed to remain in regular contact over the years. Ito air-
mailed a hundred orchids from his private greenhouse the
day after her son's murder two years ago. Her favorite
flower. He remembered.

Ito stepped up to his ball and laid the custom-fitted
EPON driver head next to it. His fingers tightened on
the grip, then loosened, then tightened again.

"Bah! You're in my head!" Ito laughed again, stepping away from the ball.

Myers didn't say a word. She just kept smiling.

"You're more Japanese than I am, I think," he said with an impish grin. "You never attack your foe straight on."

"You know I'm not your enemy. We've been friends too long."

Ito pointed a gloved finger at Myers. "You see? That's exactly what I'm talking about. No self-respecting politician ever comes out and talks about politics directly. Maybe you should run for president of Japan."

"But Japan doesn't have a president," Myers said, playing along.

"But if it ever did, I'd be the first to endorse you. After all, you were a magnificent American president. Don't you agree, Katsu?"

Katsu Tanaka stood silent as a statue by the golf cart, his fingers laced precisely around the grip of his driver. His thick, well-groomed hair was perfectly kept in place. Wide shoulders and thick arms stretched the red polo shirt neatly tucked into his creased slacks, the collar buttoned up to the throat, hiding an old tracheotomy scar.

President Lane wanted Myers to meet with Ito, but Ito needed her to meet Tanaka, his most powerful political ally and a member of his cabinet. Tanaka was not only a member of Japan's House of Representatives but also the parliamentary senior vice minister of foreign affairs. Whatever Myers and Lane had in mind, Ito knew Tanaka would eventually play a key role.

"Madame President was one of the most interesting presidents the Americans have ever had." Tanaka allowed himself the slightest smile. "You're even more popular since leaving office than when you were in it, despite your low profile. Perhaps your popularity is because your reforms proved to be the correct ones?" Tanaka's English was Oxford accented owing to a study-abroad program he had participated in during his university days.

"The budget freeze was the most important reform I put in place. Congress still has yet to pass a true balanced-budget amendment, but neither presidents Greyhill nor Lane nor Congress has dared undo it."

"Amending constitutions is a difficult task, but sometimes necessary, especially when they are horribly outdated, don't you agree?"

Tanaka seemed pleased with himself. Myers had been briefed about him. In addition to his elected office, he also led the study group that wrote proposed legislation to change the Japanese Constitution to permit remilitarization of its purely defensive forces and change the strategic mission of the JSDF. Article 9, like the rest of the Japanese Constitution, had been imposed upon Japan by the United States after the war and technically forbade the Japanese from ever going to war to settle disputes or even maintain a navy, army, or air force. Recent "reinterpretations" of Article 9 loosened up some of the restrictions, but Ito and Tanaka were determined to rescind Article 9 altogether.

"It depends on the amendment, of course," Myers said. "The balanced-budget amendment remains a popular idea with the people, but the lobbyists are still too strong to allow the Congress to act."

"Of course, your 'no new boots on the ground' reform was also very popular. It seems isolationism is the majority sentiment in America these days. I wonder if your country will someday add its own Article 9 to your Constitution?" Tanaka grinned beneath his aviators. "After all, Article 9 is an American idea."

"Mr. Tanaka, I assure you, the United States does not want to impose its will on you in these matters."

"But it already has."

"President Lane only wants to offer his assurances and advice. We don't want the current tensions to escalate into a full-blown war with the Chinese, and neither do you. But aggressively expanding your conventional fighting capabilities is more likely to lead to war than prevent it."

"And so you would suggest we simply give in to Chinese demands? Let them make their false claims on the Senkakus?" Tanaka was referring to the leaked drone video of the Chinese stele ceremony. It made national news. Myers had seen it privately but was stunned to also see it on airport television screens after she landed. The Japanese public was livid.

"Chinese expansion must be contained. But President Lane believes there might be a third way."

"And if he's wrong?"

"Katsu! Didn't I just say that a good politician doesn't come right out and speak his mind? Please, no more politics. It will ruin our golf game." Ito shook his head, feigning disgust, but he and Tanaka were close political allies and friends. The two of them had forged a strong prodefense coalition that helped their party regain control of both houses of the Diet. Until recently, the majority of the Japanese population opposed remilitarization, but recent Chinese aggression had dramatically changed the political climate.

Tanaka laughed. "That's why you're the prime minister and I'm only a lowly legislator. I was never good at subtleties. Forgive me, Madame President."

"What's there to forgive? We're all friends here. You both know I'm also friends with President Lane, and not to be too subtle about it, he wants you to know that he stands committed to honoring our mutual-defense treaties and that we will stand with you in the face of any aggression."

"That's very reassuring," Ito said. "President Lane said

the same thing to me in our phone call last month. It would be helpful if he would make that announcement publicly or at least on Chinese national television." He laughed at his own joke as he addressed the ball again.

His grip tightened. The club turned. The ball cracked against the metal face and rocketed toward the fairway. It landed a yard behind Myers's tee shot.

"The wind must have caught it," Myers said. She found that male egos were more fragile on the golf course than just about anywhere else, especially when playing against women golfers. Good manners normally required that Ito and Tanaka allow their esteemed guest to win the round, but Myers and Ito had long since killed that custom on the fairways and putting greens in Colorado.

"The ocean winds around here are very problematic. But the truth is, I just missed the shot." Ito laughed. "Or perhaps I should have let you hit the ball for me instead?" He pointed at his ball in the fairway. "But at least it's safe, isn't it? That's the important thing." The prime minister picked up his tee.

"Yes, it is. That's why your plan to build a larger, more powerful navy isn't in your best interest."

"How does having a more powerful fleet make us less safe?" Tanaka asked. He lit a Marlboro.

"You know it will raise tensions all over Asia, especially with the Chinese. At best, you'll provoke an arms race. The Chinese will match you ship for ship."

Tanaka grunted. "Tensions, Madame President? The Chinese are always tense. It's in their blood. They were tense when they started the First Sino-Japanese War in 1894. They became even more tense when we defeated them." He took a long draw on his cigarette. "We haven't built a navy since 1945, and yet, they are engaged in a massive shipbuilding program despite our lack of naval assets. We only spend one percent of our GDP on defense, less than Bangladesh and Burkina Faso in percentage terms. Simple observation leads to only one possible conclusion. China is the only threat to the region, and it is the Chinese who are raising tensions now, not us. And if you don't mind my saying, a lack of U.S. leadership in the region isn't helping to lower tensions, either."

Myers bit her tongue. She didn't need a history lesson or a lecture on the current state of affairs. When she was president, she read her Presidential Daily Brief first thing every morning before she sat through the oral presentation with her security team, peppering them with questions. She remained well versed in global politics and, by extension, history. But her mission over the next few days was to win over Ito and Tanaka, not assuage her own ego. "The Chinese naval buildup is a response, in part, to their concern about our navy, which safeguards Japan and all of our other allies in the region."

Tanaka blew out a cloud of smoke. The breeze whisked it away. "And yet, even as the Chinese expand their navy, your government is cutting back on its ships and crews to pre–World War Two levels. And, of course, Beijing's good friends, the North Koreans, just acquired their first MIRV. With just that one missile, they could obliterate our largest cities within minutes of launch."

Myers had read the reports. The CIA believed the North Koreans were deploying the third-generation Chinese-designed DF-41, a MIRV missile with up to ten independently targeted nuclear warheads. That same missile could reach the continental United States as well. Whether the Chinese gave it to them or the North Koreans stole it through their own formidable cyberspying program was still being debated.

The former American president glanced over at her friend Ito, hoping that he would reel in Tanaka, who was pouring it on pretty thick. But Ito's mischievous smile told her that this was a deliberate game of good cop, bad cop.

Tanaka continued. "With all due respect, some of us fear that America is no longer committed to our security. But our enemies remain totally committed to our humiliation, if not our destruction. We want peace."

"As do we," Myers said.

"We can hope our enemies will give it to us or trust you'll never fail us. Or we can rely on ourselves. I believe the motto of the British Royal Navy is *'Si vis pacem, para bellum.'* When Japan is allowed to have its own navy again, it should adopt the same motto."

"Which means?" Ito asked.

"'If you want peace, prepare for war,'" Myers answered.

Tanaka grinned. "Yes. A most remarkable president."

Ito nodded. "Besides the security issue, Margaret, the truth of the matter is that building more ships will be good for our stagnant economy. You had your TARP and your quantitative easing to get you out of harm's way in 2008. A naval rearmament program will be a huge stimulus for us."

Tanaka adjusted the glove on his hand. "Don't forget, we've been struggling for twenty years since our financial crisis. We call them the Lost Decades. And if you don't mind my saying, a great deal of your economic activity is centered around defense spending. Why shouldn't we be allowed to create jobs for our people in the same way as well?" He flicked his cigarette away and marched over to the tee box.

Myers knew Tanaka was right. The Japanese stock market had fallen much farther and harder in 1990 than the U.S. stock market had in 2008, and they still hadn't fully recovered; in fact, the Nikkei had begun contracting again recently. It was also true that tens of thousands of

Americans were employed in high-paying defense-related jobs. That was one of the reasons the budget freeze had caused so many political headaches. In many cases, defense spending really was just another hidden form of welfare spending. Too many unnecessary military bases and weapons systems were still funded because congressmen feared losing their jobs to angry unemployed defense workers voting their pocketbooks. Of course, the purpose of the budget freeze was to weed out the unnecessary spending. Unfortunately, Congress still too often cut the most important programs in favor of the pork barrel projects that kept them reelected.

"Do you understand the significance of the drone video?" Ito asked Myers, as he stood next to her, watching Tanaka. "We have always been willing to share the undersea resources with China. They are the ones who want it exclusively." He grunted. "Typical of them." Ito distrusted all other Asians, especially the Chinese.

Myers lowered her voice, whispering, as Tanaka addressed his ball. "I'm surprised you allowed that video to be shown. It has only inflamed public opinion and made your negotiating position with the Chinese that much more difficult. That's not like you." Myers had a great deal of respect for Ito. Like her, he was a reformer. He wanted to clean up corruption in Japanese politics and even took the unpopular stand with his party to denuclearize Japan after 3/11—the Fukushima nuclear disaster. Even Tanaka opposed Ito's stance on the nuclear issue.

Ito shrugged. "I didn't allow it to be shown. Frankly, I thought perhaps your government leaked it. It was your man Pearce on the sub who recorded it."

"Troy Pearce is completely trustworthy. He would never do such a thing without authorization and, I promise you, President Lane would never do anything to embarrass you or put pressure on your government. You know me. You know I shoot straight."

Ito gently raised his hand to signal that Tanaka was taking his swing. The club smashed through the ball. It launched into the air like a mortar round and dropped ten yards past Myers's ball. His longest drive of the day.

"Where did that come from?" Ito burst out laughing. "You've been holding out on us."

Tanaka grinned. "Just lucky." He picked up his broken tee. "Did I hear the name Pearce?"

"Yes, we were just talking about him."

"I'm looking forward to meeting him," Tanaka said. "We were scheduled to meet tomorrow, but I was just notified by my office that he had to postpone. Very disappointing."

"I apologize, Mr. Tanaka. Something terribly important must have come up." Myers couldn't imagine what that could be. She and Troy had carefully prepared for tomorrow's meeting with Tanaka, the most powerful member of Ito's governing coalition. Two other important guests were also invited. "Mr. Pearce is also a friend of the president, and he would never want to disappoint him or you. I apologize for him on his behalf."

"I'm sure we can make new arrangements," Ito offered. "Shall we finish our game?"

"Yes, of course," Myers said. Tanaka nodded.

Ito laughed. "Good! Because I'm still three strokes ahead, and I intend to win this match. And as you both know, the losers buy the drinks!" Ito signaled to the three female caddies standing discreetly away, dressed in their traditional long-sleeve shirts, pants, and oversize hats, to bring the golf bags. Myers was glad they were allowed to use electric-powered carts to carry their bags over the steep hills. In the old days, Ito told her, the caddies were young women from local farms who hauled the heavy bags over their shoulders like sacks of rice.

Ito threw his driver into his bag as Tanaka wiped the grass off his club head.

Myers glanced out over the idyllic Pacific coastline, lost in the crashing waves.

Where was Pearce?

FIVE

NEAR THE VIETNAM-CHINA BORDER
HOA AN DISTRICT, VIETNAM
3 MAY 2017

Bullets smashed into the tree as Pearce and the others ran past it, racing down the brightly moonlit hill for cover. Automatic fire cracked behind them higher up on the mountain. Pearce felt the familiar adrenaline rush, the slowing of time, the heightened senses. Nothing new. No fear. Just an urgent desire to avoid a 7.62 slug exploding in his brainpan.

Not the mission he thought Lane had given him.

Pearce dove over a massive fallen tree trunk, the woman and the lieutenant right behind him, barking orders in a comms unit.

A sharp rock dug into Pearce's hip when he hit the ground but he barely felt it.

Pearce crouched against the ancient timber for cover as another burst of hot lead jackhammered into it. The wood trembled against his shoulder.

The lieutenant swore. Pearce didn't speak Vietnamese. Didn't need to. Saw it on his sweating face in the dim light. The ambush killed three of his men. Probably more.

And they were next.

The firing up above them stopped. The last gunshot echo faded.

The young Communist infantry officer instinctively turned to Pearce, his elder, an important man with a reputation. The worry in his face said that this was his first taste of combat. His searching eyes asked Pearce if it was safe to move now.

Pearce recalled the moments before. The tough Vietnamese infantry sergeant who had stared daggers at him when he approached the crashed drone on top of the hill. The small circle of enlisted men, rifles loose in their grips, ridiculously young, scanning the tree line, smoking cigarettes. Dr. Pham, his guide and translator, as pretty as she was earnest, introducing him to the lieutenant.

Dr. Pham nodded at the drone. "Do you recognize it?"

Looked exactly like a Predator. It wasn't.

"Yeah. The Pterodactyl. Chinese."

Above, a familiar sound.

Muffled rotors whipped the treetops.

Machine guns fired, shredding the three soldiers nearest him in a plume of blood.

Pearce snatched the woman's wrist and bolted down the hill.

Now they were stuck behind this log.

Too fast, too quiet, too disciplined for regular soldiers.

Special ops. Pearce was certain.

He ought to know. He'd been one of them, years ago. He and his best friend, Mike Early. God rest him.

The Chinese were good.

But back in the day, he and Mike were better.

Dr. Pham warned Pearce the Chinese might try to recover the drone on the trek up the long winding hill. He believed her. Apparently the lieutenant didn't. The lieutenant looking to him now for answers.

Pearce shook his head. His silence itself a warning. Not safe yet. Signaled with his fingers. Soldier talk.

They're out there. Hunting.

The lieutenant checked his illuminated watch.

What the hell. You late for a movie? Pearce wanted to say.

The lieutenant whispered in the ear of the researcher. She nodded. Leaned over to Pearce. He smelled her sweat. Felt the heat of her body. A strange intimacy in a dangerous place.

She whispered in his ear.

"He says we must leave now. He will cover us."

Pearce shook his head. Whispered in her ear. "Not without him."

She glanced at Pearce, frowning. Leaned in close again. "He says we must go now, so we go."

The lieutenant gave a short, curt nod. An order. His eyes, a plea. *Save the girl.*

Pearce nodded. *Okay.*

The lieutenant pulled back the bolt handle on his well-oiled assault rifle, slowly, quietly, not making a sound, then reversed it just as silently, putting a round in the chamber. Another curt nod to Pearce.

The lieutenant leaped to his feet and opened fire, spraying the tree line above them.

"Run!"

Pearce grabbed Pham's wrist again and dragged her away from the roaring AK-47. They made it a few steps. Pearce heard the familiar pop of suppressed fire.

The lieutenant cried out. Stopped firing.

"NO!" Pham broke Pearce's grip and turned back up the hill.

The young lieutenant was down.

Her brother.

The mission was now officially a goat fuck.

Pearce grunted and reversed direction. Laid a massive hand on her back and pushed her down into the dirt. Fell on top of her. Growled in her ear.

"Shut up. Stay here."

She nodded wordlessly.

Pearce listened. The lieutenant moaned ten yards up ahead. No other sounds. The birds and bugs had more sense than people.

Pearce bolted tree to tree, squatting low. His thighs burned. Knees creaked. He was too old for this shit.

But he loved it.

Saw Lt. Pham on the ground. Crept toward him.

A twig snapped.

Pearce reached for his pistol. Not there. The Vietnamese colonel took it back at the base. "You won't need it," he said.

Shit.

Pearce leaped for Pham's rifle, lying in the leaves, still charged. Rolled. Fired. Three shots. Mag empty.

But it was enough.

The Chinese operator clutched his throat, fell to his knees.

Pearce threw down the rifle, dashed for Lt. Pham. Heaved his light frame over his shoulder and ran like hell.

Pearce and Dr. Pham cleared the tree line on a dead run, the wounded lieutenant still slung over Pearce's back. Rotor blades up on the mountain behind them strained. *Pulling up the drone wreckage*, Pearce thought.

The low, hellish moan of jet engines blasted the night sky. Deafening.

A pair of Vietnamese twin-ruddered Sukhoi fighter-bombers roared toward the mountain. Seconds later, an eruption of boiling liquid fire. The night sky burned an angry orange, licked by a cauldron of flame, like a scene from one of Pearce's favorite movies. He wanted to shout, "I love the smell of napalm in the morning," because he was a sick bastard, but he didn't. Dr. Pham wouldn't get the joke, or if she did, she might be offended. Besides, he'd smelled napalm in the morning and he hated it. The stench of burned flesh and gasoline always made him want to puke.

Twenty minutes later, Pearce found himself in another movie scene. The lieutenant was lying on the chopper deck, medics at work. Plasma, Cipro, bandages. They moved slowly now, kept checking his pulse. A good sign. Leg wound. Like Daud's, a friend, long ago in another place. At least this one would live.

Pearce settled in his seat, soaked in his own sweat and Lt. Pham's blood. Secretly, he was pleased. Sitting in the helicopter, door flung open, watching the moonlit canopy of trees slide below his feet. He'd always wanted to visit Vietnam, the country and the war that had so defined his father and, by extension, him. As a kid, he had always wondered what his dad's war had been like. Now he knew. The experience had nearly killed him. Still, it was a gift.

He wondered what the old man would've thought had he seen his only son riding shotgun in one of Charlie's helicopters on a secret mission to help the communist government of Vietnam. Or running full tilt with a VPA lieutenant on his shoulder, saving him from certain death.

Not hard to guess. His old man would've shit bricks then punched his lights out.

Pearce smiled.

Dr. Pham fell into the jump seat next to him. Her long hair danced in the air rushing through the cabin. She still wore a canvas pouch slung over her shoulder. The Pterodactyl's CPU and a few other electronic components were stashed inside. She said something. Pearce couldn't hear her. He pointed at the headset next to her. He pulled on his.

"Thank you for saving my brother," she said, her voice an electronic whisper in the roaring noise.

Pearce shrugged.

She tried to tuck her flying hair behind her ears but it wouldn't stay. Even though she held a Ph.D. in aeronautical engineering, was a senior drone researcher at the Vietnam Academy of Science and Technology, and an obviously brave and loyal patriot, she was still a woman, and a beautiful one at that, even if she was smeared with mud and blood.

"We wanted you to see for yourself that the Chinese violated our national airspace and how they continually invade our territory."

Pearce nodded. "You knew they'd come for it."

"Of course. Just not when. You weren't supposed to be there when it happened, but you took so long to get here."

"Bad travel agent." Pearce couldn't explain to her that he had just come from a Japanese diesel submarine in a secret operation in the East China Sea.

Just then the helicopter swooped over a small town. Dr. Pham pointed at it. "Cao Bang. Very famous. Do you know it?"

Actually, Pearce did. Cao Bang was the site of the last battle in Vietnam's 1979 war with China, where a hundred thousand Vietnamese militia and border forces humiliated a much larger regular Chinese army in less than a month of bloody fighting. Pearce had written a paper on the Sino-Vietnamese war in one of his undergraduate courses at Stanford and studied the battle of Cao Bang intently in a modern warfare graduate seminar, a classic.

"So your military was here waiting for the Chinese to

arrive on top of that hill. A trap. They show up; you drop the hammer." *Just like Cao Bang*, Pearce thought.

"Precisely." Her bloodshot eyes stole another glance at her wounded brother. "My brother was in charge of co-ordinating the air strike."

"Don't worry. He'll be fine. He just won't win any dance contests."

Pham smiled a little. "You're a medical doctor, too?" All she knew was that Pearce was a very important person in the American government and a drone expert. Her superior in Hanoi instructed her to treat him with the utmost respect and mistakenly referred to him as Dr. Pearce.

"In a previous life, I had some combat medical training." He pulled his mic closer so she could hear him better. "Tell him when he wakes up that he did a good job."

"Thank you. I will."

Pearce shook his head. "He won't believe it, though. He lost his men. But tell him anyway. Tell him I said so."

The Chinese had been warring against the Vietnamese for more than two millennia, but for the most part, the Vietnamese people, through sheer determination and force of arms, had maintained a relative cultural independence from the Han warlords on the other side of the rugged border. But like Japan, Vietnam had island disputes of its own with the PRC, especially over the Spratly and Paracel Islands in the South China Sea and for much the same reasons as the Japanese: oil, gas, and national sovereignty.

Pearce had his own run-in with the Chinese a few years ago in the Sahara. Hunted two of them down. Exacted a brutal payback for killing Mike Early and Mossa, the Tuareg chieftain who had helped him find himself again.

"When we return to Hanoi, I would like you to be my guest at the academy. We now produce six of our own drone systems. I would very much like your comment on them." She was clearly proud of her country's achievement. He didn't have the heart to tell her that he knew their indigenous drones still relied on imported engines and propellers.

"I wish I could."

"Another secret mission for your government?"

Pearce smiled. Wouldn't answer.

"First time in Vietnam?"

"Yes."

"Then you must come back. It is not like this all the time. It is a beautiful country with friendly people."

That's what his dad had said, too, in rare moments of reflection. "I definitely want to come back."

"Please do. And please call me. My brother and I would be honored to show you our nation at its best."

"I just might take you up on that."

"Is there anything I can do for you in the meantime? Anything at all?"

Actually, there was. He explained the situation. Gave her the names.

"It won't be easy. I'll see what I can do."

"Thank you."

"It's the least I can do."

Pham pulled off her headset and leaned her head back against the seat and closed her weary eyes. She fell asleep instantly.

Pearce stared into the night, lost in a thousand memories.

SIX

He smelled lilacs in her hair.

Troy held his sister tightly, breathed in the cloying smell of the cheap shampoo. Marichelle's favorite. She was two years older than Troy and almost as tall. Best friends.

Troy let go. "Call me when you get there."

"Soon as we get to Grandma's. I'll call every Sunday, I promise." Marichelle was teary eyed and snotty. Dark hair and eyes like their dad.

Troy nodded. "Be careful out there, okay? Any guy messes with you, I'm gonna kill him."

She shook her head. "You can't protect me if you're not there, tough guy."

Her words stung. They were supposed to.

Thirteen-year-old Troy Pearce was just under six feet tall and a hundred and forty pounds, mostly sinew, with a rebellious lick of jet-black hair falling over his clear blue eyes. The sturdy rough-hewn cabin behind him was small but tidy. His grandfather's, on his dad's side. Troy had never met him. His dad said if you knew the cabin, you knew him.

Marichelle started to say something, but stopped. She wanted to beg Troy to come with them again, but it was no use. They had already fought about it last night.

He had to stay. Dad needed him.

She had to go. Mom couldn't take it anymore.

And that was that.

Troy glanced over at his mom leaning against a faded yellow Datsun two-door squatting in the dirt driveway. No hubcaps. A long way to California in a beater car like that. His mother was dark and pretty, with his same blue eyes, but tired. Her arms were crossed, a natural pose. She'd been on defense a long time.

He caught her eye. She smiled. More tears. She wiped her face with her hand and fell into the car.

He remembered her promise. "We'll come back when he sobers up," she said.

Troy knew she meant it. Didn't mean much, though. His dad had his demons.

The Datsun fired up.

"I gotta go," Marichelle said.

"Send me a picture of your surfboard when you get one."

"Yeah, right," she said, sniffling. "Take care of Dad, okay?"

"I will."

"Take care of yourself, too."

"I will."

"Promise?"

"Promise." He smiled. "I'll make another one, too."

"What?"

"I ain't ever having kids, I swear."

Marichelle laughed, wiping her eyes. "Me neither." She kissed him on the cheek one last time, then scampered to the Datsun. "Bye."

Troy watched the yellow car disappear through the

trees in a cloud of dust, heading for the distant highway. His heart sank.

He headed for the cabin, his feet heavy as lead. Pushed his way through the door. Saw his dad passed out at the kitchen table, his forehead perched in a plate of spaghetti, an empty bottle of Jack by his elbow. Another crumpled foreclosure notice on the floor.

"Didn't even say good-bye, asshole," Troy whispered, as he lifted up his dad's head and gently set it on the table. He snagged up the empty bottle and tossed it in the trash.

The hell of it was, he'd always wanted to go to California.

SEVEN

The teenage VPA private tapped the jeep's horn to clear his way through a knot of Chinese tourists crossing the busy street. Pearce rode up front with him, but the kid didn't speak any English and Pearce couldn't parley in his tongue, either. The Soviet-era UAZ jeep they rode in from the base brought back memories of Cella.

The first time he saw her was in the reticle of his night-vision scope as her UAZ slewed up a snowy hill in the middle of a blizzard in the Afghan mountains. He wondered how she was doing and where she was. He walked away from her once in order to serve his country in the Global War on Terrorism. It was a miracle he found her again out there in the Sahara all those years later. Strange that he would also rediscover his calling to serve his nation in the same desert with her. He loved Cella, but he loved his country, too, and he was a warrior. He wanted both. It broke his heart that she refused to follow him. She had to be true to herself, she said.

So did he.

It was nearly midnight in Hanoi, and Pearce was exhausted after a long damn day that had nearly gotten him killed. The VPA medics on the helicopter had checked him for wounds and injuries, but there were none save for the purpling bruise on his hip about the size of his fist. Sore as hell, but nothing broken. A hot steaming shower and room service was all the doctoring he would need, along with twelve hours of dreamless sleep.

Hanoi at night was the back lot of a movie studio, an eclectic anachronism clogged with extras and props from a dozen motion pictures. Even at this late hour, there were gawking European tourists with knockoff Gucci purses, peasant women in conical hats toting shoulder-pole baskets laden with fruit, street vendors squatting around open braziers grilling skewers of meat, traffic cops in pith helmets yelling at teenage hipsters racing past on their gleaming Japanese motor scooters.

The art department had been busy, too. The ancient yet modern city was an absurd pastiche of Communist flags and neon signs, pedicabs and BMWs, KFC chicken franchises and French colonial slums. It was all too much and too familiar to Pearce. He'd grown up poor in the mountains of Wyoming but wound up fighting in the sprawling urban squalor that fueled the Global War on Terrorism. Hanoi was like most other third world capitals he'd been in. He noticed an intense pride in the few Vietnamese he'd met so far. The poor Communist government of Vietnam had won the war against the mighty Americans and the French before them, but clearly capitalism had conquered Hanoi along with the rest of the country. A Pyrrhic victory, indeed.

Just when Pearce thought the side trip to Vietnam couldn't get any more surreal, his jeep pulled up to the hotel Dr. Pham had booked for him. It seemed like a bad joke told in poor taste. Or it was corporate marketing at its best. Maybe both.

The Hanoi Hilton was, technically, the Hilton Hanoi Opera Hotel, built next to the old yellow and white

French colonial opera house. From his top-story window, the opera house looked like a garish yellow wedding cake. The hotel itself was nice enough, comfortable and clean like any stateside Hilton with the familiar amenities, granite tops, glass shower, and, most important, a soft bed instead of a cramped and cold tiger cage. When he arrived, he resisted the temptation to ask the bleary-eyed check-in clerk for the Admiral Stockdale suite.

Pearce planned on using the extra day layover to recoup and process. The president's office had already rescheduled everything Pearce had painstakingly arranged back in Japan before he had even landed back in Hanoi. He owed the president a brief on his mission today, but Pearce's CIA training told him to assume his room was wired. His experience with Jasmine Bath taught him that nothing and nowhere were safe. Pearce would lay out the details of his Vietnam adventure to the president when he got back to Japan. There wasn't much to report. The Vietnamese confirmed what Lane already knew from his intel sources. China was pushing the limits of international civility, to put it mildly. And the Vietnamese weren't interested in parting with the Chinese hardware that Dr. Pham had retrieved from the crash site. It was all probably stolen American technology anyway.

A quiet and efficient room service had set his covered food tray on the dining table by the time Pearce emerged from the steaming shower wrapped in a buttery soft but undersize microfiber bathrobe. Pearce had chosen the fragrant Australian beef baked in bamboo for his entrée, accompanied by a bowl of pho chicken and noodles and a sweet taro dumpling in coconut milk for dessert. He could've ordered a bottle of Yamazaki 12 single malt from the bar for the price of a small car, but he'd laid off the booze since Mali. He went for the bottled water and green tea instead.

After wolfing down his food, Pearce stood on the balcony with his tea and watched the traffic below, still thrumming at the late hour. *Another city that doesn't sleep*, he thought. Another reason to hate cities. He missed his cabin in the woods. Wondered if he'd ever see it again.

His mind drifted back to the wiry VPA sergeant on the mountain and the way he had glowered at Pearce, hatred flaming his eyes. Pearce understood that kind of rage. It usually got the better of him, too. He hunted down and slaughtered Zhao and Guo for killing his friends Early and Mossa. He'd dropped many more bodies on a few other continents for lesser offenses over the years. Too many. Even if they were sonsofbitches.

He lost a lot of friends, too. People he'd served with, bled with, loved. Early. Johnny.

Annie.

He figured he was just getting old. It was getting too hard to keep losing people. It was a helluva lot easier to not let anyone back in. An occupational hazard.

Pearce wondered how many of the sergeant's relatives had been killed by American troops and planes, shot or bombed or napalmed into oblivion. More than a million North Vietnamese soldiers and Viet Cong fighters had been killed by allied forces. Tens of thousands of civilians, too, if not more. No wonder that sergeant hated his guts.

But then again, how many of his father's friends had been killed by the NVA and the VC? Those vicious bastards had murdered hundreds of thousands of innocent civilians during and after the war. The Vietnamese Communists were just as ruthless as the murderous Pol Pot regime and all the other killing machines that had marched under the red banner over the years. Lenin, Stalin, Mao. Mao, the bloodiest of them all.

Now America and Vietnam, former combatants and ideological enemies, were trading partners and burgeoning allies. All that blood and death apparently couldn't stem the tide of strip-mall capitalism. *Why did all those people have to die in the first place? Why can't the politicians cut out the killing and the bullshit and just get straight to the money and leave the rest of us alone?*

The bile rose in the back of his throat. Pearce hated politics. He suddenly felt the urge to bail out of there and hightail his ass back to Wyoming. He'd lost too many friends in Afghanistan and Iraq because of politics. Annie's death was the worst. And his dad. Agent Orange probably caused his dad's brain cancer, but it was the lousy VA hospital service that actually killed him.

But Pearce knew he wouldn't run away. He'd made a promise to Myers and Lane to serve again. More important, he'd made the promise to himself. He loved his country despite its faults, most of them connected to the idiots running Capitol Hill. Most Americans were decent, hardworking people. So were most Vietnamese or Iraqis or even Chinese, for that matter. In the U.S. it was the elected representatives and the high-dollar lobbyists and the Wall Street bankers who kept pissing in the punch bowl.

But Myers was different. He knew that the moment he met her. Thank God Mike Early begged him to come on board and help her administration. He quit the Global War on Terrorism because self-serving politicians made decisions that benefited only them and killed people he cared about, including Annie. Myers was a politician, too, but not like the others. She put her country ahead of her own political career. That was rare. That was worth throwing in with. Yeah, she was something else. Remarkable, really. Pearce was grateful that he'd gotten to know her better since then. Not many people could say they were close friends with an ex-president. Especially a damned good president like her.

President Lane was a good one, too. Myers had introduced them. It was easy for Pearce to throw in with him as well. Without public servants like Lane, the United States was doomed—the world's largest banana republic. Men and women like Lane and Myers needed all the help they could get from guys like him. "Ask not" was Lane's campaign theme. Lane was mocked and derided for it, but he really believed it. So did the people who had voted him into office.

So did Pearce.

He offered to lend Lane a hand. Wasn't sure what that entailed. He figured it would be connected to his war record, his drone expertise, so he wasn't surprised when Lane asked him if he wanted to revive Drone Command, but Pearce held off. Heading up a vast new federal bureaucracy sounded like slow torture. Pearce knew how fast and nimble he could operate as a private contractor. The thought of all of those self-serving congressional committee chairmen peering over his shoulder pining for pork barrel handouts made him cringe.

But Lane and Myers said they also needed some help on a political matter. Pearce demurred, said he wasn't a politician. Said yes anyway.

Duty and all that.

Standing on the balcony, sipping the last of his tea, he knew his real mission had barely begun and that he'd already nearly gotten killed doing it.

He could only imagine what was waiting for him out there in the dark. Didn't matter. That was the job.

EIGHT

Tanaka sat behind his desk in Japan's version of the White House, the ashtray in front of him crowded with butts. He flicked a gold-plated Dunhill to light another cigarette as his personal cell phone rang. He recognized the incoming number. A vice president of TEPCO, the Tokyo Electric Power Company. He took a long drag before picking up.

"Yoshio! How are you, my old friend?"

"I'm well, Tanaka-*san*. Sorry to bother you."

Tanaka didn't like the worried tone in his voice. "What's wrong?"

"That American was snooping around again. Asking more questions."

"The *Issei*? Yamada?"

"*Hai*. Dr. Yamada, from the University of Hawaii. I confirmed with an associate at the Ministry of the Environment. Unofficially, of course. Dr. Yamada's story checks out. An environmentalist group contracted with Dr. Yamada and his research team."

"More Fukushima nonsense?"

"*Hai.*"

Tanaka took a thoughtful drag. "What did Yamada want to know?"

"The usual. I assured him personally that our cleanup efforts were proceeding according to plan. He said he was well aware of our efforts. Very strange."

"Strange? How so?"

"He said he was friends with one of the foreign deconstruction crews. August Mann's team, with Pearce Systems."

"Pearce? Troy Pearce?"

"*Hai.*"

"Anything else?"

"No, sir."

"Keep me posted if this Yamada character shows up again. And keep your eyes on the Pearce Systems people."

"Is there a problem? Should I dismiss them?"

"Not yet. But have your internal-security people pay close attention to them."

Tanaka hung up the phone and stabbed out his cigarette. More Westerners snooping around the Fukushima facility. Either environmentalists or spies. Japan didn't need either, especially meddling do-gooders. Humiliating. Japan would fix the problems. His country needed energy independence and nuclear power was the key.

And this Pearce fellow. Ito informed him that he brought Pearce Systems in for a drone demonstration, but he wasn't aware Pearce was involved in Fukushima as well. He knew that drones and robots were being deployed in the hazardous cleanup. Pearce Systems had the best drones in the world, so it made sense. But this was quite a coincidence.

Tanaka lit another cigarette. Picked up the phone and called an acquaintance in the intelligence service. Time to find out more about Pearce.

NINE

The twin-hulled catamaran raced across the water at thirty knots, a decent speed for a sixty-foot-long research boat. Clear sky and calm waters made for a perfect demonstration day.

Pearce stood on the high rear deck behind the tinted-window wheelhouse. He could feel the pulsating diesel engines in the soles of his feet. The open deck offered a 270-degree view of the empty sea-lanes on all sides. Standing next to Pearce admiring the view was Vice Admiral Sanji Hara of the JMSDF, dressed in blue digital camouflage and dragging on a cigarette. The short, barrel-chested Hara was an outspoken proponent for constitutional reform and naval rearmament, one of the few JMSDF flag officers to openly side with the Ito administration on these controversial issues. His recently published best-selling book, *The Rise of the Red Khans*, warned against China's insatiable territorial ambitions, chronicling its ancient lust to possess the Japanese islands since the time of the Mongol empire. Winning him over to Lane's perspective would be a real coup.

Clutching the rail next to Hara was the very tall and

soft-spoken Dr. Nitobe Ikeda, director of NEDO, the Japanese version of DARPA. Ikeda rose through the ranks of a research department in one of Japan's largest technology conglomerates before accepting the NEDO directorship. Reviving the Japanese economy in the face of its impending demographic winter was foremost in Ikeda's mind, according to the dossier Pearce read.

Myers and Tanaka finished out the complement of guests for today's demonstration. The weather, at least, was cooperating. Towering cumulus clouds sailed like dreadnoughts across a sunny blue sky. The catamaran's powerful diesel engines churned up a sparkling white wake in the deep blue water behind them. A sealed launch tube angled up from the center of the otherwise unclut-tered wheelhouse deck.

"*Carolina Blonde*?" Myers asked. She flashed a mis-chievous smile. "Must be quite a story." She didn't know much about Pearce's former love life, but Cella was one of the most beautiful women she'd ever met, not to men-tion rich and brilliant. She'd seen her up close, admired her medical skill and personal courage. Knew all about her history with Pearce, too. Also knew the Italian doctor refused to follow him back to the United States. She was a closed chapter in his life, but no doubt there were many others like her in his past. That would make for an inter-esting read, she imagined.

Pearce shrugged, feigning innocence. He was glad Myers was comfortable enough with him to tease him. "Kenji named the boat, not me. You'd have to ask him." Dr. Kenji Yamada was one of his closest friends, but the illustrious marine scientist was a notorious rake.

"A beautiful day for a boat ride, Mr. Pearce," Tanaka said. "I don't suppose you brought along any fishing gear?"

Pearce smiled. "No such luck." Pearce wished he had.

He was as familiar with a fishing rod as he was with an assault rifle. He'd used both all over the world. Unfortunately, catching fish wasn't on the agenda today. At least not the kind that swim under the water.

"My grandfather took me out on his fishing boat when I was a small child," Hara said. "I've sailed these waters for over sixty years now."

"The Japanese people are always nostalgic for the sea, even if they have never sailed in a boat," Ikeda said. Pearce leaned forward to hear him better, his gentle voice barely above a whisper. "We are an island nation. The ocean is our past and our future. Nearly everything we buy or sell sails across the waters."

"Which is why we need a powerful navy to defend the sea-lanes," Hara grunted. "A true blue-water navy."

"The admiral is correct," Tanaka said. "The United States became a great economic power because it acquired great naval power, and it became a naval power because it was bordered by oceans just as we are."

Myers and Pearce exchanged a furtive glance. It was going to be a long day.

"The United States Navy is committed to the concept of open sea-lanes for everybody, especially our ally, Japan," Myers said.

"And our navy is undergoing its own technological changes. I hope to show you the future of naval warfare today," Pearce said.

Admiral Hara spun around, gazing up into the sky. "When will we see these drones of yours, Mr. Pearce? The morning is getting late."

"Funny you should ask, Admiral."

The other Japanese instantly raised their eyes, scanning the skies. Nothing. But Hara's eyes, conditioned by years of keeping watch, spotted something on the water in the distance to the north. He pulled his binoculars to his eyes. "A surface vessel, ten to twelve meters in length, coming in fast, straight toward us. Sixty knots at least."

Ikeda pointed excitedly to the east. "Another boat. Also coming fast."

Tanaka called out two more, from the south and west.

The camouflaged vessels ran so fast that half of their mono hulls were out of the water, waking like drug-running cigarette boats screaming across the Gulf of Mexico. "Chinese warships!" Tanaka called out. "What are they doing here? These are Japanese waters!"

Pearce's catamaran was only a few miles off the south-western coast of Japan, far closer to South Korea than the Chinese mainland.

The four boats sped furiously toward their ship. They were clearly on a collision course.

"Pearce! Take evasive action!" Hara barked.

"I'm no sailor, Admiral. I'm a grunt."

"Tell your captain!"

"Please, be my guest." Pearce nodded at the door to the wheelhouse. He hadn't given his guests a tour of the boat.

Hara charged over to the door and flung it open. He whipped around.

"There's no crew!"

"No, I guess there isn't."

Tanaka's eyes narrowed. Ikeda laughed.

"Troy—" Myers tugged on Pearce's arm. The speeding boats were less than a hundred yards away, their roaring engines rattled the air. Just seconds to impact.

Pearce smiled at her. "What?"

At the last possible second, each boat veered just enough to pass the catamaran fore and aft, port and starboard, spraying the deck with water. The catamaran's twin hulls sliced through the checkerboard of frothy wakes they left behind.

The Japanese ran to the rails, watching them each turn in a synchronous clover leaf.

"No pilots," Tanaka observed.

"Those are Katanas. One of the latest autonomous surface vehicles. They're fitted with anticollision software, so we were never in any danger. And, of course, we can take control of them at any time."

"Impressive," Ikeda said.

The admiral grunted skeptically.

The Katanas took up positions one hundred yards directly north, south, east, and west of the catamaran, assuming the identical speed of the much larger vessel.

"Our vessel is designated as a mother ship. The Katanas are synced with our control center. If needed, we could designate one of the Katanas as the mother ship or transfer control to an entirely different vehicle—air, land, sea."

"Why only four Katanas?" Hara asked.

"Just a convenient number for the demonstration today. In practice, you could sync dozens, even hundreds of ASVs together, depending on your computing and bandwidth capacities. Swarming algorithms give them independent combat-decision capabilities as well. And, of course, almost any manned vessel can be converted into an ASV."

"What is the advantage of deploying a mother ship?" Tanaka asked.

"If you want to operate continuously in open waters with smaller vessels like the Katanas, they'll need regular refueling, restocking of weapons, and maintenance. Also, the Katanas are multimission platforms. A mother ship can store a variety of weapons and surveillance systems, and hot swap them out as mission requirements change. Missiles, machine guns, cannons, you name it."

"But you have no crew!"

"In real-time combat, this vessel would have a full complement of human crew to carry out the tasks that automated systems still can't accomplish. But for today, it's just us. Please, follow me."

Pearce led the group into the wheelhouse where, ironically, there was no wheel. A single captain's chair with joysticks affixed to each arm sat empty in front of the command console—a bank of sonar, radar, and video monitors—along with communications gear and other sensors. Not all of them were active.

Pearce pointed at the captain's chair. "Admiral, if you would do us the honors."

The admiral fought back a grin as he mounted the chair. Pearce pressed a button on the command console. "You have the helm."

The admiral gently gripped the joysticks as he scanned the gauges and monitors in front of him.

"Feel free to maneuver the vessel. She's very responsive."

The admiral worked the joysticks. The catamaran made a decisive port turn.

"Please observe the Katanas," Pearce said. He pointed at the radar screen.

The Katanas moved in sync with the catamaran. Hara made another turn, sped up, slowed down. The ASVs matched him move for move. Myers noted the wicked Gatling guns affixed to the decks of each Katana.

Hara grunted his approval.

Pearce said, "I'm taking control of the helm." He pressed the button again, and the joysticks went limp in Hara's hands. The *Carolina Blonde* returned to autopilot and resumed its course.

"How does this vessel know where to go when it's on autopilot?" Myers asked.

"Think of it like a Google car. All you have to do is set

the GPS coordinates and the ship will do the rest, utilizing all of the same data points that a human captain would—weather, tides, winds, other vessels, you name it."

"So you are dependent on satellite systems? What if the Chinese deploy their ASAT weaponry? Knock them out of space?" Hara asked.

The upper deck exploded on Pearce's command with a rush of air as the pneumatic launch tube thrust a Switchblade drone into the sky. The command console's HD video monitor instantly kicked on. The catamaran and the four Katanas appeared on the screen in real time, wakes trailing their hulls.

"An aerial drone like the one above us now can be used for visual navigation or as a comm link to other vessels with satellite access. A drone like a Global Hawk could be used as an AWACS platform, too. UAVs and AAVs can also be linked to form comm networks if necessary, and high-altitude drones can perform like satellites. In other words, GPS is great, but it's not absolutely necessary to function."

Ikeda nodded approvingly. "This is exactly the direction NEDO is taking. We firmly believe that the future of commercial oceangoing trade will be vast fleets of automated container vessels, both above and below the water." He turned to Tanaka and the admiral. "With all due respect, Japan's economic future will be better served by a buildup of our commercial robotics capabilities, not combat vessels."

Tanaka's eyes narrowed. He turned to Pearce. "Dr. Ikeda was a compromise choice to head up NEDO. Some of us wanted it to follow the DARPA model, pursuing advanced technology to solve complex defense problems. Unfortunately, our party was forced to make an alliance with the NKP, and one of our concessions was Dr. Ikeda."

Ikeda nodded. "The NKP is a Buddhist party, Mr.

Pearce. We are much more pacifist than some of the militarists in the LDP." His soft voice now carried a biting
edge. "We believe the purpose of NEDO is to pursue
peaceful civilian applications of advanced technology. We
are not opposed if some of those technologies have purely
defensive applications. But war is never the solution to
any problem."

Hara grunted again. "That depends on who starts the
war. Who do you think will have more problems if the
North Koreans decide to smash Tokyo with their nuclear
missiles? Or Fukushima? Us or them?"

Tanaka barked at Ikeda in Japanese. Pearce assumed it
was a blue streak. Hara jumped in. Ikeda's whispery voice
rose to a near yell against Hara's sharp staccato tirade.

Pearce felt a headache coming on. He warned Lane he
was no politician. Not only had he not won them over to
the president's point of view, now they were screaming at
one another. He'd spent months setting up the demonstration. Begged favors from every vendor he did business
with, twisted the arms of those he didn't. Even convinced
a highly reluctant U.S. Navy to part with some of its most
closely guarded tech to try to pull off today's mission.

Myers saw the frustration in Pearce's eyes. His demonstration was clearly failing. A massive Japanese naval ar-
mament program would likely lead to war with the
Chinese. If Pearce could convince Hara, Tanaka, and
Ikeda that drones were a viable third way, war with China
might be both avoided and prevented.

Pearce's eyes pleaded with Myers. *You're the politician.
Fix this.*

"Gentlemen, please. I believe there is something else
to see," Myers said.

"Apologies, Madame President," Ikeda said. "But perhaps I have seen enough. Your autonomous capabilities
are impressive, but those Katanas are still vessels of war.

My agency is only interested in peaceful commercial technologies."

"If the sea-lanes are closed by Chinese warships, you
won't have any commerce!" Hara said. "For that, we
need our own powerful fleets."

"There are other ways to defend the sea-lanes than
building new missile cruisers and aircraft carriers," Myers
insisted. "Drone systems like the Katana can be deployed
for convoy escorts, antisubmarine warfare, mine sweeping, surveillance—"

"But these are still military operations in which people
will be killed," Ikeda said. "Preparation for war inevitably
leads to war. A man with a hammer always looks for a
nail."

Myers nodded sympathetically. "I understand your
perspective, Dr. Ikeda, but imagine deploying Katanas as
escorts against pirates for vessels delivering emergency
food supplies to places like Somalia. Or patrolling drone
ships could be used for search-and-rescue operations, or
drug and smuggling interdiction. And drone vehicles like
these could deploy nonlethal sonic technologies like
LRAD sound cannons or other crowd-control devices.
Painful, yes, but not fatal."

Pearce was grateful Myers was here today. They made
a good team.

Pearce turned to Hara. "Drone vessels would be cheaper,
faster, and more efficient in a wide variety of deployments,
combat or commercial. My company develops systems for
both, but my expertise is in the security area. Unmanned
systems will protect the lives of sailors who would otherwise
be put in harm's way. Autonomous and unmanned systems
are not only an alternative to conventional weapons systems, they are also the future of combat."

"And commerce." Myers smiled at Ikeda. "I admire
NEDO's emphasis on commercial applications. I'm the

CEO of my own software-engineering firm. I appreciate the importance of business. We seldom fight wars, but we conduct business every day, don't we?"

Ikeda nodded. "Exactly. And war is not necessary! But economic growth is vital to the nation."

"I agree. In the long run, robotics and other automated systems will prove to be even more disruptive in business affairs than they will in the military sphere. Military drones, however, will help prevent the wars that will allow commerce to prosper, and if needed, fight them, too."

The admiral's face darkened. "The Japan Maritime Self Defense Force is legally not allowed to have a navy. Our ships are only used for defense. But that is precisely our problem. We must absorb the blows of the red giant until he exhausts himself. That is not a strategy for surviving a war, let alone winning one. But thanks to the leadership of patriots like Vice Minister Tanaka, that might soon change. A powerful fleet is our best defense against Chinese aggression. I don't see how your little toy boats can provide enough offensive power to counter the Chinese navy."

"These 'toy boats,' as you call them, are just one example of what ASV technology can achieve. But for now, let's see what the Katanas might be able to do. Please look at the radar screen. I'm extending the range of the radar unit."

A new blip appeared on the screen a quarter mile away. "That's a solar-powered surface drone. It's currently used to measure water temperature. But for now, let's pretend it's a Chinese patrol boat."

Pearce approached the radar screen. He tapped the blip, then pressed a button on the console.

The twin 560-horsepower engines on each of the Katanas erupted into full power, throwing rooster tails of water behind them.

"Please watch the video feed."

Myers, Tanaka, and Hara hunched over the screen. Ikeda stepped back from the group, sulking. Nobody noticed the catamaran's deck had stopped vibrating. The *Carolina Blonde* was slowing down.

Within moments, the four Katanas swarmed the small orange research vessel, flat like the solar panels that powered it, floating on the ocean surface. Four Gatling guns opened up and shredded the flimsy device in less than a second. The gunfire echoed over the water as the boats turned to resume their picket stations.

"Not much of an attack or a target, I grant you, but you can begin to see the power of fully autonomous swarming. The computers can make faster tactical decisions than a human can. And in a gunfight, the fastest draw always wins."

"And if the Chinese deployed drone swarms against us?" Tanaka asked.

"There are counterswarming algorithms, too. Also, AAVs and ASVs can coordinate their swarm and counterswarm attacks from the air and water."

"One of the greatest threats the Chinese possess are their diesel submarines. How can drones combat them? They are becoming increasingly difficult to find and track," Tanaka asked.

"And the Chinese have now begun long-range Pacific patrols with their Jin-class fleet, also difficult to detect." Hara had been briefed by the U.S. Navy. China's newest nuclear submarines carried JL-2 SLBMs with a forty-five-hundred-mile range. If launched from the Western Pacific, those nuclear-tipped missiles could strike deep into the continental United States. The Jin-class ballistic missile submarines were now China's most lethal nuclear threat.

Pearce reached over to the blank sonar screen and

tapped it. It came alive. A sonar signature appeared a thousand yards behind them. "Looks like we're being tracked by a submarine right now."

Hara and Tanaka blanched.

"Please follow me to the rear deck." Pearce led the way. Ikeda came, too, with Myers right behind him. They all reached the broad lower deck on the fantail just as a trihulled trimaran AUV broke the surface. The *Carolina Blonde* slowed to a crawl.

"That, gentlemen, is the Leidos ACTUV, the antisubmarine warfare continuous trail umanned vessel. It can track a submarine for thousands of miles continuously up to ninety days—longer in the future—by deploying electro-optical sensors, hydro-acoustics, pattern-recognition software for navigation, and both short- and long-range radar. Imagine a fleet of those deployed at the mouth of every Chinese submarine base, and another ACTUV fleet in reserve to relieve each of them, handing off the tracks. You'd never lose sight of another Chinese submarine, including the Jin-class boomers."

Pearce turned to Ikeda. "You and my good friend Dr. Kenji Yamada will be glad to know these vessels limit the use of their sonar to avoid harm to marine animals like whales. In fact, our company has already been deploying AUVs similar to this one to track whale pods as they migrate around the globe."

Tanaka pointed at the ACTUV. It remained a thousand yards back. "Does that thing have torpedoes?"

"Not that particular unit. But, of course, the same AUV technologies can be applied to fully armed attack subs and ballistic-missile submarines." Pearce glanced at Ikeda. "Research submarines, too."

"It's all very impressive, Mr. Pearce," Ikeda said. "But please tell us, if drones are the future of warfare, why is your own Pentagon cutting back on drone programs?"

Ikeda's ingratiating smile was starting to annoy Pearce. He was right, though. Too many fighter jocks and sub drivers felt threatened by unmanned systems. He glanced at Myers again. *Bail me out.*

"Some of our generals believe that drone warfare is not as suitable for some of the missions they are currently planning for, and so they are shifting resources to other kinds of programs. But the U.S. Navy is still fully committed to systems like the X-47B." Myers was referring to the bat-winged, carrier-based unmanned aircraft, part of the UCLASS drone development program. Privately, she worried the navy was loading the X-47B up with so many noncombat mission responsibilities that it would lose its effectiveness as a UCAV—an unmanned combat aerial vehicle, its original mission design.

Hara sucked air through his teeth, pulled his cap off, and rubbed the back of his head, thinking. "I'm still not convinced, but it was a good try. You Americans always know how to put on a good show."

"Well, thanks, Admiral. I always try to entertain the troops. If you don't mind my asking, what is it that still bothers you?"

"To tell you the truth, I just don't believe you." The fully stopped catamaran rocked in the gentle swells. The Katanas had stopped moving, too, naturally. They bobbed a hundred yards away on the four points of the compass.

"What don't you believe?"

"All of these devices you demonstrated today. They are very impressive in peacetime. Nothing is at stake. But if we were truly at war right now? Where would you rather be standing? On a ten-thousand-ton guided-missile cruiser or on some plastic drone tub like this one?" Hara stomped on the deck with the sole of his combat boot for effect.

"That's a fair question, sir." Pearce motioned for Hara

and the others to join him at the rail as he pressed a remote-control unit in his hand, activating a sonar pulse from an antenna on the bottom of the catamaran's port hull.

"I value my hide and prefer to let machines do the dangerous stuff." Pearce motioned toward the water. Everyone glanced in the direction he pointed.

"For the sake of argument, Admiral, let's pretend for a moment that my 'drone tub' is a ten-thousand-ton steel cruiser."

The catamaran jolted as the surface of the water broke violently. A five-foot-diameter sphere burst into view just ten feet away from the catamaran like a breaching whale. The bright red sphere bobbed in the waves but remained in place, obviously tethered.

"That's our latest prototype of an upwardly falling payload. If that sphere was loaded with high explosives, it would function like a mine and explode, sinking our cruiser. Of course, a UFP can carry a wide variety of conventional, nuclear, biological, or chemical payloads. Each equally destructive."

"These UFPs can be stationed almost anywhere on the ocean floor, hidden and easily activated autonomously or on command, transforming the ocean floor into a kind of missile range, taking out any submarine or surface vessel that passes within range," Myers said. "And their cost is extremely low compared to the larger manned systems they're designed to take out."

"And so you would weaponize the entire ocean floor with these bombs?" Ikeda asked.

"Not necessarily. A UFP can have nonlethal applications as well. High-powered microwave payloads or even chemical EMPs could fry electronic components. In the case of our 'missile cruiser,' HPMs and EMPs would disable the missiles before they launched rather than sinking the cruiser itself. That way, you're killing warheads, not sailors."

Hara and Ikeda turned back toward the giant red sphere, still hotly debating.

Tanaka approached Pearce. "A most impressive demonstration today. Quite enlightening. But, I'm afraid, unconvincing to my colleagues or myself."

"It's not just a show. The fact is, the nation that leads in drone technologies will be the safest and most prosperous in the coming decades."

"You were full of surprises today," Tanaka added. "Perhaps you will indulge me in a surprise of my own?"

Pearce hated surprises. In his experience, surprises had a way of getting people killed. But he'd put off the powerful politician for a few days to carry out his ad hoc Vietnam assignment. Myers explained that Tanaka was offended by the delay in the demonstration, so Pearce knew he couldn't offend him again.

"Yes, of course. I love surprises."

Pearce wanted to kick himself. He hated lying. But the mission called for it.

Maybe he was becoming a politician after all.

TEN

The last bell rang and Troy dashed for the bus. Hadn't heard a word the teacher said the whole last period. Was only counting the minutes on the clock until he could make his way back home.

Longest bus ride ever.

He leaped out of the bus as soon as the doors opened, hardly touching the steps. Jogged through the snow until his lungs hurt from the frigid air, then kept jogging some more. When he finally got winded, he pushed on, hands dug deep in his coat pockets, handfuls of snow crashing into him falling from the branches above.

Dad had fixed up the cabin extra nice for Christmas. The tree was lit; the air smelled like fir. The place was spotless, too.

Troy pushed through the door. He could smell a red velvet cake in the oven for Marichelle and the meatloaf for dinner, his mom's favorite. His dad was cooking a lot these days. Clean and sober for seven months.

"You need any help?" Troy asked.

"Just don't track any snow in here," his dad said, salting a boiling pot on the stove.

"You got it."

Troy had already pulled off his boots and coat in the mudroom. He tossed his backpack on his bed, then headed back out to the living room to warm up in front of the crackling fire.

"How was school today?" his dad hollered from the kitchen.

"Great," Troy said. And he meant it. He made his way into the kitchen and opened up the fridge.

"Can I get something to eat?"

"Sure," his dad said. "But don't get too full. Your mom and sister will be here soon."

Troy smiled. Couldn't help but notice the grin spread all over his dad's face, too. He was all cleaned up and decked out in his best work shirt and jeans. Even wore an apron. Unbelievable.

He was really proud of his dad, the way he got his act together. Mom was right after all. Leaving his dad was the best thing for him. Made his dad wake up, make some choices. Even get some help. It had been a year and a half since they'd seen them, except for a few Polaroids Marichelle had sent. He wondered how tall she was now.

Troy grabbed a milk jug and filled a glass to the brim, then made himself a peanut butter sandwich while his dad tossed potatoes into the boiling pot.

"I said don't get full, son."

"No worries," Troy said, his mouth full of sandwich. He was three inches taller than his dad already and still not yet fifteen. A bottomless pit for a stomach.

"Soon as you're done, will you set the table?"

"Sure."

"Settings for four."

Troy grinned, his mouth full of mushy peanut butter sandwich. "Yeah, I kinda figured that out."

"Don't be a wisenheimer."

They both knocked around in the kitchen for the next half an hour.

Tires crunched in the snow outside the cabin. Troy and his dad exchanged a nervous glance.

"They're early," his dad finally said. A tinge of anxiety in his voice. "Dinner's not ready."

"But it's good that they're here," Troy said.

"Yeah, you're right," his dad said, smiling. "That's really good!"

His dad pulled off his apron and dashed out of the kitchen through the mudroom, Troy hot on his heels. His dad flung the front door open.

A state trooper's car was parked next to his dad's old truck. A grim-faced trooper trudged toward them through the crunching snow. His shoulder mic crackled with radio traffic.

"Excuse me, sir. Is this the Pearce residence?"

Troy's dad shifted uncomfortably. "Yes, sir. Can I help you?"

"Is your wife named Helen?"

His dad's face paled.

Troy's head swam. Barely heard the trooper's words.

Two hours ago.

Eighteen-wheeler.

No survivors.

ELEVEN

"You wonder why Dr. Ikeda and Admiral Hara were so resistant to your presentation?" Tanaka asked. "This is why."

Pearce, Myers, and Tanaka stood at the foot of the stone obelisk marking the hypocenter, the ground location of the atomic blast fifteen hundred feet above that devastated the city on August 9, 1945. A series of concentric circles emanated from the spot that also contained a cenotaph memorializing Nagasaki's dead.

Pearce stared into the grim afternoon sky. Imagined the blinding blast and the mushrooming cloud directly above his head, the pressure waves crushing the city, and walls of fire incinerating the bowl-shaped valley. Felt his skin tingle as if he could feel the deadly radiation still lingering in the air.

Tanaka had already shown them several of the other statues and monuments in the Peace Park, but the severe austerity of the hypocenter memorial was the image that most impacted Pearce. He found himself speaking more quietly than usual, if at all, while he walked the grounds. He'd felt the same way at Pearl Harbor and Arlington

National Cemetery, too. Only then, he felt both reverence for the dead and their sacrifices, and a profound sense of patriotism. Here, he felt only sadness for the civilian victims of an apocalyptic war.

Myers, too, resisted the temptation to succumb to the solemnity of the place, though she was clearly moved by it. That so many people died in a blinding, momentary flash was almost too much to comprehend.

Tanaka sensed the Americans' resistance.

"My seat in the Diet represents this city. My family traces its history back more than three hundred years here." Tanaka pointed at a fragment of brick wall on the radius of the far circle. "That's a remnant of the Urakami Cathedral, the largest Catholic church in Asia before it was destroyed by the Fat Man. Nagasaki was the center of the Christian faith in this country when it was obliterated."

Pearce wanted to ask, *And whose fault is that?* But he bit his tongue. He was a soldier on a diplomatic mission, not the captain of a debate squad.

"My maternal grandmother was praying in that crowded cathedral on the morning that Fat Man exploded, killing everyone inside. I'm sure you know the statistics for the rest of the city, the tens of thousands who died instantly, and the tens of thousands more who died of radiation, burns, and disease over the next months and years. What happened here so many years ago isn't a theory for me or my colleagues, or even a historical fact. It's a deeply personal event that changed all of our lives."

"War is terrible," Myers offered, not wanting to offend Tanaka. But she felt much the same way as Pearce did. You started it, we ended it.

"Yes, it is terrible. That's exactly the point of this monument. Unlike some of my colleagues on the right, I don't blame America for this tragedy. Of course, many historians now agree that the atomic strikes weren't necessary to end the war, but at the time, perhaps, it was not so obvious."

"There are other ways to kill," Pearce said, instantly regretting the comment. He was referring to the Rape of Nanking when Japanese soldiers killed perhaps as many as three hundred thousand Chinese—many of them innocent civilians—with just bayonets, rifle butts, and bullets. Unlike the Germans, too many Japanese not only glossed over their many war crimes, they also sometimes even denied them.

"Yes. Humans are terribly creative when it comes to destruction. You Americans have always been brilliant in your application of technology to war. I didn't bring you here to evoke any kind of sympathy for my people. But I don't think you Americans appreciate the true destructiveness of that war on my nation."

"I've seen war up close and personal," Pearce said. "You don't need to tell me how shitty it is."

"Yes, of course. President Myers told me about your battlefield bravery. I admire that more than you know. But what do your people know about total war? Your cities have never been burned, your civilian populations decimated. That is something altogether different."

"We don't fight wars to expand our territory. We fight wars to protect our freedoms and the freedoms of our allies," Myers said.

"Yes, you do. And you fight those wars with the latest technologies, whether drones or nuclear weapons."

"Once a war begins, you sure as hell fight to win it with everything you have," Pearce said.

Or should, he thought.

Tanaka nodded. "Of course. And so you are the first nation in history to launch a nuclear attack. But we were the first to suffer it. Like the Israelis, we say, 'Never again.' Dr. Ikeda wants to wish war away through complete disarmament. Men like him would even abolish the JSDF. Admiral Hara, on the other hand, wants to push it away through the prime minister's policy of proactive pacifism. Either way, both are reacting to the destruction of this place."

"Admiral Hara is risking another nuclear attack if he succeeds in pushing forward a massive arms race with China," Myers said. She wanted to say, *And so are you.*

"Admiral Hara believes in deterrence, just like the United States does. Why else does your country maintain the world's largest military?"

"Our military is as large as it is because we take our treaty obligations seriously, including the one we have with Japan," Myers said.

A group of uniformed Japanese schoolchildren approached the park. Tanaka's security people ushered them away.

Tanaka turned to Myers. "May I ask you a personal question regarding your time as president?"

"Of course."

Tanaka glanced back up at the obelisk that pointed at the darkening sky above them. A storm was on the way. "Is there anything you wouldn't have done to protect your people?"

"I'm a patriot. I love my country. Yes, I would've done anything to protect her. Still would."

"Which includes avoiding nuclear war, doesn't it?"

"Of course. Nobody wins in a nuclear exchange."

"And yet, American nuclear doctrine only prevents war by promising war. That seems irrational."

"Mutual assured destruction has served us well since the '60s. For rational actors, MAD works because the prospect of it is so terribly irrational."

"And, in your opinion, the American nuclear umbrella truly covers Japan?"

"We're totally committed to your nation's defense."

"Even to the point of war with China?"

"Of course. We're only as secure as our alliances. If we fail our allies, we fail ourselves."

"And, as president, you would have willingly traded Los Angeles for Osaka in a nuclear confrontation with China simply to honor a treaty commitment with my country?"

"If the Chinese thought otherwise, war would be more likely."

"But how does sacrificing the people of Los Angeles protect them?"

Myers thought about the war photos she'd seen earlier that day. Nagasaki a desolate ruin. Burned corpses, crushed homes. She thought about Los Angeles after a nuclear strike, or even Denver. Her precious Colorado forests ablaze with fire. It sickened her.

"The president is the president of the whole country, not just a single city, as well as its commander in chief. As much as I would hate it, I would sacrifice one American city to save all the others in our alliance."

Tanaka smiled thinly. "Yes, I'm sure you would. But would President Lane?"

"Without question. Why do you doubt his commitment?"

"I don't. But you understand why other Japanese might not be as confident as I am?"

"We count on the wisdom and influence of men like you to help us guarantee the peace."

"President Lane won his election with your help, did he not?"

"Not exactly. I was happy to advise him informally,

suggest political allies from both parties he could trust. But he ran his own campaign."

"He also ran on no new boots on the ground, didn't he?"

Myers nodded. "Yes, but what that means is no new, unnecessary, undefinable, unwinnable wars. Our alliance with Japan doesn't fall under that definition."

"May I ask you a personal question?" Pearce said.

Tanaka nodded. "Of course."

"I understand that you're still in favor of nuclear energy, even after the Fukushima disaster." Pearce glanced around the ground-zero monument. "Even after this. I would think Japan would be the most antinuclear country on the planet."

Tanaka visibly tensed.

"Yes, I understand your confusion. But it's quite simple, really. Unlike the U.S., Japan has few natural resources. We import all of our energy. Complete energy independence is an economic and strategic necessity if we wish to remain a sovereign, independent country. Only nuclear energy offers us that prospect."

"But a catastrophic nuclear event could destroy your country," Myers said.

"Admiral Hara intimated the North Koreans could strike the Fukushima complex with their new missile. That would be far more devastating than Hiroshima and Nagasaki combined," Pearce said. "Fukushima might be your undoing."

"Freedom isn't free. Isn't that what you Americans always say?"

"We say a lot of things," Pearce said. "Especially things that can fit on a bumper sticker."

"The bomb that was dropped here ended the war between us. Do you know what began it?" Tanaka asked.

"Pearl Harbor," Myers said without hesitation.

"And what caused Pearl Harbor? An American oil embargo against Japan. So you see, Japanese energy independence is as vital to your national security as it is to ours."

Tanaka glanced at the fading sky. "The storm is almost here. We should leave."

Pearce checked the sky. Dark clouds boiled overhead. Tanaka was right. The storm would be breaking soon.

TWELVE

The forty-three-foot-long blue and white marine salvage boat bobbed heavily in the choppy waters. Rising Sun pennants flapped on wires that ran the length of the ship high into the rigging, and an enormous Rising Sun flag flew on top of the heavy winch on the fantail. They all flapped in the crisp breeze like a flock of red and white gulls hovering over the ship. Patriotic banners proclaimed SENKAKU ISLANDS BELONG TO JAPAN! in kanji ideographs and hiragana phonetic script and English.

A half-dozen crewmen were near the winch and dive gear, guiding a submerged diver to the exact location of the Chinese stele so they could haul it up. The men all wore Rising Sun headbands, mostly college students and activists from the mainland. Locals crewed the boat.

A small aluminum skiff with an outboard motor ran circles around the dive boat, also flying colors. The driver in the rear wore a Rising Sun headband as did his passenger, who stood uneasily toward the bow, shooting video.

Patriotic music blared from a portable digital player at their feet.

A boat horn blasted in the distance. The men on the dive boat looked up. Someone shouted and pointed.

A red and white fishing trawler split the blue water against its high prow. Rusted and weather-beaten, the ancient sea hag had two dozen old car tires serving as fenders. Black smoke belched out of a short stack. Fishing trawlers were common out here. But this one was plowing straight at them.

One of the Japanese crew shouted and waved to the video boat to check it out. The driver gunned the big outboard motor and raced toward the approaching rust bucket. The little skiff bounced heavily in the waves, tossing the amateur cameraman to the deck. He righted himself on the bench and straddled it, clutching it tightly between his thighs for balance. He put his eye to the camera's rubber cup to keep the trawler in sight. He hit the record button, then the zoom.

The camera swept over the trawler's decks and rigging that were crowded with fishermen in slickers and coveralls. Each held some sort of crude weapon—aluminum bats, wooden clubs, hunks of lumber. The cameraman caught the faded white letters on the bow. A Chinese boat for sure.

The cameraman shouted to the driver to get back to the dive boat. The little aluminum skiff spun on a dime. The driver banked a steep turn in the water, nearly spilling both of them out in his panic. They got within shouting distance of the salvage boat, yelling out dire warnings.

The Japanese crew erupted in their own panicked shouts as they scrambled over the decks, looking for weapons or shelter. A lookout called out the quickening distance as the rusted Chinese trawler barreled closer. The men on the winch engaged the motor, raising up the diver as quickly as possible without inducing the bends. The captain couldn't start the engines. The spinning props would have fouled the dive lines or, worse, shredded the diver. He shouted orders at the inexperienced volunteers to hurry.

The Chinese trawler reversed its engines hard and cut the wheel sharply. The ancient hulk deftly swept sideways, running parallel to the dive boat just yards away.

The Japanese captain blasted his horn in vain, hoping the Chinese boat would push away at the last second. He wished he had an automatic rifle instead of the .38 Smith & Wesson revolver he kept beneath his bunk. He ran for it anyway.

The trawler's engines cut completely but the ship's momentum carried it forward. The two steel hulls thundered on impact, throwing one of the Japanese crew overboard and tumbling others to the deck, shouting in terror.

The Chinese fishermen leaped aboard the dive boat, laughing and cursing. They were large men with hard, flat-iron faces and feral eyes. They swung their bats and clubs with a practiced efficiency, cracking ribs, knees, and skulls as they swarmed the decks and flooded into the cabin and below deck. The few Japanese who offered resistance or even dared take a swing were mauled by the larger men, some taller by a foot—Mongols.

The Japanese volunteers fell to the deck when struck, balling up, trying to protect themselves from the heavy boots and clenched fists smashing their faces and kicking their guts. The crew who tried to hide were hauled out into the open and bitch slapped until they bled, and the few who made it below deck were beaten even more savagely. A gunshot cracked inside the captain's quarters. The few coherent Japanese flinched at the sound but the Chinese were unfazed.

Within ten minutes, the entire crew was subdued, re-
duced to a heap of quivering bloody worms writhing on
the deck. Radios and other electronic equipment were
smashed to pieces. Two Chinese went below the water-
line, disabled the engine, cut the fuel lines, smashed the
controls.

All of the Rising Sun headbands were ripped from
their owners and tossed over the side with a laugh, along
with the patriotic banners, as other Chinese crewmen
leaped from their trawler and secured the Japanese dive
boat with ropes. The rest of the marauding Chinese
scrambled back aboard their vessel and the trawler towed
the dive boat five kilometers away, dragging the hapless
diver behind it a hundred and twenty meters below the
surface like a baited hook.

The small skiff trailed on the water behind them, keeping its distance. The driver fished out the first crewman
who had been tossed off the dive boat when the ships
collided. The two of them barely managed to haul up the
furious captain, who was cursing the Chinese despite his
broken jaw after he had been thrown overboard like a bag
of garbage.

Through it all, the excited cameraman never wavered.
He caught everything on his Sony digicam, filling up the
flash drive, eager to upload the savage imagery on the
Internet as soon as he got to shore.

THIRTEEN

It was Lane's first trip to the Pentagon as president.

Hell, his first trip ever.

The enormous five-sided structure was synonymous with American military power. In reality, the seven-story building was 3.7 million square feet of office space connected by seventeen and a half miles of corridors. Its most important occupant was a civilian bureaucrat, the secretary of defense, who ran the federal government's oldest and largest bureaucracy, and the country's single largest employer, with more than two million active-duty and civilian personnel.

Big bureaucracy, big office building.

The most important room in the Pentagon office complex was the Joint Chiefs of Staff (JCS) conference room, long known as the Tank, located on corridor nine in the outermost E ring on the second floor (which is really the main floor) near the river entrance.

The legendary Tank was where the highest ranking flag officers of the U.S. armed services hashed out the most important security issues of the day.

Today was unlike most days in the Tank. In a symbolic

gesture, President Lane left the White House and crossed the Potomac in order to meet with the chairman of the JCS and the other service chiefs.

Ironically, despite their supreme military ranks, none of the service chiefs had any operational authority, including the chairman of the JCS. Only the president and, by extension, the secretary of defense, could order troops, ships, and planes into battle. Civilian control of the military was a central tenet of Western liberal democracies. Militaries were by their nature antidemocratic and, presumably, a threat to democratic institutions if left unchecked. Democracies were also peaceful.

Or so the theory went.

In reality, the DoD and the respective military branches were far more risk averse than their elected counterparts, especially since the failure of Vietnam. In recent years, it was usually the Pentagon that had to be dragged into war by presidents, not the other way around. The Pentagon prepared for war but, whenever possible, did everything in its power to avoid it, in part because the politicians often went into war without a clear sense of the goals or conditions for victory. The men and women who did the actual fighting and dying were loyal to the core but had very little interest in sacrificing themselves in unwinnable wars.

Despite their merely advisory role, however, the chiefs carried a great deal of weight with their respective services as well as with Congress. If they spoke, you listened, even if you were the commander in chief. Especially if they spoke with one voice.

Today they did.

The chiefs were concerned. War between China and Japan appeared imminent. And because of America's de facto treaty obligations and strategic interests, that meant war between China and the United States. A war that must be avoided at all costs. And it could only be avoided, in their opinion, by confronting the PRC with a significant show of force. This they all agreed upon. But that was about it.

Many urgent questions remained. The chiefs wanted answers and time was running out. The president had choices to make.

Now.

This was Lane's first foreign policy crisis. It would set the tone for the rest of his administration and communicate to America's friends and enemies around the world what kind of global leader the inexperienced young president would be. Khrushchev's perception of JFK's weakness at their first meeting in the 1961 Vienna summit led directly to the Cuban Missile Crisis in 1962, just a trigger pull away from World War III.

Lane's problem now was his continued policy of "no new boots on the ground." His critics feared this sent a clear signal to America's enemies that the United States was withdrawing from its strategic responsibilities—the moral equivalent of waving a red flag in the bull's face, if not a white one. But his opponents also knew the American people were tired of war, and "no new boots" was wildly popular.

Lane stared at the constellation of stars as he entered the Tank. As a former air force captain, his first instinct was to salute, but he resisted the ingrained habit. After all, he was the boss now. He was the first president since George H. W. Bush to have served in active-duty combat. But Lane still felt the butterflies in his gut. Nearly two hundred collective years of distinguished and accomplished military service sat in front of him. Four earned doctorates and eight master's degrees between them, too. Flag officers were notoriously political creatures, but these were also extremely serious people.

His decision to hold the line on the federal budget freeze initiated during the Myers administration didn't win him any friends in the room, either. Military budgets were frozen in place despite the Pentagon's endless clamoring for increased funding to meet ever-increasing global threats.

Lane was accompanied by Secretary of State Gaby Wheeler, Secretary of Defense Bren Shafer, and National Security Advisor Jim Garza. These were serious people, too, in their respective spheres. And political.

The JCS agreed to meet privately, without the usual crowd of vice chairmen, staff officers, and other "horse holders" in attendance. Introductions were dismissed, formalities set aside. Stout navy coffee was served along with tea and bottled water as the chairman took his customary seat at the head of the enormous blond conference table. The other chiefs sat in their flanking positions. President Lane took the seat on the far end, flanked by his civilian coterie.

Secretary Wheeler played video clips of subtitled Japanese newscasts, along with shaky handheld Internet video of the Chinese trawler's attack on the Japanese dive boat. Everyone had already seen them, but Wheeler wanted the events fresh in their minds. The Chinese had kicked the hornet's nest. Hundreds of Japanese marched in angry protests throughout the nation, among the largest and most violent demonstrations in the postwar period.

"The Chinese claim the Japanese attacked them first, earlier in the day. Claim the Japanese tried to ram them, drive them away from one of their prime fishing grounds," Wheeler said. "It's all bullshit, of course. Including the official protest they've sent to Tokyo."

"The CIA analyzed the video and identified at least two of the so-called Chinese fishermen as members of the

Ministry of State Security," Garza said. "A boatload of bad-ass leg breakers sending a message."

"It's a helluva message," Chairman Onstot said. He was a four-star air force general with a chest full of combat medals, badges, and ribbons, all earned the hard way. "The Chinese have staked out a claim and they intend to defend it."

"No one was killed, thank God," Wheeler said. She didn't add that the diver was still in critical but stable condition at a local hospital.

"It was an act of violence nonetheless. And probably the last one without bloodshed. The next step will be escalation," Shafer said. He'd already been through the ringer with the JCS earlier as they laid out their frank concerns over recent Chinese actions. The SecDef largely agreed with their assessment, but even the chiefs weren't entirely unanimous on a course of action, which was why he insisted the president meet with them today.

Shafer was a former chair of the Senate Armed Services Committee, the perfect person to bridge Lane's political and experiential gap. Lane was viewed by establishment Washington as a country rube from Texas despite his six years in Congress, armed only with boyish good looks, a second-rate state university degree, and an excellent combat record.

But it was the four-leaf clover shoved in Lane's pocket the old hands most deeply resented. Dumb luck had won him the presidency in their opinion.

If Senator Fiero's campaign hadn't been sunk by the mysterious and incriminating Bath leaks, she'd be the one sitting in the Oval Office today, not Lane. Fiero was a known commodity. Easy to work with. She understood how the game was played.

Likewise his presidential predecessor, Robert Greyhill, whose reelection campaign was doomed from the start thanks to the self-serving betrayal of his vice president, who was caught on tape recommending the execution of the American war hero Troy Pearce. Pleading ignorance of Gary Diele's crimes only made former president Greyhill appear even more incompetent and out of touch than he was commonly portrayed.

That left Lane, a genuine outsider, as the last man standing. He beat Greyhill handily despite the hundreds of millions of dollars of soft money poured into Greyhill's campaign coffers, but Lane won with less than half of eligible voters participating.

Shafer's role was to groom and guide the new president into a prudent course of action. The power players behind the known faces in Washington—the money men from Wall Street, Silicon Valley, Hollywood, and even overseas—needed to be sure that Lane could be counted on. Shafer all but guaranteed it.

Shafer genuinely liked Lane and was charmed by his clumsy campaign rhetoric, even when he stole the line from JFK's famous inaugural, "Ask not what your country can do for you, ask what you can do for your country." It was a hateful message for the rabid left wing of his party—the social-justice warriors, fourth-generation welfare moms, and Occupy Wall Street progressives—but centrist Democrats and moderate Republicans loved it.

Lane was worried. China was, without a doubt, a regional threat and increasingly a global one as well. The conventional solutions to the China problem didn't interest him—ignoring or provoking them would only lead to an escalation of the crisis, if not war. That's why he turned to Pearce and Myers for a private brainstorming session months ago, and that's how the three of them came up with their current plan. Huge payoff, low risk—except for Pearce and Myers. Both of them understood the risk. Accepted it without flinching.

Lane turned to Chairman Onstot. "Okay, General. Let's lay this thing out."

The chairman flashed a digital projector. A regional map appeared. He highlighted features with a laser pointer.

"The Chinese are clearly becoming more aggressive, not only in the East China Sea, but in the South China Sea as well, pushing out to the so-called nine-dash line. The nine-dash line—"

"—is the Chinese historical claim to the waters and territories in the region," Lane interrupted. "Disputed by every other nation in the area." He wasn't about to let the chairman treat him like a junior officer at an ROTC luncheon. "Move on."

"It's also part of the First Island Chain Doctrine," the chairman continued, somewhat humbled. He ran the laser pointer from the Malay Peninsula in the south to the Kamchatka Peninsula in the north, touching on Taiwan, the Philippines, and the Japanese islands in between. "In the event of war with the United States, Chinese military doctrine calls for preemptive strikes on all of our naval and air bases and other significant assets, including carrier groups, in this geographic chain of archipelagos in order to secure the Chinese mainland from American attack."

"The strategic importance of the East China Sea to Chinese military doctrine can't be overstated." This from the marine corps commandant.

"Beyond expanding its nuclear capabilities, the primary emphasis of China's massive military buildup over the last ten years has been to develop weapons and assets that will enable them to carry out the First Island Chain Doctrine," the admiral said. "That's the primary reason they've acquired their first aircraft carrier and pushed their conventional ballistic-missile programs forward. As I'm sure you're well aware, Mr. President, the Chinese have been increasing their annual defense spending by double digits over the last decade, even as we've been cutting back, both in terms of spending, but also in actual force reductions, especially in naval assets. They're getting stronger even as we weaken."

"But President Sun is a reformer, not a hardliner," Wheeler said. "Our ambassador has met with him several times. Assures me he's a reasonable man."

"I'm sure he is, but like you said, he's a reformer. He's had to pick and choose his battles. In order to wage his domestic anticorruption campaign, he's given a freer hand to the PLA and the foreign policy hawks. The Chinese economy has its own problems, and securing ECS resources for themselves will go a long way to sort those out."

"So why not let the Chinese secure the ECS?" Garza asked. "How is our national security threatened by this move?"

Lane picked Garza to be his NSA because the former Green Beret was unafraid to ask the hard questions.

"Because Japan will feel forced to respond," Wheeler said, nodding at the silent looping Japanese video on the screen. "Imagine if China suddenly claimed the Gulf of Mexico and all of its natural resources as sovereign Chinese territory. We'd feel compelled to respond vigorously, especially if Chinese warships suddenly turned up outside Houston or New Orleans."

The marine corps commandant nodded in agreement. "And if the Chinese grab the ECS, they'll feel emboldened to grab the South China Sea as well. Maybe even Taiwan."

"Okay, Taiwan, the Philippines, the Spratlys—let China take it all. How does that actually threaten us?"

"Don't you know the history of Red China? Murdering tens of millions of their own in the Cultural Revolution? Their ground war against us in Korea, their proxy war against us in Vietnam?" The marine general's voice seethed. "China is our greatest geopolitical challenger. A world dominated by Communist China is a world that none of us in this room want to live in."

"Ever heard of Tibet?" Wheeler asked, sarcasm dripping.

"So, I'm hearing domino theory 2.0, is that it?" Garza was throwing Vietnam right back in their faces. "You're fucking kidding me, right? Next thing you'll tell us is that we have to win their hearts and minds."

Lane tried not to laugh. The Tank was famous for its frank discussions. Garza was laying it on thick, but Lane had told him to. He needed to see where the chiefs really stood.

The chief of naval operations leaned forward, clasping his hands together. "Fifty percent of global merchant fleet traffic passes through the South China Sea, much of it making its way north to the ECS. Oil tanker traffic in these disputed waters is three times greater than the Suez Canal and more than five times greater than the Panama Canal. We're talking about China seizing control of the majority of global commerce. Does that sound like the Chinese are fucking kidding, Mr. Garza?"

Garza raised a hand in mock surrender. "Okay, just checking. If we're going to war with the Chinese, I just wanted to be sure it was for a damn good reason."

So did Lane. *Good job, Jim.*

"So we're back to sending the Chinese our own message," Shafer said. "And we're running out of time. I spoke with my counterpart in Tokyo earlier this morning. He says Prime Minister Ito's hand is being forced by this video. Their cabinet is moving into crisis mode. He said if we don't act forcefully and immediately, they will."

Wheeler countered. "I say we make a strong public

statement, explicitly condemning the Chinese actions yesterday. Pledge our support to the Japanese."

"Words won't be enough for the Japanese or our other allies," the marine general said. "And the Chinese might just laugh us out of the room. This whole conflict is about naval presence. Force."

The chairman was as grim as a hanging judge. "The Vietnamese have a saying, 'You can't put out a nearby fire from a distant well.' If we don't show up in force in the area immediately, we'll shake the confidence of all our allies in the Pacific. Even NATO. Hell, maybe the whole world."

The room quieted as everyone processed the implications of the chairman's statement.

Lane was lost in his own thoughts. He was the commander in chief of the most powerful military in all of human history. He wasn't nearly as qualified as any of the men in this room on defense and security matters, and yet the Constitution vested him, the president, with the authority to wage war. If the chairman was right, maybe a global war really was possible. Sounded crazy to even think that. But Lane had read his history, and few heads of state in Europe in either 1914 or 1939 were prepared to think about the unthinkable before it happened. Two global wars resulted.

"And that's why you want a show of force as soon as possible?" Lane said.

"Yes, sir," the chairman said.

"And what are the options?" Lane asked.

"We're divided, Mr. President. I believe sending the *George Washington* carrier battle group to the area is the wisest course of action. The *George Washington* is based in Yokosuka, Japan."

Lane saw the marine corps and air force chiefs nodding in agreement.

"But the navy has its reservations," the chairman added. He turned to the chief of naval operations.

"The Chinese have pursued an aggressive A2AD anti-access/area denial capability. We believe they've achieved a significant breakthrough in their antiship missile technologies. The DF-21D and YJ-12 missiles are proven and reliable conventional antiship systems capable of taking out an aircraft carrier. However, we have our own anti-missile defense systems in place that we believe can deal with those threats—provided the Chinese don't overwhelm us with sheer numbers."

"Is that likely?" Lane asked.

"Not at the moment, especially in the northern reaches we're talking about. Down south toward Taiwan, well, that's a different matter."

"But the admiral has other concerns," Shafer said.

"Our biggest concern is the Chinese deployment of the Wu-14, a hypersonic, maneuverable, conventional missile warhead. Not only is it fully capable of taking out an aircraft carrier, but it travels at such a high rate of speed we have no means to defend against it at the present time. My concern is that if you send the *George Washington* into harm's way we might just lose it. That would send an even stronger message to our allies than doing nothing at all."

"Of course, the DIA doesn't believe the Wu-14 is actually operational," the marine commandant said.

"The CIA hasn't confirmed it, either," Shafer added. "Nor have any other national intelligence agencies."

Lane sighed. "Why the hell not?" It wasn't really a question. Lane had heard all the excuses before in his PDBs. He also agreed that China was America's most challenging strategic threat and the Wu-14—if it actually existed—the most dangerous conventional weapon in their arsenal.

"We don't have HUMINT near it, and their cyberdefenses are impenetrable," Shafer said.

The air force general wasn't through carpet bombing the navy's argument. "It's just not feasible that the Chinese have it, at least not an operational version. We've been trying to crack the HGV nut since the '80s and still can't make the damn thing work. The physics behind it are just too hard to engineer around."

"That doesn't mean the Chinese haven't figured it out," the admiral said. "They say they have. They've even leaked the videos of their tests."

The marine general scoffed. "Pure propaganda. They're at least five years away. Think about it. What a coup for their intelligence service if they can make us believe they have the Wu-14 when they actually don't? They could scare us out of the Pacific for the cost of a porno movie."

"I'm not willing to bet the lives of five thousand sailors on your theory," the admiral snapped. He turned to Lane. "Are you?"

"What about a preemptive strike against their DF-21 platforms?" the army general asked. "Seems like the easiest way to defeat the Wu-14 system."

"But those are mobile missiles," the air force chief said. "Besides, the DF-21s have almost twice the combat range of our F-35Cs. You'll need to use longer-range assets like sub-launched cruise missiles to effect the strike."

"The Chi-coms would start crapping golf balls if we lit up their radar screens with cruise missiles. They'd think we were launching a preemptive *nuclear* strike," Garza said.

"Not to mention that a preemptive strike without just cause is illegal under international law," Wheeler said.

"And that would start a war, which, according to our Constitution, you explicitly don't have the authority to do," Garza said. "Unless you consider the Chinese an imminent threat to the United States."

"Which it isn't," Wheeler added. "Technically, it's Japan that's in imminent danger, not us."

"There are other options," the marine commandant said. "The Wu-14 relies on satellite systems for guidance and navigation. We could launch ASAT missiles and take out their satellites."

"And start a space war with the Chinese, who would take out our satellites," the air force general said, shaking his head. "We're far more dependent on space assets than they are."

"Or disrupt the kill chain," the army general said. "Disrupt the links between the satellites and the missile."

"How?" Lane asked.

"Cripple their command and control systems through conventional or cyber attacks."

"And you're confident we can do that?" Lane asked.

"Technically, yes, I believe it's entirely possible."

"And you're confident enough that you're willing to risk one of our carriers and the lives of the sailors on board?"

The army general hesitated, weighing the evidence in his mind. "Frankly, no. The Chinese would know these were points of vulnerability and would have probably prepared defenses against them in advance. We wouldn't know if our efforts were successful until after they launched the vehicle."

"Not acceptable," the admiral said.

Lane took a sip of coffee, processing the conversation. He leaned toward the chairman. "So what you're telling me is that the best way to prevent a war with China is to threaten war with China?"

"Yes." The irony wasn't lost on the chairman or anyone else in the room.

Lane turned back to the admiral. "But the only way we can safely deploy the *George Washington* is to first launch a preemptive strike against the Wu-14?"

"That's my assessment, sir."

"If you can find it," the army general added.

"So we have to start a war to prevent it," Garza said, shaking his head. "Or roll the dice and hope the Chinese are just bluffing."

Lane turned back to Shafer. "And we're talking about provoking a regime that's already proven itself recklessly aggressive?"

The secretary of defense nodded grimly.

"And yet, backing down or doing nothing would only embolden them in their recklessness? Threaten our existing alliances?"

The secretary of state nodded in agreement.

Wheeler added, "And if we don't act quickly and decisively, the Japanese will start their own war, dragging us into it anyway."

Lane addressed the whole room. "In other words, we're damned if we do and damned if we don't."

"That's about the shape of it," the chairman said. "A Texas longhorn–size dilemma."

"So my options really are war on Chinese terms or war on our terms. Push the *George Washington* into harm's way and see if the Chinese strike—or launch a massive preemptive cruise-missile strike without cause to protect our carrier from a missile that may or may not actually exist?"

"And then there's the North Koreans and their MIRV missile testing," Garza said, grinning. "Who knows what those batshit crazies will do."

Lane tented his hands, calculating.

"Your decision, Mr. President?" the chairman finally asked.

Lane wasn't exactly sure. He'd already cast his lot with Pearce and Myers. With nothing but two bad choices in front of him, they were his only hope of avoiding either. But if they failed, it looked like World War III was all but certain.

He prayed they wouldn't. But they needed time.

Time he didn't have.

FOURTEEN

Helmeted Chinese riot police stood shoulder to shoulder against the screaming crowd, eyes burning against the tear gas blowing in their faces from the shifting winds. The front ranks clung desperately to their wire-mesh shields that had gaps between the steel rods just large enough for fingers to grasp—a distinct design flaw now made apparent as rioters seized the mesh and pulled on the tops of the shields like mountain climbers. A few succeeded in leaping over and stepping onto shields held aloft like a roof.

The police were under orders to not open fire with their weapons, but they swung their batons with abandon, trying to break the fingers clawing through the mesh or busting the ankles of the men overhead.

More than two thousand Chinese nationalist protestors shouted and surged at the wavering green police line. Black smoke choked the air as two overturned Toyota sedans burned and dozens of small fires crackled with piles of Japanese flags.

A sea of Chairman Mao posters and red and gold PRC flags hovered over the rioters' heads. A thick, bald-headed man with Chinese flags painted on his face shouted in a megaphone. "For the love of our homeland! War with Japan! War against the invaders!"

The grim Japanese ambassador stood in the second-floor window watching the riot, a secure cell phone pressed against his ear as he gave a live description to his boss, the foreign minister back in Tokyo. He also confirmed similar riots in Shanghai, Tianjin, Guangzhou, and Shenzhen. Japanese restaurants, department stores, and manufacturing facilities were looted; Japanese citizens were harassed on the streets and even assaulted. Japanese-brand televisions, computers, and appliances were being smashed in stores and on the sidewalks.

Two embassy staffers standing next to the ambassador shot official videos with Canon video cameras while other frightened staffers shot home videos on their cell phones.

The ambassador and foreign minister both agreed. The real danger wasn't the rioting. The Chinese government would never allow spontaneous protests to erupt on the streets. Tiananmen Square was proof of that.

Vice Chairman Feng watched the riots unfolding on his television. He lit a cigarette.

He had to give the MSS its due credit. The bumblers had nearly killed the Japanese activists on the dive boat two days ago. He'd seen the video footage shot by the Japanese and posted on the Internet. His explicit orders were to simply scare off the Japanese civilians, not beat them into comas.

But at least the MSS handled the controlled rioting at home well enough. State security had worked tirelessly over the last forty-eight hours to fan the flames of Chinese national outrage. Marathon television broadcasts of old newsreel footage, elderly victim interviews, and state-sponsored feature films depicting the Rape of Nanking, the invasion of Manchuria, and other Japanese wartime atrocities in China and elsewhere in Asia blanketed the airwaves. MSS social-networking agents overwhelmed the Internet, flooding blogs, websites, and the Chinese version of Twitter, Weibo, with virulent anti-Japanese propaganda and calls for vengeance even as they bullied, blocked, or secretly arrested citizens who dared suggest calm, reason, and peace.

The MSS social-networking campaign worked flawlessly. They convincingly portrayed the Chinese fishing trawler as the victim of a Japanese assault, and the old slogans about the Diaoyu Islands being stolen Chinese territory were on the lips of half a billion people. Chinese newscasts repeated the most recent public opinion poll: 57 percent said that war with Japan in the next few years was inevitable. Of those, 79 percent said that it was both necessary and good.

The polls were unsurprising. The Communist Chinese government had spent the last six decades demonizing Japan and its vicious assault on the Chinese mainland before and during World War II. In addition, every Japanese success in the postwar period was depicted as being at the expense of the Chinese people even as Japanese contributions to Chinese development in the post-Mao years were ignored. The ongoing narrative of China's victimhood by the entire world, especially by the West and particularly Japan, was constantly promoted throughout the Chinese education system. It was a shrewd calculation by the Party leadership. The greater China's humiliation at the hands of foreigners, the greater the victory—and hence legitimacy—of the Party as it restored China's fortunes and sacred honor to their previous glory. They freely taught the ancient Chinese concept of *tianxia*, the idea that China was the center of the world, the highest civilization according to the Mandate of Heaven, and that everything and everyone under heaven owed obeisance to the greatest of all human societies.

It wasn't terribly difficult for the MSS to tease the smoldering public hatred of Japan into a roaring fire. The trick was not letting it burn out of control. The prospect of a billion angry citizens rising up was even more worrisome than the prospect of war with Japan or even the United States. MSS operatives were at the scene of each of the riots, carefully and quietly directing events, even restraining the most overzealous. The local police departments had been warned not to fire on any Chinese citizens under penalty of extreme sanction. This wasn't a humanitarian concern. The last thing Feng wanted was for the crazed monster of a public riot to suddenly turn on the authority of the state. Nearly thirty years later, the government was still living down the nightmare of Tiananmen Square. The Chinese people and their innate desire for freedom was still the greatest threat that Feng and the ruling class most feared.

Feng stabbed out the cigarette in his ashtray. *Now the Japanese will know how serious he is about the Diaoyus. They might resent the loss of the islands and their revenues, but now they'll fear opposing China even more.*

FIFTEEN

"You seem distracted tonight," Prime Minister Ito said.

Myers was. A splitting headache. But worse, she couldn't stop thinking about President Lane's urgent text. The Pentagon meeting didn't provide any new answers. She told Pearce, of course. No one else. Time was running out.

It was her last scheduled evening in Tokyo, and she and Pearce had been invited to Ito's home for a private soirée of entertainment and food, all of it quite traditional. Ito's lovely young wife joined them, along with Tanaka and his equally intimidating spouse. Pearce and Myers were the third couple, or so it seemed. Despite her throbbing headache, Myers looked stunning in her form-fitting black-sequined evening gown, and Pearce was quite handsome in his hand-tailored gray suit. A striking pair. Their comfortable friendship could have been mistaken for intimacy. They all sat in leather club chairs around a large hammered-copper cocktail table in Ito's expansive library.

"I'm still thinking about the Noh play we saw tonight," Myers said. Ito had invited a troupe of Japan's finest Noh actors and musicians to perform for his honored guests.

"What is it that most captivated you?" Tanaka's wife asked. Her eyes were searching, imperious. "The singing, perhaps? It must sound strange to Western ears."

Everything about the play was strange to Myers. The atonal chorus, the carved masks, the drums. Her eyes drifted to the full suit of samurai armor standing in the corner. It had been worn by one of Ito's ancestors in battle long ago.

"I'm still amazed that there is no director for the play and that the actors have only one rehearsal. And yet, everything was so well choreographed. The singing, the music, the blocking."

"The oldest Noh plays are more than seven hundred years old," Prime Minister Ito said. "Each play, and each part in the play, has been passed down through generations of actors who continue to study. It is a collective effort, but each actor has a duty and responsibility to his or her own role. No two performances are ever the same, either for the actors or the audience. Each is completely unique."

"Of course, more Japanese have listened to Simon and Garfunkel than they have to Noh music," Tanaka lamented. "Even the Carpenters are more popular."

"Noh is difficult," Ito's young wife insisted. The former actress and model was an inch taller than her husband, even with his towering shock of gray hair. She turned to Myers. "How many young Americans prefer Shakespeare to *Duck Dynasty*?"

"Not enough." Myers took a sip of bourbon. The glass trembled slightly in her hand.

"What about you, Mr. Pearce? What did you think of the ghosts and monsters tonight?" Ito asked. The play, *Nue*, featured the ghost of a slain monster.

"Or about Japan itself?" Tanaka asked, taking another sip of Jefferson's Presidential Select, Myers's new favorite Kentucky straight bourbon whiskey. She'd brought a bottle of the double-gold winner for dinner tonight, a gift to the prime minister. A nod to their friendship and shared tastes.

Pearce shrugged. He was as uncomfortable in his suit as he was being in a room with politicians. It felt more like a court-martial than an evening of entertainment. He knew he could undo any good work he'd accomplished so far by saying just one stupid thing.

"I can't get over the contrasts," Pearce finally said. "Your nation is both ancient and modern, the best of both. But it seems like an irreconcilable contradiction in some ways."

"You are more right than you know," Tanaka said. "We are losing our history and culture to Western modernity. We are losing ourselves."

"Don't listen to him." Ito laughed. "He's old-fashioned. He'd like to go back to samurai swords and emperor worship."

"We've lost something in the embrace of the West," Tanaka said. His red eyes saddened. Myers wondered if he'd been drinking too much. She watched him down several shots of sake at dinner, and now he was working on his second bourbon.

Myers wanted to ask the prime minister to turn down the air-conditioning. She felt the sweat beading up on her forehead. Her head was throbbing now.

Mrs. Ito smiled. "In your previous travels here, Madame President, have you heard of the term *nihonjin-ron*?"

Myers wanted to dislike the pretty former actress. But she was devastatingly charming and sharp as a tack. "No, I'm sorry."

"It's our ongoing national conversation, a question we keep asking ourselves. 'What does it mean to be Japanese?'"

"You must be having the same conversation in your country," Tanaka's wife said. "Open borders, mass migration, globalism. Is it true that in some cities it is illegal to fly an American flag now because it upsets the foreigners living there?"

"I've never heard that," Myers said. But she was telling only half the truth. More and more apartment complexes, businesses, and even universities were putting greater restrictions on anything that smacked of "American" because of the fear of offending foreign-born residents and customers. Shameful, in her opinion.

Tanaka smiled. "My English is terrible. Maybe you can help me. I've just heard of the phrase 'undocumented citizen.' What exactly does that mean?"

Myers forced her own smile. They both knew that Tanaka's English was faultless. "Some people in my country feel that the term 'illegal alien' is pejorative and prefer the term 'undocumented immigrant.' But even more progressive people are now using the term 'undocumented citizen' to fully legitimize the illegals' status and pave the way conceptually for them to vote, hold office, and enjoy every other right of a citizen."

"Doesn't that destroy the meaning of citizenship?" Ito's wife asked.

"Some would say so," Myers said.

Tanaka shook his head in disbelief. "The purpose of the state is to protect and provide for its citizens. If you change the definition of 'citizen,' aren't you changing the definition and purpose of the state?"

"Possibly."

Tanaka's wife refilled her empty glass. "Political correctness is killing your country."

"I think every country today is struggling with the concepts of nationality, citizenship, status, and rights. Globalism is erasing national borders. The free flow of money, communications, commerce, and labor are all making borders less and less relevant to the lives of most people in the West," Myers said.

"And you support this idea of globalism?" Tanaka asked.

"No," Myers said. "But it's here."

"Why?"

"Economies of scale. Ease of commerce. Profits, ultimately," Ito said. His family-owned business earned most of its cash overseas, and his past work with the trade delegation only confirmed this.

Pearce took another sip of club soda, hating like hell he'd given up the booze. "Corporations are also part of the problem."

"But you are the head of an international corporation!" Mrs. Ito said.

Pearce smiled. "Which makes me an expert."

"How are corporations a problem?" Ito asked.

"American corporations depend on the United States to protect their interests at home and abroad, but more and more of them are relocating their headquarters to other countries with lower tax rates. They want the benefits of American government without having to pay for it. Their only loyalty is to their own profits, not the country that sustains them."

"But it's the responsibility of corporations to earn a

profit, isn't it?" Mrs. Tanaka asked. She was the daughter of one of the wealthiest industrialists in Japan.

"Of course. But not at the expense of the national interest."

" 'What's good for GM is good for America!' " Ito said, his familiar smile brightening his face. A famous American misquote.

"I say what's good for America is good for GM," Myers countered. "American corporations used to show loyalty to the nation instead of just to themselves. Of course, that's how too many American citizens feel, too. Their only loyalty is to themselves. They don't want to pay any taxes, but they want to have all of the benefits of government."

"That's why I support a national draft," Pearce said. "Everybody should pay taxes, and everybody should serve the country either in a military outfit or some kind of public service."

Myers nodded her agreement.

"Ask not what your country can do for you, ask what you can do for your country," Ito said, repeating President Lane's campaign slogan.

"Exactly," Pearce said. President Lane hadn't called for a national draft, but Pearce decided then and there he'd raise the subject with him when he got back.

Assuming he ever got back. The mission was far from over, he reminded himself.

Mrs. Ito raised a finger. "Perhaps nations are no longer needed. Some believe nationalism is the cause of all of our problems, not the solution."

Myers licked her tingling lips. "Individual rights are defended by national government. If we lose the state, we lose our freedoms and our protection."

"Oh. So a nation does have the right to defend itself,

then." Mrs. Tanaka said. It wasn't a question in her tightly woven mouth.

"Yes, of course. The only question is how," Pearce interjected. He decided to play his role tonight, awkward as it was. Myers clearly needed him to. "Alliances are even more important than tanks and planes."

"So we can count on the United States to send the *George Washington* into the East China Sea tomorrow?" Tanaka asked.

"I'm sure the president and his security team are discussing their options even as we speak," Pearce said. He instantly regretted it. He knew that Lane had decided against the move. At least for now. Tanaka already knew this. Lane would have communicated directly with Ito if the carrier group was on its way.

"My husband says that your drone demonstration was very impressive," Mrs. Tanaka said.

"But not persuasive," Pearce said.

"On the contrary. My hope is that NEDO and our self-defense forces will now more enthusiastically embrace drone combat technologies, thanks to you." Tanaka smiled. "But, of course, not at the expense of conventional systems."

Myers rubbed her hands together, her eyes focused on her numbing fingers.

Pearce saw this. So did everybody else. Myers appeared to be drunk. Pearce wanted to keep the room focused on him. He asked Tanaka, "So what do you think is the main difference between Japan and the United States?"

Tanaka set his empty glass down. "We Japanese take pride in our uniqueness as a culture. You take pride in your uniqueness as an idea."

"We try to take the best ideas of every culture and incorporate them," Pearce said. "My research director is of South Asian descent, the head of my IT department is a Scot, a German heads up my nuclear deconstruction division, and my UUV specialist was actually born in Japan."

But we seem to celebrate the worst of cultures, too, Pearce wanted to say.

Tanaka tented his fingers. "We also define ourselves by our history, even as you ignore yours. The Imperial House of Japan is the oldest monarchy on the planet. Emperor Akihito traces his lineage back to the Emperor Jimmu, more than six hundred years before Christ. My own family scroll dates back to before the Normans invaded England, and my wife's even further." Both Tanakas beamed with pride.

Pearce couldn't even name his great-grandparents. Knew his dad's dad only through stories. "History has its advantages and its burdens."

"That depends on how you remember it," Ito said. "Hitler and Stalin understood the power of history and the power that came with changing it according to need."

Pearce wanted to point out the controversy of Japanese history books glossing over wartime atrocities but decided against it.

"Our history is the history of immigrants. I believe it's one of the reasons why we still produce the most patents every year."

"How did mass immigration work out for the Native Americans, I wonder?" Mrs. Tanaka asked, not even trying to hide her smirk.

"Our population continues to grow, thanks to immigration. Japan has the opposite problem, doesn't it?" Pearce asked. Japan's demographics were collapsing. The old were living longer than ever, and the young had little interest in childbearing, and a growing number even abstained from sex altogether. Of course, ethnic Europeans throughout the Western nations and the former Soviet Union were depopulating as well.

Tanaka chuckled. "As Dr. Ikeda suggested, we feel that the revolution in robotics and automation will solve that problem. Robots won't bring failed cultural values into our society, won't go on the public dole, won't bankrupt our pension plans, won't strike for higher wages and benefits. Neither will they crowd our prisons, as so many immigrants do."

Pearce clenched his jaw. He hated this shit. Tanaka kept baiting him. He'd rather throw a punch or just get the hell out. But this is what he signed on for. Better to change the subject.

"Our danger is that we're losing our sense of national identity. We've left it up to each person to decide for themselves what it means to be an American," Pearce said. "And with fifty million foreign-born residents, that means a lot of different opinions."

"Then we are more alike than I imagined," Tanaka said. "Both of our countries are under assault."

Tanaka's wife whispered in Japanese. *More like a growl*, Pearce thought.

"I apologize. My English is so terrible. My wife informs me that the better word for 'assault' is 'transformation.' But at least you have the freedom to choose your destiny. Without the authority to defend our national interests, we must rely on good allies like the United States to dictate to us what our national interests must be."

"Or China," Mrs. Tanaka snapped. "Did you see the television news about the riots?"

"Frightening," Myers said, slurring the word. Her bourbon glass sat empty by her elbow. Pearce frowned.

"Orchestrated," Mrs. Ito said.

Ito shook his head. "Politics. What a shameful way to ruin a lovely evening."

"Politics is the world. We can't escape it," Mrs. Tanaka said. "Might as well face it head on."

"Thursday," Myers said, standing, wobbly. "El Paso."

Everyone else rose with her, surprised. Was the evening over?

"Excuse me, Margaret?" Ito said.

Myers extended a shaking hand to Ito, then crumbled to the floor at his feet.

SIXTEEN

Flashing digital cameras lit up the room like a Milan fashion show. Photographers shouted questions in Japanese and English, a cacophony of noise and blasting lights. Television crews were there, too.

So much for keeping her appearance in Japan private.

Myers fought to keep her practiced smile, taught to her by her campaign manager in her first run for governor of Colorado. It never failed her.

Standing next to her was the white-coated hospital president, the chief of surgery, the chief of the endocrinology department, and the three nurses who assisted in the procedure, all smiles. Prime Minister Ito was there, too, along with Tanaka and Pearce.

Ito signaled for the press to quiet down. He spoke in Japanese first, then English. "President Myers would like to make a short statement." He nodded in her direction.

"Thank you, Prime Minister Ito. First of all, I want to thank the wonderful staff of this amazing hospital for their excellent care. Everyone has been extremely kind to me, and they have provided world-class medical service to me. I am forever grateful." She bowed slightly toward the

Chiefs on her left and the Indians on her right. They bowed in return, in some cases, a few times, enthusiastically.

"Because of their excellent care, I am in perfectly good health. I had a very slight incident of insulin overdose last night and passed out. Fortunately, my good friends were there to call an ambulance and I was rushed over here immediately."

To his credit, Ito gave strict orders to the ambulance crew and his staff that Myers's identity was to be strictly guarded. But someone tipped off the Japanese press and set off a media firestorm.

Just as Myers had hoped, actually.

Ian McTavish's anonymous tip to several local media outlets did the trick. Pearce's gifted computer genius could break into almost any computer system in the world, but in this case he didn't need to. Simple text and e-mail messages to news-starved reporters was all it took.

The media questions came fast and furious. What was the former president doing in Japan? Why wasn't this widely known? Was she on a secret mission? Was her visit in response to the Chinese attack on the Japanese dive boat? Does this mean the United States will be coming to the aid of Japan now? Will a carrier be dispatched? Myers deflected each question, as did the prime minister who promised an "off the record" conversation later with the press in attendance.

Myers continued.

"I was diagnosed with adult-onset type 1 diabetes just over a year ago. It's an extremely rare condition, and I have been able to manage it quite nicely thanks to my personal physician and endocrinologist back home in Denver. I'm afraid that I didn't monitor my insulin and glucose levels closely enough in the last few days, and this induced a hypoglycemic reaction. Too much fast-acting insulin and not enough carbohydrates, I've been told. I was rushed to the hospital and treated, and within an hour, I was fully recovered. But it was at that time we decided to take the unusual step and install a bionic pancreas."

The press gasped at the words "bionic pancreas" and began shouting questions louder and louder over one another to catch Myers's attention. Once again, Ito quieted them down. Myers continued.

"I'm going to let Japan's leading endocrinologist, Dr. Hironaga, explain the technology behind the bionic pancreas. She is far more qualified than I am to answer your questions. Thank you."

Myers bowed slightly again to the press out of respect, and Ito signaled his security staff to clear a path. They led the way out for Ito, Tanaka, Myers, and Pearce as the press peppered Dr. Hironaga with questions about the bionic pancreas. She was happy to explain the device components and their respective functions.

As per her security briefing, however, Dr. Hironaga was careful not to reveal the fact that the high-tech wireless device was manufactured by Pearce Systems.

SEVENTEEN

Feng jabbed the volume button on his HD television. The party music pulsing on the other side of the door was deafening. He could barely hear what Myers was saying. He barked an order at his aide, who rushed back out of the media room. A tidal wave of noise assaulted Feng's ears when the aide opened the door, worsening the stabbing pain behind the vice chairman's eyes.

Feng fell onto an overstuffed leather couch, his head still swimming with liquor. His aide shouted on the other side of the door and the music dropped by half. Better.

His English wasn't very good. He didn't understand the words "bionic" or "pancreas." No matter. He'd have translated transcripts on his tablet within the hour. More important than the words were the pictures. Former president Margaret Myers was in Japan, standing next to the fascist Ito and his lapdog Tanaka.

The vice chairman raged. What was Myers doing in Japan? Was Lane sending some kind of message to the

Japanese? Was she there to lend America's support? Perhaps negotiating a new secret treaty?

Another wave of techno beat rushed through the opened door, and just as quickly it subsided.

Feng seethed. Why hadn't he been informed of Myers's presence in Japan? He swore. Another MSS failure.

Soft hands reached from behind the couch and began massaging the tension out of his neck.

"So much stress. You need to relax. Come back to the party."

The soft hands belonged to an even softer feminine voice. A Thai boy, eighteen years old, pretty and fey. One of Feng's favorites in his stable of young androgynous consorts.

"You don't understand," Feng said. He closed his eyes for a moment against the raging headache. The soft hands on his neck felt good.

"Who's the white lady?" The Thai drove his moist palms deep into Feng's shoulders.

"No one for you to worry about," Feng said. "Just shut up and rub."

"My pleasure."

Feng opened his eyes just in time to watch Myers, Ito, and Tanaka depart the press conference. He snapped off the television and tossed the remote. The MSS was becoming increasingly inept. He would have sacked Huang Yong long ago, but the minister had powerful friends on the Central Committee.

Worse, Huang knew all about Feng's financial ties to Mao Island and the ECS initiative, partly because Feng had paid Huang substantial sums of money to support it. Like so many other relationships among the ruling elite, Feng's web of corruption extended widely, with each strand of the web terminating in a rope around the neck of the man or woman being paid off with dirty money. In

Feng's case, dirty petromoney. If Feng pushed Huang off the cliff, he would only break Feng's neck on the way down and drag another hundred conspirators tied behind him. It was the Party's version of mutual assured destruction.

Huang could still prove useful for the time being, but Feng was determined to find a way to rid himself of the fat fool. He never forgave Huang for not discovering his nephew Zhao's killer. Feng had a blood debt to repay and Huang's failure was standing in the way.

"My head still hurts," Feng whimpered.

The Thai padded around to the front of the couch. He wore a brightly flowered silk kimono. He opened it. Nothing underneath but his smooth pale skin and swelling manhood.

The Thai knelt down between Feng's legs, unbuckled his pants.

"I know how to fix it."

Feng's throbbing headache was soon relieved.

EIGHTEEN

She howled like a wounded moose.

Troy heard the pounding against the thin trailer wall all the way out here. Whoever his dad had dragged home last night was either having a stroke or a really good time. At least no one else could hear it. They lived too far outside of town at the end of a dirt track.

He checked his watch. Less than an hour until school started. No way he'd make it there on time this morning, but it couldn't be helped. He was facing expulsion. Too many tardies and too many unexcused absences. They didn't understand.

Troy still had to change the oil and plugs on the big Husqvarna chainsaw after he finished sharpening it. It was running like crap. His fingers were still numb from the early morning cold. He left his gloves in the trailer like an idiot, but he couldn't go back and get them now that his dad and his new lady friend were back at it, and knowing his dad, that could take a while.

Troy was careful to count eight drags of the chainsaw file for each tooth and even more careful to keep the file at the same angle as the tooth, just like his dad taught him. Failure to do either meant the saw wouldn't cut straight. It was tedious but important work. Work his dad wasn't getting done lately, like a lot of other things. If he and his dad didn't clear the stand of dead trees by the end of the week, they'd lose their Forest Service contract, and work was hard enough to come by these days. All the damn environmentalist lawsuits had practically shut down the lumber work on federal lands, and the Gulf War recession had crushed timber prices and demand. The job they were doing was chickenshit, but it was the only work they'd had this year and maybe likely to get for the rest. But between his drinking and his whoring, Troy's dad was proving to be an unreliable supervisor in their failing two-man operation.

The women he didn't care about so much. The death of Troy's mother had hit them both hard. It was the drinking that was going to kill his old man. In a way, it had killed his mother and sister. Why his mother had decided to leave Troy with his drunken father he'd never know. He'd probably be dead if she hadn't, but this wasn't exactly living, either.

Troy finished up the chainsaw and stored it in the back of the rusted out pickup with PEARCE LUMBER crudely stenciled on the side. He thought about driving it to school, but then his dad wouldn't be able to work today, and work was more important. A vice counselor threatened to expel him if he had one more tardy, but it just couldn't be helped.

Twenty minutes after the woman's howling stopped, Troy headed back in to wash up. He made his way past the unfamiliar bright orange hardtop Jeep Wrangler and pushed through the door of the single-wide trailer. A coffeepot wheezed on the yellowing Formica kitchen coun-

tertop. The aroma was strong and sweet, masking the
stale cigarette stink that permeated everything. He heard
the shower running.

He washed the grease off of his hands with Ajax and
hot water in the kitchen sink and toweled off just as his
dad's bedroom door swung gently open. The woman's
dirty blonde hair was still wet. She gasped.

"Oh, honey. You scared me," she whispered, shutting
the door quietly behind her. "Your daddy went back to
sleep. Let's not wake him up."

"Nah, don't want that." Troy grabbed a chipped coffee
mug out of the cabinet. "Coffee?"

"Please. I thought I'd make some before I run off.
Hope you don't mind."

The woman was closer to his age than his dad's. Plain
face. A nice smile, though. She seemed familiar. Wide
hips, big chest. Just his dad's type. She wore a brightly
patterned polyester dress down to her thighs with black
tights. Must've been the one she wore last night, too, but
the polyester didn't hold wrinkles so you couldn't tell.

"You don't recognize me, do you?" she asked.

He shook his head, embarrassed for her. Prayed she
wouldn't ask his name. He sure wouldn't ask hers. What
would be the point?

An awkward smile. "Doesn't matter." She squeezed
past him in the narrow galley kitchen on the way to the
living room to fetch her coat and boots. "Excuse me,
honey."

Her breasts brushed against his back. Troy wasn't sure
if that was on purpose or not. It wouldn't have been the
first time. Women had their fantasies, too. His dad said he
was good-looking like his mother, sometimes proudly,
sometimes mocking. Troy's dark hair was straight and
thick, and he wore it long, to his dad's chagrin. But it was
his blue eyes that grabbed most women. Since the sum-

mer, he stood just over six feet tall, but his size-fourteen feet suggested there was more to follow. He was still boyishly thin, with long, ropey muscles and a broad back, hardened by years of swinging an ax with his dad. His father was just five-eight, with dark curly hair and dark eyes that women like this one couldn't resist—cold-blooded eyes that could steal away a lesser man's courage. He was wide in the hips and shoulders like a fireplug, heavily muscled, and his powerful arms were slathered in tats drawn by the best ink artists in the Philippines.

Troy pulled down another mug and poured coffee into both.

The woman flopped on the couch and pulled on a boot. "Hope we didn't make too much noise this morning. Hated to wake you up." She blushed a little.

"I was outside doing some work. Didn't hear anything."

"Aren't you going to be late for school?" She pulled on the other boot and grabbed her coat.

"They won't start without me."

She giggled. "You're a funny kid." She pulled on her coat and took the steaming cup of coffee Troy offered her. She sipped it. "Can I make you some breakfast or something, honey?"

With what? The fridge is empty, lady.

"No, I'm fine. Thanks."

The woman saw the clock on the wall. "Shit. I'm gonna be late. Can I give you a ride to school?"

Troy saw the clock, too. If he left now with her, he'd only be late for gym, and the PE coaches didn't give a shit. But this being nice stuff was getting on his nerves. These women always wanted to be nice to him. Like somehow being nice to him would get them closer to the old man. Stupid. And he didn't want them around anyway.

"I've got it covered. But thanks."

"Suit yourself."

She set the cup down on the counter and started to tell him something but thought better of it. Troy figured it was along the lines of "Tell your dad to call me," but maybe she was smart enough to realize that would never happen. She pushed through the trailer door and headed out to her Jeep.

Troy felt stupid. He should've taken her up on her offer for a ride, but he didn't want anything from her. Or anybody else, for that matter. *People only cause you problems.*

The Jeep engine coughed into life and the transmission clunked into first gear as Troy grabbed a couple of pieces of stale bread from the cupboard. He smeared two big gobs of peanut butter on them and washed them down with coffee before heading to the bathroom to brush his teeth. He'd shower later at the school gym. Hotter water.

He pulled on a heavy flannel shirt out of the laundry basket and sniffed it. Not too bad. Found his backpack and slung it over his shoulder. His tiny room was crammed with dog-eared paperbacks and a 1959 Collier's encyclopedia set he bought at a garage sale for twenty dollars when he was a freshman. His twin bed was perfectly made with a single wool blanket and sheets so tight you could bounce a quarter off them. His dad was a lot of things, but a slob wasn't one of them. He insisted that his son make his bed "the army way" every morning to start his day. "Bed's made tight, the day goes right," his dad always said.

His dad said a lot of shit that didn't make sense.

Troy made his bed this way now because he actually liked it. It also avoided an unnecessary fight with the old man. There were plenty of necessary fights to go around.

Like trying to get his dad to take his meds. "Don't need 'em" was what he'd say if he was in a good mood. "Shut the fuck up about the goddamn meds" was the more common response. They were probably expired by now anyway. Troy had done his own research into the subject of PTSD at the small public library and managed to convince his dad last year to go to the VA for an evaluation. But his dad never followed up and never took his meds, so he kept cycling down, as deep as the next whiskey bottle would take him.

Troy laid his hand on the doorknob to open his father's door but stopped. If his old man needed to sleep, better to let him sleep. He'd be home right after school and the two of them together would get more done if his dad was rested up than he would working by himself all day without Troy, tired and hungover. And Troy didn't like the idea of his dad running those saws by himself, especially if he was having Mr. Jack Daniels over for lunch.

Troy shut the front door behind him and began the long trek to school. With any luck, he'd hitch a ride once he got off the dirt track onto the main road. His feet were already sore, cramped inside the too-small boots he got from Goodwill last week. He was probably an idiot for turning down that lady's offer for a ride. His dad would've laughed at him, but he had his own rules to live by.

NINETEEN

Troy was more than an hour late by the time he arrived on campus, a collection of cinder-block boxes strung together by covered walkways, typical school architecture from the 1960s. Troy never found a ride to hitch and had to hike all the way in. His still-hungry stomach grumbled for more food that wasn't going to be coming anytime soon. For two bucks he could get a deep-fried bean burrito and a chocolate milk, but he didn't have two bucks, and he wasn't a mooch.

He qualified for the school lunch program, but his father wouldn't allow it. "Pearces don't beg."

Pearces also didn't make their son's lunch, either, Troy thought, as he crossed through the faculty parking lot. The third-period bell rang and he knew he was in trouble. Out of the corner of his eye he saw Mr. Felcher, a vice principal with a serious hard-on for misfits like Troy, who had warned him just last week that his next tardy would get him expelled.

Troy ducked behind a two-door Chevy Nova at the last second and ran crouching between cars like a rat in a maze, finally making it onto campus without Felcher seeing him. The covered walkways were still jammed with students knotted in cliques of jocks, theater nerds, cowboys, cheerleaders, ROTC—groups he never belonged to. Troy bolted at full speed toward the temporary trailers on the far side of the campus, weaving in and out of the foot traffic with effortless grace. His PE coach last year begged him to join track, but Troy didn't have time for extracurriculars at all. If he wasn't working with his dad, he was hunting or fishing, in season and out. He wished the high school offered letters in rifle, bow, and fly rod. He'd own 'em all.

The door to his math class was shutting when Troy arrived breathlessly. He grabbed the handle.

"Excuse me."

Susan Morrow, the math teacher, was on the other side. Brown pantsuit, glasses, hair in a bun. She was in her forties and pretty, but trying to hide it.

"Troy Pearce. So glad you can make it."

"Sorry, ma'am." The other students were already dropping backpacks, popping binders, pulling homework. Troy moved toward his desk. Morrow tugged on his shirt.

"See me after class."

"I can't be late—"

"I'll write you a hall pass."

"What's this about?"

"You're failing."

Pearce shrugged.

"And that, young man, is your problem."

Troy paid more attention to his gurgling stomach than Morrow's math lesson. She was a gifted teacher, but Pearce hadn't done the homework. He glanced over the assignment, just in case she called on him. She always seemed to know when he hadn't put in the work. For whatever reason, she left him alone today.

The bell rang and the other kids poured out of the bungalow, but Pearce remained behind as ordered. Morrow motioned for him to join her at the seat next to her desk. She opened a file folder as he fell into the chair.

"Do you know why you're failing this class?"

"I dunno. Maybe low self-esteem?"

Morrow stifled a laugh. "You missed the midterm on Wednesday. That means your grade is zero right now. If you fail this class, you won't graduate, and if you don't graduate, you can't go to college."

Troy shrugged.

"You're still planning on going to college, aren't you?"

"No. Why?"

Morrow frowned. She had cornered Troy a year ago and read him the riot act. Told him how smart he was, that he needed to go to college. She even paid for him to take the SATs.

"What do you mean you're not going to college? Are you thinking about the military?"

Troy snorted. *Hell no.*

"No, ma'am."

"What's so funny?"

"Nothing, ma'am. Just wasn't planning on a military career."

"What are your plans after school?"

"Today? Or after I graduate?"

She gave him the stink eye. "What do you think?"

Troy softened a little. "Work with my dad."

"Does he own his own company?"

"Yeah."

"What does he do?"

"Lumbering."

"Mills are going out of business all over the place these days. There's no future in that."

Troy felt the heat rise in his face. Tamped it down. "We're doing okay. Can I please go now?"

"Look, I shouldn't do this, but I can let you make up the midterm."

"Thanks." Troy stood to leave.

"But you have to take it today. After school."

"I can't. My dad and I have this job we're working on—"

"It's your only shot. Today after school or not at all."

Troy felt a surge of adrenaline kick in. Fight or flight— or both. She was boxing him in. He couldn't miss work. But he couldn't fail, either. His old man would kill him. Not that his dad ever gave a damn about his grades or parent-teacher conferences or anything else having to do with his academic life. "Winners never quit, and quitters never win" was another one of his father's slurred pearls of great wisdom.

What could he do?

"That's not fair. I need to study for it." It was a weak play, he knew, but it was all he had.

Morrow frowned. "You already had the chance to study for it, remember? Not that you need to. You scored a 770 on the math portion of the SAT. Why you're not in honors calculus I'll never understand. If I were your mother, I'd be furious at you."

But you're not, so shut the fuck up and quit screwing with my life, he thought. He didn't dare say it. His dad would beat the shit out of him if he did.

Troy glanced out of the window. Saw one of the lady gym teachers marching by in sweats and a whistle around her neck, her nose buried in a sheaf of papers. Wide hips, large breasts, dirty blonde hair.

She glanced up just then. They locked eyes. She smiled thinly, blushed, and hurried away, ashamed. Troy grinned.

"Something else funny?"

"No, not really. But now I'm really late for fourth period."

Morrow scratched on a note pad. Handed it to Troy. "Here's your hall pass. See you at three thirty."

Troy took it. "Thanks."

"Troy, I'm serious. Three thirty or not at all. It's your life."

Yeah, I kinda figured that out, Troy thought, but still kept his mouth shut.

He bolted out of the door onto the walkway. When he reached the faculty parking lot, he crumpled the hall pass and tossed it in a trash can and headed for home.

TWENTY

The vessel was the first drillship ever constructed in a Chinese shipyard, though it relied heavily on a Norwegian corporation for its automated dynamic positioning (ADP) system. The *Tiger II*, the second ship launched in the series, was no exception. ADP allowed the vessel to find and maintain a fixed position in deep water without the need for anchors or other fixed assemblies typical of many deep-water drilling platforms. Proprietary computer algorithms used the data gleaned from motion and vertical and draught reference sensors along with the ship's hydro-acoustic navigational system to automatically fire bow and stern thrusters as needed, putting and keeping the forty-five-thousand-ton drilling vessel in place at sea without human intervention. The *Tiger II* needed to remain perfectly positioned in order to begin and sustain drilling operations. Unnecessary movement would destroy the drill assembly as it bored into the ocean floor and, worst-case scenario, cause irreparable damage topside, even possibly sinking the ship.

The blue water boiled beneath the red-hulled vessel as

the azimuth thrusters fired, driving the vessel sideways and leaving a perpendicular wake. The oil derrick loomed more than two hundred feet above the center of the deck, far higher than the rear-mounted helicopter pad. The guided-missile destroyer *Kunming* circled on patrol in the distance, keeping a careful watch on the much larger but vulnerable drillship.

A massive bloodred, gold-starred PRC national flag perched on top of the derrick, and a forty-foot-long flag was painted on both sides of the ship. Feng didn't want any confusion about the nationality of the mobile drilling platform.

The *Tiger II* captain, her first officer, and the entire crew were civilian employees of the Chinese National Offshore Oil Corporation. CNOOC was owned by the PRC government and was the third-largest oil producer in China. The CEO of CNOOC was a protégé of Vice Chairman Feng's, who mentored the younger man before he left his high-ranking position at CNOOC to begin his political career. In fact, the CEO owed his position to the personal intervention of Feng, who used his political clout to guarantee the appointment. Feng maintained close relations with CNOOC and several other oil concerns, most of which were populated with strong political allies or Feng family members, including his murdered nephew, Zhao Yi, who had been the president of the Sino-Sahara Oil Corporation until he was assassinated by unknown killers in Mali.

The captain and her bridge crew were all proficient in computer systems. Two of her officers were dedicated computer specialists, while she and her first officer and the deckhands below were also seasoned sailors. The oil-drilling operations were run by a separate supervisor with his own handpicked operators, but even he and his gang of roughnecks were under her authority. The drilling supervisor stood silently by her side as the captain watched the video monitors detailing thruster direction, propeller RPMs, and engine status.

A few minutes later, the ADP system computers signaled that the *Tiger II* was finally in place. The captain nodded to the drilling supervisor, signaling that his work could now begin. They were both devoted members of the Party and loyal CNOOC employees, so they took on the potential risk of an American or Japanese attack on their operations with stoic pride. Feng characterized their actions today as heroic and every bit as important as a military victory in China's quest for energy independence. The knowledge that they would also each be granted one percent of gross revenues from the rig operation in perpetuity—paid into untaxed secret offshore bank accounts—was equally motivating.

Perhaps more so.

TWENTY-ONE

ON BOARD THE *LIAONING*
OFF THE COAST OF ZHANJIANG, GUANGDONG,
    CHINA
SOUTH CHINA SEA
APPROXIMATELY SEVEN HUNDRED MILES
    SOUTHWEST OF MAO ISLAND
10 MAY 2017

Admiral Ji, commander of the East Sea Fleet, stood twenty feet above the carrier flight deck on the open-air observation deck of the *Liaoning*'s superstructure for an unobstructed view of today's flight operations. The air thundered with the roar of turbofan jets and stank of jet fuel despite the buffeting South China Sea winds.

Ji stood next to Admiral Deng Zilong, the commander of the South Sea Fleet. Admiral Ji was only an observer of today's exercises, since China's only operational aircraft carrier was technically under Deng's command. But the two men were former shipmates, old friends, and, most important, allies in a cause greater than themselves. Like Ji, Deng believed President Sun's anticorruption reforms were too little too late. The Communist Party's corruption and ineptitude threatened the very legitimacy of the state and the Party. Failure to forcefully and decisively resolve the ongoing Uyghur rebellion, the latest Hong

Kong protests, or the reunification with Taiwan threatened China's hard-won unity. They both fervently believed that only a corps of uncorrupted military officers
led by the unwavering Admiral Ji could prevent China
from falling into prerevolutionary chaos and return her
to greatness in the twenty-first century. Standing next to
Ji was Captain Augusto Da Costa of the Brazilian Navy.
He served as a liaison to the PLAN and as a consultant
in naval air operations. Da Costa was the former commander of Brazil's only aircraft carrier, the French-built
Clemenceau-class *São Paulo*.

A turbofan jet screamed as it went full power.

"Gentlemen, you are about to witness history," Deng
said.

The catapult fired. A Lijian (Sharp Sword) unmanned
combat vehicle rocketed forward. A second later, the
black delta-winged aircraft bolted off the ski-jump forward flight deck and screamed into the sky.

The flight deck crews in their color-coded uniforms
exploded with cheers and applause.

The Chinese admirals grinned and shook each other's
hands, as well as the Brazilian's.

"Congratulations, Admiral," Da Costa said in heavily
accented English. "It is a new world today."

"Thank you, Captain. Your government has been in-
strumental in our success. China will not forget your
friendship."

The swarthy Brazilian nodded his appreciation. His
people had been circumnavigating the globe for five centuries since the Portuguese explorer Magellan first sailed
around the world and the tiny Iberian nation became the
first global superpower—a naval superpower—founding
colonies all over Africa, Asia, and Latin America, including
his own native country. The Chinese-Brazilian military
connection was a natural one. The BRIC nations—Brazil,

Russia, India, and China—were the four largest developing economies in the world, rapidly gaining on the declining West. They shared many interests, including escaping the economic imperialism and political domination of Europe and the United States. In recent years, they had strengthened their political and economic ties; military relations quickly followed.

"There it is," Ji said, binoculars pulled tightly to his eyes. "Two-hundred-eighty degrees, about five kilometers up."

The other officers turned their binoculars in the same direction.

"I see it," Da Costa said. "Amazing!"

"Once again, the Americans have given away their advantage," Deng shouted in the stiff breeze.

"As Americans usually do," Ji said, grinning.

Deng was right. The Americans were the first to successfully launch an unmanned vehicle from a carrier deck. The Northrop Grumman X-47B was also a delta-winged carrier-based jet aircraft. Originally intended to be a true unmanned combat aerial vehicle (UCAV), the X-47B would have carried the latest air-to-air missiles and stealth technology for air superiority combat missions. But the U.S. Navy changed the X-47B's mission profile to UCLASS, an unmanned carrier-launched surveillance and strike system designed for antiterror operations in low-threat environments. Essentially turning the X-47B from a world-class automated fighter into a glorified Predator.

The Chinese weren't about to make that mistake. Ji understood that lethal autonomous robotics—LARs—were the future of drone combat. The Americans were fools. Just one more reason for Ji to loathe them. He'd been raised by his mother to hate the Americans with every fiber of his being. His father, an army major, was killed fighting U.S. Marines during the Korean War. An unforgivable sin in his mother's home.

A second Sharp Sword rolled into launch position as the first UCAV made the landing approach for the deck.

"A completely autonomous landing?" Da Costa asked, still incredulous.

"The entire flight plan is run by the computer," Deng confirmed. "The next step in the program is combat operations." Deng wondered if the Chinese cyberwarfare specialists who had managed to steal so many American defense secrets had been able to pilfer any combat software yet. The Americans spent tens of billions of dollars developing new systems like the X-47B and yet allowed the Chinese to steal them for free. It was no accident that the Sharp Sword looked nearly identical to the American UCAV.

A loudspeaker croaked in Chinese above their heads. Ji translated for Da Costa. "Prepare for landing!"

The approaching Sharp Sword lined up toward the angled retrieval deck, dropping its gear. Today the fighter carried no weapons, but if the next few days of testing proved successful, that would change. Moments later, the wheels kissed the runway. The drone's tailhook snagged the third arresting wire and the Sharp Sword screeched to a halt. Again, the crew burst out in applause. The most dangerous moment in a naval aviator's life outside of combat was the carrier landing. Even in good conditions, it was a hazardous undertaking. At night, in poor weather, or extreme sea conditions, it was nearly impossible for all but the most skilled aviators. The *Liaoning* had lost several manned aircraft in the last few years during such landings. Hardly unusual given that China was still learning how to run carrier operations. The advent of the Sharp Sword would accelerate their progress exponentially in the decade to come. Even America's manned

F-35C, the carrier-based version of the Joint Strike Fighter, was designed around a JPALS system, utilizing GPS and navigational software for "hands off" approaches and landings in inclement weather and adverse conditions.

But UCAVs had other advantages over manned aircraft. Like other manned systems, a significant amount of weight and technology was devoted to pilot safety and survival. Humans were incredibly fragile, particularly in combat environments. Humans required sleep, food, waste elimination, and even oxygen at high altitudes. Human pilots could also panic, become distracted or fatigued, or suffer wounds in flight operations, causing them to hesitate or falter while making crucial combat decisions. Decision delays of just fractions of a second could cost the pilot his life—or worse, the air battle or even the war—as fragile, imperfect humans in heavier aircraft competed with emotionless, faultless UCAVs flying far beyond human endurance at faster speeds, traveling longer distances, making sharper turns, executing coordinated swarming maneuvers, and firing larger numbers of missiles at their human counterparts.

A light flashed on the weatherproof phone-console panel attached to the rail. Deng picked it up. Listened. Handed the phone to Ji. "For you, Admiral."

Ji thanked him and took the call. Ji nodded, smiled. "Excellent." He listened further. His face darkened. "Yes, just as we discussed. You have it on my authority." He hung up the phone.

Deng narrowed his eyes, a question. *Problem?*

Ji shook his head imperceptibly and offered a small reassuring smile. *No. Everything was proceeding exactly according to plan.*

TWENTY-TWO

The *Tiger II*'s deck was a beehive of noisy energy, the clamor of ringing hammers, growling diesel engines, straining cables. Arc welders hissed, throwing sparks, as supervisors shouted orders, urging speed as pipes, fittings, and a thousand other crucial pieces came together to begin the process of drilling on the ocean floor several hundred feet below—a cakewalk for the experienced deep-water crew.

The commander of the *Kunming* hung up the bridge phone. His orders from Admiral Ji in the preparation of the mission were clear, and now he confirmed them again verbally. He'd known the admiral for more than twenty years and knew him to be an honorable man. The kind of man an officer would willingly follow into combat, into the very mouth of hell itself. But the commander also knew that the decision he was about to make would change the course of his life and, perhaps, the life of his nation if the enemy didn't react the way they were sup-

posed to. And if military history had taught him anything, it was that the enemy seldom obeys one's wishes.

No matter. If the operation went sideways, the commander knew his life would be forfeit, but he comforted
himself in the knowledge that Ji would take the blame
first. That was why the commander believed Ji was the
man best suited to lead China, not the moneygrubbing
pigs in Beijing.

The commander pushed open the steel hatch and
stepped out onto the flying bridge. Held the binoculars
to his eyes. Saw the delta-winged Multimodal Volant surveillance drone high above, no doubt recording everything.

The commander stepped back into the bridge, took
his command chair. Picked up his phone.

"Lieutenant Liu, do you still have the target on your
scope?"

"Aye, sir!" The lieutenant was one deck below in the
CIC, a darkened room of two dozen video monitors and
computerized combat stations. The commander hated it.
Thought it looked like a video-game parlor.

"Then . . . engage."

Before the commander hung up the phone, a single
TY-90 missile roared out of a rotating deck launcher, arc-
ing into the sky like a bolt of lightning in reverse.

The first shot in the battle of Mao Island, he thought.

He doubted it would be the last.

TWENTY-THREE

"You may have lost your privacy, but at least you're in the Chairman's Suite now," Pearce said. He stood at the floor-to-ceiling window, staring at the bright lights of Tokyo's bustling business district. He sipped a hot green tea.

"Comped, too. One of the perks of fame. That poor hotel manager was embarrassed that he didn't recognize me when I checked in." Myers sat on a large sectional, also enjoying hot tea. The suite was tastefully modern. Very *Mad Men*, Japanese-style. Glass, stone, wood.

"He's probably just as concerned about your security. You've got the whole floor to yourself—including guards stationed at both ends of the hall."

"And you," Myers added.

"I'm not on his payroll."

"You should be."

"He couldn't afford me."

Pearce fell into the cushions opposite Myers. "You sure you're okay?"

She smiled, nodded. Her tired eyes said otherwise. "Part of the job description."

"I must've missed that part about you possibly dying."

"It's what we agreed to," Myers insisted. But she was touched at his obvious concern.

"Not exactly. But you pulled it off perfectly."

"Thank you. I don't remember much after we went into the library."

She took another sip of tea. The bionic pancreas was functioning as expected. Not only in her body, but in the worldwide press attention they'd hoped to receive. Now everybody on the planet knew that a bionic pancreas wasn't nearly as high-tech as it sounded. Clearly, the former American president could never again walk through an airport security scanner without setting off the alarm bells.

She wore on her body two Tandem t:slim insulin pumps connected to separate infusion sets, a Dexcom CGM monitor, an embedded glucose sensor and transmitter that monitored her bloodstream, and an iPhone streaming the data every five minutes, running a patented algorithm that drove dosing decisions. Nearly three hundred times a day, the iPhone broadcast Bluetooth dosing commands to the pumps according to the insulin levels in her bloodstream.

Hardware, software, smartphone, sensors. Myers was loaded for bear. But at least the bionic pancreas had completely automated the monitoring and dosing functions that every other type 1 diabetic had been forced to figure out manually for decades. No more stinging finger pricks for blood samples, no more nasty needles chasing veins. Best of all, no more mistakes or miscalculations that could result in under- or overdosing—the kind of thing that could land a diabetic in the hospital battling a coma or worse.

But both of them knew that in Myers's case, the overdose wasn't an accident. After consulting with her endocrinologist, she fasted for twenty-four hours, ate very few carbohydrates before or during Ito's dinner, injected twice as much "fast" insulin as was normally prescribed, and waited for the inevitable results.

In typical Margaret Myers overachiever fashion, she nearly overdid it. The goal was to pass out. When the ambulance arrived, she was on the edge of a diabetic coma.

Myers reached for her iPhone, didn't feel it. A momentary panic. She glanced over at the wireless charging pad. Saw it there. Relaxed again.

"When did you learn you were diabetic?" Pearce asked. "Type 1, right?"

"They call mine type 1.5. It falls somewhere between type 1 and type 2. LADA is the official term."

"Latent autoimmune diabetes of adults," Pearce said.

"If you already knew the answer, why'd you ask?" Myers said. She was secretly pleased that he'd taken the trouble to do the research, but she played it cool. "That's what lawyers do when they cross-examine witnesses."

"It's rare, isn't it?"

"Very. I'm just lucky, I guess. I was first diagnosed two years ago. Handled it fine with diet and exercise until my pancreas shut down about a year ago."

"And here you are."

"Make lemonade, I always say." She held his gaze for a moment then turned to her tea, slightly embarrassed.

"Excuse me," Pearce said. He headed for the restroom.

Myers watched him amble away. His gait was powerful and athletic even at this late hour. Though in his forties, Pearce still had a fantastic physique and excellent health. For the first time since they met, she felt like damaged goods. Her body was letting her down, which only reminded her that he was several years younger. Not that she was vain—she didn't really think about her age all that much. She'd been strong and healthy since working her father's cattle ranch as a little girl all the way through high school, along with lettering in three sports. She always ate right, exercised. Never looked her age. Not even now.

She grinned. Okay, maybe she was a little vain. It was hard to imagine a man like Pearce wanting to be physically intimate with an android like her with her pumps and needles and monitors. Not exactly Victoria's Secret stuff. He'd probably think he was making out with one of his drones.

Her smile faded. She remembered sitting in the doctor's office two years earlier. The LADA diagnosis hit her hard that morning. She had spent the first few minutes staring at the lab results and feeling sorry for herself. A real pity party. Life wasn't fair. She had already lost her husband and her son, and now she was losing her health.

And then she realized it was true, life really wasn't fair, and that she'd had a far better run of good fortune than most, even though most of that luck had been earned through hard work and taking big risks. Her dad had taught her a lot. Life was like a temperamental horse. Discipline worked wonders. But even the best horse still crapped in the barn every now and again. By the time the doctor came back, she had decided to pull up her big-girl panties and get on with it.

Pearce returned and sat back down across from her.

"Nice bathroom. Size of a basketball court," he said.

"There's two more of them, should the need arise."

"We're certain Feng saw the broadcast," Pearce said. The androgynous Thai had confirmed it verbally an hour earlier, according to Lane. "Now what?"

"We wait."

"I hate waiting." Pearce drummed his fingers on the cushions, thinking. "You ever like a guy who wasn't paying attention to you?"

Myers fought back a grin. *You have no idea.*

"Yes. In college, there was someone."

"How did you get him to pay attention to you?"

"Easy. I ran into his car in the parking lot at the student union. I was driving an old Buick at the time. Did a fair amount of damage, as I recall. I left a note with my name and number."

"How did that work out for you?"

"Asked me to marry him six weeks later."

"Your husband?"

She nodded. "He was a really good guy."

"No doubt." Pearce smiled. The laugh lines deepened around his dark blue eyes. "So now we just have to find ourselves another Buick."

TWENTY-FOUR

When Myers and Pearce arrived at the new business-jet terminal at Narita International Airport, everything was waiting for them, including one of the new HA-420 HondaJets. As soon as Pearce dropped his American Express Black Card onto the counter, a small army of uniformed agents suddenly appeared and swiftly expedited all the necessary legal, flight, and insurance documents for today's scheduled round trip to Taiwan's Taipei Songshan Airport. A courteous young flight steward served Myers a French press of dark Arabica coffee and a plate of *matcha* cookies in the executive lounge while Pearce conducted his preflight inspection of the HondaJet with a company official. An hour later, she and Pearce were airborne.

Why'd you pick the HondaJet?" Myers whispered in the headset.

"Because I own one," Pearce said. "Judy taught me how to fly it."

"I liked her."

"Me, too."

Judy Hopper had been his personal pilot and was the best flier he'd ever met, but she turned out to be a great flight instructor as well. She brought him along on single-engine prop planes before finally promoting him to the HondaJet, a magnificent lightweight aircraft with a state-of-the-art cockpit featuring flat-panel displays with touch-screen flight planning and navigational controls.

Pearce thought about Judy a lot lately. Her piloting skills saved his life back in Algeria. Myers's, too. He hoped she was happy in her new life as a missionary's wife in Africa. Wished she was flying the plane today. It would improve their chances of surviving greatly.

Pearce and Myers were flying at nearly five hundred miles an hour, bypassing Nagasaki Airport on their way out over the northern reaches of the East China Sea, heading roughly southwest toward the island nation of Taiwan.

The digital navigational panel displayed their GPS location and registered flight path, circumscribed by narrow red bands that warned against veering off course. The terminal agent explained that the air lanes between Japan and Taiwan weren't safe beyond the red zone owing to certain recent political developments. She was either too polite or too afraid to say that the Chinese now considered the area their national airspace and that planes entering it were subject to being shot down without warning.

Pearce had previously marked the location of Mao Island on his digital map—a designation still unrecognized by every government in the world save North Korea and Cuba. The HondaJet was locked firmly in the middle of the designated flight path, nearly due south of the disputed new island.

He glanced over at Myers strapped into her padded leather seat. Whispered in the headset. "All set?"

Myers nodded. "You betcha." She glanced around the high-tech cabin. "Not exactly a Buick."

"Actually, Honda calls this ride the Civic of the Sky."

Pearce turned the yoke and pressed the rudder pedal into a sharp, smooth turn heading due north. A moment later, cockpit alarms sounded as the navigation screen flashed a warning signal repeated by a female voice in their headsets. "Entering disputed airspace. Return to designated course."

Pearce tapped the touch screen, killing the alarm bells and warning signals. His radio buzzed. An incoming call from a traffic controller, no doubt. He ignored it.

"There." Myers pointed at the windscreen. On the far horizon they both saw the two-hundred-foot-tall oil derrick looming high above the deck of the Chinese drillship. She tapped another screen and a forward camera began feeding a live image of the drillship into a video monitor.

Pearce nodded toward the west. Far below, the wake of the *Kunming* missile destroyer, keeping a distant watchful eye.

"Looks menacing, even from here," Myers said.

"Heading down."

Pearce eased the yoke forward until the digital altimeter read just one thousand feet. From this height, ocean-going container ships looked like toy boats.

"We should have their attention now," Myers said. Her gut tingled.

"We got it the moment we entered their airspace. That destroyer has already painted us." Pearce and Myers were informed by Tanaka personally about the Volant drone getting shot down the day before. Didn't exactly boost Pearce's confidence in today's mission. He wished the civilian HondaJet had missile-lock alarms and electronic countermeasures.

Pearce held his course steady until they passed directly over the drillship. His palms sweated. The radio call signal flashed again. Myers nodded for him to take it.

Pearce put the incoming call on both headsets. An angry voice in broken English screamed in their ears. The *Kunming* ordered them to return to their airspace immediately or risk being fired upon.

"Better do what the man says," Myers said. "He sounds very displeased."

Pearce snapped off the radio, then banked the aircraft to the northeast in the general direction of Japan.

"Think that will calm him down?"

"We'll see," Myers said.

Pearce held the long, looping bank steady, dropping his altitude at the same time. The wide blue ocean grew larger. Soon, the red-hulled *Tiger II* filled the lower half of the windscreen.

"This idea feels dumber by the minute," Pearce said.

The HondaJet roared directly over the derrick again. They were low enough to see the crew scrambling over the deck. Pearce hoped it was out of sheer terror.

"I should've been a fighter pilot," Pearce said. "Get to fight sitting down."

"You might get your chance," Myers said. She pointed at the radar screen. A red blip was screaming toward them at Mach 2. More than fifteen hundred miles per hour.

Pearce slammed the throttles into the firewall and banked hard right and down, straight toward the deck.

"Troy—"

Pearce put the HondaJet twenty feet above the water, low enough that he'd slam into the side of an oil tanker if one got in his way. Luckily, nothing in sight. He glanced at the radar just in time to see the red blip directly on his six a half mile back—

The air exploded like a shotgun blast as a twin-tailed

Shenyang J-16 Red Eagle strike fighter rocketed past them, five hundred feet above their heads. Pearce felt the tiny HondaJet buck in his hands from the turbulence above. He and Myers watched the Chinese fighter pull into a near vertical climb and disappear into the late morning sun.

"That was too close for comfort," Myers said.

"Maybe being a grunt isn't so bad after all." He kept his eyes on the radar scope. The blip reversed direction, heading back toward where it came from at a high rate of speed. "We just might be out of the woods."

"That was reckless," Myers said.

"Me or them?"

She glared at him. "Both."

Pearce tapped the HondaJet's yoke. "We needed a Buick. At least I didn't hit anything."

"Is that—" Myers pointed at the radar screen.

The red blip reappeared behind them again.

And gaining.

Pearce tapped a video screen. A rear-facing camera pulled up. Incredible. The Chinese fighter flew just above the deck, trailing a vapor cone as it cut deep trenches of water behind it. His computer said the bogey was sub-sonic.

Pearce made a quick calculation, speed and distance. He held direction for three seconds, cut his throttles back to near stall speed, banked right.

Wrong move.

The big J-16's afterburners exploded again, roaring past them at supersonic speed, pulling a wall of pressure in its wake. The turbulence was too great this time. It grabbed one of the HondaJet's wings and flipped it as if it were tossing a coin. Pearce fought the yoke and rudder pedals, got it righted. The stall alarm screamed. The plane yawed and pitched. Pearce fought the controls, but before he could slam the throttle forward, the engines died. He keyed the radio.

"MAYDAY! MAYDAY!"

He kept the nose up as long as he could. Sixty knots and falling. He pointed the jet at a distant trawler. Prayed it was Japanese.

"BRACE FOR IMPACT!"

They hit the water.

Hard.

TWENTY-FIVE

The plane skipped like a flat rock on a rippling pond. Seawater sprayed over the windscreen as they jerked against their safety belts. The HondaJet shuddered until it finally came to a halt.

Judy taught Pearce that ditching a plane on smooth water was as likely a survivable event as a crash landing on flat dirt. The trick was to get out fast.

"We've got thirty seconds. Go!" Pearce shouted, as he unbuckled the safety straps. He wasn't sure if that was all the time they had, but he didn't want to wait around to find out.

Myers quickly popped her safety-strap releases and climbed out of her seat, racing for the exit door. Pearce pointed at the life jacket strapped to the bulkhead, a safety regulation for commercial jets flying over open water.

"Strap that thing on. I'll grab the raft." Pearce felt the plane bobbing in the water but didn't get the sense it was sinking.

Yet.

"Got it," Myers said, pulling the jacket out of its harness. She tossed one to Pearce then grabbed one for herself.

"Thanks." He pulled it on as he scrambled for the emergency locker. He yanked it open and found the inflatable raft folded into a solid yellow square.

Myers struggled to pull on her life vest.

"Need help?"

"No, I got it," Myers said. "But I should've paid more attention when the flight attendant was demonstrating it."

"I thought you were the flight attendant."

She laughed, snapping the buckles into place. "That's the other problem."

Pearce grabbed the raft out of its container and stepped toward the cabin door.

"All set?"

Myers nodded. "Good thing for you I like to swim."

"May not have to," Pearce said, patting the heavy yellow rubber. He dropped the uninflated raft at his feet and grabbed the lift handles on the cabin door and raised them. The door swung open easily, the bottom of it still a few inches above the water.

"So far so good," Myers said.

Pearce grasped the raft's red inflation handle in one hand and tossed the square out with the other. It splashed in the water several feet away and Pearce tugged on the inflation handle, activating a compressed-air cylinder that instantly inflated the raft. Pearce secured the tether line to the door handle and pulled the raft back close to the door. The plane had already sunk five inches and the raft was now even with the cabin door opening. Water began lapping into the entrance.

"After you, Madame President."

"Don't forget to bring the peanuts and sodas," Myers said, stepping gingerly into the bobbing raft.

Once she was securely in, Pearce leaped in after her and cut the rope with a utility knife provided in the raft kit. He handed her one of the two short paddles and they pushed away as fast as they could from the plane to avoid getting dragged down with it.

The plane remained relatively stable, the nose sinking by degrees as water flooded in. Pearce pulled out his emergency satellite phone and dialed up the air traffic controller at Ishigaki Airport, which was located on a small island about a hundred miles south of his position. The controller informed him that they had been tracking their flight since leaving Narita International Airport and that a JMSDF rescue helicopter was already on its way.

"Now all we have to do is wait," Pearce said.

Suddenly, Myers was overwhelmed with the magnitude of what had just happened. A Chinese fighter jet had just thrown them out of the sky, nearly killing them. She shuddered violently, as if badly chilled.

Pearce gathered her up in his arms, shielding her from the ocean breeze.

But she wasn't cold.

"Won't be long," he promised.

She nodded, happy to be held in his strong embrace.

"Did you find what you were looking for?" Pearce asked.

"And then some. That sonofabitch could've killed us."

"But he didn't."

"Thanks to you," Myers said. "If only that pilot knew he just did us one hell of a favor."

TWENTY-SIX

Tanaka gripped the bars of the dip station in his powerful hands. A leather belt cinched around his waist held a fifty-pound weight by a chain that dangled below his knees. He leaned forward and lowered himself until his elbows were at ninety degrees, then thrust upward, pecs and triceps exploding with power until he was fully extended. He repeated the move again and again, watching himself in the wall-length mirror, careful to keep the heavy weight between his legs nearly motionless with his perfect form. Sweat poured off his face as his arms and chest burned with lactic acid. An aide pounded on the door of his private gym.

"Enter!"

Tanaka pounded out the last brutal rep, then set his feet on the platform to relieve his exhausted arms.

The aide ran over, bowing deeply, begging forgiveness as Tanaka unchained the dumbbell and dropped it onto its rack with a clang.

"What is it?"

The aide explained. Myers's plane had crashed an hour ago in the East China Sea. Either shot down or forced down by a Chinese fighter jet.

"Dead?"

"No, sir. Rescued by one of our helicopters just a few minutes ago."

Tanaka dismissed the man and mopped his soaking-wet face with a towel. The gym door shut. He was alone.

Tanaka burst into laughter.

It would have served the Americans right if she had been killed. They had taunted the dragon, and the dragon snapped. Americans were arrogant fools.

He grabbed a seventy-pound dumbbell from the rack and sat in a chair with a low padded back, starting his first set of triceps extensions, slowly lowering and raising the heavy weight behind his head. He could already feel the burn.

An old familiar rage welled up in his gut as he lifted. *The Americans dare to tell us how to defend ourselves? They can't even win their own wars, but presume to tell us how to protect our nation? Arrogant bastards.*

Tanaka squeezed out the last rep and dropped the weight into his lap.

As bad as the Chinese were, at least they were honest, Tanaka thought. They hated Japan and everything it stood for, especially since Japan had proven itself superior in every regard. Their hatred wasn't just public; it was public policy.

But Tanaka deeply resented America. It paraded around as if it were a rich benevolent uncle at a birthday party. But in Tanaka's mind, America was a tyrant and a hypocrite. The United States had murdered hundreds of thousands of innocent Japanese citizens during the war in order to terrorize his country into submission, and now they have the gall to wage a war against terror?

Tanaka raised the weight back over his head, began the next set of reps, slow and steady. The seething anger energized his muscles.

The Americans forced a treaty on us, he fumed. *Wrote our Constitution. Forbade us to have an army or navy. They might as well have castrated every Japanese male while they were at it. But worst of all, America destroyed our sacred culture by forcing Americanism on us, ripping out the heart of Japan by relegating the divine emperor to the status of just another privileged royal. The very essence of what it meant to be Japanese was our culture. By destroying our traditional culture, America destroyed Japan itself.*

There was no doubt in Tanaka's mind at all.

Japan's only hope for survival as a nation and a culture was the destruction of both China and America.

Tanaka pushed the dumbbell faster and faster. Eight reps, nine reps—

Japan didn't have the ability to destroy either the U.S. or China.

But they had the power to destroy each other.

Tanaka powered through another five reps. He shouted as he raised the dumbbell for the last rep, his arms trembling with fatigue, muscles failing with complete exhaustion. Tanaka roared a low, open-throated shout from deep within, releasing his last ounce of spiritual energy. The weight rose, millimeter by millimeter, until it finally cleared the back of his head. He lowered the heavy weight into his lap, grinning ear to ear. He stood and tossed the dumbbell into the rack.

It suddenly dawned on him. Myers had shown him the way.

He laughed again, clapping his hands. *Hai!*

She had shown him the way.

TWENTY-SEVEN

Myers stood at the window, arms crossed. Watched the traffic six stories below.

Pang Bo, the Chinese ambassador, stood behind her a respectful distance away. Hong Kong–tailored suit, Rolex watch, frameless glasses. His security people remained outside the door, over their protest. Pearce stood in the corner, glaring at the tall, well-groomed ambassador.

"My government is extremely grateful that you suffered no permanent injuries, Madame President."

"That hardly seems possible, since your government obviously tried to kill me."

"We were unaware of your presence on the plane, I assure you. A plane, I might add, that violated Chinese sovereign airspace—"

Myers laughed. "Are you kidding me? Mao Island? It's a false claim under false pretenses."

"It's a perfectly legitimate claim that has been fully documented and presented to the appropriate international authorities for verification."

"International authorities you bully or bribe into your sphere of influence."

"China enjoys the same right as other nations to protect its borders, territories, and economic zones. We're confident that the international community will eventually see things our way."

Myers turned and faced Pang. A smug grin was plastered on his face.

"Because of the heightened state of tension between our two nations, I'm willing to keep this matter as private as possible, Mr. Pang. But I demand a full, official apology from your government for that reckless, senseless attack on our airplane."

"Forgive me, Madame President, but it's impossible to apologize for an act that wasn't committed. We made no attack on your person, and had we known you were on board the aircraft, we would have taken extra precaution. But your aircraft was specifically warned to remain on its scheduled flight plan and that leaving the designated flight corridor could result in a shoot down." The ambassador's grin widened. "But as you witnessed, the Chinese people showed great restraint, and our pilot didn't fire any weapons."

"Good thing I wasn't flying over Tiananmen Square."

Pang's grin fled.

"My government hoped that my appearance here at your hotel room would sufficiently convey our deepest concern for your well-being."

"Your government is going to get us into a shooting war."

"The Chinese people have no wish for war."

"Then why are you trying to steal the oil reserves in the East China Sea?"

"One cannot steal from one's self."

"Tell me, Pang, who's the idiot behind this Mao Island business? I know President Sun. He's far too smart to do something this radically stupid."

The ambassador's jaw clenched. He opened his mouth to speak but decided against it.

Now it was Myers's turn to grin. "Did I hit a nerve?"

"I believe President Sun is in complete agreement with the current policy."

"How uninformed do you think I am? He's not the one behind all of this. It's Feng, isn't it?"

The ambassador frowned briefly, surprised at her insider knowledge.

"Vice Chairman Feng speaks for many in our government. The East China Sea belongs to China. That is a historical fact and a current reality."

"My advice to you is to tell President Sun to call off his dog Feng before the Sixth Fleet steams into Shanghai harbor with all guns blazing."

"Highly unlikely, Madame President."

Myers laughed. "Why? Because of the Wu-14? It's a joke, and we both know it."

"I am not a military man, but I have been assured of its capabilities."

"My government knows for a fact that it's a fraud. We can't even produce one. And since all of your country's military advancements only come from stealing ours, I'm completely confident the Wu-14 is nothing more than a two-bit bottle rocket."

"Spoken like the former president of a failing superpower."

"You're an arrogant man representing an arrogant country. Someone needs to teach you both some manners."

Pang's pallid face flushed crimson. Myers had scored a direct hit.

"Perhaps I have upset the president. Please forgive my intrusion today. I will take my leave."

"If I don't get an apology from Feng personally within twenty-four hours, I'm contacting President Lane."

"I will convey your message." Pang turned to leave. He fumbled with the door, unnerved by Pearce's glowering eyes. He finally got it open and slammed it shut after him, fuming.

Pearce approached Myers. "A little rough on him, weren't you?"

"That's the point. It's not enough to find a Buick. You've got to crash it into your man, remember?"

TWENTY-EIGHT

The headquarters of the Chinese Communist Party and the vast bureaucracy known as the State Council were located behind the ancient red walls of Zhongnanhai, the ornate imperial leisure garden of China's resplendent emperors.

Vice Chairman Feng and Admiral Ji stood uncomfortably in President Sun's executive office. The squat, balding technocrat sat glumly behind his massive mahogany desk, his small hands folded quietly in front of him. Four red phones, a single black phone, a row of sharpened pencils, an empty yellow writing tablet, an iPad, and a recent family photo of Sun, his wife, and his daughter were the only items on the fifteen-foot-wide expanse.

Behind Sun, a wall-length bookcase of identical construction as the desk, each shelf neatly stacked with legal, political, and chemical engineering texts, reflecting Sun's accomplished professional background. Above the bookshelves, a reproduction of the ten-inch-tall, seventeen-foot-long scroll painting *Along the River During the Qingming Festival*, the most famous work in all of Chinese history. The thousand-year-old painting by the master Zhang Zeduan depicted the prosperous economic life of the Song Dynasty. Sun's administration referenced the painting as often as possible. It was a clear message conveying the peace and prosperity of an era before both Western colonialism and the brutality of Maoist Communism, the perfect metaphor for Sun's reform programs.

Feng quietly seethed, waiting for the hapless president to croak out some blathering inanity. Sun looked like a sleepy toad with a bad comb-over, his oily face and hands riddled with liver spots. Dark bags underscored his heavy-lidded eyes, which blinked behind thick prescription lenses wedged into large, unstylish frames.

Sun's inexorable rise to power had always frustrated Feng. The rancid little bureaucrat had an excellent reputation as an efficient and effective administrator, but he possessed little in the way of charisma or personal presence. His singular virtue was his determined, stubborn spirit. Like dripping water, he invariably wore down his opposition, less by force than by persistence. His unassuming demeanor caused many to underestimate him. His anticorruption reforms at the local and state levels were insignificant as far as Feng was concerned, but it was surprising that Sun survived the ordeal at all. Even the bottom-feeders in China's ruthless political ecosystem were dangerous. Sun was the compromise choice of a slim majority within the Politburo and the Standing Committee to become China's latest version of a reform president. His alliances were shaky at best. In Feng's estimation, Sun's days were numbered, especially when the nation would come to rally around him in the coming weeks when the oil would begin to flow from the Mao Island project and the American navy was driven out of Chinese territorial waters for good.

President Sun had summoned—*summoned!*—Feng and Ji to his office today with a terse summary of the meeting's agenda and a copy of Ambassador Pang's troubling report.

"I believe the Mao Island project is becoming too dangerous to continue," President Sun said. "It must be shut down immediately."

Feng tensed. "But Mao Island drilling has just begun. You're well aware of the oil and gas reserves we shall capture if we don't lose heart."

"The risk of war with the United States is greater than the reward of continued operations."

"The risk of war poses no danger; only war is dangerous. And the Americans will avoid a war with us at all costs," Admiral Ji said.

"You nearly killed an American president yesterday. Do you think the Americans wouldn't have retaliated if you had ended her life?" Sun asked.

Admiral Ji raised his hands in protest. "It was an accident. Had she announced her presence, we would have dealt with the situation differently."

"I'm afraid the Standing Committee agrees with me, gentlemen. Not you."

President Sun was the first among equals as one member of the seven-member Standing Committee, the ruling body that controlled the Communist Party of China. The Communist Party of China, in turn, controlled everything else, including the government and military. The Standing Committee met at least once per week and sometimes more if a particular crisis arose. Their decisions were reached through debate and consensus, but once made, they were final. President Sun was the legal head of all three branches of government—party, executive, and military. All of the members of the ruling class, no matter their bureaucratic or military titles, were members of the Party, and the Standing Committee controlled the Party.

President Sun was also the chairman of the Central Military Commission, which controlled all the branches of the military. But Sun's chairmanship was more ceremonial than actual. Vice Chairman Feng was the true head of the CMC, and General Chen, the other vice chairman, was Feng's paid lackey. As powerful as he was, however, Vice Chairman Feng wasn't yet a member of the Standing Committee. He had attained his position as vice chairman of the Central Military Commission three years before Sun rose to the presidency, and though Sun legally could dismiss Feng, he didn't have the political muscle to do so. Feng's densely woven web of alliances and secret bank accounts had proven too difficult to crack even for the determined Sun.

"The Standing Committee may agree with you," Feng said, "but the Central Military Commission certainly does not." He started to tell Sun that he knew the secret Standing Committee meeting had split four to three on their recent vote because three of the Standing Committee members were on Feng's payroll, as were half of the Politburo, who elected the Standing Committee, but there was no point in tipping his hand now.

"Vice Chairman Feng is correct," Admiral Ji said. "The PLAN is quite in favor of our current direction."

"And the PLAN is willing to risk a catastrophic war for a few gallons of oil?" President Sun asked.

"The Americans don't want war and neither do we. But there will be no war because the Americans won't fight us," the admiral insisted.

"Did you bother to read Ambassador Pang's report?" Sun demanded.

"Of course. Myers is mistaken. The Sixth Fleet wouldn't dare challenge us."

"She's a failed president of a failing nation," Feng said. "What does it matter what she thinks?"

"It matters because she's a close friend of President Lane's. My sources tell me she helped him win power. That means she has influence over him." Sun leaned forward. "And she wants an apology from you, Feng. A personal apology."

Feng was lost in thought. It suddenly occurred to him that Myers might be his best option yet. "If you were certain that the Americans would not oppose us, would you support the continued drilling at Mao Island?"

"Do you take me for an idiot? Of course I would. The amount of oil and gas located there would virtually guarantee our energy independence in the coming decade," Sun said. "But you can't guarantee the Americans won't attack us."

"Myers said the Americans don't believe the Wu-14 is operational. You also said she has influence over Lane. If I can convince Myers the Wu-14 exists, she'll convince Lane. And if Lane believes we have it, the U.S. Navy will, and the U.S. Navy will never risk an aircraft carrier, especially for the sake of Japanese oil interests."

"Vice Chairman Feng is exactly right," Admiral Ji said.

Feng relaxed, knowing he'd already won. "So let me propose this. I'll invite President Myers to meet me in person, and I will apologize to her face-to-face."

"Where and when?" Sun asked.

"At Admiral Ji's headquarters," Feng said. "Where the Wu-14 is currently located."

President Sun unfolded his hands and leaned back in his chair, thinking.

"Yes, that might just work."

"I'll make the arrangements immediately," Feng said.

Once Myers saw the Wu-14 in person, the Americans

would be convinced of its existence. China might just win this war without firing a shot.

"Do so, and keep me informed," the president said, picking up a phone. He waived a spotted hand, dismissing the two men.

"As you wish," Feng said.

Feng glared at Sun's flaking scalp. He made a mental note as he left. The first thing he'd do when he took over this office was to have it thoroughly disinfected.

TWENTY-NINE

A curtain of heavy snow fell in thick flakes. Troy slammed the brakes in front of the bar, nearly plowing into the back of a familiar custom pickup, a '66 Chevy 4x4 painted midnight black with orange flames raking the hood.

Troy leaped out of his own beater truck, leaving the motor running and windshield wipers slapping. He dashed through the front door just in time to see his dad smash a man in the mouth with his hammering fist. A gout of blood spewed out of the taller man's bearded mouth as he howled in pain. There were two other men on the floor already, one crawling toward a table, the other out cold. Troy prayed he wasn't dead. The air was hot and fetid and clouded with blue smoke. A honky-tonk steel guitar wailed on the jukebox.

"I'm calling the cops now, Troy," the barkeep hollered. He slammed a rotary phone on the bar. Started to dial. "Get your old man outta here."

A towering bear of a man shouted at the barkeep, six-foot-six if he was an inch and three hundred pounds. Big gut, bigger arms. Steel-toed boots and an ugly pockmarked face. "Fuck that. He started it, I'm gonna finish it." He grabbed the rotary phone off the bar and yanked it hard, pulling the cord out, and tossed it across the room. The bell rang when it smashed against the wall.

"I shit bigger 'n you, you fat fuck," Troy's dad slurred. He was nearly a foot shorter and half the weight of the hulking brute. He started coughing fiercely.

"Fuck him up, JoJo!" A heavy woman in leathers horse-laughed, a cigarette dangling in her blistered mouth. She was perched precariously on a bar stool beneath a crumbling beehive of bleached purple hair matching the color of her lipstick and fingernails.

"That's the idea, honey." A wiry man with bad teeth and biker tats grabbed a pool cue.

"Put that down," Troy growled. He'd grown in the last two years. Six-foot-two, two hundred pounds of hard ax-swinging muscle.

"You gonna make me?" the wiry man asked.

"Are you shitting me? Put that damn thing down or I'll shove it up your ass."

Troy's dad wobbled on unsteady feet. "I don't need your help, son. Get out!"

"Yeah, get out, son. Get out!" JoJo mocked, belly laughing. So did half the barflies crowding around the edges. JoJo reached into his oil-stained Levi's. Pulled out a quarter and tossed it at Troy. "There's a pay phone across the road. Call an ambulance. Your daddy's gonna need it."

The quarter hit the cigarette butt–littered floor at Troy's feet.

"Idiot." Troy picked up a chalk-stained cue ball from the pool table. Held it like a baseball. Pointed at the wiry biker. "Put that stick down now. We'll clear out."

"I'm not going anywhere." Troy's dad glowered at him.

"Only to the morgue, little man." JoJo stepped closer.

"You tell him, JoJo!" the purple-haired woman bellowed, hoisting a beer.

Troy threw the cue ball hard. It thudded into the skinny man's chest right above the heart. He cried out. The pool cue in his gnarled hand clattered to the floor. He clutched his chest like he was having a heart attack and doubled over.

Troy was on him in an instant. Grabbed the man by his greasy hair and smashed his face with an iron-hard fist. The cartilage in the man's nose cracked like a snapped pencil, gushing blood all over Troy's shirt before he collapsed in a heap, howling and clutching his broken face.

Troy turned to his dad. "Let's get out of here."

"I'm not going anywhere."

"What the hell's wrong with you?" Troy marched over and grabbed at his father but he got shoved back hard.

"Touch me again and I'll put you down, you little son of a bitch."

"You tell him!" the big woman shouted, laughing again.

"Get him out of here, Troy. I mean it!" The bartender held an old police billy club in his hands now, still hiding behind the bar as a shield.

"Dad, please."

The man who had crawled under a table to escape his beating earlier suddenly leaped up behind Troy's dad and wrapped his arms around him. Before Troy's dad could break the armlock, JoJo lunged with a beer bottle from his blind side, swinging it like a hammer. It smashed against his dad's skull with a sickening thud. The rock-hard bottle didn't break.

His dad moaned and fell to his knees, reaching for his bleeding scalp.

JoJo turned and charged Troy, bottle held high in the air. He swung down just as he reached Troy, but Troy stepped into him, throwing a perfect punch into the lunging man's face, doubling the strength of the blow. JoJo's head snapped back like a Pez candy dispenser as his feet swept out from under him. He crashed to the floor, knocked out cold.

Troy turned just in time to see his dad collapse to the ground, his unblinking eyes staring straight back at him.

THIRTY

The freighter was nearly forty years old and looked every year of it on the outside with its peeling paint and rusted hull, but that was a convenient disguise. The old freighter's cargo hold had been lavishly refurbished for an entirely new purpose, fit for princes and champions.

Tanaka sat next to Kobayashi-*san*, the most powerful yakuza boss in Tokyo, in the premium seats with the best view, high up, like a caesar at the coliseum. Half of Japan's eighty thousand yakuza pledged allegiance to the Kobayashi-*gumi*, the most vicious and well-funded crime syndicate in the country.

Tanaka had known Kobayashi for years and owed much of his political career to the wise old yakuza. But Kobayashi had never invited Tanaka to one of these fabled events before, which, until tonight, Tanaka believed were only an urban legend.

Kobayashi had founded his *gumi* the old-fashioned way back in the '70s, through extortion, gambling, and prostitution. But his organization entered the ranks of the superwealthy by securing bank loans from Japan's most respectable institutions back in the bubbling heyday of the '80s, when banking regulations were lax and property values were soaring.

But when the great Japanese miracle bubble burst and the economy crashed, Kobayashi's unsecured bank loans were nowhere to be found, having been made by shell companies with no traceable records connected to the wily boss. When the dust finally settled on the real estate crash, Kobayashi bought up prime Tokyo real estate in the early 2000s for pennies on the dollar, becoming one of Japan's largest legitimate commercial landlords. He was known in police circles by the code name the Realtor.

The yakuza organizations were not unlike the *keiretsu* conglomerates that dominated Japan's domestic economy, the powerful interlocking corporate relationships that forged the crony-capitalist system known as Japan, Inc. The yakuza organizations became natural allies with several of the largest Japanese *keiretsu* conglomerates and, in turn, with their political connections. The yakuza achieved in Japan what the American mafia could only dream of by several orders of magnitude. The Chicago mob connection to the Kennedys paled in comparison.

In recent years, tough laws cracking down on yakuza activities and their associations with political and corporate elites had significantly curtailed the smaller *gumi*s. But Kobayashi's organization flourished behind its gilded corporate doors and secure political connections.

But old habits died hard for the well-heeled gangster, and he kept his hand in the more traditional lines of the family business, especially gambling. In fact, gambling gave birth to the yakuza concept hundreds of years before; the name itself was derived from the numbers in a card game that indicated a losing hand. Despite his European-tailored suits and two-hundred-dollar haircuts, the now urbane Kobayashi was still a street gambler at heart—and a cold-blooded killer. Once a year he hosted the Golden Sword tournament on this ship, a sign of his nostalgia for all things Japanese and the old yakuza ways peopled with hard, violent men who fancied themselves the luckless sons of *ronin*—masterless samurai.

The polished bamboo floor was surrounded by three rows of plush leather bench seats, each row higher than the first, all with a clear view of the arena. The audience sat cross-legged in the traditional manner, and each was served the finest gourmet food and beverages available between bouts. The price of admission was one hundred ounces of gold. Kobayashi no longer trusted the fiat currencies of Japan or the West—but the one-hundred-twenty-thousand-dollar ticket price was pocket change for the assembled audience, most of whom were other yakuza bosses, including several of Kobayashi's most trusted lieutenants. But the audience also included two Saudi princes, a Russian oil magnate, and several other respectable billionaires, along with a few select guests, including Tanaka.

Stable owners brought at least one fighter to the tournament and some brought several. Even though the real money would exchange hands in the betting, it was the victorious stable owner of tonight's tournament who would win a samurai sword crafted in pure twenty-four-carat gold—a useless instrument in combat, but of inestimable worth in bragging rights alone.

Tanaka watched the current bout eagerly. The two men squaring off were former national kendo champions, Japan's famous nonlethal sword-fighting martial art practiced all over the world. Traditional kendo combatants were covered from head to ankle in safety equipment—protective face masks, head gear, body armor, padded gloves—and wielded flexible bamboo-slat swords. International Kendo Federation (FIK) bouts were safe, and winners were determined by a point system based on landing harmless blows to the opponent.

But the Golden Sword was anything but a sanctioned FIK tournament.

The two past champions on the floor fought with only grilled face masks and wielded *bokuto*—samurai swords fashioned from the hardest known woods available. Battles were won when an opponent quit, was knocked unconscious, or was killed, the latter two easily accomplished with *bokuto* wielded by highly skilled swordsmen. Most preferred the long *katana*, but some fought with shorter *wakizashi* and even knife-sized *tanto* blades, sometimes one in each hand.

Without fear of injury or death, FIK bouts were almost dancelike in their careful choreography, each combatant seeking openings to swiftly score points with a tap of bamboo. But in the Golden Sword tournament, a single "point" scored with a wooden sword blade usually meant cracked teeth, broken bones, or a split skull and thus the end of the bout.

A large digital clock counted down the five-minute limit on bouts. Combatants who failed to score a single blow were given a second three-minute bout. If no points were scored then, both were eliminated from the tournament and banned for life, which bore the greatest shame. Some unfortunates suffered harsher treatment later by their temperamental stable owners. But the rewards for winning fighters were mind-numbingly staggering. More than one millionaire would be made on the killing floor tonight, though perhaps at the cost of an eye, limb, or brain injury.

The two champions circled each other in short, sharp steps, both wielding long wooden *katana*. Suddenly, gut-wrenching screams exploded as both men lunged in a lightning-fast strike. The swords clacked like gunshots when they struck, swords flashing and striking again and again. The champion in black—a Korean—staggered under a blow to his left shoulder by the Japanese fighter in red, but not before he landed his own hard strike against the other man's helmet. Both men fell away, reeling in blinding pain, swords held up defensively. The clock was ticking down. Less than one minute to go.

The Japanese fighter ripped the helmet off his head and flung it aside. His hair was matted with blood where the blow landed.

The audience erupted with wild applause.

Kobayashi lit a fresh cigarette from his current one. A doe-eyed Russian girl refilled the yakuza's glass with bubbling Cristal.

"Is that one yours, Kobayashi-*san*?" Tanaka asked, nodding at the Japanese fighter.

The yakuza chuckled, his eyes still fixed on the killing floor. "Looking for an inside scoop?"

Tanaka laughed. "No. Your humble servant doesn't have enough gold to make a wager."

"I can loan you any amount you need."

"Thank you, sir, but no."

Kobayashi slapped his knee, laughing loudly. "You always were the smart one, Tanaka! That's why I like you, even if you aren't a yakuza."

"I'm not worthy of such an honor."

Kobayashi howled again. "You're a politician, that's for sure!"

Both men knew that Tanaka was highborn and pure Japanese, but Kobayashi was the son of a Chinese mother and a poor working-class Japanese father. Many yakuza were ethnic outcasts of non-Japanese heritage, despite being third- or even fourth-generation inhabitants of Japan. Unlike in America, being born in Japan didn't automatically make a person a Japanese citizen. Kobayashi never admitted to his shameful Chinese heritage, only to his legitimate Japanese blood. His untold wealth bought him the respect he needed from the poorer purebreds like Tanaka who needed either his muscle or cash—or both.

The digital clock flashed thirty seconds. A loud alarm bell began blaring like a klaxon, marking the countdown.

"Watch!" Kobayashi shouted, his aged eyes filled with childish delight.

The Japanese lunged at the Korean, a war cry screaming from his mouth, eyes crazed, sword raised high above his head for a killing blow.

The Korean raised his sword to block, but the Japanese checked his swing and pulled back at the last second. He cursed the Korean, called him a coward, his voice booming, amplified by pure adrenaline. The clock ticked off fifteen seconds.

The Korean circled cautiously. The crowd booed and jeered. The Japanese lowered his sword to his side and mocked the Korean's mother, his manhood, his paternity. The clock ticked five seconds to go.

The Korean shouted a bloodcurdling curse and grabbed his helmet with his left hand. In the second it took him to clear the mask from his face, the Japanese lunged again, sword held in both hands, thrusting straight forward. The sharp tip of the wooden blade plunged into the Korean's unprotected throat, cutting off his scream. He dropped his *katana* and instinctively grabbed the blade plunging into his neck. Too late.

The Japanese shouted his *kiai*, ramming the wooden tip in as deep as he could, legs pumping hard, forcing the Korean backward until the Korean tripped over the first row of seats, scattering the bettors, the Japanese fighter on top of him, throwing his full weight on his sword until the Korean's neck snapped in two with a crack.

The buzzer blared. Bout over.

The audience screamed with bloodlust, joyous, even the losers.

The Japanese lifted his bloody blade high, spreading his arms wide, face beaming with pride. A shower of gold and silver coins crashed on the floor at his feet.

Kobayashi shook his head in disgust. "No honor in that."

Tanaka nodded his agreement. "He acts like a filthy American footballer after a goal."

Kobayashi shook his head. "I fear for our young people. They have lost their way." He took another drag on his cigarette.

"Then it's our responsibility to teach them the old ways before it's too late."

"Too late? How?"

"I know you're a learned man and pay attention to the affairs of the world."

Kobayashi grunted, accepting the compliment. "The Chinese again?"

"Yes."

Kobayashi thought about that as he watched the Korean's corpse being ceremoniously carried away. Several towel boys slid onto the floor and mopped up the blood and sweat.

"Will we be at war soon?"

Tanaka nodded. "Yes. It's almost unavoidable."

A voluptuous African woman with short-cropped, blazing red hair approached carrying a silver platter of freshly sliced sashimi. She described the extremely costly tray items in faultless Japanese.

"Almost unavoidable?" Kobayashi pointed at three different plates of sashimi. The girl set them down in front of him and flashed an offering smile at Tanaka. He waved her away and she left with a small bow.

"War can be avoided, *Oyabun*. But it will not be easy."

Kobayashi lifted a piece of fatty *otoro* tuna with his chopsticks and dropped it into his mouth. The sweet belly meat practically melted on his tongue. He pointed to the plate, indicating Tanaka should take some. He did.

"What about Ito?" Kobayashi asked.

"He's an American lackey, a monkey on a leash. The fool will stumble into war and drag us all the way to hell. Unless you help me."

The old yakuza nodded. Yakuza were famously patriotic and ultranationalistic, a common trait among organized-crime elements the world over. Even the Chinese Communists were known to have employed the lawless Triads in patriotic service to the world revolution.

"What must be done?"

Tanaka laid out the details of his plan as the next combatants entered the ring. Three men in green strode in from one side of the ring like a street gang, rough and unmannered. Their dark bare torsos were shredded with thick cords of sinewy muscle and slathered in bright yakuza ink, but heavy grilled kendo masks hid their faces. They took up positions on the far side of the circle, flashing their wooden swords back and forth as if flicking at flies, impatient for battle. Tanaka guessed the yakuza fighters were mixed-race Okinawans.

"Sounds risky. What's in it for you?"

"Nothing, *Oyabun*."

"Not very smart. So what's in it for me?"

"Even less. Perhaps worse." They both knew that Kobayashi was putting his entire organization at risk by throwing in with Tanaka's plan.

"So what would that make me?"

"A patriot."

Kobayashi nodded his head, calculating. Finally, he snapped his head curtly. *Hai!*

A lone fighter entered from the opposite side of the room, each step an act of ceremonial grace. He wore a traditional kendo uniform—a *keikogi* with three-quarter-length sleeves over his torso, and the pleated skirt known as a *hakama*. Both were dyed in traditional indigo blue. A white and red "sun circle" Japanese national flag was sewn on the back. His mask was tucked under one muscled arm. His face was stalwart and handsome like one of the samurai soap-opera stars seen constantly on Japanese television, but his thick black hair was styled in a crew cut, the bristles stiff and dense. He pulled on his mask with ritual precision and carefully adjusted the wooden *tanto* tucked in his belt.

"This will be something special," Kobayashi said. He nodded toward the lone Japanese fighter. "That man has never been defeated."

Tanaka was a martial artist himself. He saw clearly that the disciplined Japanese was the superior fighter and certain to win in spite of being outnumbered by the Okinawan rabble.

The referee approached, dressed in the traditional long-skirted garb of a kendo judge. He was short but powerfully built, and his pencil mustache was tinged with gray. He pointed at the clock with a folded fan until it flashed five minutes. He raised his arm. The combatants bowed to one another. The referee slashed the air with his hand and the bout began. The audience shouted.

The three yakuza fighters backed up and spread out equidistant as the Japanese advanced into the center. The yakuza fighters swiftly spread out even farther, forming a three-pointed perimeter around the Japanese swordsman.

The Japanese stood rock still in the center of the arena, dropping his head to his chest, resting his *katana* on the top of his helmet mask almost as if he were praying.

The yakuza fighter directly in front of him glanced up at the clock. Twenty seconds had already elapsed. He shouted to his compatriots and the three men inched forward, their feet never leaving the wooden floor, trying not to reveal their positions, trying to move in sync so as to arrive at the same destination at the same time.

Cautiously, deliberately, they each inched closer and closer. The audience was dead silent. Not even the *tink* of glasses or silverware. The closer the yakuza fighters got, the farther forward everyone in the audience leaned.

When the yakuza fighters got within slightly more than a sword's length distance, they all shouted as one and charged, *katana* slashing wildly. The Japanese twisted, parried, turned, spun, and swung faster than anything Tanaka had ever seen. Sword strikes clacked like a string of firecrackers. The yakuza fighters fell back. The Japanese stood firm.

The audience applauded.

To his practiced eye, it seemed to Tanaka that all the yakuza strikes were blocked. If any landed, the Japanese hadn't shown it. No signs of injury. But Tanaka noticed the bleeding knuckles on the hand of one of the yakuza fighters, and another one was shaking out an obviously injured wrist.

The yakuza fighters regathered their wits. This time, they moved in a circular motion around the Japanese, coordinating their speed and distance by shouting to one another in short, crisp, singular vowels, as much to confuse the Japanese as to organize their next attack. The shouts bounced back and forth like an echo while the Japanese kept his head bowed to the ground.

The yakuza fighters circled cautiously as the seconds

ticked off. When one of the Okinawan fighters crossed directly in front of him, the Japanese fighter vaulted forward, slashing down hard at his head. The Okinawan held his sword up in defense, but the crashing blow from the Japanese was so forceful that the fighter's own wooden blade cracked into his skull, buckling his knees and breaking his scalp. He staggered badly.

When the Japanese leaped into the frontal attack, the other two yakuza fighters charged at him from the sides. By the time they reached him, the Japanese had already broken the first man's nose and managed to duck and turn in a vicious sweeping motion, raking the other men's knees with his own blade.

All three yakuza fighters howled in pain and fell back, even as the first man tried to stanch his bleeding scalp with a palm pressed firmly against the top of his head.

The audience applauded again.

Wounded and humiliated, the three Okinawan fighters retreated to the outermost edge of the fighting circle while the Japanese returned to the very center.

The clock clicked off the four-minute mark.

The Japanese lifted off his mask and tossed it aside.

The three yakuza fighters exchanged nervous glances with one another through their masks as the Japanese raised his long *katana* parallel to his torso near his right shoulder like a batter at the plate.

All three yakuza screamed in rage and charged the Japanese. He pulled his short *tanto* out of his belt in a flash and spun, using both blades as a shield against the falling blows. The three yakuza crashed into him, blocking his arms, keeping him from making powerful thrusts, but they were in too close. The Japanese punished them with his elbows and knees.

But the Okinawans landed their own blows, too, finally drawing blood on the handsome unmasked face before they fell back, gasping for air, trembling with rage and pain. They took up their far positions again, preparing for the final assault.

The Japanese shook his head to clear it. Blood stained his indigo *keikogi*. He signaled to the referee, who, in turn, glanced up at Kobayashi. The yakuza overlord nodded his approval, and the referee shouted a command as his hand thrust into the air with an open fan, signaling a time-out. Rare, but legal. A privilege for the Japanese fighter, a former Golden Sword tournament champion. The clock stopped.

The audience jeered, especially the white *gaijin*.

Tanaka scowled. The foreigners had no manners.

The Japanese retreated to his starting position and set his *katana* and *tanto* down on the polished bamboo floor. He untied the belt to his *keikogi* and pulled it off, revealing his heavily muscled upper body. It was covered in vivid inks, too: gods and monsters in brightly colored hues. But Tanaka admired the dragon on his chest the most. Its monstrous gaping mouth filled his upper torso while scaly green arms extended down his biceps and forearms, ending in vicious claws in the palms of his hands that ran the length of his outstretched fingers.

The Japanese clapped his hands twice and three retainers ran out in traditional kendo garb, each carrying a black case. They bolted over to the exhausted Okinawans and fell at their feet, setting each case down, then opening it and, while remaining in a bowing position, holding up a razor-sharp carbon steel *katana* high enough for each yakuza fighter to take hold of.

The audience went insane. The betting pool exploded. Tanaka watched Kobayashi toss a cool million into the pot, tapping out the bet on the tablet with his yellowed fingertips.

The Okinawan fighters glanced at one another through their masks. What would they do? The metal swords were an obvious insult, but they had already proven overmatched against the lone Japanese fighter. They were proud Okinawans and hated the purebred mainlander now openly mocking them with his haughty smile.

Tanaka couldn't believe his eyes when, a moment later, all three yanked off their masks and tossed them across the arena floor.

"He's lucky they're rash," Tanaka said.

"Luck is a woman."

Each yakuza fighter picked up his steel sword from the case extended to him, and the retainers bolted away.

The referee barked a command and the combatants took up their original positions opposite one another. The yakuza fighters gained confidence with each passing second, their hands gripping hard steel while the Japanese fighter held only wooden blades.

The referee held his hand high to restart the bout. The Japanese threw his *tanto* aside.

The crowd cheered madly. The betting pool added another two million.

The referee cast a glance at Kobayashi, who nodded his approval. The referee chopped his hand down hard with a shout. The clock resumed its countdown.

Thirty-two seconds to go.

The audience leaped to its feet, howling and clapping as the four opponents squared off. The three Okinawans circled the man in the middle, slowly tightening the noose. The Japanese raised his wooden *bokuto* high above his head, shouted his war cry, and lunged at the man in front of him.

But the Okinawan didn't move.

The Japanese slashed his wooden sword toward the man's skull just as the Okinawan dropped to one knee and held his own razor-sharp blade above his head, braced on each end by his wiry hands.

The steel blade absorbed the blow. The wooden sword bit deeply into the razor-sharp edge—so deeply that it stuck for just a fraction of a second.

A fraction of a second the Japanese fighter didn't have.

Just as he managed to free his *bokuto*, two finely honed carbon steel edges slashed across his back, opening his flesh as if they were boning a fish. The Japanese screamed in agony and whipped around only to be slashed again across his broad chest. Blood poured out of the dragon's voracious mouth as his body crashed to the floor.

The crowd stood in stunned silence, including Tanaka. But Kobayashi sat grinning like a Buddha.

"I don't understand," Tanaka said. He saw Kobayashi betting heavily. He assumed he'd been betting on the Japanese.

"There's the man we need to lead your operation," Kobayashi said.

Tanaka glanced at the three yakuza on the arena floor, pacing around the corpse and laughing like hyenas over their kill. Tanaka couldn't decide which one he meant.

"Him." Kobayashi nodded toward a large man standing in the audience on the far side of the area. The big Okinawan was fat like a *sumotori* and wore his long hair in a ponytail. Voluminous black silk pants and shirt couldn't hide his enormous girth, and the heavy gold chains around his neck were nearly lost in the folds of fat.

"Oshiro-*san* is the one you can count on," Kobayashi said.

"Why him?"

"Those are his boys. Rough, but fearless."

"Impressive," Tanaka said. "Those Okinawans are better trained than I realized."

Kobayashi nodded. "Good fighting dogs are always trained. Oshiro-*san* keeps his men vicious, effective, and obedient." And then he laughed. "But those Okinawans are crazy, too. Crazy enough to do what needs to be done."

THIRTY-ONE

Myers and Pearce tried to relax in their plush leather seats despite the blaring sirens outside that were muted by the armored chassis and bulletproof glass of the twenty-foot-long Red Flag L8 limousine. An armed military escort raced in front and behind them as the convoy roared past the open gate, sentries erect, saluting Admiral Ji's flags snapping just above the big bug-eyed headlights of the gleaming black vehicle.

After landing at Ningbo airport in Feng's private Gulfstream G150, the convoy whisked Pearce and Myers out of the bustling city over the bridge to the naval facilities on the southern side of Zhoushan Island. Myers kept eager eyes on the buildings, equipment, and personnel speeding past her window, taking it all in. They finally reached the four-story headquarters and rolled to a stop, the sirens suddenly cutting off like a slit throat.

A scowling PLAN lieutenant commander yanked open the limousine door and motioned for Pearce and Myers to follow. He marched them into the building and up three flights of stairs, where they were greeted by two hulking armed guards. The lieutenant commander barked an order and the guards opened two heavy steel doors with synchronized precision. Still unsmiling, the PLAN officer shot a stiff open palm toward the open doors, bidding the two Americans to enter. They did, and the doors closed silently behind them.

Admiral Ji and Vice Chairman Feng stood in front of Ji's desk, an ornately crafted piece of antique captain's furniture. Ivory-eyed sea dragons held up the four corners of the mahogany desktop. Paned windows overlooked the harbor.

"Madame President, Mr. Pearce, thank you for coming. I trust your journey was a pleasant one?" Feng asked. He approached Myers with an extended hand.

Pearce grabbed it instead. "Thanks, it was."

Feng's plastic smile didn't budge as his hand was caught in the vice grip of Pearce's handshake.

"This is Admiral Ji, the commander of the East Sea Fleet."

Ji nodded deferentially to Myers. "Welcome, Madame President."

"Coffee? Tea? Something to eat?" Feng asked.

"No, thank you. We didn't come here for the food or the hospitality," Myers said.

"I admire your frankness. A hallmark of your presidential administration," Feng said. "Please, be seated." He gestured toward the four club chairs arranged in a circle.

The Chinese and Pearce went to sit down, but Myers proceeded over to the window. Her eyes scanned the ships tied up to the piers. Two diesel submarines, a missile destroyer, several smaller ships. Civilian dockworkers and sailors serviced the vessels.

"Lovely view. I can't wait to see the *George Washington* pulling into your harbor."

"President Myers, please," Feng said.

"Of course." She took the last remaining seat.

"It was good of you to take the trouble of coming here," Feng said.

"It was terribly inconvenient. I hope it will be worth my valuable time."

"I don't think you'll be disappointed," Feng said.

"That's what you promised on the phone."

"First things first. I offer my apologies for what happened to you and Mr. Pearce the other day. Our pilots are trained to be aggressive, but had they known someone as important as you was in the vicinity, they would have restrained themselves."

"So if I had just been a member of the American proletariat, my death would have been acceptable to you?"

"Or a working stiff like me?" Pearce asked.

"Tensions in the area are high, and the Japanese are increasingly belligerent. We will not tolerate any Japanese violations of our national airspace," Admiral Ji said. "For the sake of peace."

Pearce tried not to laugh out loud. "Yeah, right."

"Our apologies to you as well, Mr. Pearce. Your friendship with President Lane is noted, as is your incredible success as a security company. Drone warfare, correct?" Feng said.

"My company does far more civilian consulting than military these days. There are many more opportunities in the private sector for unmanned vehicles."

"Perhaps then you are familiar with the Wu-14?" Ji asked.

"Yes, of course," Pearce said. "Or at least the rumor of it. From everything I've read, you don't have the technical capacity for it."

"Isn't that why we're here?" Myers asked. "I assumed that's the real reason why you invited us."

"The primary reason was for me to apologize to you in person, just as you demanded from Ambassador Pang." Feng's eyes narrowed.

"And so you have. I suppose it would be rude of me not to accept it."

"Thank you," Feng said.

Myers smiled. She doubted Feng understood the English language well enough to know that she hadn't technically accepted his apology.

"Our country does not wish to fight a war with the United States," Admiral Ji said.

"Of course you don't. You'd lose," Pearce shot back.

The admiral's face flushed. He wasn't used to subordinates speaking to him that way. Or anybody else, for that matter. "Perhaps. And perhaps not. As we are both nuclear powers, the possibility of even a small conflict escalating into a total nuclear confrontation is too great. In that event, we would both lose."

"And if we're both not careful, the Japanese will drag you into war against your will. You would do well to advise President Lane to keep the Japanese on a tight leash," Feng said.

"The Japanese are our good friends and allies, and we don't abandon our friends or our allies in a time of crisis. That's a promise straight from President Lane. Tell that to President Sun."

"I will convey your message to him directly, empty though it might be," Feng said. "But I admire your, how do you say, chutzpah?"

Myers checked her watch. "It's getting late."

"And I have another promise to keep." Feng stood, straightening his tailored Mao jacket. He gestured sternly toward the steel doors, now open and flanked by armed guards.

Myers and Pearce exchanged a glance.

Looked like Feng had called their bluff.

THIRTY-TWO

The dimly lit air-conditioned room was filled with computer monitors and handheld tablets along the periphery. In the center of the cavernous space stood a massive digital chart table with two dozen uniformed faces hovering around it, focused intently on the digital ships and aircraft coming into virtual contact on what Pearce assumed was the East China Sea.

Myers could hardly believe her eyes. Three-dimensional aircraft were flying over the table as three-dimensional ships sailed on the virtual sea.

"Holographs. Impressive." Myers and Pearce stood next to Admiral Ji and Feng on an elevated platform that gave them a bird's-eye view of the chart table. "When did you steal that from DARPA?"

Admiral Ji ignored her insult.

An oversize three-dimensional holographic representation of an oil rig glowed in bright red near a small collection of islands in the center of the map.

Pearce pointed at the oil rig. "The Senkakus."

"The proper name is the Diaoyu Islands," Vice Chairman Feng said through clenched teeth. "Unless you prefer the Japanese mispronunciation."

Pearce counted fifteen ships steaming from the coast of China and saw what appeared to be an American carrier battle group hovering off the southwestern coast of Japan. Overhead stereo speakers carried what Pearce guessed was chatter between pilots and ships' crews.

"This is live?" Pearce asked.

Ji pointed at a ten-foot-wide 4K HD digital screen on the far wall. A live satellite image popped on. An overhead view of an aircraft carrier and the nearly two dozen support ships that surrounded it in real time.

"Do you recognize it, President Myers?" Ji asked.

"The *George Washington* carrier battle group, stationed out of Japan."

"Correct."

The admiral barked an order. The overhead satellite image zoomed in to the deck of the *George Washington*. F/A-18 Hornets and F-35Cs were lined up and taking off in combat launch operations. The detail was incredible. Myers could read the letters on the vests of the multicolored flight-deck crews scrambling on the tarmac. A bloodred target reticle suddenly appeared, centered on the carrier deck.

A junior female PLAN officer at the chart table shouted an order. Another officer answered back, followed by a dozen more.

A missile launch roared in the loudspeakers overhead, drowning out the chattering voices.

On the chart table, a missile rose from a mobile launcher on the coast of China. The missile track arced high above the table. It disappeared into the unlit ceiling. The Americans were mesmerized.

Admiral Ji pointed at the HD digital screen. The *George Washington* image was still live. "Watch the screen, please."

Suddenly, an explosion ripped into the *George Washington*. The carrier erupted in flames.

"Oh, my god!" Myers shouted.

The holographic *George Washington* on the chart table burned furiously, listing to one side.

The room erupted in cheers and applause. Ji and Feng clapped their hands approvingly at the officers below them as the lights popped on. The chart table went blank and all the holographic images disappeared. But Ji let the burning hulk of the *George Washington* continue to blaze on the HD screen.

"We find that realistic war-gaming exercises between deployments keeps our fighting officers razor sharp," Admiral Ji said.

"Was that your idea of a joke?" Myers seethed.

"Merely a demonstration of the kinds of exercises we run in this room twenty-four hours a day," Feng said. "I apologize if it upset you. It was only intended to inform you."

"Very realistic," Myers said, calming down.

"We have these kinds of training facilities at every headquarters base now and in every regional military district. Of course, we have even more advanced training facilities in Beijing," Ji said.

"And that's your proof the Wu-14 actually works?" Pearce said. "A video game?"

"A fourteen-year-old kid with Final Cut Pro and his daddy's laptop could replicate that video," Myers added.

"But that 'kid' wouldn't have access to a live satellite image of the *George Washington*, which you saw with your own eyes," Feng said.

"Our CGI team superimposed the graphical images of fire and explosions. We find these effects help to add to the realism of the exercise. It gives great satisfaction to our men and women when they make a kill," Ji said.

"But to answer your question, Mr. Pearce, no, this is not our proof. It is only meant to show you that we have already incorporated the Wu-14 into our battle plans. And now you see the likely outcome of any confrontation with a U.S. carrier group."

"Then show us the real proof," Myers said. "Or quit wasting our time."

She hoped with all of her heart the Chinese were bluffing, but a sick feeling deep in her gut told her to expect the worst.

Unfortunately, her gut was never wrong.

THIRTY-THREE

They all stood inside the massive hangar. Myers and Pearce were kept at a distance from the flat, cone-shaped Wu-14 suspended on a sling hanging from a crane. Its dull black hull made the arrow-headed shape all the more menacing. Several white-coated technicians and blue-uniformed personnel hovered over the Wu-14's open service doors, tablets and notebooks in hand. Ji had explained that as soon as the checklists were completed the Wu-14 would be lifted onto the body of the nearby DF-21D mobile missile and fitted into place where its warhead normally resided.

"That's it?" Myers asked. "Looks like a prop from a *Star Trek* episode."

"That is the Wu-14." Feng beamed with pride. "It is a true revolution in military affairs. The end of the era of aircraft carriers. The end of American naval power projection capabilities as we have known it."

"Don't count your chickens just yet," Myers said. "It still hasn't been tested in battle."

"We have concluded seven tests with earlier prototypes, all successful," Feng said.

"And all of our computer simulations agree. The Wu-14 is completely operational," Ji said.

"Seeing is believing," Myers said. She began stepping past one of the scowling navy guards, who gently shoved her back with the stock of his rifle.

Pearce leaped over and slammed two hands into the surprised guard's chest. The guard started to raise his rifle but Pearce was too fast, knocking the barrel aside with his right hand and smashing the man's face with the heel of his left hand. Blood exploded out of the guard's nose like a crimson party favor. The violent confrontation took all of two seconds. Before the guard's knees hit the pavement, five other guards rushed at Pearce, pointing their assault rifles at his chest.

Admiral Ji shouted in Mandarin. The seething guards stepped back, lowered their weapons.

Pearce raced over to Myers. "You all right?"

"Been kicked by horses a lot tougher than he is." Myers glared at Feng. "Still trying to get me killed, I take it?"

Feng was horrified. "You are an impetuous woman!"

"Better get used to it," Myers said. "There's a lot more like me where I come from."

"The Wu-14 is top secret. You're not allowed to approach it," Admiral Ji said.

Myers grinned. "Try and stop me."

She stepped past the kneeling guard, blood seeping out of his cupped hands. She patted the top of his head as she walked by. "Get some ice for that, son."

Admiral Ji whispered violently to Feng. Feng shook his head, whispered back, "Leave her alone."

Feng, Ji, and Pearce hurried after Myers. Thirty long strides and she was near the Wu-14, but another guard came swiftly forward, accompanied by an officer with a security wand in his hand. Myers saw the dead stare of a killer in the guard's eyes. Halted in front of him.

Myers turned to Feng. "Do I get to take a look or are we going to start World War Three right here in this hangar?"

"I forbid it!" Ji said. Feng shook his head at the admiral. *What can it hurt?*

The admiral cursed in Mandarin and looked away, humiliated by the rebuke and the poor manners of the former American president.

"By all means," Feng said, palm extended toward the Wu-14. "Get as close as you like."

Admiral Ji nodded at the officer with the wand in his hand, the same kind used for airport security screenings. The wand beeped violently as it waved over Myers's torso. The officer shouted angrily.

"You are carrying spy equipment!" Ji blurted.

"Don't you watch the news?" Feng asked, exasperated. "She has a bionic pancreas system implanted in her body. She's no spy." Feng stepped closer to Myers. "May I see your phone?"

Myers reluctantly handed him her phone.

"I don't trust phones. Too many interesting things can be done with them," Feng said. He glanced at the key pad. "Your security code, please?"

"F-R-E-E."

Feng typed it in using only his thumb. He flipped through the various app icons. Found the bionic pancreas app. Opened it.

"I see it dosed you just three minutes ago."

"I wouldn't know. But I sure feel terrific."

"May I keep this until you leave?" Feng asked.

"Of course. Just don't turn it off—unless you're trying to kill me."

"Wouldn't think of it." Feng nodded to the guard to let her pass. Myers shouldered past the intimidating hulk and marched over to the Wu-14.

"Wait up," Pearce said.

The guard blocked his path.

"Not you, Mr. Pearce," Feng said. "You own a drone company, yes?"

"I'm just a simple businessman."

"I'm afraid I don't trust you. I must ask that you remain here."

"And if I don't?"

"Admiral Ji will order the guards to kick your teeth in."

Pearce glanced around. A dozen guns were pointed at him.

Pearce shook his head, frustrated. "Fine."

Myers stepped right up to the hypersonic glide vehicle next to one of the technicians, who glanced at her quizzically and backed away, confused. The other scientists and technicians stopped what they were doing and watched the brazen American woman inspect their country's most top secret missile.

"This is outrageous," Ji hissed.

"Don't be foolish. This is exactly what we wanted," Feng whispered.

Pearce didn't speak a word of Mandarin, but he understood the basics of their exchange. Thus was it ever between military men and their civilian leadership.

He wasn't paying attention to the technicians, one of whom was a homely middle-aged woman in a lab coat who was staring at Pearce intently.

A minute later, Myers marched back over to Pearce and the others.

"Satisfied?" Feng asked.

"How many rubber bands does it need to fly?" Pearce asked.

"I'm no aeronautical engineer, but it looks real enough," Myers said. "God only knows if it actually works."

Admiral Ji handed her a thumb drive. "All of the test

DRONE COMMAND   193

data and video clips are on this. Give it to your best analysts. It will convince them."

"I'll pass it along," Myers said, pocketing the thumb
drive.

The middle-aged woman who had been scoping out
Pearce grabbed Feng by the arm and pulled him off to
the side. Myers's eyes tracked the two of them.

"Data can be faked," Pearce said. He was drawing on
his past experience with Jasmine Bath, who not only stole
volumes of data, but also planted false and doctored evidence during her cybercrime career.

"Starting tomorrow, you'll know if the data has been
faked or not," Feng said.

"How's that?" Myers asked.

"Tomorrow, China announces a red line around the
territorial waters of Mao Island and the surrounding East
China Sea. Any ship that dares cross it will suffer the
wrath of the Wu-14."

"If you think we're bluffing, try us," Admiral Ji said. A
broad smile wrinkled the skin around his bulldog eyes.

Myers wanted to slap the smile off of the admiral's
face. He was too damn confident.

And confident sons of bitches like him went to war.

She noticed the woman and Feng were in a heated
conversation. Feng kept stealing glances at Pearce.

Myers got that feeling in her gut all over again.

Time to get the hell out of Dodge.

THIRTY-FOUR

The Red Flag L8 limo coasted to a smooth stop in front of Feng's private Gulfstream jet, along with its armed escort. Soldiers leaped out of their vehicles. Myers and the others climbed out of the limo, Admiral Ji in the lead. Avgas and brine scented the ocean air.

Feng shouted over the Gulfstream's turbines, which were winding up.

"Please convey our message to President Lane. China does not want war with the United States, but neither will we back down from a fight. You are well advised to leave the Japanese to fend for themselves. Why risk your carriers for a fool's errand?"

"I'll be speaking with President Lane as soon as we land. What he decides to do is his business, not mine. I can only give him my opinion."

"And what is your opinion?" Admiral Ji asked.

"That pride cometh before a fall."

"What do you mean by that?" Feng asked.

"It's in the Bible. I don't suppose you've read it."

"Of course I have. I just wasn't sure whose pride you were referring to."

"Don't say I didn't warn you." Myers glanced at Pearce. "C'mon. Let's get back."

"No, not him," Feng said. He pointed an accusing finger at Pearce.

"What are you talking about?" Myers demanded. Chinese rifles were suddenly leveled at Pearce.

"I have a few questions for Mr. Pearce about his time in Mali."

"What questions?" Myers asked.

"That's between him and me," Feng said.

"Don't be ridiculous. You can't detain him. He's an American citizen."

Feng's eyes narrowed. "You are an arrogant ass, Madame President, which is no crime, but Pearce is an American spy, and he will be detained until further notice!"

Myers got in his face. "I dare you to try and take him." She jabbed a finger into his chest. "I dare you personally."

Myers was at least an inch taller than Feng. She wanted him to hit her. Get him to lose his cool, maybe get cashiered right out of government service.

"Get on the plane, Margaret," Pearce said.

"Not without you."

A guard's heavy hand landed on Pearce's shoulder.

"Call the embassy," Pearce said. "They'll straighten this out. You need to go."

"They wouldn't dare—"

"Your health, Margaret. Please."

"What about it?"

"Your health. The doctors still want to monitor you, remember?"

Feng chuckled as he pulled out Myers's iPhone from his pocket.

"Yes, your health." Feng unlocked the phone. Found the bionic pancreas app. Clicked on it. Graphical sliders for dosing insulin and glucagon appeared. Level indicators pointed to normal glucose levels.

"You will walk onto that plane immediately or else I will have you bound and gagged and thrown onto it like a sack of cabbages," Feng hissed. "And on your flight back home, you will experience a tragic malfunction of your bionic pancreas, falling into a deep coma and dying before you land."

It was Admiral Ji's turn to laugh.

Myers regretted not slapping the shit out of him earlier. But Pearce was right. She had to go.

"Fine," Myers spat. "Just give me my damn phone." She held out a trembling hand.

Feng slapped it into her palm. "A wise choice. Please give President Lane my warmest regards."

Myers stepped closer to Feng. The guards shifted nervously.

"Anything happens to Troy, you'll have to answer to me."

Feng smiled. "Little dog, big bark."

"Get going, will ya?" Pearce said. "Before this psycho changes his mind."

Myers's jaw clenched. She fought back tears. She remembered watching Troy spin like a top, blood spurting from his scalp before he hit the tarmac in Algeria. She thought she'd lost him then. She couldn't bear the thought of losing him now. But she had to leave.

"I'll call the president as soon as I land," Myers said.

"Just let Ian know I won't be home for dinner," Pearce said.

She nodded, smiled bravely, and jogged up the stairs.

The cabin door slammed shut behind her as she fell into a seat, her face close to the window. She watched three guards force Pearce to his knees and pat him down for weapons as they jammed his hands in a pair of Plasti-

Cuffs behind his broad back, then raised him up and manhandled him into the back of a covered vehicle.

The Gulfstream shuddered as it began to pull away. She watched helplessly as Troy's truck raced away from the tarmac.

She prayed. *God save him. Please.*

She punched the seat next to her.

Or else.

THIRTY-FIVE

As soon as the plane taxied to a halt, Myers shoved her way past the fawning Chinese cabin attendant and dashed down the staircase to the tarmac. She climbed into the rear passenger seat of an American Chevy Suburban and was greeted by the driver and the security muscle—both Pearce Systems employees and both women—who remained up front, weapons secured under their seats.

The Suburban sped past the terminal gate as Myers speed-dialed President Lane on a secured phone in the back of the vehicle.

"Margaret, it's good to hear your voice."

"Thank you."

"I take it everything went as planned?"

"Not exactly."

"Did you see the missile? Is it legit?"

"Yes, it's real, and it looks legit. Ji handed me all the test data to back up his claim." She handed the thumb drive to the security guard, Stella Kang, as she spoke. Stella loaded the drive into a USB port on a secured wireless transmitter and began uploading the data.

"Our analysts will tear into it as soon as they get it," Lane said.

"Won't be long. Let me know what they find."

"Of course. So you were able to get eyeballs on the Wu-14?"

"Even laid my hands on it."

"Outstanding. So what's the problem?"

"They kept Troy for interrogation. Called him a spy."

"You think the mission's blown?"

"No, or I wouldn't be here now talking to you."

"They must have suspected something."

"Maybe." Myers was thinking about the woman who had taken such a keen interest in Troy back in the hangar. "And maybe not."

"So long as you're safe."

"It's Troy you need to worry about. We've got to get him out of there fast."

"You know we can't do anything to jeopardize the operation."

"You can't leave him there."

"Pearce would understand."

"I don't. He's my friend, and yours. And he's an American, damn it. That used to mean something."

"There's a bigger picture here."

"Don't tell me about a bigger picture. I've sat where you're sitting, remember? But you don't leave a man behind, ever, no matter what it costs."

Lane hesitated. She was right, of course. "I'll have Gaby pick up the phone and see if she can get to the bottom of this."

"No offense, but they don't call the State Department Foggy Bottom for nothing. I need you to get on the phone yourself."

Lane wanted to chew her ass out. How dare she speak to him that way? But he owed her everything, and his dad raised him to believe that the man with the greatest power had the greatest opportunity and responsibility to serve those under him. All of the bowing and scraping and *yes, sirs* he'd been subjected to over the last several months in office had inflated his ego more than he wanted to admit.

"You're right. I'll call President Sun directly. I can't make any promises and I won't jeopardize the mission. But I'll do whatever I can."

"So will I."

"Margaret—"

Myers hung up the phone.

There were very few days she regretted resigning from the Oval Office.

Today was one of them.

THIRTY-SIX

Myers shot through the door of her suite with Stella Kang hot on her tail. The young Korean-American woman was one of Pearce's top small-drone operators, earning her skills during a couple of tours flying Ravens in the U.S. Army. Since the death of Johnny Paloma, Pearce relied more and more on Stella for his personal security detail.

"Ready to get to work?" Myers asked. She had called ahead and told Ian about Pearce's status.

"Ready," Ian said in his thick Scottish brogue. Pearce's IT division chief was normally located at corporate headquarters in Dearborn, Michigan, but Pearce wanted Ian close by for this op. The former IT executive turned his considerable computer skills to antiterror operations soon after losing both of his legs in the 7/7 bombing attack in London. He was one of Pearce's most formidable weapons.

"I'll be just another minute. I hope you've ordered room service for yourself while you were waiting."

"Indeed, I did. Thank you."

"You, too, Stella. Get something for yourself. There's Fiji water and Sapporo in the fridge."

"I'm fine for now, ma'am, but thanks." Stella was worried about her boss. Troy was the best employer she ever had, but also a good friend. She knew what the Chinese were capable of. Her family barely survived the brutal Communist Chinese invasion of the Korean peninsula in 1950. They had passed along the horror stories of rape and slaughter to their children and grandchildren.

Myers marched into her bathroom and opened a drawer. She removed a small metal case the size of a pack of cigarettes and opened it. Inside was a small rubber insertion/removal device used for glass contact lenses. She picked up the little rubber suction cup and leaned close to the wall-length bathroom mirror, carefully touching each lens with the suction head and removing them from her eyes. The hard lenses were embedded with wireless cameras and sensors, making them, in effect, contact-lens cameras. She placed both glass lenses back into the metal case and closed it. She rubbed her itching and irritated eyes for a few moments. Her eyes were used to the soft, permeable contacts she normally wore. Myers grabbed a bottle of saline solution and flushed her eyes out, then pulled out a pair of old reliable eyeglasses to give her aching eyeballs a rest.

Myers headed back to the living room, where Ian was set up and laid the case next to his laptop. "Ready when you are, Ian. Do I need to take off my blouse or anything?"

Ian blushed, the inbred reaction of three hundred years of Presbyterian modesty coursing through his veins. "No, ma'am. We'll manage."

Not that he would've minded. *She was a wee smasher.*

Ian opened up the first app on his laptop and connected wirelessly to Myers's insulin pump that served double duty as a hard-drive storage device for the contact-lens video camera. Sensors embedded on the lens surface allowed Myers to shoot video just by blinking her left eye. Her right eye was a toggle switch, allowing her to zoom in tight or go wide at fixed focal lengths. Unfortunately, audio wasn't available.

"There's a woman I shot in the last few minutes of the visit at the hangar. I need you to jump ahead and capture her image."

"Does she have something to do with Troy's predicament?"

"That's what I need you to figure out as soon as you can."

Myers had captured incredible footage of the Ningbo naval base, along with its equipment and personnel. She thought DARPA would be particularly interested in their war-gaming setup and the three-dimensional holographic board that DARPA had been developing for years. More important to the mission, she'd grabbed several minutes of extreme close-up shots of the Wu-14.

While the video footage downloaded, Ian opened up another app on the insulin pump hard drive. Before Myers left for Ningbo, Ian had loaded it with three powerful self-propagating bots—hacker software he'd taken from the late Jasmine Bath's incredible cyberwarfare arsenal and then modified for this mission.

The first bot broke into the Wu-14's CPU and downloaded its operating software. By analyzing the Wu-14's software architecture, Ian could determine whether or not the HGV was fully operational on the basis of the software program's integrity alone. The added bonus was that a complete download of the Wu-14's operating software would provide him with a virtual blueprint of its hardware design and functionality. Knowing how the Wu-14 worked and whether or not it was fully functional was the primary purpose of their clandestine mission.

The second bot was designed to move from the Wu-14

computer back into the Chinese mainframe controlling it and spreading out from there. This would not only give Ian a big-picture view of the Wu-14's mission-control operation but also, with any luck, the entire Chinese missile program. The bot would also find and download any test data or other physical evidence the Chinese had collected on the Wu-14, once again allowing him to confirm or deny the Wu-14's operability.

The third bot was written for Pearce. President Lane was not made aware of its existence, let alone its purpose. It would lie dormant inside the Wu-14's computer and wouldn't activate until the Wu-14 was powered up and connected with its mission-control computers.

When Lane, Myers, and Pearce first conceived of the plan to steal the Wu-14's secrets, Lane had recommended simply knocking the HGV out of commission with an implanted virus. Myers explained to him that the Chinese would not only debug the missile computer and get it back online, they'd also probably figure out she was the one who had infected it, and they wouldn't get a second chance to get a peek inside. It was riskier in the short term to leave the missile operational—if, indeed, it was— but for the long term, it was the better play.

"Downloading now," Ian said. "Should take only a few minutes."

Myers watched the progress bar begin to inch its way across his screen. She walked over to the well-stocked bar and poured herself two fingers of Maker's Mark. She downed it in a single throw, then poured herself another. She wanted to scream. Wanted to get back on the plane and fly to Ningbo or Beijing or whatever shit hole they were hiding Pearce in and tear it apart brick by brick until she could find him.

"Got it!" Ian shouted. The first bot had successfully copied the Wu-14's operating software.

Myers sighed. "Thank God."

"I can't wait to dive into this."

"After we analyze the video."

"Yes, ma'am."

Myers hoped it was worth it. Hoped everything they'd captured was worth Troy's life.

She doubted it.

She hoped Ian could identify the woman. She was obviously connected to Feng, but how? If Myers could figure out that connection, it might give her the tool she needed to save Troy. She couldn't wait for Lane to help him. If she were still president, she wouldn't have taken the chance of blowing the mission, either. She'd give it a few more days if she were him.

But she wasn't.

She had seen the look in Feng's eyes. Troy didn't have a few more days.

He might already be dead.

THIRTY-SEVEN

It was late and the president didn't feel like heading back downstairs to the office. Mrs. Lane was already in bed with the flu and the kids were long since asleep, so the president made his phone call in the Lincoln Sitting Room on the opposite end of the residence. The room was maintained in an elegant Victorian style, and though it was completely opposite his personal taste, the history of it was oddly reassuring, and he found himself utilizing it more and more. The chief usher told him that it had been Nixon's favorite room and that the former president had an exact replica of it built in the Nixon Presidential Library and Museum.

The call was taking a long time to go through. A proud UT Austin alum, Lane wore white-and-orange Longhorn workout shorts and a Longhorn T-shirt. He paced the thick pile carpet in his bare feet. Walking and talking was an old habit. He never sat still and talked on the phone if he could help it. The wireless phone headset was his best friend these days. He wondered if he was the first president of the United States to speak with the president of China barefoot. He couldn't imagine Nixon in his bare feet, not even in bed. His mind was prone to such musings at this hour. Finally, the White House operator came on line.

"Mr. President, President Sun is on the other line."

"Thank you."

The two most powerful men in the world hadn't yet met in person or even spoken on the phone. Lane had been briefed earlier about Sun and his precarious political situation, triangulating between forces opposed to military-and-corruption reform and his own tenuous pro-reform alliances. Lane imagined that Sun wasn't available earlier in the day when he first called because Sun was huddled up in an emergency meeting with his most trusted advisors over the Pearce fiasco. Lane left a terse and unambiguous statement for Sun: We need to discuss the Pearce matter immediately. No point in playing the game of whether or not Sun knew about it. Even if he didn't know about it, he'd certainly put his staff to work on it. When the president of the United States calls and demands an explanation, it behooves most world leaders to respond as soon as possible, including Sun, even if China was the world's largest economy.

Once connected on the phone, the two presidents exchanged formal pleasantries, then got down to business. Lane expressed his deep concern about Pearce's safety and well-being, both of which were assured by Sun. Lane then demanded to know where he was being held in custody.

"My understanding is that he is not in custody because he has not been arrested," President Sun said. "He is only being detained for routine questioning."

"Under whose authority? Feng's?"

Sun was a malleable bureaucrat at heart, but he was not accustomed to such effrontery, not even from an American president.

"I am confident that Vice Chairman Feng has legitimate reasons for detaining Mr. Pearce."

"What reasons?"

"I'm not certain. Inquiries have been made, but Vice Chairman Feng has been unavailable. I just dispatched a personal messenger to hand-deliver my request."

"I need you to know I'm holding you personally responsible for Mr. Pearce's safety."

"I'm hopeful the matter will soon be resolved to our mutual satisfaction. Unless, of course, Mr. Pearce really is a spy. And if that is the case, I shall hold *you* personally responsible for his fate."

The phone clicked off.

Lane hung up. He cursed.

Pearce was fucked, and it was his fault.

THIRTY-EIGHT

Lane stood barefoot in the kitchen of his private residence, one of three in the White House. His kids and sick wife were still in bed, sound asleep. He flipped over the sizzling grilled cheese sandwich, its edges dripping with cheddar and Gouda. A real no-no in the Lane household as far as calories and fat were concerned, but exactly what the doctor ordered, especially after his phone call with President Sun.

He'd screwed up, but it was a screwed-up situation all around. He'd made an idle threat and Sun had called him on it, but he needed to say something other than pretty please. Both men knew Lane wouldn't risk starting a war over the detention of one individual, and Sun's reference to Pearce possibly being a spy was chilling. The Chinese didn't coddle foreign nationals who committed crimes on their soil. They had recently executed several South Korean, Japanese, and even British citizens for drug-related offenses, even over the diplomatic protests of those governments.

Lane dumped his grilled cheese on a plate, snagged a

Revolver Blood & Honey beer from the fridge, and headed for the kitchen table.

He took a bite of the hot sandwich, sucking up a long string of gooey cheese like it was a piece of spaghetti. Chewing, he thought more about his conversation with Sun, but something else was bothering him.

The labor secretary had delivered more bad news earlier in the day about current employment stats, especially labor participation rates. They were continuing to fall. More and more Americans were simply giving up looking for work, and the great middle class was shrinking. The growing income disparity wasn't merely a social-justice issue, it was a matter of grave political and economic concern. A thriving capitalist democracy depended on a thriving middle class. A few wealthy people standing on a wide base of impoverished masses was a formula for social unrest, economic catastrophe, and maybe even revolution.

It was the Texas congresswoman Dolly Waddlington who had been giving him the most hell on the subject of the middle class in the last few weeks. The fiery little Republican was infamous for the safari trophy heads hanging on her office walls, each identified with a brass plaque listing the location and date of her kill. Her favorite was the giant snarling Eurasian boar. She shot the charging three-hundred-pound beast between the eyes with a .357 Magnum revolver less than three yards away before it could rip her to shreds with its gruesome yellow tusks. She named the murderous pig ISIS.

But it was the political hides she'd skinned over the years on both sides of the aisle that impressed Lane. An unapologetic nationalist, Waddlington had been blistering his ear on the phone for weeks now about the pernicious Chinese trade deficit that ran in the hundreds of billions of dollars year after year. Besides locking out U.S. firms from their markets with unfair regulations, manipulating the yuan-dollar relationship, and their virulent industrial espionage program, it was cheap Chinese labor and bad American tax laws that really fueled the trade disparity. No wonder China's economy was now the largest in the world.

As a Democrat, Lane bristled at the idea that his party continuously put the interests of multinational corporations over the average American worker, hiding behind the gilded skirts of the big labor unions who themselves should have been fighting against America's crippling trade deficits with China and the rest of the world. But most of the big union bosses were as corrupt as many of the congressmen he'd worked with on both sides of the aisle. Some of the very biggest corporations making the most obscene profits from cheap overseas labor were the Democrats' biggest contributors. Historically, the Democratic Party had been the champion of labor, but in the last two decades, the labor they were championing was foreign, particularly Chinese.

Many of the same millionaires and billionaires in his party who complained—rightly—about gross income inequality were partly to blame for the crisis. The middle class was being decimated by so-called free-trade agreements and, worse, the pursuit of profits at the expense of people and the nation. High-tech corporations like HP, Facebook, and Microsoft decried the shortage of American engineering talent, which simply wasn't true. Lane had seen the numbers. Every year, twenty-five thousand freshly minted American engineering graduates couldn't find STEM employment. But the high-tech companies kept clamoring for H-1B visas—fast-ticket entry for lower-wage technical talent from abroad—even as they were laying off tens of thousands of high-wage American employees year after year, exporting their jobs to lower-paying foreign labor markets.

Just like the Republicans, too many Democrats gladly

signed on to legislation that incentivized job exports and eagerly encouraged unfettered immigration, legal and otherwise. Those two policies alone were enough to decimate the great American middle class and trap the working poor. Lane was proud to be an old-school Kennedy Democrat, the party that used to work hard for working Americans instead of working hard to get reelected. He was determined to right the ship.

Lane took a swig of his beer. The sweet bite of the Revolver's blood orange peel was a perfect match to his savory grilled cheese.

He thought about his meeting back in the Tank. Something nagged at him. The United States was spending tens of billions of dollars every year preparing for a potential war with China. So why in the hell are we even trading with them? The answer sickened him.

By locating their operations in China for the cheap labor—and in order to avoid the labor regulations that protected American workers—too many American corporations had unintentionally helped fund China's massive military expansion, including the Wu-14 that now threatened America's carrier fleet, which, ironically, protected the sea-lanes that enriched those American corporations and their officers in the first place.

Lane was also the proud son of a proud Vietnam veteran. Like most thinking Americans, Lane understood that the values of communism, like those of radical Islam, threatened human rights and freedoms. Tens of millions of Chinese had died under Mao's reign of terror, and that was no accident. Communism was to Mao what fascism was to Hitler. America would never have traded with Germany after the war if the Germans hadn't renounced fascism, and yet the Chinese government not only had never renounced communism, but it also still actively promoted and defended it.

It was time to put a stop to all of it.

The Wu-14 situation was the first problem at hand, but that was only a symptom of a much bigger issue. It was clear to him now he had to find a way to completely transform the Sino-American relationship. Either China was a friend or a foe. It couldn't be both. If he could somehow help Sun push through his reforms, China might become a trusted ally instead of a strategic competitor. But how could he help Sun at a time like this?

The original mission he initiated with Pearce and Myers was to secure the design of the Wu-14. But the mission profile suddenly changed in his mind. If Pearce was going to die, it needed to be for something more significant than just a missile blueprint. Unless the Sino-American relationship changed, the Chinese would inevitably build a more powerful missile in preparation for future conflict anyway.

The path was now clear in his mind. Lane wouldn't lose the chance to change China and make America more secure in the process. He'd do whatever it took, even if it cost him the presidency. Or worse.

So be it.

THIRTY-NINE

BRIGGS CEMETERY
JACKSON, WYOMING
APRIL 1993

The backhoe roared as the caretaker gunned the engine,
dropping the last bucket of dirt onto the grave. The
air smelled like exhaust fumes in the dimming light. Not
very ceremonial, but efficient. Hand digging was too ex-
pensive these days and the cold slope was hard and rocky.
The caretaker didn't usually run the backhoe until after
the family had already left with the flowers and their
friends, but there weren't any of either at his dad's
gravesite. Troy didn't have anywhere else to go just yet so
he stood around and watched.

A tall man in a gray windowpane sport coat and a car-
dinal rep tie approached from the bottom of the hill,
stopping to the side. He had neatly trimmed silver hair
and a mustache to match, with sharp green eyes. He
looked like an executive or maybe even a college professor. The man watched the backhoe bucket pound the
mound of dirt with a heavy metallic clang. When the
backhoe finished, it pulled away, heading clumsily
through the weeds for the maintenance shed. The man
with the silver hair made the sign of the cross. Noticed

Troy watching him. The man nodded curtly, a sign of respect. Turned and left.

Troy had no idea who he was. Not one of the VA doctors, that was for sure. He knew every one of those sons of bitches. They wouldn't dare show their faces here today. He checked his watch. It was time to keep a promise he'd made to himself.

FORTY

Fat JoJo sat spread-legged on a stool, hovering over a customer. His thick fingers deftly guided the tattooing needle over the man's forearm, filling in the details of a flaming skull. Two of JoJo's men had draped themselves on the torn vinyl waiting seats, thumbing through worn biker mags and smoking cigarettes. They were both heavily tatted—a perk of the job. One was tall and lanky with wild, bushy hair. The other was shorter and broader like a fireplug, his shaved head offset by a scraggly goatee and a silver-skull earring. JoJo's custom '66 Chevy 4x4 was parked out front, riding high on its six-inch lifted suspension and thirty-six-inch knobby tires, still midnight black with orange flames raking the hood.

Troy marched into the shop, straight toward JoJo. The fat man didn't budge. Kept working his needle.

JoJo's tallest man leaped up to block Troy's path. "Wait your turn, bud—"

He swallowed the last syllable as the heel of Troy's hand crashed into his jaw, snapping his mouth shut and shattering his front teeth. He grabbed his face, stifling a scream. The other man jumped to his feet but didn't make a move toward Troy, who was four inches taller.

Troy stood over JoJo, hands flexing. JoJo motioned for his customer in the chair to get up, which he did, then he raced outside. The heavy skin artist shut off his needle and finally looked up. "What the fuck is this?"

"My old man is dead."

"I heard. Something about a brain tumor. That's too fucking bad."

"You hit him on the head when he couldn't fight back, you cowardly shit."

"And you knocked me out cold. I figured we were even."

"You figured wrong."

"You want me to throw him out?" the other man said.

JoJo laughed. "If you can."

The shorter man reached behind a counter and grabbed a baseball bat. Pointed it at Troy. "Get the fuck out now."

Troy glowered at him.

The man raised the baseball bat up, ready to swing. "You think I'm kidding?"

"You're wearing an earring," Troy said. "I thought maybe you wanted to kiss me."

The bald-headed man shouted and raised the bat over his head as if he were going to chop Troy down like a tree. Troy charged at him and caught the bat above the man's gripped hands before he could bring the bat down. Troy easily twisted the bat around and grabbed the barrel and handle, the man stupidly still holding on to the bat, trying to win the wrestling match. Big mistake. Troy easily pushed the smaller man back toward the chairs against the wall until the man fell into one. Troy kept pushing the bat against his throat until the man's face turned red and he finally let go. Troy pointed the bat at him. "Don't move."

Troy turned around with the bat in hand, ready to start pounding JoJo with it. But JoJo had other ideas. He stood by the doorway, pointing a long-barreled Colt .357 Magnum at Troy's chest. A smile twisted his pockmarked face.

"Looks like a robbery to me. Self-defense, too." His fat thumb moved toward the hammer to cock it.

A hand grabbed the pistol around the cylinder, locking down the hammer, then wrenched it hard in a vicious 180-degree turn. The heavy steel pistol twisted so fast it broke JoJo's wrist and trigger finger.

JoJo dropped to a knee, yelping, his fractured hand empty of the gun that was now in the steady grip of the man from the graveyard.

Troy raised the bat to brain JoJo.

"Troy," the man said. The authority in his voice checked his swing.

"What?"

"He didn't kill your dad."

"What's that to you?"

"He isn't worth going to jail for."

"He needs to pay for what he did to my old man."

"He just did. He won't be inking anybody for a while now with that broken hand."

"Nobody asked you."

The man's fierce green eyes didn't ask anything, either.

"Listen to him, boy," JoJo hissed, teeth clenched in pain.

Troy looked around. The two other men had hobbled to the back of the shop, tending their wounds, no longer a threat. He gripped the bat tighter. Wanted to piñata the fat man's skull and watch the candy spill out.

"Knowing when you've won is half the battle." The

tall man opened the pistol cylinder and dropped the big shells onto the floor. "Killing him will only hurt you in the long run. Trust me, kid. If I thought he needed killing, I'd do it myself."

They left JoJo on the floor, alive.

But two minutes later, JoJo's big custom pickup with the orange painted flames was burning to the ground.

The man had to give Troy at least that.

FORTY-ONE

They sat in a booth at the back of the empty diner. Troy was wolfing down his second Denver omelet while the man smoked a cigarette. He'd introduced himself on the steep, winding drive through the Teton Pass. Said his name was Will. Knew his dad a long time ago.

They'd eaten in silence since arriving an hour before, a few miles out of town, just in case JoJo changed his mind and came looking for trouble in one of Troy's familiar haunts.

Troy scraped up the last bits of egg and hash browns with his fork and shoveled them into his mouth, then pushed the plate away. A middle-aged waitress with puffy eyes and an easy smile cleared away the mess, then refilled Will's coffee cup and Troy's Coke. Will gave her a wink and she nodded, her cue to stay away for a while.

"Thanks for back there," Troy finally said. The first words he'd spoken since they'd left JoJo's shop.

Will nodded, sipping his coffee. "Sorry about your dad."

"How'd you know him?"

"The war."

"You were in the army, too?"

"Not exactly. But we served together."

"CIA?"

Will smiled. *Bright boy.*

"Your dad was a good man. It was a bad war."

Troy shrugged.

"He ever talk about the war?" Will asked.

"When I was a kid, he talked about it more. Not so much lately."

"But he was living it, wasn't he?"

"He was having a hard time. PTSD, I think."

"He try the VA?"

"He preferred self-medicating. Jack Daniel's mostly."

"I'm sorry I wasn't there for him. He saved my ass more than once. He ever tell you about the tunnels?"

Troy nodded. "When I was little. Gave me nightmares. Didn't give me all the details."

Will did. How a local Viet Cong commander got wind of Will's marriage to the daughter of a prominent South Vietnamese politician in a Catholic ceremony—a particular affront to the godless Communists. Six weeks later, they killed Mai and her family when Will was away on assignment.

"I recruited your dad's unit to help me hunt the bastard down. Found out he went underground, along with his VC platoon. Barracks, hospital, you name it, it was all down there. We finally found the tunnel entrance and your dad was the first one in."

Will described the hand-to-hand fighting in the dark. And their capture.

"Dad was a POW?"

"Not exactly. After they roughed us up, they stripped us of anything of value, looking for intel. Lost the only photo I had of my wife. Even stole my crucifix. Then they shipped us off to a regular NVA camp to get us to Hanoi, but a Green Beret unit intercepted us before we got there."

"Wow. I had no idea."

"I have other stories about your dad if you ever want to hear them. You know, he was about your age when he was over there. He had a big brass pair on him, and then some."

Troy was lost in thought, imagining his dad's ordeal under the cramped earth. He shuddered. "Yeah, maybe someday."

"I only just heard through the grapevine he'd passed. What happened?"

"He got in a fight one night. That fat fuck in the tat shop, JoJo, hit him in the head with a bottle, knocked him out cold. I took Dad to the county hospital to get him checked out. They did X-rays, found a tumor. Doc asked me about his overall health. I described some of the symptoms. The doc thought maybe the tumor had something to do with Agent Orange. Referred dad to the VA."

"And the VA didn't do its job."

"Told him the tumor was inoperable. Gave him six weeks to live. Handed him a bunch of pain pills and wished him luck. He died like a fucking dog."

"The VA is a crapshoot. Sometimes you get lucky, sometimes you don't."

"He used to say he was the luckiest guy in the world. The only problem was that it was all bad luck."

Will grinned. "He was a funny guy."

"So how'd you handle it? I mean, the war and all."

"One day at a time." Will lit another cigarette. "Don't be too hard on him. He lost a lot back in the jungle. We all did."

"Seems to me he brought it all home with him. Drove my mom away, that's for sure."

"Yeah, I heard about that. I met her once. A beautiful gal. Your dad was crazy about her."

"He was just fucking crazy. She couldn't take it any-more."

"Wars don't just hurt the men who fight them. I'm sorry you and your mom were collateral damage. You had a sister, too, didn't you?"

"Yeah. I did." Troy's face darkened.

Will clapped a hand across Troy's broad back. Nothing to say.

Troy came back to the present, took another swig of soda.

"So what are your plans now?" Will asked.

Troy drained his glass. The ice crashed against his mouth. He wiped his face with his sleeve. "Work, I guess."

"What about college?"

"Me? Nah. I dropped out of high school my senior year. Never graduated."

"I know. I saw your school records."

Troy frowned. "How?"

Will smiled. "I used to be a spook, remember?"

"Oh, yeah. That's right."

"You're a smart kid. You should be in school."

"I'm not going back to high school. Forget that."

"No. I'm talking about university. A real one. Ever thought about Stanford?"

"Are you kidding me? I couldn't get into there. I don't have the grades, and I don't have the cash."

"What if I could get you in?"

"How? Unless the CIA runs the admissions office."

"Not exactly."

Will pulled out his wallet. Handed Troy a business card. "I'm a research fellow at Hoover. I've got a little pull with the dean of admissions. Your SAT scores are strong enough to get you in with the right academic reference."

"What reference?"

"Me."

"Even if I could get in, I couldn't pay for it."

"I can get that covered, too."

"I'm not a charity case."

"I didn't say you were. But Stanford's loaded. They put scholarship money aside for students like you. And I've got a friend who lives in Palo Alto. Paraplegic. Needs someone to cut the grass, wash the car, that sort of thing. Has a garage apartment and three squares a day he'd swap out for the labor."

"What's the catch?"

"No drugs, no booze. Keep your nose clean and your grades up, or at least passing."

"Why me?"

"Why do you think?"

Troy looked at the card again. DR. WILLIAM ELLIOTT, NATIONAL SECURITY RESEARCH FELLOW, THE HOOVER INSTITUTION, STANFORD UNIVERSITY.

"What if I fuck it up?"

"The only way you can fuck it up is if you don't try."

"I dunno. It's been a long time since I was in a classroom, and I wasn't very good at it."

"It's not like high school. You'll be around the brightest students in the country, learning from some of the best faculty in the world. I'll get you set up with any tutors you might need, but I doubt you'll need them."

Troy shrugged. "I don't know."

Will slid out of the booth and stood up, opening his wallet.

"Think about it. You've got my card. Even if you decide against it, you can call me any time for any reason. I owe your dad at least that." He dropped forty dollars onto the thirteen-dollar check.

"Thanks for dinner, Dr. Elliott." Troy stood and stretched. "And for everything else."

"Just Will." He held out his hand.

Troy took it. A good grip.

"Take care of yourself, sport. And think about what I said."

"Yes, sir. I will."

He did.

FORTY-TWO

Bright light exploded in Pearce's eyes beneath the hood. An illusion. The second strike against his face in as many seconds. The hand was soft, but heavy, like a dead fish. It belonged to the shouting woman hitting him. He couldn't see her but he sure as hell could smell her.

WHACK!

Another blow, more lights. He assumed the flashing lights meant his retinas were detaching.

"C'mon, lady. That all you got?" Pearce shouted, almost grateful for the beating. He needed the distraction. He was half out of his mind with claustrophobia beneath the hood.

Someone snatched it off. Pearce blinked. Wanted to cry out of sheer joy. He hadn't seen real light since he'd been cuffed and tossed into the back of that truck. His eyes adjusted as he squinted. A big Mongolian goon stood off to the side, the hood in his hands, a pistol on his hip. Feng stood back, smiling, smoking a cigarette. The woman looked familiar. She had been at the test facility. Wasn't wearing a lab coat now. A lady's peasant coat, like Feng's, but not tailored. She looked like Chairman Mao with small breasts, only uglier. Now she stood just a foot away from him, leaning over, red-faced, squawking in Mandarin.

"Zhao! Zhao!"

"Sorry lady, me no hablo Esperanto."

Another slap of her hand.

Pearce shook it off. Swore he felt his brain knocking around in his throbbing skull. He already had a headache from dehydration and lack of sleep. The pounding from the angry lady was only making it worse.

"What's her problem?" Pearce asked.

Feng blew out a long, thoughtful cloud of smoke as he twisted the cigarette in his fingers. "She hates you." He took another drag.

"If she only knew me. Then she'd really hate me."

WHACK!

"Guo? Zhao!" the woman shouted.

"Shit! Lady, seriously?"

She raised her hand again. Pearce stiffened for the blow. Feng spoke a single word. Her hand stopped in midair. She muttered curses under her breath.

"So what does she want from me?"

"She wants to know if you knew two men named Guo and Zhao."

Pearce had to decide what cards to play. He knew he was seriously hosed and it worried him. He tried to calculate the speed of the truck and the time he spent riding in the back of it from the moment they tossed him into it, but for all he knew, they could have been driving in slow circles around the base. The only thing he knew for sure was that once they arrived wherever they were they descended forty-two steel steps that clanged beneath his boots. The descent spiraled in a long, slow circle, and the air was cooler. But that was about it.

In Iraq he'd been in some bad places in the hands of some real shitbirds, but what kept his spirits up back then was knowing that even badder friends with evil intent always came to rescue him. Pearce knew nobody was looking for him now, at least not on the ground.

He could try talking his way out of this thing but that was a long shot at best. He didn't have any leverage, and the only Mandarin he knew were the menu items at the Chinese buffet near his condo in Coronado.

The only real question in Pearce's mind was: How much damage was going to be inflicted, and could he keep his wits about him in order to keep from revealing Myers's real mission? No telling, especially if they resorted to chemical interrogation or something even less civilized. His only hope was that they would knock him unconscious or, better yet, beat him to death before he accidentally spilled the beans.

Pearce shrugged his aching shoulders. His hands were still cuffed behind his back. The only time he hadn't been cuffed in the last few hours was in order to relieve himself, but that had been a while ago.

Here goes nothing.

"She said Guo? Zhao?" Pearce asked, frowning at Feng through a swelling eye.

Feng nodded. "Yes."

The woman stared daggers at Pearce, listening intently.

"Hard to say. I've killed a lot of Chi-coms in my day. You kinda all look the same to me."

The woman slapped him three more times. One of her jagged fingernails scraped across Pearce's cheek, drawing blood. Her face was so close to his he could smell her rancid breath.

"Crikey, lady. Ever heard of Listerine?"

"Have you ever heard of manners, you filthy white bastard?" she asked in faultless English.

Pearce was shocked. Should've guessed she was bilingual. "What?"

WHACK!

The hulking Mongolian goon laughed at Pearce, muttered something in Mandarin.

Pearce tasted copper. He spit. Bloody drops hit the cement floor. He turned to the goon. "What's so funny, numb nuts?"

"You," Feng said. "He thinks a middle-aged woman is going to beat the big American to death with her bare hands. He's probably right."

Pearce flashed a bloody grin. *That's the idea.*

The woman got in Pearce's face and screamed, clenching her fists. Veins bulged in her forehead as flecks of her spittle splattered on his chin. He stared at her crooked yellow teeth with an insolent smile.

The barrel-shaped woman deftly reached inside a coat pocket and produced a spring-loaded blade. In a single move, she snicked it open and plunged it straight at Pearce's throat. He stared hard at her. Wouldn't let her see him flinch.

Fuck you, lady. See you in hell.

Feng's hand caught her wrist at the last possible second, the blade an inch from Pearce's jugular. She howled in protest as Feng pried the knife out of her hand. The security guard rushed over and wrapped a massive arm around her throat, twisting her other flailing hand behind her back. Firm enough to restrain her but gentle enough to not cause the prominent scientist injury.

Feng barked an order and the goon wrestled her toward the steps, but not before the woman managed a swift kick into Pearce's shin, cursing in Mandarin at the top of her lungs. Even after the heavy metal door clanged shut at the top of the winding staircase, Pearce could hear her howling.

"You need to teach your wife some manners, Feng."

"Dr. Weng is not my wife."

Pearce looked Feng up and down, grinned. "Yeah. You look like the kind of guy who eats his noodles from the other side of the bowl."

"Excuse me?"

"Doesn't matter. What was her problem?"

"You killed two of her colleagues while in Africa, Guo and Zhao."

"An occupational hazard. For them, I mean."

"It is written, 'He that lives by the sword, dies by the sword.'"

"Depends who's got the bigger sword. Want to compare?"

"We both know you're CIA."

"Former. I'm a private contractor now."

"A convenient cover. The CIA doesn't let field agents quit. This is well-known."

"Well-known? Where? In comic books?"

"You came here to spy."

"On what? The Wu-14? You invited us here, remember? Bad way to keep a secret, inviting a former American president and a former CIA operative to see the damn thing. But we both know you don't want it kept secret. Just the opposite."

"You came here to steal the Wu-14."

"Steal it? How? By shoving it up my poop chute and waddling out of here?" Pearce flashed a mischievous grin. "That's more up your alley, isn't it? Pardon the pun."

Feng's eyes narrowed, waiting for his rage to pass.

"Why are you here, then?"

"I'm providing security for President Myers. She refuses Secret Service protection."

"Why would she do that?"

"She likes her privacy."

"If you're her security, I'd say you failed."

"Me? You're the one in deep shit. President Lane won't take kindly to kidnapping an American citizen."

"A citizen? I thought you were his friend."

Pearce shrugged, wincing at the pain in his shoulders. "Yeah, I guess so."

"A friend of the president's who happens to be a CIA agent on a secret mission, spying on the People's Republic."

"I think we covered that already."

"Do you think I'm stupid?" Feng asked.

"If you don't already know, I'm sure as hell not going to break the bad news to you—"

WHACK!

Feng's delicate, well-manicured hand slapped Pearce's face.

"Dr. Weng wants to kill you," Feng said. "I'm tempted to let her."

"Why don't you?"

"I personally abhor violence. I'm a businessman. I prefer to negotiate."

"So let's negotiate. Let me out of these cuffs, and we can talk."

"If you don't tell me what I want to know, I'll let Dr. Weng slit your throat. Or worse."

"Go ahead, but only if you want the wrath of the U.S. military to fall on your head."

The vice chairman laughed. "Now who's the idiot? Ever heard of Dr. Afridi? Sergeant Hekmati? Reverend Abedini? Your government is notorious for leaving their people behind, sometimes indefinitely."

Pearce knew the names well. The first was the Muslim doctor sentenced for treason and left to rot in a Pakistani jail after helping the United States find and kill Osama bin Laden. The second was an American marine sergeant abandoned in an Iranian jail for years. The third was an American Christian cleric seized and tortured by Iranian thugs. All three incidents were stains on America's honor. In each case, the American government held the cards it needed to play to win their release. Pakistan was a corrupt regime heavily dependent on American largesse to survive. Iran had other vulnerabilities.

"A previous administration. Lane is different. Think Teddy Roosevelt."

"We both know who really runs your government. The puppet masters who pull the strings would never allow Lane to upset the apple cart."

"You don't know Lane. And you shouldn't mix metaphors."

"I know that trillions of dollars in trade, loans, and profits all depend upon a healthy relationship between China and the United States. Do you think the worthless life of a single American CIA spy is worth all that?"

"There are things even more valuable than money, even in a capitalist society."

"You're quite right. Knowledge is far more valuable than money, in any society. And you have some of the most valuable knowledge of all."

The heavy steel door swung open. The security goon slipped back in and shut it behind him. One of his eyes was shut and purpling.

Pearce laughed. "Hey, tough guy. Punching above your weight class again?"

The Mongolian glowered at Pearce as he trotted down the staircase.

Pearce motioned with his pinned wrists. "Yeah, Lurch. C'mon, untie my hands. Let me show you what a real punch feels like."

The security guard muttered under his breath and stepped toward Pearce, flexing his massive hands.

Feng shouted an order and the Mongolian froze in his tracks, then retreated to his spot in the corner. Feng turned back to Pearce. "You're a drone expert. There's much you can teach us."

"I'm no expert. I don't invent the damn things. I just run a contracting company. We deploy drones, sure, but mostly off-the-shelf stuff."

"Dr. Weng told me your company is the best in the world at what it does."

"And she'd be right."

"Is that why you're in Japan? To give Japan advanced drone technology?"

"Like I told you, I just came to provide President Myers with personal security."

"And what is her mission?"

"You'd have to ask her. Far as I could tell, it was just business. You know, filthy capitalism. Just like you billionaire commie bastards love."

"You're not going to leave this place, ever. You do understand that, don't you?"

"If you're going to shoot me, do it now." Pearce flexed his shoulders. "I've got an itch I can't scratch that's killing me."

Feng laughed. "Kill you? No. You are too valuable alive. I'm going to extract every last secret you're hiding in that thick skull of yours. We both know you can't stop it. And unlike you, I'm not constrained by the Geneva Convention or the ACLU. I have no qualms about crippling you for life or blinding you. Even if I decide to let you go, you'd still be maimed and your government wouldn't be able to do a thing about it, nor would I suffer the least consequence. Do you understand how perilous your situation truly is?"

"I think I've caught the gist of it. But I'm not much of a talker. So stop wasting your breath."

"I have a technician who will not only make you talk but also, perhaps, even sing, as the saying goes. I should like that."

"Don't get your panties in a wad. I don't do Broadway show tunes if that's what you're hoping for."

Feng barked a command to his security guard. The big Mongolian slapped the black bag back over Pearce's head.

Pearce wanted to scream. His mind clawed at the claustrophobic fear rising in his throat; only a sheer act of will kept him silent. For now.

"I'll be back in a few hours and we'll begin our first session. Until then, I want you to imagine the worst of all possible pain and know that it will pale in comparison to what I have in store for you."

"Room service is that bad, eh?"

Feng's cell phone chirped. He checked the screen and motioned violently toward the stairs. A few moments later Feng and the Mongolian disappeared, slamming the steel door behind them.

Pearce sat in the rickety chair, shoulders aching, shrouded in the lightless bag. The room was silent now except for his heavy breathing. He didn't want to hyperventilate. Fought to control it. The bag was stuffy, close. But that wasn't the worst. He felt like a miner trapped a thousand feet below the earth when the lights go out and the roof caves in. He prayed Ian would find him before the sightless black dragged him down into madness. He focused his mind on the one possible thing that could save him: the Pearce Systems tracker embedded in his gut.

It was his only hope.

FORTY-THREE

S till no luck."

Ian's charming brogue had softened recently, Myers noticed. Too long in the States. "Can't you do anything?"

The Scotsman shook his head solemnly. "If Troy is behind a thick wall or underground, we'll never find his tracker signal, and unless they move him quickly out in the open, he'll be lost for a while. We're losing the satellite feed in ten more minutes."

Myers paced the room, hardly noticing the plush carpet beneath her bare feet. She'd lost her husband and her son, and nearly lost Pearce almost two years ago in the Sahara. She'd cradled his unconscious body in her lap as Judy Hopper corkscrewed the plane through the air, making their escape. She couldn't bear the thought of seeing him like that again.

Her laptop dinged. She raced over to it.

"Found her!" Myers shouted. An automated search of a classified photo database finally identified the woman in the video. Ian made a screen grab and tossed it into the NSA search engine. Maybe Lane couldn't do anything to rescue Pearce at the moment, but at least the president could open up classified government resources for them with a phone call.

Ian rolled his chair over to the coffee table serving as Myers's desk. "Dr. Weng Litong. Yes, I've heard of her. She runs the PLA's robotic-weapons development program."

"Makes sense she'd be in the same building with the Wu-14," Myers said. "What's her beef with Troy?"

"There's no telling." Ian tapped a few keys. Ran a loop of Myers's video showing Weng whispering into Feng's ear and Feng's reaction. "Whatever she said to Feng sent him up. The question remains, what did she say?"

Myers shook her head. "Too bad my video camera couldn't capture audio."

"Bollocks! My head is up my proverbial arse. We don't need audio." Ian stood on his robotic legs and rushed over to his laptop on the dining-room table. The original video clip was on his hard drive. As he pulled it up, Myers came up behind him.

"What are you looking for?"

Ian paused the video clip just as Weng's face came into view. He enlarged the image so that the faces of Weng and Feng filled the screen. He played the video again. Watched her lean over, whisper in his ear. Her face slid behind Feng's head then slid back into view. Feng frowned violently, whispered back. Weng nodded. Spoke again, turned aside, hiding her face.

"She didn't want anyone else but Feng to hear what she was saying," Myers said. "Too bad we can't hear it, too."

Ian grinned. "Oh, but we can." Ian clicked his mouse and pulled up another program. A translucent square popped up in the middle of the screen. He dragged it over to Weng's mouth and tapped a couple of keys. "That will lock the target to Weng's mouth."

"What for?"

"A lip-reading software program."

"Are you serious?"

"MI5 has been using one for years in coordination with the nationwide CCTV network. I suspect the FBI uses one, too."

Myers knew that the Brits had installed millions of closed-circuit television cameras in public areas like subway stations, airports, and street intersections over the years, and millions more were in private use. She read one estimate that there was one CCTV camera for every eleven British citizens. Like her own miniature video camera, however, those systems often didn't have audio. Lip-reading software was the next best thing, and maybe better, since it allowed the observer to pick and choose the conversations they wanted to hear.

Ian clicked on a few icons and the Feng-Weng loop ran again with the lip-reading software window automatically tracking Weng's mouth.

"Not sure how this is going to help unless you speak Mandarin," Myers said.

"Not a problem. I have a—"

"Translation program, of course." She patted him on the shoulder.

A few minutes later, Ian pulled up the transcript. "Sorry, ma'am, it reads like gibberish. But there are some useful fragments."

Ian was right. The lip-reading program obviously didn't function when Weng's mouth was turned away or was hidden behind Feng's head, but it managed to grab a few words: Zhao, Mali, Pearce, Guo, Congo.

"Those make any sense to you?" Ian asked.

"Troy was in Mali, certainly. I don't know about Congo. I assume Zhao and Guo are names of people? Or places?"

"Good question. Let me try a couple of searches." Ian ran a search program that sought links between the names Feng, Zhao, and Guo. Myers popped a K-Cup into a Keurig brewing machine while she waited. "What would you like to drink, Ian?"

"Oil," Ian finally said. "And blood."

"Excuse me?"

Ian strode over to her with a sheet of paper in his hands. "It appears as if Feng and Zhao were both close relatives in the oil industry. Feng was his uncle. Tea, if there is any, thank you."

Myers pulled another K-Cup for tea and popped it into the brewer. "Was?"

"Zhao Yi is dead. Killed in an elevator accident in Mali in 2015."

"What's that got to do with Troy?"

"Zhao was heading up the Sino-Sahara Oil Corporation in Bamako, Mali, when he was killed."

"Where Troy was. If Zhao was connected in any way to Mike Early's death—"

Ian nodded grimly. "My thoughts exactly."

"But it was an accident, right?"

"A particularly violent one, apparently." Ian knew that Pearce wouldn't leave any evidence behind unless he wanted to send a message. Otherwise, an apparent accident made perfect sense.

Myers took a thoughtful sip of coffee. Troy never told Myers about any kind of revenge killings after Mike Early's death, but she knew Pearce had killed Ambassador Britnev for his role in her son's murder a few years earlier—a violent, foolish act on Troy's part, but one for which she was eternally grateful. Troy's fierce sense of loyalty was only superseded by his thirst for justice, particularly for those to whom he was loyal.

"And this Guo person?"

"Nothing's come up yet. Maybe it's not a person, or not a person easily found."

"Like a special operative?"

"As good a guess as any."

"There were Chinese special forces operators in the desert. They're the ones who killed Mike and Mossa." Myers had never met the fearsome Tuareg chieftain, but she felt she had after Troy's colorful and emotional description of him.

"Then there's the other link, if any. If Guo was an operator involved in their deaths, Troy would have taken him out, too."

"So if Weng fingered Troy for the deaths of those two men, it still doesn't make sense that Feng would grab him, does it? It's a ballsy move just to get revenge."

"Revenge, honor, hate. Pick one or all. Feng knows there's nothing we can do about it."

"You don't think Feng would hurt Troy, do you?"

"Why not? What would President Lane do about it?"

"Nothing, at least for the moment." Myers had already spoken to Lane. He recounted his conversation with President Sun. He was apologetic but firm. He wouldn't leave Pearce behind, but Pearce needed to sit tight for now. Time was against them. They both knew Pearce would agree. But then again, time wasn't exactly Pearce's friend, either, Myers realized.

"What about the CIA?" Ian asked. "Pearce was one of theirs. Could they mount some kind of operation? Kidnap a Chinese agent, offer a trade?"

"Troy isn't one of them anymore. He quit the Company, and they don't forget that kind of thing. And when it comes to the Russian and Chinese security services, the CIA never wants to go to the mattresses."

"Excuse me?"

"Sorry, a *Godfather* reference. 'Going to the mattresses' means going to war. The spooks never want to play roughhouse. Spying is a gentlemen's game despite what you see in the movies. More like hide-and-seek, not MMA cage fighting. If the CIA snatches one of theirs, then they snatch one of ours, and back and forth it escalates until some real damage gets done. Best to avoid that kind of thing, or so they believe."

"But if Pearce is a private citizen, then shouldn't he be afforded some kind of diplomatic protection?"

"Did you forget why he was really there? If they suspect him of spying, he won't have any protection."

"He's in for a rough time of it. President Lane understands that, certainly?"

"Of course he does. If I was president, I'd be forced to leave Troy in Chinese hands, too. At least, until everything else got sorted out."

"I suppose you're right," Ian conceded, as he took a sip of hot tea.

"But then again, I'm no longer the president of the United States, am I?"

"Sorry, ma'am, I'm not following you."

"There's a phone number I need you to get for me. It's a long shot, but it just might work."

FORTY-FOUR

Twenty wide-eyed schoolchildren oohed and aahed with grim curiosity as the whalers' sharp pole blades sliced thirty-foot-long slabs of pink blubber. Other whalers pulled back the thick strips of skin and fat with their hands as if they were peeling a twelve-ton banana, only this banana was gray, with eyes and a wry smile.

It was the annual harvest of Baird's beaked whales in a small Japanese whaling village on the Pacific coast. The children in their bright-blue school uniforms and yellow caps chattered excitedly. Another whale had been dragged up the bloody cement ramp from the water to the open-walled slaughterhouse.

"That's disgusting." The forty-three-year-old vegan and nuclear physicist scrunched up her pretty California surfer-girl face.

Yamada shrugged. "It's a four-hundred-year-old tradition."

"Tell that to the whale."

"I would, but I don't think he'd hear me." Yamada watched two of his American graduate students wolfing down fried whale morsels and guzzling ice-cold bottles of Asahi beer.

"For a world-class whale researcher, you don't have much empathy for the poor things," the woman said.

"I've devoted my life to them, but I don't value them above people. A small local harvest like this is no threat to the species. It's the big floating kill factories that need to be stopped." Yamada didn't tell her that in his radical youth he had sabotaged Soviet whaling boats.

A whaler sliced deeper into the carcass, revealing the dark meat and viscera.

"I'm think I'm gonna be sick." The blonde researcher stepped away, looking for a bottled water to soothe her queasy stomach.

Dr. Kenji Yamada looked more like a surf bum than a world-class marine scientist, with his dark tan and long silver ponytail. His handsome face was framed by a well-groomed platinum beard. He had been born in Japan to Japanese parents who immigrated to Hawaii when he was a young child, but he was thoroughly American and a naturalized citizen. His parents, now long since dead, were buried in a lonely Japanese cemetery on Kauai. They raised him proudly steeped in Japanese culture, tradition, and language, all three of which he closely embraced in his middle age. He was their only child, and he was childless—an unspoken disappointment for his parents, who wished for grandchildren to tend their graves and join them in the next life.

An old fisherman shuffled up with a whale fin neatly wrapped in folded paper. Yamada bowed his gratitude. The two men conversed happily in Japanese. Yamada felt the warm sun on his face, smelled the sea and the salt air. The life of the happy little village coursed in his blood. For a moment it felt like home.

*   *   *

Yamada listened to the soft snoring of his vegan physicist sound asleep next to him and the water chucking against the cabin bulkhead.

Yamada's research boat was owned by Pearce Systems, but he leased the vessel for a dollar a year from Troy under a special arrangement. Yamada and his lab was Pearce Systems' primary UUV development team, building and testing new underwater drones for use in oceanographic research, especially whale migration. Drones that Pearce Systems later sold or deployed in both civilian and military applications.

Yamada hadn't spoken to Pearce in months. Their friendship was strong enough to weather any storm, but watching Pearce kill Jasmine Bath with one of his own turtle-shaped UUVs had wounded Yamada deeply. Yamada accepted the use of his vehicles for security purposes, though he was a pacifist. But murder for revenge was something else. He knew Pearce was a violent man, but he had never seen it up close. Bath deserved her fate, no doubt, but Yamada still couldn't condone it. He feared it was bad karma for his old friend.

Earlier that day, the vegan researcher had threatened to blow chunks all over him if he didn't break down the whale fin sample for her to do an assay, so he did. There was no question now. The whale meat was laced with cesium-137 and the fin bones contained strontium-90, notorious for mimicking calcium. These were just two of several known radioactive isotopes dumped into the air, ground, and waters around the Fukushima nuclear facility that were turning up in fish, plant, and even human subjects all over the Pacific, even as far as the west coast of the United States. Cesium had been found as far as two thousand kilometers away and more than five thousand meters deep just thirty days after the accident. How much more, how far, and how pervasive the subsequent nuclear contamination had been hotly debated. His contracted research mission was to try to answer those questions more definitively.

It would take her some time, but the vegan physicist would be able to determine if the nuclear contaminants came from Fukushima once they got back to the university. Before coming to the University of Hawaii, she had worked at Los Alamos National Laboratory in the technical nuclear forensics (TNF) department, but since the surfing was better in Hawaii than in New Mexico, she decided to move. She had her priorities.

When the 9.0 magnitude earthquake and resulting forty-six-foot-tall tsunami struck the six reactors of the Fukushima Daiichi nuclear facility on March 11, 2011, all hell broke loose. By any measure, the Fukushima nuclear catastrophe was the worst peacetime nuclear event in history, surpassing Three Mile Island and even Chernobyl. The magnitude of the damage was such that Germany's chancellor, Angela Merkel, a Ph.D. in quantum chemistry, ordered all of Germany's nuclear plants to be shut down and deconstructed as soon as feasible.

Within just a few days of the catastrophe, celebrity physicists and antinuclear activists called Fukushima a planet-killing event. Three of the six nuclear cores had melted down—down into the Earth's crust, some speculated. Of course, no one knew for sure. It was too dangerous and too difficult to get inside any of these wrecked facilities, even with robotics systems. But all three cores contained plutonium-239, one of the most toxic substances on the planet, a radioisotope with a half-life of twenty-four thousand years. More than fourteen hundred fuel rods, also loaded with plutonium, were at risk of fire and explosion. The fuel rods alone could pump fourteen thousand times more radiation into the atmosphere than was released by the Hiroshima bomb.

The dire warnings gained credence as the incompetence and deceit of both TEPCO (the utility company managing Fukushima Daiichi) and the Japanese government became apparent. Revelation after revelation proved at least some of the fears. Three hundred tons of groundwater passed through the contaminated facility every day straight into the Pacific Ocean, and the level of radiation of the groundwater was exploding exponentially. More than eighty thousand gallons of highly contaminated water from within the facility had been pouring into the Pacific every day since the earthquake. A dime-size bit of cesium-137 evenly distributed over a metropolis like New York City would render it uninhabitable.

Yamada devoured everything he could about the catastrophe when it first occurred, especially the Japanese sources, but also the scientific articles as they began to emerge. It was a very mixed picture. Even environmentalist organizations like Greenpeace said that concerns over Fukushima were grossly exaggerated, and other sources he trusted said that the massive amounts of radiation released into the Pacific were being safely diffused and that little environmental damage had or would ever occur.

And yet . . . he wondered. In Hawaii, he had caught a few fish that tested for low levels of radiation—nothing dangerous. But the concentrations of cesium were far higher than he had ever seen before. And there were other reports of high rates of cancer suddenly occurring in people around Fukushima and even among the crew of the USS *Ronald Reagan*, which had been dispatched to Fukushima for disaster-relief efforts. Independent sources—unknown, unaccredited—reported much higher levels of radiological contamination on the American west coast than "reliable" sources stated, and they further documented birth defects in animals and fish in a wide variety of regions.

Most disturbing, antinuclear activists in Japan were receiving death threats from right-wing opponents even as the Japanese government was cracking down on "irresponsible" reporting of Fukushima events. And the conspiracy theorists had one argument in their favor. If Fukushima really was a planet-killing event, would the governments of the world even admit it? If they did, the resulting global panic would crash markets, collapse economies, and ignite civil chaos. Governments had every reason to hide the truth until a solution could be found. Or so the alarmists concluded.

But Yamada discounted alarmists in general. Too many science debates today were being driven by political orthodoxies and other agendas rather than scientific inquiry—and even credible "deniers" were ruined. Yamada believed the facts should determine the argument rather than the other way around. As far as he was concerned, the world had enough real problems to deal with. The truth about the real dangers of Fukushima would be eventually known, but only if dedicated marine scientists like him used their skills to pursue that truth, and the truth was always to be found in the hard data.

When a private nonprofit environmental organization requested Yamada and his team do some independent radiological survey work in Japan's Pacific waters, Yamada agreed. So far, what they had discovered was worrisome. Fukushima radiation was definitely pluming throughout the region, popping up in a number of locations and species that hadn't been reported before.

Radioisotopes had fingerprints. With the comparison samples they had already collected, his vegan physicist could determine if the butchered whale had picked up cesium and strontium from Fukushima or some other source. She explained to him that a TNF physicist was like a good sommelier who can determine not only the vintage of a great wine, but also the exact field it came from because of the soil composition.

Several anonymous tips from sources within the Japanese government and even TEPCO had aided their detective work in the last few weeks as their efforts became more widely known. At first, the anonymity of the sources bothered Yamada, but he understood. Fearful of losing their high-paying jobs—an increasingly scarce commodity in Japan—these concerned engineers and bureaucrats were also worried about appearing to defy the consensus on TEPCO's handling of the crisis—or the government's.

Yamada sighed. He couldn't go back to sleep. Thinking about Fukushima made him think about death, which made him think about his parents, whom he'd come to miss terribly in the last few years. He had an active social life—his married friends, many of them younger, envied his carefree childless lifestyle—but in truth he was alone in the world, a middle-aged man facing his mortality for the first time. He resolved to visit his parents' graves when he got back home, and even pray over them and burn incense, and find some way to console their spirits. Until then, he had work to do. He checked his watch. It was still an hour before dawn.

He slipped out of bed as quietly as possible and padded in his bare feet toward the galley to make coffee. His cell phone buzzed. He checked it. Another text message, anonymous as usual. GPS coordinates.

And the promise of an unbelievable discovery.

FORTY-FIVE

Disko Dschungel squatted on the fifth floor of a crumbling prewar warehouse overlooking the Spree River in the Kreuzberg section of Berlin. It was equal parts *Blade Runner* chic and bad '80s chrome-and-neon disco.

In Jianli's drug-addled state, it looked like a spaceship had crashed in the middle of a futuristic dance club. The music alternated between heavy electro beats and ethereal space music. The twenty-thousand-square-foot space was centered around a circular bar that was ringed with a lighted dance floor, the colors throbbing and shifting according to the beats of the music. There were precious few dancers, however; most of the clientele clustered in the constellation of tall black vinyl booths scattered like satellites around the floor.

The club owner was a friend of Jianli's, a Chinese national and fellow princeling seeking to make his way in the world beyond the reach of his own powerful and equally disapproving father. The club was a favorite of other wealthy Chinese expats along with an internationally diverse collection of well-heeled, fully entitled, disaffected youth. A wide variety of hallucinogens was available for purchase along with the finest selection of distilled spirits in central Europe. A three-star Michelin chef in the kitchen served up the best and priciest bar food anywhere.

Jianli's two favorite bodyguards sat in the booth with him, sipping sparkling water and keeping a careful eye on their besotted charge. His studies at Humboldt University of Berlin were going well enough, but it was the nightlife that most intrigued the handsome nineteen-year-old, especially the wide availability of willing young women. Disko Dschungel was his prime hunting ground. The members-only club carefully recruited some of the most attractive and eager women on the continent by giving them access to some of Europe's wealthiest and rebellious young men.

Jianli's bleary eyes were captured by the leering gaze of a stunning blonde standing at the bar. Next to her was an equally spectacular mixed-race woman, smoky and lithe, who was also locking eyes with him. Jianli felt the heat rising in his loins. He whispered to one of his guards who slid out of the booth and made his way to the bar.

Thirty minutes later, the two scowling guards were standing at the bar while the two women sat with Jianli, bookends to his swelling libido. They devoured sweet buttery lobster and cold champagne between bouts of laughter and short teasing kisses. Jianli couldn't believe his luck. He had enough experience with whores to know these weren't paid professionals. They were fashion models shuttling between European capitals on an extended contract. They seemed genuinely interested in him and that was the most stimulating thing of all. Suddenly, two swift, skillful hands reached under the table and teased him with promises of pleasures still to come. A swift nod to his bodyguards, and the threesome fled the club, head-

ing for the armored Mercedes limo parked in the base-
ment.

The ancient freight-elevator doors creaked open and the
guards stepped out first, heads on a swivel. The base-
ment was clear of foot traffic and Jianli's Mercedes limo
was parked in a separate VIP area reserved just for him.
One of the perks of being a regular as well as being the
son of one of the most powerful men in China.

The guards nodded all clear and Jianli ushered the
women out with him, his arms wrapped around their
waists. They clung to him like drunken sailors on a pitch-
ing deck in a high storm, giggling and purring with each
step. When they reached the limo, one of the guards
opened the rear door and ushered Jianli in. When the
blonde girl tried to enter, he blocked her with his hand.

"What the fuck is this?" she asked in slurred but effortless German.

The bodyguard spoke no German but easily inferred
the question. He motioned with his fingers at her small
clutch.

"Jianli! What's this all about?"

Jianli leaned out. "Sorry, my love, but he's just doing
his job."

The blonde glanced over at the other steely-eyed
guard, certain that the bulge in his coat pocket wasn't an
oversize smartphone. He held a security wand in his
hands. "Fine." She handed him her purse and he fingered
through it. Found her cell phone, pulled it out.

"Hey! You can't have that!" She snatched it out of his
hands.

"Sweet, if you want to come with me, you need to give
him your phone. He'll keep it safe in a special box. It

blocks signals so that it can't be used to track us, that's all. He'll give it back later, I promise."

"I don't know about all of this," she said, as the other guard wanded her firm, curvy frame.

Jianli flashed his most charming smile. Rattled a pill bottle. "If you're a good girl, I have some candy for you."

That caught her attention. She reluctantly handed her cell phone over and climbed next to Jianli after the other guard gave his approving nod. The blonde scrambled in with a giggle and playfully climbed over Jianli's lap to make room for her friend.

The other girl hesitated, apprehension gripping her stunning green eyes. Jianli tried to coax her in with his hypnotic smile. The dark-skinned girl was the one he truly wanted. She looked like a young Halle Berry, an effect she clearly cultivated with her tight-fitting clothes and short-cropped hair.

"Please?" he asked in English. The woman spoke no German.

"Don't be such a baby. We'll have so much fun!" the blonde said, laughing.

Jianli held out his hand. So did the blonde. "Maybe it will be like Barcelona." Her eyes twinkled.

The dark-skinned woman allowed herself a small smile. "Gee, I hope not. I couldn't walk for a week after that." She dropped her cell phone into the bodyguard's open hand and let the other one wand her down. After the all clear, she clambered in. The doors shut, the guards climbed in and the Mercedes sped out of the parking structure with tires squealing.

The Mercedes sped westward on the crosstown highway toward Jianli's recently built high-rise penthouse in Charlottenburg. It was after two in the morning and traffic was light, especially at the usual exit for Loschmidstraße. Jianli had already popped a Viagra and was eager to go, but a police barricade on the deserted street brought them to a standstill. Police lights splashed against the windshield like blue strobes, and a beefy Berlin police officer flashed his bright LED light through the driver's window, tapping the bulletproof glass with the heavy metal casing.

"Show him your papers," Jianli commanded from the back. The sooner they got through this, the sooner he could get into action.

The reluctant driver hit the automatic-window button and lowered the glass, handing his passport and driver's license out the window, never hearing the muffled pop of the silenced 9mm hollow-point bullet that blew his brains out.

At the sound of the muzzle blast, the blonde threw a sharp elbow into Jianli's face, cracking the cartilage in his nose and blinding him with pain while the other woman stabbed his guard through the ear with a razor-sharp plastic blade.

The two women hustled young Jianli out of the backseat as the two other men posing as Berlin police made preparations to move the Mercedes and dump the bodies.

The blonde nodded at the blood on her friend's hand. "You okay?"

"Not mine." The dark-haired woman wiped her hand on Jianli's tailored shirt, then carefully removed from his wrist the white-gold Patek Philippe watch he'd been fingering nervously all night. She knew it contained a tracking device. She smiled at the thought that some lucky homeless Berliner in urine-stained coveralls would soon be wearing a ten-thousand-dollar Swiss timepiece.

Thirty minutes later, the Mercedes was dismantled and parted out in a local Bosnian chop shop and the two

Chinese corpses were incinerated by a crematorium under a blind contract with Mossad.

On the other side of town, Tamar Stern and her blonde comrade made the final arrangements for a live video broadcast from a safe house in a heavily treed suburb off Königstraße on the far west side of the German capital. Tamar covered herself head to toe in black athletic wear and a balaclava, and used brown contacts to hide her striking green eyes. She knew the moment the video feed went through that her life would be forfeit if the Chinese MSS ever discovered who she was. They might anyway. She was willing to take that risk.

Had to.

FORTY-SIX

Vice Chairman Feng checked his Patek Philippe watch. It was nearly time to begin Pearce's interrogation. He'd discovered through the years that simply leaving a man alone with his worst fears was sometimes enough to break him. He doubted the former CIA special operations group officer would cave so easily, but an active imagination coupled with a sleepless night without food and water would at least soften him up. His ultimate goal wasn't to just extract information from him, but to turn the big American into a useful thrall. Feng's government was making great advances in drone technology, but someone with Pearce's practical knowledge could help greatly in furthering their tactical and strategic deployment.

A panicked knock rattled Feng's door.

"Enter!"

A young army lieutenant dashed into the room, one of several trusted aides and the newest. The handsome young officer was the son of a key Politburo ally and a vigorous paramour. If the boy's father ever discovered his son's behavior, he would be disowned, which only bound him more tightly to Feng.

"Sir, there's an urgent message for you on your private phone." He thrust the smartphone into Feng's hand. The threatening text message was terse and included both a private URL and a password.

"Who else has seen this?"

"No one! I swear."

Feng's searching eyes examined Lieutenant Chin's strong but anxious face. "Good. See that it stays that way."

"Yes, sir. Of course."

The vice chairman dismissed him with a wave of his hand. After the door shut, he removed a private laptop with special security features designed by his own cyberwarfare specialists to thwart any attempts to monitor his online activity. He hoped it worked as well as promised.

Feng tapped in the URL and password, and within moments a live video feed appeared on his screen. A masked figure clad in black appeared. Feng was more curious than angry. The threat was insulting enough. But the fact that this man felt he had to hide himself—gloves, mask, sleeves—was proof that he was afraid of Feng's power. That meant he was smart—or at least wisely cautious.

"Who are you?" Feng demanded.

"My name doesn't matter," the voice said. The tone was eerily ethereal and low, masked by an electronic filter. "You have Troy Pearce in your custody. I want him released immediately."

Feng knew he was dealing with a professional. Possibly even a national-security operative. The masked bandit was smart enough to realize the vice chairman was deploying voice-detection software to try to identify him after the video call.

Feng smiled. "So afraid of me that you can't even use your real voice? That won't help you. My security services are probably already racing to your location—"

"For your sake, I hope not. They would only find a list of the names of the sons of Party officials you've seduced over the years, including Lieutenant Chin."

Feng's jaw clenched. *Who is this bastard?* How could he have possibly known about his most recent acquisition?

"Have I struck a nerve, Feng Yongbo?"

"You're wasting my time," Feng said. "You obviously have a few resources at your disposal, so you know it's the families of these young men who will be compromised and shamed by these false accusations, not me."

"I assure you that I have more than a few resources at my disposal. All I want from you is for Troy Pearce to be released immediately."

Feng chuckled. "You Americans. So arrogant. So demanding. Perhaps I'll release Pearce to you. Perhaps I'll mail him to you in a bag chopped up like a chicken prepared for the wok. What do you say to that?"

The masked figure on his screen held up a razor-sharp KA-BAR combat knife. "Strange that you should mention chopped up."

The figure waved the ominous blade, motioning for the camera to follow. Feng began to despair. The walls were bare and the rooms empty. Every precaution had been taken to not reveal the least possible detail about the hidden location. Furniture, calendars, photos, newspapers, wallpaper prints, and even room dimensions or window types could provide enough clues to locate them. Definitely trained professionals.

The camera followed the shadowy figure into a room. Feng gasped.

His naked son was hanging upside down from a rope attached to a heavy wooden beam in the ceiling.

"Jianli?" Feng said, leaping to his feet.

The figure touched the tip of the blade against the boy's smooth flesh and flicked it just enough to spin him gently and also nick the skin. A tiny drop of blood welled up just above the navel.

Feng's lined face tightened with anger. "You're a fool to touch my son like that."

"So I have your attention?" The electronic voice reverberated over Feng's laptop speaker.

The vice chairman calmed himself down. The American wouldn't dare harm his son. "You're risking all-out war. Many sons will die because of your crimes, including you."

"I'm risking nothing. I'm not an American. I work for cash. You release Pearce; I release the boy; I get paid. It's a simple business transaction."

"Release the boy now and I'll triple your price," the elder Feng promised. "Fail to release him, and I swear I'll find you and skin you alive."

The figure rotated Feng Jianli's body so that his broad chest faced the camera. "Poor choice of words." The masked figure lightly dragged the knife blade across young Feng's skin. A razor-thin line of pink flesh opened up and blood seeped out, quickly creeping toward his bruised face.

The vice chairman smiled. "Blood doesn't scare me. Perhaps I'll drain Pearce of his when we're finished. I know I'll be bathing in yours soon enough."

Feng leaned forward in his chair, his face pressed close to the camera. "Of course, a woman knows all about blood, doesn't she?"

FORTY-SEVEN

Tamar's spine tingled. How did he know her gender? She'd read up on the vice chairman. His ruthless climb to the top of the Party hierarchy was well documented, but she hadn't anticipated a cold-blooded sociopath with near psychic abilities.

She took a deep breath. It didn't really matter. She owed Troy Pearce everything. He was the only man she trusted as much as she had her beloved Udi, who had been brutally murdered a few years before in an operation to stop the Iranian Quds Force in Mexico.

When Margaret Myers called her in panicked desperation about Troy's kidnapping, Tamar was only too glad to help in any way she could. So was Mossad, Israel's feared security service. Pearce had been a great friend to her and Udi over the years, as well as to Israel, providing valuable assistance when called upon. Pearce's CIA service in Iraq had earned him serious street cred within Israel's intelligence and counterterror community. They were all glad to throw in to help out an old friend who never asked for favors, especially when the request came from the former president of the United States, another staunch ally of the Jewish people. Tamar welcomed the chance to pay back a few of her debts to Troy. Tonight's gambit was a high-risk ploy and neither she nor Mossad were confident it would work with the elder Feng, but they all agreed it was worth the gamble because Pearce's life hung in the balance.

"Nice try, Feng. Let's see how cool you are after your baby boy here is bled out like a pig."

Feng laughed. "A minor cut. A little blood. I think you're gutless."

"Feng, Feng, Feng. Words have consequences. Haven't you learned that yet?"

Tamar reached over to young Feng and grabbed his scrotum in her gloved hand. She laid the knife blade at the base of the sac. Blood from his chest cut now spilled all over his face. He screamed.

Tamar raised the blade high.

"STOP! You win!" Feng shouted. Jianli was his only son. The Feng family name and fortune would pass through him. Vice Chairman Feng's only sense of eternity was the family bloodline. If his son should die or, worse, be castrated, the family line would perish and so would a hundred generations of his family name. Pearce wasn't worth it. He would have to find some other way to get his vengeance for his nephew Zhao. He never really cared for the arrogant and insufferable young fool anyway.

Tamar kept the blade held high. "Make the call now. Release Pearce immediately. I want him on a plane within the hour, heading for Japan. When I receive confirmation that he's arrived safely, I'll release your son. Until then—"

Tamar swung the blade hard. The rope split. Young Feng hit the floor with a howl.

"I'll be sure nothing else happens to your son."

She cut the transmission, silently breathing a sigh of relief.

Young Feng whimpered, curled up at her feet.

She kicked him in the ribs to get him to shut up.

He did.

A door opened. Another masked figure stepped in. Tossed Feng's clothes onto the floor.

"Get dressed and be ready to move," the blonde said.

Now they had to wait for the vice chairman's confirmation.

Tamar prayed the Chinese hadn't somehow managed to track their location. If they did and sent a team to snatch the boy, Pearce was dead.

And so were they.

FORTY-EIGHT

The big fish flapped lethargically in the bottom of the net as Yamada spilled him out onto the deck. He reached down and pressed his finger against the smooth rubbery skin and flipped a switch. The robo-fish stopped flapping. Yamada and his team used a wide variety of sensors to detect, measure, and, in some cases, retrieve radioactive elements in the water, including the autonomous robo-fish. His research mission was to determine the range and extent of contamination resulting from the Fukushima disaster. So far, the tip that had sent him and his crew out here hadn't panned out, which was strange, because his anonymous sources had proven utterly reliable before.

Yamada lifted the four-foot-long robo-fish and hauled it belowdecks for processing in their miniature lab. Its software was programmed for autonomous swimming, diving to specific depths at regular intervals, and recording data as it went. The young woman running his onboard IT department would handle the data download and analysis. Part of the robo-fish's skin provided data collection—a kind of flypaper for chemical elements, including cesium-137. Samples would be drawn and analyzed by another grad student when they got back to the mainland. But for now, Yamada would subject it to a simple scan to see if any radioactivity could be detected. He wanded the robo-fish's entire body with a handheld Geiger counter. Nothing. He began to think the whole trip out this way was a wild-goose chase. Maybe the bad guys had fed him a false lead to get him away from the real evidence he had been gathering earlier.

"Kenji, report to the bridge." The voice on the loudspeaker was urgent—one of his grad students was piloting the boat today.

Yamada dashed up the ladder and made his way to the enclosed cabin above the main deck.

"What's wrong?"

The bearded young man pointed to the northeast. A fishing trawler. "Been tracking him on our radar scope. Getting awfully close."

The rusted trawler ran a parallel course. Looked like it would pass by, but with little room to spare. Their research ship was dead in the water, waiting to retrieve several other submersible sensors, including two more robo-fish.

"Did you raise him on the radio? Try to wave him off?"

"He's not doing anything illegal, technically. I thought I'd call you first."

Yamada grabbed a pair of high-powered binoculars. Adjusted the furled focus ring. He scanned the vessel. Booms, drums, winches. "Definitely a fishing trawler." His glass stopped on the big red flag with the five golden stars on the fantail.

Yamada lowered the binoculars, frowning. They were out of the shipping lanes. Hadn't seen much of any traffic the last few days.

"It's a Chinese vessel, isn't it?" the pilot asked.

Yamada nodded.

"You think we're in any danger?" They had all heard about the Chinese trawler attack on the Japanese dive boat several days earlier. Yamada made sure to keep his American flag flying at all times.

"Has he altered course at all?"

"Not since I've been tracking him."

Yamada scratched his head, an old nervous habit. If they moved too far off their current location, it would take them a lot more time to retrieve the other submersibles, even with their autonomous homing capabilities. If they held their position, they would be all packed up and heading back to Nagasaki for the night in less than an hour. "We'll stay put. We aren't in any danger unless that trawler changes course."

Twenty minutes later, it did.

FORTY-NINE

Floodlights bathed the tarmac where Feng's Gulfstream taxied to a stop. The stars overhead were hidden by a bank of low clouds.

Myers's hair whipped in the brisk ocean breeze that chilled her to the bone. The cabin door opened and the stairs deployed. Her heart skipped a beat when Pearce finally emerged in the doorway. As soon as he stepped onto the tarmac, the stairs behind him were lifted and the door shut. A moment later, the turbines whined as the plane began to taxi away.

Pearce's broad frame was only a shadow as he crossed the asphalt. It took everything in her not to run to him because that was the kind of thing only silly women did in bad Hollywood movies. The American ambassador, Henry Davis, was with her, along with a navy corpsman stationed at the American embassy.

Troy emerged out of the shadows into the light of the hangar. Myers gasped. His unshaven face was badly bruised. One of his sleep-deprived eyes was red and blackened. Dried blood stained his collar. The horrible memory of Pearce's head wound in Algeria flooded over her.

Bad movie or not, she ran to him.

"Troy—"

She wanted to gather him up in her arms and hug him, but she was afraid to touch him. She gently laid her hands on his shoulders.

He smiled. "Hey."

She stood back. "What did they do to you?"

"A couple of love taps. No big deal." He lisped a little. His lower lip was swollen.

"No big deal? You look like you walked into a wall," Myers said.

"You should see the other guy." Pearce laughed. Winced again. Didn't want to tell Myers the other guy was actually a middle-aged woman who used his head for a punching bag.

Myers and the navy corpsman steered him toward a bench near the hangar wall. The corpsman broke out his medical kit.

"Can I get you anything?" the ambassador asked. "What do you need?"

"A shower and a change of clothes for a start. I'm kind of ripe."

The corpsman flashed a light in both of Pearce's eyes.

"How's your head? Headache? Dizzy?"

"No." Pearce lied. His head hurt like hell, but he'd be damned if he was going to spend the night in a navy hospital.

"Anything broken?"

"No."

"How about a belt?" The corpsman pulled a silver flask from his coat and held it up.

"Don't tempt me."

The corpsman pocketed the flask and pressed two fingers on Pearce's inner wrist, feeling for a pulse, counting the beats while staring at his watch.

"How badly did they beat you?" Myers asked.

"I've had worse, believe me. I'm fine, really."

"Heart rate is good," the corpsman said. "They hit you with anything? Electric shock? Any wounds?"

"Just my ego. Honestly, I'm fine."

The corpsman closed up his kit. "I'd like to get you to the base clinic for a full exam or even the local hospital if you'd prefer."

"All I need is that shower. Maybe a steak, medium rare." Pearce stood and stretched, working out the kinks.

"I'm filing a formal protest with my counterpart in Beijing first thing in the morning," the ambassador said. "Lot of good it will do."

"Does Lane know I'm back?" Pearce asked.

The ambassador nodded. "Called him the moment your plane landed."

Pearce looked at Myers. "How'd you get me out of there?"

"Called a friend of yours. She was very persuasive." Myers didn't know the ambassador well. Even if she did, she didn't want to admit to an official in the Lane administration that she'd instigated the kidnapping of a Chinese national on German territory by an Israeli secret agent. "I'll fill in the details later."

Myers turned to the corpsman and the ambassador. "I need a moment, please." They both nodded and stepped away per their prior arrangement. When they were out of earshot, Myers took one of Pearce's hands in hers.

"I'm okay, really," Pearce said, smiling through the pain. Myers loved the way the corners of his eyes crinkled up when he smiled like that.

"Troy, I've got some bad news."

Pearce's smile disappeared. "What?"

"It's your friend, Kenji Yamada."

FIFTY

The young Japanese medical examiner carefully pulled open the refrigerated stainless-steel drawer and stepped quietly back.

Pearce took a deep breath. He pulled back the crisp white sheet. His blood pressure plunged. It felt like the floor was falling out from beneath his feet.

His old friend Kenji Yamada lay there, his pale, bearded face oddly serene, his body butchered. Yamada's corpse had been cleaned after the examination but not repaired. What remained of it was ghostly pale from blood loss, almost blue. Giant gashes had sliced him open across the chest and stomach. His left arm was practically severed just above the elbow, barely connected by a skein of milky white tendons, badly frayed. Most of the meat was missing from both thighs, exposing white shattered bone. After years in combat, Pearce had seen worse—some of it inflicted by him. But Kenji loved life and living things more than anyone else he'd ever known. Seeing his mangled corpse numbed Pearce to the quick.

"The cause of death appears to be a massive blow to the back of the head by a blunt object," the examiner said in excellent but thickly accented English. "Perhaps a pipe or even a piece of heavy wood."

"The other injuries?"

"In my estimation, the lacerations on the upper torso were caused by propeller blades. The same for the left arm, possibly."

"And his legs?"

"Sharks."

Pearce nodded. He'd seen enough.

The examiner replaced the sheet with ceremonious precision.

"My condolences."

"Thank you."

"He was your friend, yes?"

"Yes."

The young examiner nodded grimly. He slowly pushed the drawer shut. The metal glides whispered as the drawer disappeared into the wall. The door shut. The tiled room echoed with a heavy metal *click* as the locking mechanism engaged.

The medical examiner finally turned to Pearce, his dark eyes furious. "The Chinese must pay for this."

Pearce nodded.

They would.

Pearce was greeted in the waiting room outside of the morgue by Myers, Ambassador Davis, and Tanaka.

"I'm very sorry for your loss, Mr. Pearce," the ambassador said.

"It was good of you to come at this time of night." Pearce glanced at Tanaka. "Both of you."

"All of Japan grieves with you, and for your friend Dr. Yamada." Tanaka bowed slightly.

"Thank you. Kenji was a good man and a good friend."

"My government is outraged," Tanaka continued. "We consider the attack on Dr. Yamada as an attack upon us as well. He was a naturalized American citizen, but he was born on Japanese soil."

"He loved America and Japan equally."

Tanaka turned to the ambassador. "The United States must do something more than lodge a formal protest."

"President Lane is meeting with his cabinet even as we speak."

"If your government will not act to defend Japan, it must at least act to defend itself."

"I'm inclined to agree," the ambassador said. "I'm sure President Lane will be contacting Prime Minister Ito shortly."

Tanaka's phone vibrated. He checked it. "Please, you must excuse me." He shook Pearce's hand. "Again, my condolences." He nodded to Myers and the ambassador then put his phone to his ear and listened to his message as he walked out of the room.

"I understand he has no living relatives?" the ambassador asked.

"He was never married and has no children. His parents passed away years ago. They're buried in Hawaii."

"We'll make all the necessary arrangements to have him flown home," the ambassador said. "I'll contact your office for the particulars."

"Thank you."

"I'll be waiting in the car," the ambassador said.

After he cleared the room, Pearce asked Myers, "What do we know for sure?"

"Five dead, one survivor. One of the dead was a Japanese national. The survivor is adamant that it was a Chinese vessel. A fishing trawler. Recognized the flag."

"Just like that other attack," Pearce said. "I'm guessing this is all over the news?"

"Not yet. The government convinced the local news stations to spike the story for at least twenty-four hours for national security reasons. There's no video and the lone survivor is at the hospital in a private room under protection. She's agreed to not speak to anybody about what happened yet. She's a brave girl."

"How badly is she hurt?"

"Broken arm, exposure. And . . ."

"They raped her."

"Yeah."

Myers nodded grimly. "If the Chinese want a war with us, this should do it."

Pearce frowned. "Yeah, it should." He felt the old familiar rage welling up inside his gut. But something held it in check. Killing Americans in Japanese territorial waters right now would likely lead China into war with both countries. The Chinese would know that. Maybe their leadership had finally lost their minds. Decided now or never, like Tojo did when he lashed out at Pearl Harbor.

Or maybe they hadn't. This wasn't a sneak attack. It was an assassination. And then he remembered.

World War I had started that way, too.

FIFTY-ONE

Vice Chairman Feng had commandeered the security chief's own office and threw him out, waiting for the phone call for news about his son. He paced the floor like a nervous cat, smoking furiously. The intercom rang. "It's the Berlin embassy, sir."

Feng snatched up the receiver. "Jianli!"

"I'm sorry, sir. My name is Liu. I'm the station chief."

"Where's my son?"

"He's been sedated. Doctor's orders."

Feng's grip tightened on the phone. Perhaps Jianli's kidnapper had castrated him after all. "Was he injured?"

"Traumatized. Just crying, mostly."

Feng winced. That wouldn't do. But his son's cowardice couldn't be helped now. At least he was safe.

"Have him contact me the minute he wakes up. As soon as he's fit to travel, he's to return home—even if he protests. Understood?"

"Yes, sir."

"And if anything happens to him between now and his arrival, I'll hold you personally responsible. Is that clear?"

"Perfectly."

"To whom have you spoken of these matters?"

"No one, just as you ordered. Only one other agent was with me when we picked him up. And the doctor, of course."

"Make sure they understand the importance of silence. If one word of this gets out—"

"I'll be held responsible."

"I'll have you all shot."

Feng slammed the phone into its cradle. The image of his naked son hanging like a pig in a slaughterhouse clawed at his heart.

He pulled his secure cell phone from his pocket and punched the speed dial for Admiral Ji. He'd teach those American bastards a lesson in humiliation. Drive it deep into their ugly round eyes like a burning spike.

FIFTY-TWO

The rays of the rising sun shot through the towering cumulonimbus on the horizon. A sign, surely.

Sanjuro Sakai sipped the steaming cup of tea, his clear eyes transfixed by the morning sky. The weather report said it would be a clear day, no rain, slight breeze from the west.

Another sign.

Sanjuro had lived a full and interesting life. He was eighty-nine years old and in perfect health. It was a miracle. Born in 1928, he was just seventeen years old when the war ended. If the war had lasted another day, he wouldn't have survived it. His parents and sister didn't, perishing in a fire set by American incendiary bombs.

After the war, Sanjuro fed himself by selling scrap metal, then he apprenticed in a small-engine repair shop. Within a decade, he owned it and began designing his own motors. He sold a patent. Married. Started a family. Started another company.

His wife gave him one son and three daughters before she passed. His children gave him ten grandchildren and five great-grandchildren. An unusually large family in Japan these days. His son grew the company into an international firm worth millions. His daughters all earned university degrees. His grandchildren were educated abroad. They, in turn, had grown the business even larger and diversified it. His entire family was wealthy, comfortable, and close. They worshipped the ground Sanjuro walked on because everything they enjoyed had all come from his hand.

A fine life indeed.

But his blessings didn't end there. All of his life he loved to fly. His vision was still nearly perfect and he was Japan's second-oldest licensed pilot. Never a crash.

And today was a good day to fly.

But Sanjuro was no fool. Life begins and it ends like the rising and the setting of the sun. He turned his attention to the ancient black-and-white photographs on the small table near his bed, a shrine of memories. Family and friends long gone. He missed them. He stroked his long silvery mustache.

Soon, he thought.

Sanjuro felt the ocean breeze battering his wrinkled face. He could smell the salt. It made him feel young again. Flying always did. The electric hangar door opened at the push of a button. His great-grandson Ikki was already inside, fixing a GoPro camera on the dashboard of the Mitsubishi A6M. The single-engine aircraft was his favorite. A classic. An extravagant gift from his son years ago.

Sanjuro walked the plane, inspecting it. It had been recently serviced and repainted. He checked the ailerons for play, kicked the tires—plenty of air. The hangar floor was clean. No leaks. The mechanic who maintained the family's aircraft was an excellent technician. An artist with a wrench. Sanjuro expected no less than perfection from him and usually got it.

Thirty minutes later, Ikki climbed down and helped Sanjuro pull on his old flight suit, green and baggy on his ancient frame. Then he nimbly climbed the pegs in the fuselage, careful to step only on them and the pad on the wing. Once Sanjuro was inside the cockpit, Ikki followed him up and stood on the wing pad.

"You're still spry, Great-grandfather."

"Stretching and bending, every day!" He laughed and patted Ikki's round belly. "Don't forget! Or you'll be a fat man in a wheelchair way too soon."

Ikki explained to him again how to activate both Go-Pro cameras, the one in the cockpit facing him and the one on the cowling facing forward, but Sanjuro remembered everything. His mind was as sharp as his eyes. An overactive bladder was the only thing that bothered him. No matter. Today was a short flight.

Ikki pulled out his own video camera. Flipped open the screen. Held it up and hit the record button. "Ready, Great-grandfather?"

"It's a beautiful day to fly, isn't it?" He smiled like a child at play, a mouth full of crooked teeth beneath his mustache.

"Yes, it is."

They chatted briefly as Sanjuro tested the stick and rudder pedals. Ikki was Sanjuro's favorite great-grandchild, now a grown man, though he thought of him as a boy. Ikki was crazy about flying just like Sanjuro was. Sat at his feet for hours and listened to the old man's stories, especially about the war. Sanjuro talked most about the friends he lost, much younger than Ikki at the time, loyal and brave in service to the emperor. Sanjuro was grateful that Ikki was attentive to his stories. His friends would live a while longer in Ikki's heart long after he was gone, even if only as Sanjuro's memories.

Sanjuro adjusted his *hachimaki*, then pulled on his

head gear. Smiled brightly into Ikki's camera. Ikki smiled back and shut it off.

"Good luck and good flying, Great-grandfather." He patted Sanjuro's shoulder. The old man squeezed his great-grandson's hand.

"It's an easy trip. Don't worry."

Minutes later, the white aircraft lifted off, captured in Ikki's viewfinder. Sanjuro must have sensed it. He wiggled the Mitsubishi's wings, waving good-bye.

The television screen flashed LIVE! BREAKING NEWS! The two attractive Japanese television anchors, a man and a woman, spoke in rapid, breathless urgency. A video flashed on the screen behind them. A GoPro camera image of the Chinese oil-drilling ship as seen from above through the flickering shadow of a spinning prop blade.

The young woman announced, "Moments ago, Mr. Sanjuro Sakai—"

The drilling ship grew larger and larger as the camera sped toward the platform.

"Industrialist, family man, and Japan's second-oldest pilot—"

The camera plunged into the drill ship's steel deck, a last-second blur of scattering jumpsuits and steel rigging before the image cut to black.

"Crashed his aircraft today in an apparent suicide attack on the Chinese oil-drilling ship *Tiger II*, in the disputed waters of the Senkaku Islands."

The television image cut away from the anchors. Ikki's video loop filled the screen. Played again. This time with audio. Sanjuro's voice cried out as the plane plummeted toward the *Tiger II*, *"Banzai! Banzai! BANZAI!"*

The male anchor appeared on screen. "No word yet

from the Chinese government concerning the extent of the damage. A Japan Maritime Self-Defense Force spokesman just released a statement that the ship caught fire from the strike, but that the fire appears to be under control."

A new image flashed on the monitor behind them. Sanjuro's smiling face, crinkled and bright, flashing his crooked teeth beneath a rakish silver mustache. He stood in his baggy green aviator's jumpsuit and *hachimaki*—a white headband with a rising sun and kanji that read FOR JAPAN! In the background, his white Mitsubishi A6M, the fabled Zero fighter aircraft of World War II legend, gleamed in the sunlight, a bright red sun painted on the fuselage.

The anchorwoman held up a sheet of paper. Other images of Sanjuro flashed behind her, including an Imperial Army photo of seventeen-year-old Sanjuro in the same jumpsuit standing in front of the same kind of airplane, a nearly duplicate image—all carefully crafted by Ikki.

"I have in my hands a copy of the letter he gave to his great-grandson Ikki Sakai just moments before he departed on his fateful journey. It reads, in part, 'Do not weep for me. Rejoice! It is a beautiful death, to die for one's country. For today I join my brave comrades who flew their Zeros into the teeth of another invader. We are all delicate flowers, and in the end, our sweet fragrance must fade.'"

The beautiful young woman, a former actress, choked up at the last words and wiped away a tear. She continued reading, inspired. "'Japan! Do not fear the Dragon. Resist him, and he shall flee. The divine wind shall drive him from our waters. Death is not the end. Do not fear it. But shame will last forever. Fight!'"

The male anchor continued. "Sanjuro Sakai, one of

Japan's oldest living pilots, was almost the youngest kamikaze pilot in history. He volunteered as a teenager to
fly a suicide mission, but the war ended the day before
Corporal Sakai's scheduled flight could take place. His
family states that Corporal Sakai lived a long and happy
life, but in the end, he had become haunted by the memories of his young friends who had completed their missions."

The newscast continued, reviewing Sanjuro's long and
prosperous life, updating the *Tiger II*'s damage reports,
detailing the specs of Japan's most famous fighter aircraft,
the history of the kamikaze, and broadcasting several
other still images and video clips of Sanjuro and the attack. All of this had been supplied by Ikki, who stood in
the station owner's office while watching the broadcast,
toasting the owner, an old university pal, with Yamazaki
Single-malt Sherry Cask whiskey. The station owner, like
Ikki, hated the Chinese, but hated the cowardice of the
current Japanese government even more.

When Sanjuro first confided in his great-grandson that
he planned to attack the Chinese oil-drilling ship, Ikki
protested. But his formidable great-grandfather was un-
deterred, and he eventually persuaded Ikki to use his ex-
ceptional media talents to stir Japan into action against
the ancient invader through Sanjuro's sacrifice.

Ikki finally agreed. As both an obedient offspring and
an ardent nationalist like Sanjuro, he could do no less. He
planned and executed the entire publicity campaign. Besides the carefully crafted images he provided to the news
station, the award-winning filmmaker produced several
stirring videos of Sanjuro set to patriotic music, along
with footage of his final fatal flight and posted them on
the Internet.

Within hours of the attack, the videos went completely
viral—not just in Japan but all across China as well. San-

juro's death was hailed by many Japanese as the greatest patriotic act since the war, transforming him instantly into a cult hero to the masses. Sanjuro's Zero had slammed into the Chinese drillship, but his self-sacrificing death exploded in the hearts and minds of Japanese nationalists, who now revered him as the Last Kamikaze. The Japanese stock market viewed the act less favorably, dropping nearly three percent within an hour before nervous regulators suspended trading for the day.

Every Japanese news outlet carried Sanjuro's story and broadcast the video images throughout the morning. Left-wing stations that belittled or condemned the attack were themselves attacked by protestors wearing *hachimaki* identical to Sanjuro's. Patriotic rallies began springing up all across Japan. So did the counterprotests.

By the early afternoon, the brave deck crew of the *Tiger II* finally managed to put out the last flames caused by Sanjuro's strike, but they couldn't stop the raging fire that now burned all across Asia, a blaze that threatened to set the whole world on fire.

FIFTY-THREE

Myers exited the fifth-floor elevator with the American ambassador, following one of Prime Minister Ito's secretaries. The retractable roof was open to an afternoon sky. The sunlight shimmered on the white pebbles and large *aji* stones elegantly arrayed in the rock garden. The effect was instant tranquility, a splash of unadorned nature in the midst of their technology-fueled crisis. It was just another example of the ultramodern architectural marvel known as the Kantei, Japan's version of Myers's previous working quarters, the nineteenth-century White House.

The secretary led them to the prime minister's suite of offices, finally directing them to the his private conference room, where they were met by Ito and Tanaka. The room was elegantly paneled in horse chestnut and stainless steel. In the center was a round table constructed of a beautiful Japanese red cherrywood polished to a high gloss. The round shape struck Myers as particularly egalitarian, unlike the four-sided power platforms preferred in Washington and America's corporate boardrooms.

Greetings were exchanged, beverages served.

"I thought Mr. Pearce would join us," Tanaka said. "Our two nations may soon be at war with China."

Myers resented his tone. She was well aware of the gravity of the situation. So was Pearce. "Mr. Pearce asked me to extend his apologies. He's not feeling well."

"Was he badly injured while in Chinese custody?" Ito asked, obviously concerned. His famous shock of silver hair was more disarrayed than usual.

His ego, mostly, Myers wanted to say. "Nothing that a little rest won't take care of."

Technically, Pearce wasn't feeling 100 percent, but the truth was that Myers didn't want to reveal that he was conferring with someone in an even more important meeting. With any luck, he'd be able to throw off any Naicho agents who might be tailing him. Japan's intelligence service was small but well organized and proficient. Lane had offered to arrange for help from the CIA chief of station, but Pearce thought it wiser to keep as many people out of the loop as possible. Myers agreed. It would be disastrous if the Japanese thought the CIA was being deployed in an operation designed to thwart their own security service.

An assistant entered the room. "President Lane is ready."

Ito thanked her. The assistant left, shutting the door. It was just the four of them now. The meeting was top secret. Ito dimmed the lights. A moment later, Lane appeared on a wide-screen HDTV for a live teleconference.

"President Lane, thank you for taking my call. It must be very late where you are."

Lane flashed his famously boyish smile but couldn't hide the dark circles under his eyes. "It's nice and quiet around here now. Easier to get things done. Thank you for agreeing to keep our meeting today private. I'm looking forward to a frank and open discussion of all of our options."

"We are as well," Ito said. "Shall we proceed?"

"Please."

Ito nodded. "Of course, you know President Myers and Ambassador Davis."

Lane nodded. "President Myers, Ambassador Davis. Good to see you both."

Myers grinned. "It's just Margaret, Mr. President."

"And I believe you know Mr. Tanaka, the parliamentary senior vice minister of foreign affairs."

"We've never met, but I'm well aware of Vice Minister Tanaka's importance in your administration. I'm grateful he's here with us. His expertise is invaluable. How may I help you, Mr. Prime Minister?"

Ito folded his hands in front of him. "I'm sure you're well aware of the unfortunate events that have transpired today. The crash of a Japanese civilian aircraft into the Chinese drilling ship has led to mass protests across Japan and now China."

Lane nodded. "I've been apprised by the State Department of the situation. My understanding is that the protests in Osaka and Nagasaki have been particularly violent, at least by Japanese standards."

"Regrettably, Chinese businesses have been attacked—mostly smashed windows and graffiti," Ito said. "And counterprotestors have been beaten with fists and pelted with stones, but no serious injuries have occurred."

"But the situation is escalating. If the Japanese people become aroused, we can expect far more violence." Tanaka added, "We have reports that yakuza elements are getting involved. They have guns and explosives, and aren't afraid to use them." Tanaka tried to sound concerned. In fact, he was counting on his old friend Kobayashi to escalate the violence as quickly as possible. The yakuza boss had already silenced a number of prominent left-wing critics in small acts of terror that hadn't yet reached the police blotters.

"I'm even more concerned about events in China. The current violence there is far surpassing the mass protests that unfolded slightly more than a week ago. At least two Japanese nationals have been killed. Our foreign minister has issued a travel warning, urging our citizens to avoid unnecessary travel to or within China. Some Japanese citizens have already sought refuge at our embassy in Beijing."

"My understanding is that your government has issued a formal apology to Beijing for the suicide attack today?"

"Over my strong protest," Tanaka said.

Ito nodded. "Yes, but the apology was rejected."

"And the rejection has been made public," Tanaka said. "To our great embarrassment."

"Was it wise to go public with that information?" Myers asked.

"The apology and rejection were issued through back channels. Somehow, the information was leaked," Ito said.

Only an act of iron will kept a grin from stealing across Tanaka's scowling face. His people had leaked the story to one of the right-wing papers, along with one of the largest left-leaning blogs. Tanaka knew that both sides would be furious, albeit for different reasons. The more pressure he could bring to bear on Ito, the better. He thought Ito was weak, too willing to negotiate and compromise. Properly applied pressure would force him to act in the national interest.

"Our Ministry of Defense has put the JSDF on high alert," Tanaka said.

"That will only add fuel to the fire, don't you think?" Ambassador Davis asked. "The Chinese might see that as a preparation for hostilities."

"The JSDF has orders to engage in no provocative actions," Ito said. "My government is under extreme pressure to respond. My own party is ready to revolt if I don't act swiftly and decisively."

"I understand your situation, but I urge you to refrain from anything rash," Lane said.

"Rash? Our satellites indicate that the Chinese aircraft carrier *Liaoning* is preparing to set sail within twenty-four hours from its port in Ningbo," Tanaka said. "Our intelligence service reports that a PLA marine assault battalion has just arrived in Ningbo as well."

"The CIA confirms both of those reports," Lane said. "I understand your concerns. But these could all be preparations for a military exercise, not an invasion of the Senkakus."

"Would it be easier to block the Chinese from invading the islands or driving them out after they've landed?" Tanaka asked.

"Let's hope that neither situation will occur," Lane said.

"And if it does?" Tanaka asked.

That's the question, isn't it? Lane thought. *And my answer may plunge us all into war.* "The best course of action is for us to do everything we can to prevent either from happening."

"If we restrain ourselves, we give the Chinese the opportunity to deescalate," Ambassador Davis said.

"For the sake of argument, let's assume we restrain ourselves. Let's further assume the Chinese take our restraint as cowardice and decide to send the *Liaoning* and its support ships to the Senkakus, along with that battalion of marines. What will you do then, Mr. President?" Tanaka jabbed a finger at the desk, driving home his question.

"Katsu!" Ito said. In nearly whispered Japanese, the prime minister urged his friend to restrain himself. But Tanaka wouldn't relent. He glowered at the video screen.

Lane took a sip of water, considering his reply. "I know President Myers briefed you on her visit to Ningbo. She was able to confirm the existence of the Wu-14, a hypersonic glide vehicle capable of disabling or destroying an aircraft carrier. This is classified information, gentlemen, but the United States currently has no known defense against this weapon. We would throw every available antimissile defense weapon at it, but all of our computer models show that the Chinese would likely score a killing strike."

"You have other weapons in your arsenal," Tanaka insisted. "You could take out their aircraft carrier with a sub-launched cruise missile."

"A preemptive strike?" Myers asked, incredulous. "Like Pearl Harbor?"

"I was thinking about Israel's Six-Day War. Do you disagree with the wisdom of their strategy?"

Myers didn't, of course. Israel's preemptive assault on the Egyptian air force allowed it to prevail in its war against Egypt, Syria, and Jordan.

"Or perhaps we're speaking of deterrence," Ito offered. "If the Chinese sink the *George Washington*, we sink the *Liaoning*. That act alone would set back their carrier program by a decade. That threat might be enough to dissuade the Chinese from any rash decisions."

Myers shared a glance with Davis. A career diplomat, Davis had studied and lived in Japan for a decade before joining the State Department. His raised eyebrow confirmed her intuition. Ito's use of the word "we" was significant.

"My generals and admirals are urging me to avoid conflict at all costs. Once hostilities begin, there's no way to predict how far or how fast they would escalate. Even the threat of retaliation would prove dangerous in the current climate," Lane said.

Myers hated to hear Lane talk like this. It almost sounded weak and cowardly. But she knew Lane and knew his distinguished combat record. She also understood the incredible pressure he must have been under from the Pentagon. When all of your senior military advisors tell you not to do something that might start a war, you tend to listen, even if you are the commander in chief. Caution was in order. The stakes were high—the highest. If a war actually did break out, there was no guarantee it would end favorably for the U.S. Wars were notoriously unpredictable. Pearce was fond of quoting the heavyweight boxing champion Mike Tyson: "Everyone has a plan until they get punched in the face."

"I'm sure the Chinese know as well as we do about your unwillingness to do anything to provoke them. Don't you see that such passivity will goad them into action?" Tanaka insisted. "If you're not willing to show your sword, then your enemies will assume you can't use it."

"The *George Washington* and other American combat forces have been 'showing the sword' on Japan's behalf for seven decades," Myers said.

"Mr. President, let's be frank," Ito said. "If the Chinese do start hostilities, what will the United States do? If you're not even willing to threaten them now before hostilities begin, why would you be more willing to issue threats against them afterward?"

"The Chinese would know that we would have to respond," Lane said.

"What if they sink your carrier?" Tanaka asked. "Won't your response to the sinking only escalate the violence? Put even more American lives at risk?"

"The State Department doesn't believe that China would be so foolish as to provoke either Japan or the United States into a war it couldn't possibly win," Davis said. "America and Japan are two of China's largest trading partners. They have far more to lose and little to gain by starting a war over the Senkakus."

Tanaka turned toward the American ambassador. "Then why have they created this fiction about Mao Island? Why have they started drilling operations? Don't you understand? The Chinese have sent a very clear signal. They're willing to start a war. And I believe they're willing to start a war because they know you won't do anything to oppose them."

"Our intelligence sources disagree," Davis said.

"With all due respect, American intelligence has fallen short on many occasions in recent years, beginning with the notable lack of WMDs in Iraq," Ito said. "That failure of intelligence led to an unnecessary war against Saddam Hussein and a decadelong war against the Iraqi insurgency afterward. As the prime minister of Japan, I reaffirm my nation's unwavering commitment to the United States, but I don't affirm our confidence in your intelligence services."

Tanaka grunted his approval. *"Hai."*

Can't say that I blame you, Myers thought. "Let's not forget the Chinese threat about the red line that they conveniently placed just beyond the Senkakus. They said they would consider it an act of war if American naval vessels crossed it and promised to launch the Wu-14 at any carrier that did."

Tanaka threw out several other tactical possibilities that kept the *George Washington* out of harm's way, but every scenario he proposed had already been hashed out at the Pentagon. In each case, the likely outcome was war, and the only way to carry out operations against Chinese forces was with force projection and that meant deploying the *George Washington* and its battle group. The United States didn't want to risk losing either. Tanaka finally threw up his hands in disgust.

"It seems clear to me, Mr. President, that the United States has no wish for war with China. Neither do we," Ito said. He sat up straighter in his chair. "But we are determined to defend our national interests and our national honor. If the Chinese dispatch the *Liaoning* into Japanese territorial waters, I will instruct the JSDF to respond."

"Then you'll be at war with China, a war you cannot win," Lane said.

Tanaka nodded. "If one is forced to choose between honor and life, it is always best to choose honor."

The room went silent. Myers kept her eyes on Ito. He was clearly lost in thought. She'd always known him to be a rational, affable, intelligent man. But he was also a proud Japanese. Back in Denver, whenever she talked about American exceptionalism, he was quick to point out his own sense of Japanese exceptionalism. She couldn't blame him. Japan was an ancient and remarkable culture, one of the world's oldest and greatest civilizations. She knew the rational part of Ito's brain understood Lane's position, but his Japanese sense of duty, kinship, and honor inclined him toward Tanaka.

"It sounds like you're saying that you would abandon your friends in a time of war," Ito said.

"I didn't say that. But if Japan launches a preemptive strike against Chinese forces, then you limit our options and put all of us at risk. I'm asking you to trust us and refrain from any actions that might give the Chinese any reason to act against you. But you have my assurance that the United States is completely committed to the defense of Japan, no matter what happens."

Tanaka shook his head in disbelief.

"There is, of course, the matter of the North Koreans to consider," Ito said. "They've moved their MIRV to its launch pad at their test facility at Musudan-ri."

"The North Koreans are China's lackeys," Tanaka said.

Lane nodded grimly. "They aren't making things any easier, that's for sure."

"It's a strange time to test an intercontinental ballistic missile," Davis said.

"It might not be a test," Lane said.

"Then what could it be? A message?" the ambassador asked.

"They may be trying to send a message," Myers said. She took a deep breath.

"Or they just might be preparing for World War Three."

FIFTY-FOUR

Pearce!"

The African-American jail guard glowered at Troy through the cell door. Standing six-foot-seven and carrying three hundred pounds of sculpted muscle on his wide frame, he was as intimidating as he was large.

Troy looked up at the sound of his name. He was seated on a steel bench in the overnight tank for drunks, johns, and other less dangerous miscreants. He had no shirt, only athletic shorts, jailhouse slippers, and a black eye.

Keys rattled in the lock and a massive black hand guided Troy by the arm, cuffed and shuffling toward out-take processing.

Will was at the front desk signing papers. A paper bag by his elbow.

The guard unlocked Troy's cuffs. "Don't come back, kid."

"Thanks," Troy said.

Will nodded his thanks to the desk officer and tossed the paper bag at Troy. He opened it. A hooded Stanford sweatshirt.

"We gotta roll," Will said, turning for the exit. Troy followed suit, yanking on the hoodie.

The drab downtown jail facility was an unremarkable building on the outside. The kaleidoscope of broken people inside provided the color.

Will pushed open the glass door and dashed for the parking lot, Troy on his heels.

"What's the hurry?" Troy asked.

"You kidding me?"

"Oh, shit."

" 'Oh, shit' is right. Your thesis defense is in an hour. It'll take an hour and twenty to get to Encina Hall."

Will unlocked the doors to his Porsche 911 and they both fell in.

"I can't go like this. I need to change, take a shower."

The Porsche engine roared to life and Will turned around to back out. "I've got your slacks and sport coat under the hood, along with a shirt, tie, and shoes. No point in looking like a complete slob."

Troy smelled his underarm. His nose crunched. "Don't suppose you have a shower under there?"

"There's a bottle of Old Spice under your seat. Go ahead and slap some on now, use plenty of it. It's gonna be a long ride."

Will gunned the Porsche down the I-880 on the east side of the bay to avoid the traffic in San Francisco.

"What the hell were you thinking?" Will asked. "I thought you gave that shit up."

"I told you I'd quit fighting when I had enough cash. Can't exactly make serious money flipping burgers at Carl's Jr." Troy had been cage-fighting in the underground circuit since his sophomore year at Stanford. The infamous Chinese triad Wo Hop ran the illegal gambling enterprise throughout the state, especially in the Bay Area.

"You almost threw everything you've worked for out the window last night." The warehouse where Troy was fighting had been raided by the Oakland PD's gang unit.

"Still have bills to pay."

"Your dad's debts were his, not yours."

"My dad was a lot of things, but he wasn't a bum."

"That's what bankruptcy laws are for."

"He couldn't do it."

Troy leaned back his seat to close his eyes. He hadn't slept all night in the holding tank. The stink of stale urine and vomit was stronger than his fatigue. They drove along in silence for a few minutes. Will finally calmed down. Couldn't stay angry with the kid. He risked his life in the no-holds-barred cage fights to earn money to pay off his old man's debts. It was stupid, but honorable.

"So you won."

"Yeah. How'd you know?"

"I used to be a spook, remember?" Started to tell Troy that he was the one who had tipped the Oakland PD to the location, but the boy was already sound asleep, the unopened bottle of Old Spice still clutched in his hand.

FIFTY-FIVE

The three faculty members sat on one side of the conference desk and Troy on the other. The air reeked of too much Old Spice but no one said anything. Troy was better dressed in his sport coat and tie than the faculty who wore Levi's, collared shirts, and loafers.

Troy's master's thesis was brilliant but controversial. He applied a quantitative game-theory approach to the qualitative work of William S. Lind and others on fourth-generation warfare. He proved the hypothesis that 4GW was the future of conventional warfare in the third world because it was superior to the current forms of warfare deployed by the West. The Black Hawk Down incident in Somalia a few years earlier wasn't just a tragic error, he argued; it was a portent of things to come.

Troy's thesis defense for his master's degree today was a technicality, but it was also a chance for the department chair, Dr. Fagan, to get even with him. Troy had embarrassed him publicly on a number of occasions in seminars and colloquia, successfully challenging the professor's indefensible positions on security issues and his slavish devotion to political correctness.

Dr. Fagan was also an intellectual bully, and Troy wouldn't put up with it. Fagan was infamous for publishing articles in his own name that had been researched by talented graduate students in his department without giving those students proper attribution. Troy had publicly denounced that practice in faculty meetings, earning Fagan's undying enmity.

Drs. Garth and Pembroke were the other two faculty members on his thesis committee, men he deeply respected for their scholarship and integrity. He was glad they were there. Garth was his thesis advisor, and Troy had been a teaching assistant for Pembroke's undergraduate poli sci classes.

Garth opened with a softball question and Pembroke followed up with a few technical clarifications of Troy's game-theory analysis. They were both satisfied with his responses and spoke effusively about his graduate work in general and the thesis in particular.

Then it was Fagan's turn.

He waved a copy of Troy's thesis in the air.

"I don't get the title. 'Future War' sounds like a sci-fi novel, not a serious academic treatise. And for the record, fourth-generation warfare isn't the future of warfare. It's just terrorism by another name."

The sonofabitch hasn't even read it, Troy realized. He wanted to grab Fagan by the nape of the neck and toss him out of the door. How many times had he seen Fagan screaming at some poor sleep-deprived grad student for not coming to one of his seminars fully prepared?

But Will had warned Troy about controlling his temper today. Troy's goal was to get Garth and Pembroke to approve his defense and the master's degree was assured. Only two votes out of three were needed. It would be better, though, if all three committee members signed off, and better still if they would award him a superior commendation. That would require a unanimous vote, but if he got it, it would guarantee him a slot in the Ph.D. program at Stanford or anywhere else in the country he might choose. Unfortunately, Fagan's recommendation carried a lot of weight in the tight circles of top-tier academia.

The worst-case scenario would be that Troy would so lose his cool that he wouldn't provide a coherent defense of his work despite its obvious merit. That might prompt Garth or Pembroke to vote against him and delay or even deny him his master's. Garth and Pembroke, despite their tenured status, feared Fagan's power over them as department chair, a position that could make their professional lives extremely inconvenient—seven a.m. classes, odious committee memberships, extension-class assignments. If Troy was too rude or even threatening, Fagan might bully them into voting with him, literally. At six-foot-four and two hundred forty pounds, Fagan towered over the other faculty in his department, mostly narrow-shouldered hipsters or portly middle-aged golfers in penny loafers. But like most bullies, Fagan was wary enough to never try that with an alpha male like Troy despite his junior status in the department.

"As I've cited from the works of Lind, Schmitt, Sutton, Wilson, Hammes, and others, 4GW isn't just 'terrorism' or even asymmetrical warfare, though both would be subsumed under that rubric. 4GW is a whole new strategic conception of warfare, which is why I refer to it as the future of warfare. The next major war the U.S. will fight won't be with other industrial powers like China and Russia, but with nonstate actors like Hezbollah and al-Qaeda."

Fagan shook his head. "Hezbollah and al-Qaeda are

terrorist groups. You're talking about terrorism, not warfare. Terror tactics are what terrorists use when they can't
fight wars. Don't you understand the difference?"

Troy flexed his aching fists beneath the table. Watching Fagan swallow his teeth might just be worth losing
his master's. But Will had invested too much time and
energy into him these past six years. He didn't give a rat's
ass about Fagan, but he'd rather die than disappoint Will
Elliott.

"Nonstate actors use terror as part of their concept of
strategic warfare. We did the same thing at Dresden, fire-
bombing an ancient city with no military value in order
to terrorize the Germans into surrendering. If we're
smart enough to use terror to accomplish our strategic
goals, so are our opponents." Troy leaned forward. "Unless you're calling the United States military just another
terrorist group."

"You're just proving my point. World War Two was a
war between state actors. War-fighting nations can use
terror in their campaigns, but they're still fighting wars
for strategic goals. Terrorism as practiced by nonstate actors isn't a strategic concept, it's a reaction. A tactic at
best."

"The strategic goal of warfare is winning, period. And
the tactics of 4GW are aimed at undermining the will of
state actors to continue fighting, and they almost always
work. But the 2G and 3G tactics we use against nonstate
actors are almost always guaranteed to fail."

They argued back and forth for the next forty minutes,
ignoring the other two faculty who relished the savaging
Troy was giving Fagan. They were careful not to smile or
verbally agree with Troy, but they were silently cheering
inside. Troy successfully reviewed the history of
twentieth-century warfare and further explicated the
4GW concepts that Lind and the others had outlined.

Troy also sided with them on the most controversial idea of all.

"Not only will our next major war be with a nonstate actor or an alliance of nonstate actors, it will be long, costly, bloody, and we'll likely lose if we don't change our strategic concepts of war."

"That's just stupid," Fagan said. "We have overwhelming firepower and technology. We're the wealthiest and most advanced economy on the planet. No nation can stand up against us. What hope would a far less powerful nonstate actor have?"

"We had overwhelming air, land, and sea superiority in our war in Vietnam. We even had nuclear weapons. How'd that work out for us?" Troy asked. "And don't forget about the Soviets in Afghanistan. The Taliban broke them."

"Thanks to poor tactics on the part of the Russians and the deployment of advanced American weaponry like Stinger missiles by the Taliban. You know as well as I do that Afghanistan was a proxy war between us and the Soviets. We prevailed, once again proving my point."

"In order to frustrate the Soviets, we funded and armed the Taliban and al-Qaeda. They're the real enemy. The Soviet Union was on its last legs, crumbling under the weight of its failing economic system and corrupt political regime. They would've lost that war with or without our help. But now we've trained and equipped our real enemies, who are playing a very long game."

"We're not the Soviet Union. If we ever decided to go to war against the Taliban and al-Qaeda, we'd squash them like bugs. Worst-case scenario? We sit back and fire cruise missiles at their command centers and hideouts. War is about power, and it takes two parties to fight a war. Nonstate actors don't have the power to wage war with us; therefore, the next war can't be with them. End of story. To think we'd ever be in a protracted war with a low-rent organization like al-Qaeda is specious at best."

"In the West, states fight wars against states. We win when we occupy enemy territory and force their governments to sign our peace treaties. But 'terrorism' doesn't have a capital, and jihadism is completely decentralized— who would have the authority to sign a peace treaty that would end it?"

"You win the war on terrorists by killing terrorists faster than they can make them. It's as simple as that."

"No. You can only win the war on terrorism by killing all the terrorists—a genocidal war against the nonwhite, non-Western world, something we'd never do, nor should we. We'd lose that kind of war on moral grounds alone. But even if we did want to wage that kind of war, the only way to kill every terrorist is to occupy the entire globe, because terrorism is everywhere. It won't be just a long war, it will be a forever war. And we'll lose it because we don't have the will to do what it takes, and they always win by not losing. Time will be on their side, not ours. Trying to fight a 4GW war with 2GW weapons and tactics is the strategic equivalent of a nineteenth-century cavalry charge against a twentieth-century machine-gun nest."

Fagan rolled his eyes. "How do you think a bunch of third world peasants armed with AK-47s are going to stand up to our fleet of B-2 stealth bombers?"

"Women wearing suicide vests beneath their burqas are pretty stealthy, too. So are Toyotas loaded with C-4 on a crowded city street. In a war by civilians against civilians, the burqas trump the bombers."

Fagan stood. "I've got a committee meeting in ten minutes across campus."

Troy stood and held out his hand. Fagan reluctantly took it. Troy resisted the temptation to crush his moist grip. The other faculty stood as well, chairs scraping against the linoleum.

"Thanks for taking the time to hear me out," Troy said.

A smile stole across Fagan's face. "Interesting presentation. Good luck."

That's a no vote, Troy knew. Fagan was too much of a coward to say it to his face. "Thanks."

Fagan left the room. The other faculty members shook his hand and clapped him on the back.

Garth said, "Best thesis defense I've heard in twenty years. Don't worry about him. He's just mad he didn't think of your idea first. You've got my vote."

Troy relaxed. Even smiled. "Thank you."

Pembroke added, "Great job. You can easily turn that third section into a journal article. I know a couple of editors who would eat this up. I'm happy to write a cover letter for you."

"Thanks. I appreciate that."

Garth stroked his graying beard, barely hiding an impish smile. "Just one thing kept bugging me while you were talking today."

"Shoot."

"How'd you get that black eye?"

FIFTY-SIX

Will grilled thick steaks on the backyard barbecue and broke out the best whiskey in the house. Troy and his friends danced on the polished hardwood floors and toasted his success. Three of the young women in attendance made plans to sleep with Troy that night. Troy made plans to sleep with just two of them, preferably at the same time.

After feasting on succulent T-bones and corn on the cob slathered in butter, Will finally got Troy off to the side for a quiet moment. He pulled out two Cuban Cohibas, and they lit them up over snifters of Hennessy cognac.

"So, Mr. Chips, what's next? Staying at Stanford? Or is Yale still a possibility?"

Troy puffed thoughtfully for a few moments. "Neither."

"What other school do you have in mind?"

"I'm done with academics."

Will frowned. "I don't understand. You've worked like a dog these last six years. You're talented. A hundred doors are open to you. Money's not an issue—you'll get a free ride wherever you go with your academic record."

Troy blew out a billowing blue cloud. "I need to get out of the ivory tower. I want to stretch my legs, see the world. Work up a sweat, you know?"

Will's eyes narrowed. He swirled the cognac in his glass.

Troy was afraid he'd disappointed him. "Not that I don't appreciate everything you've done, Will. It's been an amazing ride and, God knows, I've learned a helluva lot, in and out of the classroom. And thanks to you, I'm civilized now, or at least some of the sharper edges have been knocked off."

Will took a sip. "It's your life, sport. You do what you've got to do."

"You understand, don't you? I grew up with chain saws and deer rifles in the Rockies, not laptops and lawn mowers in the 'burbs. I don't know if I'm cut out for the academic life. Especially if I'm not allowed to smash anyone in the mouth." Troy was still sore about Dr. Fagan's no vote. A petty, petulant stab in the back by a petty, petulant department chair.

Will chuckled. "I understand on all counts. Believe me. So what are your plans? Working on an Alaska crab boat? Backpacking across Europe? That sort of thing?"

"What I need is a challenge. An adventure. Something physical, but something important. I don't know exactly."

Will's green eyes twinkled. "I've been waiting for six years for you to say something like that."

Troy's eyes widened, shocked. "Really? I thought you wanted me to be an academic like you."

"No. All I ever wanted for you was to become truly and fully yourself. You're a really smart kid, but you're not exactly cut out for the campus lifestyle."

"Then what?"

Will laid an arm across Troy's broad back. Pulled him in close. His breath stank of cigars and sweet liquor. A smile stole beneath the neatly trimmed mustache. He whispered.

"You need to go to the Farm."

FIFTY-SEVEN

PRESIDENT SUN'S PRIVATE RESIDENCE
ZHONGNANHAI
BEIJING, CHINA
18 MAY 2017

President Sun rose well before dawn to begin a ritual he'd practiced for forty years. After finishing a simple breakfast of Earl Grey tea and two *baozi* filled with spicy ground pork, he shuffled in his slippers and silk pajamas to his den. For the next thirty minutes, he sat in his chair and played his beloved cello.

His parents were both high-ranking Party members and accomplished musicians who were tragically purged and reeducated during Mao's Great Proletarian Cultural Revolution. That ended their dream for their only child to follow in their artistic footsteps, but Sun never lost the love of music they had instilled in him from an early age. Sun was a gifted musician, a prodigy, really. But musicians and other artists—particularly those favoring Western "bourgeois" forms and instruments like his parents had—were held in some suspicion during Mao's sadistic reign, so he was guided into a career in chemistry by his grandfather that led, ultimately, to politics. He still worshipped his long-deceased mother and father; the time with his cello was time spent with their memories and the most pleasant moments of his idyllic childhood. It was also an opportunity to process the events of the coming day.

This morning, Sun took up the bow and played from memory the famous *Adagio in G minor*, improvising the part written for the first violin, his mother's orchestral seat and preferred instrument. The familiar neo-Baroque composition was a passionate, maudlin affair, but it was his mother's favorite and thus his. He needed his parents' encouragement to face the day. Today's secret meeting with select members of the Standing Committee was fraught with peril—and promise.

They would question his decision to allow Admirals Ji and Deng to embark on this reckless adventure. But he would tell them that even if he were inclined to stop them, an attack on the base or on the fleet once at sea was simply not feasible. Admiral Ji's popularity within the Party was greater than his own, and the Mao Island campaign was enthusiastically embraced by the officer corps. Besides, nothing would please China's enemies at home and abroad more than to see the PLA and PLAN turn on themselves.

But Sun understood the Standing Committee's concerns. By any measure, this truly was a reckless action, but he was of the opinion that Ji would actually pull it off. The United States would avoid war with China at all costs, if for no other reason than the fact that the Americans had been engaged in the Global War on Terrorism for more than a decade and they were exhausted. Even their armed forces were reaching a breaking point, and the budget freeze had slowed American defense spending while China's increased by double digits every year. But Sun was confident of American appeasement for another reason.

The Americans were idiots.

China's trade surplus with the U.S. was on the order of

hundreds of billions of dollars annually. China used those billions to buy American CEOs. Nothing mattered more to American executives than profits. They were more than happy to sacrifice American national interests in the name of stock prices, market share, and bonuses—all of which were tied to privileges awarded them by the Chinese government, privileges based on compliance with Chinese national interests.

American congressmen, in turn, were in the CEOs' pockets, groveling for campaign dollars and lucrative postretirement board memberships. Sun marveled at America's blindness. How could they not see that they themselves held all the cards? China was the one who had the weakest hand. Shutting down trade with China would collapse China's economy, not theirs. But the spirit of globalism and "free markets" had so infected the American political establishment that a bloodless trade war was more feared than an actual war in graveyards like Afghanistan. Capitalists would, indeed, sell him the rope to hang them with. And, apparently, they were willing to tie the noose and even pull on the other end if it meant an increase to the bottom line.

In Sun's mind, the worst-case scenario could actually prove to be a bonus. It would be a national tragedy, certainly, if Admiral Ji and his fleet were attacked by the Americans or Japanese and sunk, but in reality, the death of Admirals Ji and Deng would eliminate his two greatest uniformed opponents and permanently discredit the adventurism of the so-called patriotic militarists. Discrediting military adventurism would also allow him to push forward with his military reforms. China was spending far too much money on defense that could otherwise be spent on economic development and education for the tens of millions of Chinese still trapped in rural poverty.

Better yet, a defeat at Mao Island would end Vice

Chairman Feng's political career. Feng was the greatest civilian threat to his presidency and the strongest opponent of his anticorruption reforms. Sun and his allies believed that failure to end corruption would result in the collapse of the political and economic legitimacy of the state. Revolution, civil war, or dissolution would be the only possible outcomes. But Feng was still too strong to openly oppose.

However, if Admiral Ji and the others pulled off the Mao adventure and successfully captured the Diaoyu Islands, Sun would claim victory for himself by running to the head of the parade. By not opposing Ji, he appeared to be supporting Ji's actions, and if Ji succeeded, it would only strengthen Sun's position with him, and Ji was as fervent about anticorruption as he was. The two of them would pose a formidable alliance against Feng and his cronies. It might yet cost him the presidency, but at least China would be saved.

Sun found his fingers playing out the last high, hopeful notes of the adagio. He felt his mother's smile. He could face anything now. A soft knock on the door interrupted his thoughts.

"Yes?"

An aide entered. "I'm sorry, sir, but there's phone call for you. It's quite urgent."

Sun thanked him, told him he'd be in his office presently, and waved him away with his bow. The caller could wait. He wanted to play the last fifteen bars again.

FIFTY-EIGHT

Admiral Ji stood on the flying bridge of the *Tai Shan*, his flagship. He greeted his old friend, the rising sun, as it crested the wine-dark ocean. The cold, salty breeze stung his face, but he was warm beneath his thick woolen greatcoat. He was as happy as he could remember. Ji was a man at the peak of his powers, the admiral of China's largest invasion fleet since the days of the great emperors. Today he would make history. China would assume its rightful place under heaven, and the world would never be the same again.

The newly built *Tai Shan* was a giant 210-meter-long amphibious transport dock ship carrying a battalion of PLAN marines, two French SA 321 Super Frelon transport helicopters, and four Russian Zubr-class troop transports, the world's largest military hovercraft.

The *Tai Shan* was well guarded by its escort of Type 056 corvettes and Type 052 guided-missile destroyers, including the *Kunming*. Both classes of vessels possessed powerful long-range antiship, antiair, and antisubmarine

systems. Two diesel-powered Kilo-class submarines shad-
owed the *Tai Shan* as well. The task force wouldn't be
complete until Admiral Deng arrived with the aircraft
carrier *Liaoning* and a full complement of conventional
jet fighter-bombers along with six of the Lijian UCAVs.
Once the *Liaoning* and its support ships rendezvoused, Ji
would transfer his command via helicopter to the *Liaoning*. Per their battle plan, they would proceed toward
Mao Island and the Diaoyus, careful to not accidentally
signal that the task force was intent on the long-awaited
invasion of Taiwan. It wasn't.

In Ji's mind, the Taiwan campaign would be his
crowning achievement and the first goal of the PLA Navy
once he was installed as president of the People's Republic. Shaming the Americans into backing down over the
Diaoyus would finally convince the rest of the world that
the United States was no longer a reliable ally, and the
rebellious Taiwanese would either capitulate or suffer the
mainland's wrath in a lightning-swift war of reunification.
The Mao Island campaign was the key to China's rise and
dominance in the East. It was as bold as it was necessary,
which was why Ji was able to convince a significant number of PLA and PLAN flag officers to support the adventure, including Admiral Deng, commander of the South
Sea Fleet. Neither he nor Deng were under any delusions
that the Mao task force could withstand a direct confrontation with the U.S. Navy's vastly more powerful Sixth
Fleet—but the Wu-14 virtually guaranteed that such a
confrontation would never occur.

Ji believed the greatest threat to the expeditionary
force at the moment was President Sun. As a precaution,
the admiral had deployed a second battalion of marines
to guard Ningbo from a possible PLA attack that Sun
might mount to stop the small fleet while it was still at
base replenishing for the mission, but no such attack oc-

curred. Ji wondered if Sun's inaction was a tacit endorsement of his efforts. But Vice Chairman Feng argued that President Sun was more afraid of the blowback he would suffer for an attack on a Chinese naval facility led by China's greatest and most admired military commander. Feng also assured his allies in and out of uniform that Admiral Ji's task force was preparing for a mission to secure China's future and glory, and squashed the ugly rumor that the PLAN was preparing some sort of military junta against Sun and his reformist cronies.

A junior officer approached Ji with a cup of steaming hot tea. The young man's eyes radiated with hero worship. Ji took the tea with a grateful nod and dismissed him, cherishing the last few moments of solitude he would enjoy before he transferred his combat command to the *Liaoning*.

FIFTY-NINE

The cabinet room on the fourth floor was much larger than the prime minister's circular private conference room, matching the shape and scope of the enormous blond birchwood table in the center. The walls were a combination of birchwood and diatomaceous earth, and a window afforded a view of yet another tranquil rock garden. For Myers, the intention of the design was to induce a kind of natural serenity, but the mood in the room this morning was just the opposite.

Prime Minister Ito's entire cabinet was seated around the table in supple white leather chairs, while their assistants and secretaries stood anxiously behind them, clutching file folders, tablets, and smartphones.

Myers sat to Ito's right, a position of high honor. She wore an earpiece linked to an official government interpreter in an adjoining room. Lane had informed her about the Chinese fleet setting sail and the latest Chinese demands. The crisis was escalating, yet Lane's calm voice reassured her. For a president on the verge of war, he was amazingly composed. Another advantage of having a commander in chief with combat experience.

Lane asked her to attend Ito's emergency cabinet meeting. She agreed, of course. Anything to help. They discussed his agenda. Under no circumstances could she allow the Japanese to undertake unilateral action. She concurred, silently wondering how in the world she could possibly prevent them from doing so. Lane wished her luck.

Ito called the meeting to order.

"Today's session will be recorded for posterity, but the information discussed is top secret. Under no conditions are any of the matters we discuss in this room today to be released to the general public."

Heads nodded around the table.

"What is she doing here?" Tanaka asked, glowering at Myers.

The translator's voice echoed with Tanaka's anger. *The emphasis was hardly necessary*, Myers thought. His eyes were enough.

Ito stiffened. "President Myers is here today as my guest and as a personal envoy of President Lane. As many of you know, President Myers and I have been friends for many years. I trust her as I trust my own sister. She also enjoys the complete confidence of President Lane. We may speak freely and candidly in front of her, and I encourage her to speak frankly as well. Her role is to convey the substance of today's meeting to President Lane and his cabinet, which will be meeting shortly as well. Does anybody object?"

As both the prime minister and party leader, Ito's authority in the room was unquestioned. But anti-American sentiments were escalating around the country—it appeared as if the United States were abandoning the Japa-

312　　　　　　　　　　　　MIKE MADEN

nese to their fate. The elected officials and representatives seated in the room reflected those public sentiments.

Several shifted uncomfortably in their seats, but no one objected publicly. Tanaka already had by inference.

Ito nodded at his minister of defense. The MOD reported that the Chinese fleet was twenty-two hours away from breaching the territorial waters around the Senkakus. He briefed everyone on the extent of the Chinese ship, aircraft, and troop complement, as well as Japanese and American forces in the area.

The foreign minister then read the letter hand delivered to her office personally by Ambassador Pang and signed by Vice Chairman Feng. The letter began with a virulent protest against the "war-era suicide assault" on the *Tiger II* oil-drilling ship before launching into a reassertion of China's historical and legal claims to the disputed islands. Feng's letter then announced the arrival of Chinese PLAN marines who would occupy the two largest islands in the chain "in order to protect Chinese lives and property in Chinese territorial waters against future Japanese aggression."

The letter also demanded unobstructed passage of their ships to Mao Island and no armed resistance to Chinese landing forces, and ordered the Japanese government to turn over all of the islands in question to Chinese authority and further demanded immediate recognition of the them as sovereign Chinese territory in perpetuity.

The letter concluded ominously. "Failure to comply with our demands or violating the terms set forth herein shall constitute an act of war against the People's Republic of China." The foreign minister practically hissed as she read the last sentence. So did the translator.

"So there we have it," Ito said. "The Chinese fleet is on its way to seize the Senkakus, daring us to oppose them. We've discussed our options at length. Do nothing, wait for the Americans to dispatch the Sixth Fleet, or dispatch our own fleet to fight them."

"If we do nothing, we'll only encourage the Chinese to seize other disputed territories throughout the region," the defense minister said. "Our inaction puts several of our regional allies at risk."

The foreign minister nodded vigorously. "If we do nothing, we declare ourselves to be vassals of both the Chinese and the Americans." She waved a hand for emphasis. "Completely unacceptable for a sovereign nation."

"Our conference with President Lane yesterday made it clear that he will not dispatch the Sixth Fleet to block the Chinese," Tanaka said. He turned to Myers, switched to English. "Do you agree with my assessment?"

Myers shook her head. "Not necessarily. President Lane has personally contacted President Sun, strongly opposing the current Chinese actions. He reaffirmed our treaty commitments to Japan and reminded him that any attack on Japan was tantamount to an attack on the United States."

The aides of the few cabinet members who didn't speak English whispered translations into their bosses' ears.

"And what was President Sun's response?" Ito asked.

Myers sighed. "He thanked the president for his concerns and promised to look further into the matter."

The room exploded in a flurry of outrage. The translator did her best to keep up, but it was impossible to translate everything. It didn't matter. Myers got the gist of it. They were mad as hornets, both at China and the U.S. She would be, too, if she were in their seats. She folded her hands politely in front of her and tried to calm the room with her disarming smile. "What matters is that President Sun has been formally warned about the consequences. I promise you those consequences were heard.

President Lane also reminded President Sun that the *George Washington* carrier battle group was deployed to Okinawa two days ago for a training exercise."

"President Sun is a liar if he is saying he has no idea about what's going on," Tanaka insisted.

"What would you expect him to do? Immediately apologize and promise to withdraw his fleet? If he's behind all of this, he's not going to back down with a phone call. But if other forces are at play, he might be helpless to act immediately," Myers said.

"Other forces at play? It's Communist China. He's a dictator!" one of the ministers shouted.

The foreign minister leaned forward on her elbows. "But President Myers makes an interesting point. The letter was signed by Minister Feng, not President Sun."

"He's only covering himself in case something goes wrong," Tanaka said. "Feng will suffer the consequences of failure, but Sun can seize the credit if they succeed."

"That suggests some kind of schism within the leadership. A gap that perhaps we can exploit," Myers said.

The room buzzed again as heads leaned in close for private conferences among themselves. *That was a good sign*, Myers thought. *They're thinking about the possibilities.*

Everyone except Tanaka, who only glared at her. "Politburo politics are irrelevant. A fleet of Chinese ships loaded with missiles and marines is the reality we must address. Doing nothing is out of the question, in my opinion, and I still believe the Americans are hoping the Chinese will change their minds without the U.S. deploying the Sixth Fleet. Prime Minister Ito, I ask for a vote right now. I believe in the third option. I believe that Japan must act on its own. We should send our fleet now and dispatch our air force. We have a long and glorious history of defeating the Chinese dragon."

Ito turned to the minister of defense. "What hope do we have of defeating the Chinese fleet?"

Like many of his counterparts in the West, the defense minister was a lawyer by training and a bureaucrat with no prior military service. His background had been entirely in government, working his way up the chain of security subcommittees and chairmanships in the legislature until he was appointed by Ito to head the defense ministry. He removed his glasses and set them on the table. "The commanders of the naval and air services assure me we can mount an effective attack on the Chinese fleet, but only with a high casualty rate of ships and aircraft and only if the Chinese don't commit further air or naval assets. If the Chinese deploy long-range bombers or missiles, we risk a catastrophic defeat."

"Sakai-*san* showed us the way! Death is not defeat!" The shouting cabinet minister was a former chairman of the Izokukai, one of the most conservative public-interest groups in Japan, responsible for the care of the controversial Yasukuni Shrine honoring Japan's war dead.

"*Hai!*" Tanaka grunted. "I would rather suffer a catastrophic defeat in defense of our homeland than suffer the living humiliation of cowardice."

Half the room shouted agreement. Several others nodded. Tanaka was running the room now. Ito turned to Myers, his eyes questioning her. Myers feared the worst.

"Mr. Tanaka, if Japanese forces cross the red line, China will consider it an act of war," Myers said. "Do you want to bear the personal guilt of starting a war before Japan is even attacked?"

Tanaka laughed. "Guilt? That's a strange word coming from an American. When did Afghanistan attack your country? Iraq? Libya? Syria? Yemen? How many others? You Americans have waged war all over the planet against countries that never attacked you. If you can bear the guilt, so can I."

Myers flushed with anger. Probably the reaction Tanaka was looking for, she realized. Her job today wasn't to defend American foreign policy, right or wrong. It was to prevent a war.

"My country is able to wage war all over the planet because it has the means to do so. We have the means to defend Japan as well, and we have been committed to doing so for more than seventy years. We will do everything in our power to prevent anything from happening to Japan now during this time of crisis."

Tanaka sneered at her. "The same way your country protected the Syrian people when they were gassed by Assad? Defended Ukraine against the Russians? South Vietnam from North Vietnam? I could list a dozen examples of you Americans sacrificing your weaker allies on the altar of your own ambitions."

"Tens of thousands of Americans have shed their blood in defense of her allies for no material gain whatsoever. When has Japan ever done that?" As soon as the words left Myers's mouth, her heart sank. It was a huge insult and a terrible mistake. Her face stung with embarrassment.

The room quieted as if all the oxygen had been sucked out of it. All eyes turned to her. She lowered her gaze. She wanted to apologize, but couldn't. What she said was hurtful, but it was true nonetheless.

The long, awkward silence was finally broken by Ito's humble voice. "I thank President Myers for her frank and forthright opinions today. I have no doubt of her sincerity and integrity. She has presented the views of her nation, and I believe she wants the best for her country as well as ours. But our security, ultimately, depends on our own actions. We have relied on the United States far too long. This only proves to me once again it's time to change the Constitution and begin our rearmament program as quickly as possible, even if this crisis should end peacefully."

"Agreed," Tanaka said. Other heads nodded.

"But the crisis is still upon us. We must decide what we shall do next."

Myers was still stinging with embarrassment. She had offended everybody in the room, and in so doing had jeopardized everything, including the security of the United States. If Japan acted foolishly now, it might be because of her, and if they did, the Chinese would respond, and the United States would be at war. She took a deep breath.

"Mr. Prime Minister, please allow me to say one last thing if I may," Myers said, softening her voice to nearly a whisper.

Ito's mouth flattened. She was taking advantage of their friendship. But she was a former president of the United States, and she was here at his invitation.

"Yes?"

"The Chinese fleet is still twenty-two hours away, and as we discussed earlier, there seems to be some disconnect between President Sun and Mr. Feng regarding the deployment of that fleet. You're right to say that you and your government are ultimately responsible for the security of your nation, and I agree with you wholeheartedly that you must do what you think is right. But as a friend of Japan, I would suggest that your government refrain from any provocative action for the next twenty-two hours. At least give us that much time to continue direct negotiations with the Chinese and pursue other avenues. If we have failed to stop the Chinese from violating Japanese territorial waters, then you should act according to your own best interests."

Ito nodded, considering her words. He cleared his throat.

"In my opinion, if the Americans aren't able to persuade the Chinese to turn around or if the Sixth Fleet isn't willing to act decisively to stop them, then we should dispatch our armed forces into the region to defend the Senkakus. But we will wait for twenty-two hours before doing so." He turned to the defense minister. "I assume the service chiefs have battle plans to defend the islands?"

"*Hai.*"

"Then I want those plans on my desk within the hour. And make all preparations necessary as if we are going to war twenty-two hours from now."

The defense minister nodded violently. *"Hai!"*

Tanaka stood and began applauding. The other ministers followed. Ito remained seated, nodding his thanks. He shot a glance at Myers. *That's the best I can do.*

She nodded her thanks and prayed it was enough. In twenty-two hours, she'd know for sure whether or not Pearce had pulled everything together and what stuff Lane was actually made of.

SIXTY

Tanaka's cell phone vibrated in his trousers while he was still applauding Ito's decision. Ito was soon surrounded by the other ministers who bowed and shook his hand, congratulating him. Tanaka slipped out of the room into the hall in the confusion, heading for his private offices.

Ito's decision to give the Americans another twenty-two hours was craven. The Americans would never risk a war with China on Japan's behalf. Why couldn't he see that? Like so many Japanese, Ito had become a willing participant in his own debasement. The whole country was suffering from a collective Stockholm syndrome. The Americans had killed millions of Japanese during the war, subverted the emperor's divinity, and imposed pacifism on Japan by force of arms. And yet they acted as if America were some kind of benefactor. Japan must stand on its own two feet and assume its rightful role in the world. Only a nuclear-armed Japan would be able to do so. China, Russia, and the United States only respected force.

Even backward North Korea had nuclear weapons—and look how the United States feared them!

Of course, Ito disagreed with his views. At least Ito was willing to consider conventional rearmament and amending the Constitution. But it wasn't enough. Ito was the head of the nation and yet he had no martial spirit. That made him not only weak, but also a traitor to his culture and his people. Tanaka prayed Ito would have the guts to follow through on his promise to attack the Chinese fleet if the Americans failed to keep their promise, but he doubted it. Fortunately, Tanaka had a few reliable allies in the naval and air branches of the JSDF. If Ito wouldn't pull the trigger, they would.

Safely behind his locked office door, Tanaka checked his text message. Finally, good news. His friend at the Naicho had, in fact, been able to locate Pearce through a mutual contact in the maritime service. The American was definitely up to something. The former CIA officer was mounting some kind of operation, no doubt directed at disabling Japan's ability to defend itself against the Chinese. Like Myers, Pearce was an arrogant *gaijin*. He was also dangerous. Now that Pearce had been located, he could be dealt with. Tanaka messaged back to his friend at the Naicho to send his men home, then forwarded Pearce's location to another number. He also called his JMSDF contact and told him to alert his men to the pending action.

Unlike Ito, Tanaka wasn't afraid to shed blood in defense of the homeland. Especially American blood.

SIXTY-ONE

A vintage American muscle car rumbled up to the poorly lit side gate of the JMSDF naval base. Only one guard was on duty. He stepped out of his guard shack and leaned into the driver's open window. Two men dressed in black tactical gear were crammed inside the two-door coupe. The driver gave the password, slipped the guard a wad of cash. The guard waved them through.

Pearce and Dr. T. J. Ashley, a colleague and UUV expert, worked feverishly on the last assembly. They had just twenty minutes to finish up and get everything loaded on the fast launch if they hoped to meet the rendezvous at sea on time. Pearce's Bluetooth rang.

"Are you watching your monitor?" Ian asked.

"Kinda busy."

"You've got company."

"So take care of it."

"On it."

"But I want them alive."

Ian hesitated. "If you insist."

The two-man sniper team set up on the rooftop of the nearest building just two hundred yards away from the Vietnam-era Quonset hut where Pearce and Ashley were working. The spotter had Pearce and the short-haired woman in his scope inside the building. He whispered the exact distance to the shooter, lying prone on his belly and sighting his rifle.

"Can't miss," he said, adjusting the scope one click.

The spotter glanced down around the perimeter one last time through his scope. Didn't see anything.

"All clear. Fire when ready."

The shooter smiled. His left hand was missing a finger but his shooting hand was intact.

"Ready."

The shooter slipped his shooting hand toward the trigger guard. Two flash-bangs bounced on the asphalt roof between the shooter and spotter. Ian's whisper-quiet quadcopter sped away. Before either man realized what had happened, the flash-bangs exploded.

The yakuza awoke, his face slapped hard by a big hand. He blinked his bleary eyes furiously against the fluorescent lights blazing overhead. He attempted to move his hands to shield his eyes but couldn't. A thin plastic cable tie bit into his wrists behind his back so tightly his shoulders ached. He hardly noticed this because of the screaming headache hammering inside of his skull.

The big American lifted him up by his tactical shirt and pulled his face close to his, shouting. But the Okinawan yakuza didn't speak any English and he could hardly hear him anyway through the shrill whine in his aching ears. He glanced over at the shooter, who lay on the floor, arms cuffed behind his back, blood trickling out of his ears and nose. His shirt had been ripped away, revealing the brightly colored yakuza tattoos adorning his chest and arms.

The spotter began to panic. If he looked as bad as the shooter did, then he was truly fucked.

The American let go of the spotter's shirt and he thudded back to the floor. His eyes followed the American's combat boots as they trudged toward a worktable in the center of the room. The spotter saw the short-haired lady carrying a big sealed plastic case out of the Quonset hut. She seemed entirely unconcerned about the situation. Her indifference terrified him even more.

The American turned around, holding a pair of yellow-gripped wire cutters in his hands. The spotter's heart raced. The American marched over to the shooter and rolled him onto his stomach, exposing his cuffed hands pinned behind his back. The American was shouting again and kneeling on the shooter's spine, holding the shooter's left hand and tugging on the stubbed finger cut off from an earlier failure.

The shooter screamed, tears streaming down his face, utterly panicked. The spotter didn't need to speak English to know what the American must have been threatening. The American shoved the shooter's index finger between the razor-sharp cutting blades and began to squeeze the grips. That crazy American was going to cut off all the shooter's fingers if he didn't talk—but the spotter knew the shooter wouldn't. Then the American would come after him—

"Oshiro! Oshiro!" The spotter shouted his boss's name over and over. *What else could the American want?*

The big American turned his cold-blooded gaze toward him. Shouted something again. The spotter couldn't make it out.

The spotter saw his friend shouting at him, face twisted with rage. He couldn't quite hear him, but the way his mouth formed the words it looked like he was screaming for him to shut the fuck up.

The American dashed over to the spotter, pushing the wire cutters into his face and shouting again. The spotter felt his bladder give way, hot piss welling up inside of his pants. *What did this crazy bastard want now? To say the name again?*

"Oshiro! OSHIRO! O-SHI-RO!"

The American's livid scowl softened. He stood, touched his earpiece, then spoke. A moment later, the spotter barely heard the American say, "Oshiro." The spotter sighed with relief. He'd guessed right. The American had wanted to know who had sent them. Oshiro-*san* was his *oyabun*, the boss of his *gumi*.

The American tapped his earpiece again, tossed the wire cutters onto the table. He grabbed something and turned back around, marching over to the shooter.

Oh, shit.

The American shoved a clear plastic bag over the shooter's head, whipped out a long white plastic cable tie, and ripped it around the shooter's neck, zipping it tightly.

The shooter panicked, screamed. When he inhaled, the plastic bag sucked partway into his mouth, which only made him panic more. He exhaled until he out-of-breath inhaled again, and sucked the bag back into his mouth. The cycle repeated. The American watched emotionlessly. The breaths came shorter and shorter. The bag fogged.

The American stood and turned his withering gaze at the spotter. He stepped slowly over to him, knelt down. Held another plastic bag and zip tie in front of the spotter's face. Leaned in close. Spoke, moving his mouth slowly.

The spotter squinted, trying desperately to hear the words.

"Ya-ma-da? Ya-ma-da?" the American asked.

"*Hai!* Yamada! Yamada!"

A slew of words vomited out of the spotter's mouth, explaining that his *oyabun* Oshiro-*san* had ordered the attack at sea on the American Yamada, using one of his own fishing trawlers but making it look Chinese, just like he'd ordered. It was just a job. Nothing personal. Him? He liked Americans. Even drove an American—

A plastic bag snapped over the spotter's face, clouding his vision. He kicked and twisted as hard as he could, but the American planted a heavy knee into his chest, pinning him to the ground. A moment later, the zip tie cinched around his neck. He tried not to panic, tried to take small, measured breaths. Felt more than two hundred pounds lift off his chest as the American stood and stepped away.

The spotter rolled over just in time to watch the American jog out the door. He shouted for mercy through the fogging bag. The last thing he saw was the American's hand hitting the light switch, throwing the room into an eternal black.

SIXTY-TWO

The Situation Room had just been refurbished again, updated with the latest security and communications equipment. It looked nothing like Kennedy's original room, with its small table, paneled walls, analog clocks, and Bakelite telephones. But Lane felt the weight of history nonetheless. JFK had created the Situation Room after the Bay of Pigs fiasco, believing his administration had stumbled into a crisis and nearly a world war because he lacked enough credible information. Fifty-five years later, Lane still felt like he didn't have all the intel he needed to avoid a war with China, despite all of the computers and high-tech gear surrounding him. But he was going to have to make a decision today nonetheless.

Lane sat at the head of the rectangular mahogany table where he had control of the video monitors. The others sat in the high-backed leather chairs in no particular order, ignoring protocol. Lane was informal and preferred to keep it that way even in the Situation Room. In attendance were JCS Chairman General Onstot and the other service chiefs, along with Director of National Intelligence Pia, Secretary of State Wheeler, Secretary of Defense Shafer, and National Security Advisor Garza.

The image on the nearly wall-length HD screen opposite Lane was a live satellite video feed showing the Chinese fleet steaming toward the Senkakus. He intentionally kept all of the other video screens blank. Too much information was as big a problem as the lack of it.

Lane spoke to the speakerphone on the table. Myers was on the other end in Japan. "What's the word from your man Ian?"

"He's still running the software analysis. He isn't able to confirm whether or not the Wu-14 will actually work."

"And the bot?"

"It's found several Chinese classified test results claiming success."

The DNI chimed in. "Same as the thumb-drive data you sent us. Our analysts say it's legit, so that clinches it."

"Not necessarily," Myers said. "Ian believes it's possible all of those reports might be falsified, including the internal ones."

"Why would the Chinese file bogus test results with their own people?"

"For the same reasons our defense contractors sometimes do," Garza said. "They massage the data to get continued funding for their pet projects. Even some of the peer-reviewed science journals are loaded with bogus research these days. Everyone's out for a buck."

"Thank you, Margaret. I appreciate everything you've done."

"My pleasure, Mr. President. I'll wait for your further instructions." Myers clicked off.

"Well, you heard it for yourselves. President Myers says that if we don't send the *George Washington* across the red line and block the Chinese assault on the Senkakus the Japanese will go to war without us." Lane turned to Secretary Wheeler. "Do you concur with her assessment?"

Wheeler nodded. "The Japanese will undoubtedly go to war without us, especially now that the presence of the Chinese fleet was leaked to the Japanese press. New and larger mass protests have broken out all over Japan. If Ito doesn't act quickly, his government will fall and a militarist right-wing coalition will undoubtedly be formed. If that happens, all bets are off."

Lane turned to the DNI. "How did the Japanese media get this information?"

Pia shrugged his shoulders. "A leak in Ito's cabinet or maybe on the JSDF staff. Certainly wasn't on our end, otherwise it would've gone to an American media outlet."

"The Japanese won't be waiting for us for much longer. Our fleet guys at Yokosuka report their JMSDF counterparts are prepping for war even as we speak," Onstot said.

The *George Washington* was ported out of Yokosuka, but the carrier and its battle group were already at sea. After his meeting with the JCS at the Tank several days earlier, Lane had decided to deploy the *George Washington* to Okinawa for a "training exercise," hoping that it would prove to be enough of a deterrent to keep the Chinese at bay, but clearly the ploy had failed. The *George Washington* and its escorts were two miles north of Okinawa, which kept them safely beyond the Chinese red line, but still within striking distance of the Senkakus.

"Still no word from President Sun?" Lane asked.

Wheeler shook her head. "He's just waiting to see how all of this plays out to his advantage. Our best guess is that he's hoping to clean house when this is all over. It's a shrewd gamble."

"He's a sonofabitch for risking a war for his personal political gain."

"Like every other fucking politician," Garza said. Catching himself, he added, "Present company excluded."

"He's not the only one. The rest of the PLA is standing on the sidelines, too. They'll be the first ones to applaud if Admiral Ji pulls this thing off," Shafer said.

Lane shifted in his chair. "If we deploy the *George Washington* across the red line, will that be enough to stop the Chinese?"

Wheeler drummed her fingers on the table, weighing her response. "My gut says no. We've communicated our position clearly and forthrightly. There's no misunderstanding. If the *George Washington* doesn't deter them on the far side of the red line, it won't on the near side."

"Which only confirms President Myers's report. The Chinese wouldn't be this bold if they didn't possess a fully operational carrier-killing missile," Onstot said. "The navy sure as hell believes it. Our satellites report that a DF-21D mobile launcher at Ningbo has been prepared and is ready for launch."

"The Wu-14?" Lane asked.

"Based on what Pearce and Myers described, I would say so."

"Should we risk sending the *George Washington* over the red line?"

"The navy says not unless we're willing to do a preemptive strike on that mobile platform," Shafer said.

"Which starts the war," Garza said. "Exactly what we're trying to avoid."

"That platform might be a decoy. The real launcher might be somewhere else," General Onstot said.

The DNI shook his head. "Our intelligence reports indicate no other movement or deployment of mobile launchers outside of Ningbo, something they should've done as a decoy move if nothing else. Somebody over there isn't doing Feng and Ji any favors."

"Does that mean President Sun is sending us a signal?" Lane asked. The CIA had just confirmed that both Vice Chairman Feng and Admiral Ji were on board the *Liaoning*.

The secretary of state shook her head. "I'm not sure. Feng and Ji are thick as thieves, and the two of them together pose the greatest threat to Sun's presidency."

"You're saying he's hoping they'll go down with the ship?" Lane asked, incredulous.

"He isn't doing anything extra to prevent that possibility, that's for sure," Garza said.

Lane turned back to Pia. "What if we ask the Chinese for a forty-eight-hour delay?"

"To what end? They're determined to seize the Senkakus even if they granted us another forty-eight hours, which they likely won't."

"And if we don't do anything and allow the Chinese to seize the Senkakus and abandon the Japanese to their fate, all of our other allies in the region—Taiwan, the Philippines, even Australia—will question our commitment to them. They'll run as fast as they can to Beijing to cut their best deals before the Chinese turn their fleets in their direction," Wheeler said.

"A complete power realignment throughout the western Pacific. Hell, all of Asia, for that matter," Shafer added.

"And you'll embolden the North Koreans for sure," Pia said.

Onstot leaned forward. "For the record, the navy strongly believes that sending the *George Washington* over the red line will result in its destruction."

"So we're still at square one. Damned if we do, damned if we don't," Lane said.

"It's a lose-lose situation," Garza said. "A one-handed clap."

"Almost," Lane said, leaning back. "There's still one option."

His advisors all exchanged a glance, curious. "What have we missed?" Wheeler finally asked.

Lane smiled. "Pearce."

SIXTY-THREE

The waters surrounding the *Tiger II* were a welter of mechanical noise. The grinding metallic acoustics of the incessantly turning drill bit carried for miles beneath the waves, the bit itself driven by enormous diesel engines thrumming on deck like a slow-moving freight train. Enormous thrusters beneath the hull of the giant drillship erupted periodically, churning the sea in a delicate dance choreographed by the finely tuned electronic sensors and blazingly fast computers that kept the forty-five-thousand-ton vessel perfectly positioned in the turgid waters. Without benefit of anchors or fixed assemblies, the automated dynamic-positioning system was the only way to keep the drill assembly perfectly aligned. Otherwise, disaster.

The tired radar operator kept a bleary eye on his scope, trying to stay focused. He crushed another Red Bull can and tossed it in the garbage. It was his third double shift in as many days, midnight to four p.m. Graveyard was the worst. The most exciting thing he ever saw on his scope was the occasional school of fish passing by. He paid little attention to the small blip approaching the rig two hundred meters below the surface. But when the blip reached the spinning drill shaft, he became more interested; most fish didn't approach the noisy assembly that closely. As the blip rose, it came into underwater-camera range. He smiled. It was a manta ray, its large smooth wings flapping effortlessly in the dark waters below. Apparently, it was curious. He wondered what a manta ray would taste like. Probably like shark, which he favored. Fishing was his passion on the mainland. He wanted to cast a line off the rig's deck in his off-hours, but the tight-assed captain had forbidden it.

The manta ray passed out of camera range. The sleepy radar operator clucked his tongue in disappointment. Another long shift, boring as hell.

Until the manta ray exploded.

SIXTY-FOUR

The manta ray was actually a mantabot, another example of beautifully engineered biomimicry. Nature was the best designer and the manta ray was an ideal underwater foil, a graceful swimmer that could carry massive amounts of weight but expended little energy as it glided on its winglike pectoral fins between long, slow, powerful strokes. The mantabot's pectoral fins were constructed out of highly flexible silicon wrapped around articulating titanium bones, but its main body was an aluminum storage compartment containing onboard electronics, power supply, and payload. In this case, the payload was an electromagnetic pulse (EMP) bomb.

Pearce had earlier deployed the autonomous underwater vehicle from one of the torpedo tubes of Commander Onizuka's submarine, the *Sword Dragon*. Swimming virtually undetected until it reached the platform, the mantabot's stealthiest device was its appearance. Nobody would guess that the familiar shape of the silently swimming batoid was anything other than a manta ray, even as the mantabot breached the surface, an unusual activity for the large fish.

The EMP explosion instantly fried all the electronics on the civilian drillship—computer chips, motherboards, sensors. Every video monitor, camera display, iPod, and chip-based device was immediately taken out of service, including all the computers and sensors powering the automated positioning system keeping the *Tiger II* in place. Even the massive diesel motors were governed by computers. They shut down as well. The drill bit ground to a halt.

To the scrambling crew, it appeared as if a massive power outage had just occurred. But the automated power-backup systems couldn't bring the diesel motors or the automated positioning system back online. Within a few minutes, the churning seas battering the hull of the *Tiger II* nudged the forty-five-thousand-ton vessel out of alignment, snapping the drill assembly in half. The ship was in deep water; no anchor chain on board could reach the bottom. With no engines online, the ship was now helplessly adrift.

Thanks to his mantabot, Pearce was able to completely shut down the entire drilling operation without firing a shot or shedding a single drop of blood. The Japanese submarine crew shouted triumphantly as Commander Onizuka reported the results. He and Pearce shook hands.

"So far so good," Onizuka said.

Pearce nodded. "Yeah, but that was the easy part." He glanced over at Dr. Ashley. She understood.

Even if they managed to pull off the second half of the mission, Pearce doubted they would get out of it alive.

SIXTY-FIVE

The task force was still two hours away from Mao Island and the Diaoyu Islands. The PLAN marines were making final preparations for loading into their hovercraft, and the *Liaoning*'s fighter-bombers and surveillance aircraft were launching as fast as the air boss could get them safely into the air. The deck thundered each time the catapult exploded, throwing another multiton airplane into the sky from the angled waist ramp, while more powerful jets rocketed into the air on their own power with the aid of the forward bow "ski jump" ramp. Neither Admiral Ji nor the ship's captain was taking any chances. They were supremely confident the Americans would hesitate and offer no resistance, but putting all their aircraft in the air would serve as both a training exercise and a wise precaution.

Admiral Ji resented Vice Chairman Feng's presence on the carrier, let alone in the CIC, the high-tech nerve center where combat operations were conducted. The heavily air-conditioned room looked like the deck of a starship to Feng, bathed in blue digital light and crowded with dozens of computer monitors manned by young officers and enlisted people wearing the familiar blue camouflage uniforms of the PLAN. In the center of the room was the threat assessment display (TAD), a giant digital monitor showing the *Liaoning* in the center of the vertical transparent glass.

Feng's arrival on board ship was an obvious attempt by him to share in the glory of Admiral Ji's impending victory over the hated Japanese and arrogant Americans. When Feng's helicopter appeared on the horizon, Ji seriously considered shooting it down, but there would be ample time after the coup to deal with him and his cronies. For now, he was still a useful tool in the struggle with President Sun.

A wide-eyed lieutenant called out from his comms station. "Admiral Ji! The *Tiger II* has gone off-line. We can't raise her!"

Ji and Feng rushed over. "What do you mean, can't raise her?" Ji demanded.

"She's not answering radio calls. Text messages, e-mails, cell phones—nothing's getting through."

"Is she sunk?" Feng asked.

"No, sir. She's still on our radar."

"Contact the carrier air group commander. I want two more surveillance aircraft overhead in five minutes or I'll have him court-martialed."

"Aye, aye, sir!" The lieutenant snatched up a phone and dialed in the commander's number.

"What does this mean?" Feng asked.

"Software malfunction. Power outage. Could be any number of things," Ji offered.

"The Americans?"

Ji nodded. "Who else?"

Alarms suddenly blared throughout the CIC. The TAD flashed hundreds of inbound aerial bogies less than a quarter mile away—striking distance—coming at the ship from all directions. Automated chaff rockets exploded above decks, throwing radar-confusing aluminum clouds into the air as antiaircraft missiles and Gatling guns roared.

A bespectacled lieutenant next to Ji shouted, "We're under attack!" The room exploded with nervous chatter as operators called out status reports.

Ji laid a firm hand on the shoulder of the nervous officer. "Calm down."

"Sorry, sir."

Ji turned to another officer. "Someone get me the CAP."

"The CAP commander reports no visual sightings, but his radar has locked on to multiple targets, closing." The commander of the combat air patrol flew the latest Shenyang J-15 Flying Shark fighter aircraft, which possessed its own long-range radar, also tied into the TAD.

"Air defense. Status report," Ji said. The TAD screen exploded with dozens more aerial blips. More antiaircraft missiles roared out of their launchers above his head.

"No splashes, sir!"

"Our missiles hit nothing?"

"No, sir."

"What kind of aircraft?"

"Indeterminate, sir. Too slow for missiles."

"Super Hornets? Lightnings?" Ji feared the strike capabilities of the latest American carrier fighter-bombers, the F-35Cs.

"Too small. American CAP and surveillance aircraft all accounted for."

"Shut down automated air defenses," Ji ordered.

"Aye, aye, sir!"

"Is that wise?" Feng asked.

"We're just wasting ammunition." Ji turned around. "Damage control. Report."

"Sir, damage control reports—"

Another alarm screamed.

Dozens of red blips suddenly appeared beneath the *Liaoning*, swarming in from every point of the compass. Station operators shouted out the information on their screens.

"Contact bearing 173, distance, 1,000 meters!"

"Contact bearing 238, distance, 950 meters!"

"Contact bearing 049, distance, 1,200 meters!"

"Contact bearing 313, distance, 800 meters!"

The ship's captain called out, "Emergency flank speed!"

The other officers called out their status reports, but Ji ignored them. His eyes told him everything he needed to know.

"Torpedoes?" Feng cried out. He was sweating despite the room's low temperature.

"Too slow," Ji said.

"What then? Submarines?"

Another dozen red blips appeared as the others drove toward the *Liaoning*.

"No." Ji's calm demeanor masked his grave concern.

Feng's eyes grew as wide as boiled eggs. "The Americans have infected our computers!"

The commander in the chair next to Feng ran the ship's IT systems. "Negative. All computers are functional, no viruses detected."

Another alarm sounded. "Surface contacts, bearing 040, 122, 274!"

"I don't like this," Feng squealed. "We're vulnerable."

Ji called over to the mission-control officer. "Put the Wu-14 online. Make all necessary preparations for an immediate launch."

"Aye, aye, sir!"

SIXTY-SIX

Troy, the Wu-14 is online!" Ian's brogue thickened on the comms as his adrenaline kicked in. "The bot is active. Repeat, bot is active!"

Troy felt his blood pressure drop. Whenever extreme danger arose, his body always responded by slowing down. It brought him a preternatural calm, one of the reasons he was so effective in combat.

The third software bot that Pearce told Ian to plant in the Wu-14's onboard computer lay dormant until now. It was the only way to guarantee it couldn't be detected until this point. Now that the Wu-14 and the mission-control station on board the *Liaoning* were linked and the satellite connection was active, the bot was in play.

A video screen above the mission-control officer's head displayed the Wu-14 on its mobile launcher at Ningbo.

"All systems go. You have operational control, Admiral."

Feng dashed over to Ji, grabbed him by the arm. "Are you mad? We're vulnerable. We should retreat."

"We'll never have a better chance than this," Ji said. "The Americans will be better prepared next time."

"They appear to be prepared for us now. I order you to retreat."

Ji's mouth thinned. "A gutless mouse. I should've known."

"Don't be foolish. There's always another day—"

WHAP! Ji backhanded Feng across his jaw. The minister yelped, grasping his bleeding mouth with both manicured hands.

"Throw this coward into the brig!" Ji commanded.

Two armed guards grabbed the whimpering politician by his arms. Feng cried out as he was dragged out of the CIC, "He's a madman! Turn around before it's too late!"

"Where's the *George Washington*?" Ji demanded. Another mission-control officer had a God's-eye satellite view of the American carrier on his monitor. Joysticks and a computer screen were also fixed at his desk. He would be the one to guide the Wu-14 to its hypersonic final destination.

"The *George Washington* is still holding just outside the red line, sir. But within strike distance."

"Are they launching more aircraft?"

The officer glanced at his monitor. The *George Washington*'s deck was covered with fighter-bombers waiting to launch.

"They're holding so far."

Ji took a deep breath. The Americans were hesitating just as he predicted. They were fearful of provoking his own powerful fleet. Fortunately for him, the *George Washington*'s crowded flight deck was crammed with fully fueled and bomb-laden aircraft. That made it even more vulnerable to a missile strike.

Perfect.

SIXTY-SEVEN

Prime Minister Ito's situation room was modeled on the American one, though its video displays and electronics were superior. One of the large video displays was linked to American satellite feeds of Ningbo naval base, and a second featured a live video link to the *Liaoning* at sea, its aircraft scrambling into the air as it turned a hard circle in an evasive maneuver.

A third video monitor was used for a live video conference feed between Ito and his cabinet with President Lane and his circle of civilian and military advisors back in Washington. Other video feeds showed the *George Washington* at sea and the remote North Korean launch complex at Musudan-ri, where the North Korean's DF-41 MIRV was still on the launch pad.

Myers sat next to Ito. Pearce was still on board the *Sword Dragon* and wasn't visible to either room but was audio linked to both.

"The Chinese are panicking," Shafer said. Lane's advisors were seated around the table while he stood, pacing.

"Maybe," Lane said.

"Your handiwork, Mr. Pearce?" Ito asked. He was surrounded by his cabinet as well, along with the uniformed service chiefs of the ground, air, and naval forces of the JSDF.

"Yes, sir," Pearce said over the speakers. "My drones are only throwing large electronic signatures to fool the Chinese. So far, they're working."

"By now Admiral Ji must realize they're not really under attack," Myers said.

"But at least we've rattled their cage," Lane said on the video screen.

Tanaka shook his head in disbelief. "And when they figure out they're in no danger, won't they simply resume their assault?"

"Would you?" Lane asked.

"Of course!" Tanaka barked.

"Frankly, it's that North Korean missile that scares the hell out of me," Lane said.

"Join the club," Ito said.

A collective gasp filled the room as a flash of light exploded on the Ningbo screen.

SIXTY-EIGHT

They've launched the Wu-14!" General Onstot shouted, pointing at the screen. A cacophony of panicked Japanese blasted over the audio system. Lane's advisors sat in stunned silence.

"Cut the sound, please," Lane said to a VTC technician manning the video teleconference controls. The MIC OFF sign flashed a moment later. Lane glanced at Ito's cabinet room video monitor. Everyone there stood on their feet and pointed excitedly at the Ningbo missile launch. Lane swore Tanaka was smiling. Myers was clearly shocked.

"How long do we have, Admiral?" Lane asked.

The chief of naval operations stared at the screen. "Best guess, six minutes at most. Probably half that. Once that bird reaches terminal velocity, it will be traveling at nearly eight thousand miles an hour. Whatever you have in mind, sir, do it now."

The *George Washington* lurched into flank speed. Giant white wakes foamed behind her fantail. With two nuclear reactors cranking two hundred and sixty thousand horse-power, the hundred-thousand-ton vessel could make more than thirty knots, half again as fast as World War II–era battleships like the USS *Arizona*.

"Can the *George Washington* outmaneuver the Wu-14?" Wheeler asked. She was a foreign-policy expert, not a military one.

"We don't think so," the CNO said. "But it's damn well worth trying."

The giant American aircraft carrier began launching its aircraft, too.

"Options?" Lane asked.

"Call President Sun. There must be a self-destruct on that thing," Shafer said.

"Too late. Not sure he'd do it anyway," Lane said.

"Pearce, you said you've got a software bug planted on board?" General Onstot asked.

"Yes, sir."

"Can you crash the damn thing into the drink?" the admiral asked. "Or can we blow it up ourselves?"

"Yes. To both," Pearce said.

"Can we capture it?" Garza asked. "Guide it out into the Pacific; let the Navy pick it up off the ocean floor?" He turned to the admiral. "Would that even be remotely possible?"

"Depending on where and how you dropped it. Yeah, it's possible."

The service chiefs launched into a fevered discussion about pulling a salvage operation together on short notice.

Pearce's voice rumbled on the audio speaker. "Mr. President, I need to speak with you privately."

"The clock's ticking, sir," Garza said.

"You've got thirty seconds," Lane said. He dashed to a private secure conference room designed for just such a meeting. Lane slammed the door shut. The room's only window fogged electronically, shielding him from view.

"What's on your mind, Troy?"

"I've put an option in play."

"What option?"

Pearce explained.

Lane couldn't believe his ears.

"You're sure?"

"Ian guarantees it. That's good enough for me."

"You could've told me this before."

"Wasn't an option until the missile was launched."

"Does Margaret know?"

"No, sir."

A knock on the door. Garza's voice. "David, you're out of time."

Pearce had just handed Lane a live hand grenade. Most presidents would have panicked. But Lane wasn't like most presidents. His pilot training kicked in. John Boyd's famous OODA loop popped into his mind: "Observe, orient, decide, act." It had saved his life many times before.

Maybe it would save his country now.

SIXTY-NINE

Ji hovered over the shoulder of the mission-control officer. The computer screen was tracking the Wu-14's downward trajectory.

"Speed, Mach 9 and accelerating," the officer said. "Fifteen seconds to impact."

A second targeting screen kept the *George Washington* in the center of a red target reticle. So long as the laser targeting reticle remained fixed on the center of the deck, the HGV couldn't miss. A massive white wake trailed behind the nearly eleven-hundred-foot American carrier, which was now turning sharply.

"He won't escape," the officer said, grinning. "Mach 10!"

Admiral Ji stood, erect. Every eye in the room was focused on the main overhead screen, intently watching the hapless American carrier attempt to execute its futile escape maneuver.

Ji flushed with pride. Any second now and he would deal the Americans their worst naval defeat since Pearl—

*   *   *

The *Liaoning* erupted in a cloud of fiery steel as the Wu-14's explosive warhead plowed into the main deck at 7,680 miles per hour. The thirty-year-old carrier hull shattered beneath the thundering strike, breaking in two amidships when several thousand tons of munitions exploded, sending both halves of the broken carrier to the bottom. A thousand Chinese sailors perished in the first three seconds, another nine hundred in the next minute.

The fate of the pilots and crew of the dozens of Chinese jets and helicopters still in the air remained uncertain; they suddenly had nowhere to land.

In the Kantei's situation room, the Japanese were on their feet cheering, clapping, laughing at the flaming wreckage of the breaking hulk until Tanaka threw two fists in the air and shouted, *"Banzai!"* Several others echoed him back. Tanaka threw his arms into the air and shouted again and again, *"Banzai! Banzai! Banzai!"*

Everyone else in the room joined him in chorus, throwing up their arms, joyously crazed.

Everyone except Myers.

She still sat in her chair staring at the video screen, incredulous.

SEVENTY

The following morning, Pearce and Myers sat alone in the embassy's secured conference room. The ambassador was making preparations for Secretary Wheeler's arrival in a few hours. President Lane appeared on the large VTC screen on the far wall.

"Glad you're back safe and sound, Troy. Congratulations on a job well done. It couldn't have been easy for you."

Pearce nodded his thanks. "Nor you." He hid a yawn behind a closed fist. He hadn't slept or bathed in nearly three days.

Lane rubbed his face. Dark circles under his eyes, too. "It was the hardest damn decision of my life."

"Regrets?"

"None."

"Was this the plan all along?" There was an edge in Myers's voice. "I feel like I've been played."

"No," Lane insisted. "Our plan never changed. The goal was always to steal the Wu-14's software to determine whether or not it was operational."

"But you don't 'accidentally' gain control of a sophisticated system like that," Myers said.

Pearce reached for the coffee carafe on the table in front of him. "I had Ian write up the software. I figured once we were in there, we might as well get everything out of it we could, including operational control."

"Why didn't you tell me?" Myers asked.

"Wasn't sure you'd approve," Pearce said. Poured two cups.

"Maybe you don't know me as well as you think."

Pearce handed her a cup. "Maybe not."

"You took a helluva risk, David," Myers said. "Why didn't you just have Troy dump it in the ocean?" She took a sip of coffee.

Lane stiffened. Didn't expect to be getting the third degree from the former president. "Admiral Ji and Vice Chairman Feng were hell-bent on grabbing the Senkakus. Even if we'd dropped the Wu-14 into the ocean, they still would've invaded Japanese territorial waters. Then I would have had to commit the *George Washington* into battle. Despite the Sixth Fleet's superiority on paper, the truth is that in war you can never be certain of outcomes. I had to choose between risking American lives or taking Chinese ones. The choice was clear."

"Doesn't that put blood on your hands?" Myers asked.

"Already had that problem long before I got elected. Besides, keeping my hands clean isn't part of the job description, best as I can recall." He didn't mention it was actually Pearce who had used the Japanese submarine as a remote mission-control station, personally steering the hypersonic warhead into the deck of the doomed carrier.

"It's a bloody business, all the way around," Pearce said into his cup. "Better them than our guys."

"Agreed," Myers finally admitted. She studied Pearce's face. The lines around his eyes had deepened.

"By appearing to have knocked out their own aircraft carrier, the Chinese military is now discredited with the Politburo, and so is their adventurism. Feng's, too, for that matter. And the North Koreans can't be feeling very confident about their old ally. They've already withdrawn their MIRV from the launching pad and put it back in storage."

"The Chinese don't know we did it?" Myers frowned with disbelief.

"I reminded President Sun that the *Liaoning* was an old Ukrainian design and that the same government that built the Chernobyl nuclear power plant built his carrier. Maybe the turbines were defective. Maybe they caused a fire that led to a catastrophic munitions explosion. It's happened before."

"And he believed you?" Myers asked.

Lane smiled. "President Sun was quick to accept that explanation—a way to save face. But he asked us not to report it. I agreed. So has Prime Minister Ito. Officially, the sinking never happened. Informally, we all agreed the loss of the *Liaoning* was an unfortunate tragedy and a national embarrassment that President Sun would rather not discuss."

"But he doesn't really believe your story, does he?"

Lane shrugged. "Sun suspects we did it, I'm sure, or the Japanese. Possibly even the Taiwanese. But what incentive does he have to point a finger at anybody? We've done him a huge favor by taking out his two biggest political opponents. And the last thing he needs is a full-scale shooting war with us. Officially, we've denied any involvement. He also knows we immediately launched rescue operations, along with the Japanese, and made emergency arrangements for Chinese aircraft to land at

Japanese and Taiwanese bases. A gesture of goodwill and, I believe, the beginning of a new strategic partnership. I'm flying out to Beijing in five days for an official state visit, just as soon as Gaby and her team can make all the arrangements."

"Politics," Pearce grunted.

"Yes, politics," Lane said. "Feng and Ji were Sun's two biggest political threats, but not anymore. Now they're at the bottom of the East China Sea or in chains on their way to a secret prison somewhere, along with a half dozen other senior conspirators. And the other CMC vice chairman, General Chen, put a bullet in his brain last night. We've just handed President Sun a clear path to the military and anticorruption reforms he so desperately wanted."

"At the cost of thousands of Chinese sailors' lives," Myers said.

"The Chinese shot the bullet; we just moved the target," Pearce said.

"If Ji hadn't launched the Wu-14, those Chinese sailors would still be alive—unless he would've pressed his luck and forced us to attack. Then a lot more people on both sides would've died," Lane said. "Sun could've stopped Ji and Feng before they set out to sea. If anybody else is to blame for this, it's him, not us, and he knows it. That's why he won't make too big of a stink about all of this, no matter his personal suspicions. Otherwise, he hands his political enemies the club they need to beat him to death with."

Myers sighed, still on the fence. She wasn't certain she would've made the same call Lane did had she been in his shoes. But then again, she'd never been in combat. Men like Lane and Pearce survived by making life-and-death decisions in the blink of an eye. Even if she couldn't fully understand his decision, she knew he made it because he thought it was in the best interests of his country and the uniformed men and women who served it. Lane would always put his country before his own political career or even his reputation. That's why she had backed him in his bid for the presidency to begin with. It was a tough call in a split second and he made it for the right reasons. In the end, that was good enough for her.

"What's the purpose of the state visit, if I may ask?" Myers said.

"In exchange for deep cuts in his military spending, we're prepared to make new security arrangements in the region. Joint naval cooperation to keep the sea-lanes open, that sort of thing. Of course, pushing through Sun's anticorruption reforms is even more important. China's long-term viability as a stable growing democracy is in our vital strategic interest."

"What about Mao Island?"

"Ito says they can keep it, so long as all revenues from the drilling operations are evenly divided. He'll be joining us in Beijing, too. We have a few surprises." Lane leaned forward. "It would be great if the two of you could join us. None of this would've been possible without both of you."

Myers glanced at Pearce. He seemed lost somewhere. Maybe a memory. Or a regret.

"Yes, of course," Myers said. "Whatever you need."

"Troy, how about you? I'd like you to see the fruits of your labor. We're going to make history."

Pearce set his empty coffee cup down. "I have some business to take care of first, and I'm not sure how long it will take. But if it's at all possible, I'll be there."

"Anything I can do to help?" Lane asked.

Pearce shook his head. "I've got it under control, but thanks."

"Again, congratulations to you both on a job well done. Your country owes you a debt it can't repay."

"Duty doesn't incur any debts, Mr. President. We're glad we could be of service," Myers said.

Pearce nodded, but his mind was already on the next task at hand, sharpening an old knife deep inside of him, a ruthless blade with an endless, ragged edge.

SEVENTY-ONE

The hearse from the funeral home pulled away as the shipping container containing Yamada's remains was being carefully lifted into the cargo hold of the Pearce Systems jet.

Pearce's grim face set the flight crew on edge. Myers, too. He'd been sullen since the president's video conference at the embassy, no doubt distracted by the reality of his friend's death and the need to transport the body back home. She was surprised when he asked her to join him at the airport. More so when he asked her to come with him to Hawaii for the interment.

"Of course."

President Lane would no doubt want to brief them further before the trip to Beijing, but there was still plenty of time for that. Time for her friend Troy to process everything that had transpired in the last few days. For all of his tough talk about killing the enemy—and God alone knew how many of America's enemies Pearce had sent to hell over the years—she also knew he valued life and that killing, no matter how righteous, took its psychic toll. She couldn't fix that, but she could stand by his side and walk with him through it, no matter how long or how dark the valley set before him. He'd always been there for her. She would always be there for him.

SEVENTY-TWO

Ito's aide opened the door and Tanaka marched in, his stern face frozen in resentment. Ito tapped on a keyboard.

"You summoned me?"

"Yes," Ito said, without looking up. "Please sit."

Tanaka sat down stiffly in the chair in front of Ito's desk, folded his arms across his chest. His clothes reeked of heavy tobacco.

Ito finally finished his e-mail and logged off. He leaned back in his executive chair, relaxed but pensive, his fingers laced. He let the silence fill the room, gathering his thoughts. Finally, he spoke.

"We nearly found ourselves trapped in a war between China and the United States. If it had not been averted, we might well have been annihilated by nuclear strikes from either China or North Korea, or both."

"As I've said all along, we need nuclear weapons."

"And as I've said all along, I disagree. At least, until now."

Tanaka raised an eyebrow. "What?"

"I've come around to your way of thinking. We need a nuclear deterrent as much as any other country. Maybe more than any other country. And I'm making arrangements for that to happen."

Tanaka bolted upright in his chair, a smile plastered across his face. *"Hai!"*

Ito allowed himself a small grin. "I thought you would be pleased. I wanted you to hear it from me first."

Tanaka frowned. "But the Americans will never agree to this."

"They already have. With conditions."

Now Tanaka was really confused. "Why would the Americans suddenly agree to our having nuclear weapons?"

"President Lane and his team are reimagining American national security policy. Like us, he was both surprised and alarmed at how quickly the Mao Island affair spun out of control. He confided in me that several people in his government argued against going to war to honor their treaty obligations to us. Fortunately, President Lane is a man of honor. But he's also a wise man and is determined to do what's best for his country in the future. He understands that America will always have to come to our defense if we can't defend ourselves, including nuclear defense. He said he never wants to be put in a position again where America's nuclear shield forces him to trade Los Angeles for Shanghai to save Osaka. By giving us nuclear weapons, we can defend ourselves and free up the Americans from an unnecessary obligation."

"They will *give* us nuclear weapons?"

Ito nodded. "Yes. We both agreed that we must have them in our possession immediately and then make the announcement to the world. Unlike the West, which refuses to strike preemptively against nuclear proliferators like North Korea and Iran, our enemies would not hesitate to strike us a death blow if we announced we were just beginning to develop a nuclear arsenal."

Tanaka nodded. "Agreed." He thought further. "The Chinese will be livid. This will only worsen our relations with them."

"Perhaps not. President Sun is as eager as President Lane to rethink his security posture in the region. The PLA has become far too strong and too dangerous to his government. Thanks to the Mao Island fiasco, he now has the power to rein them in and start slashing military spending. But his security concerns are valid. In some ways, our vulnerability to North Korea's nuclear arsenal puts China at some risk, since North Korea is seen as China's proxy, which is only partly true. If we are allowed to have a nuclear arsenal, North Korea becomes an American and Japanese problem, no longer just a Chinese one."

"The Chinese people won't stand for it."

"The Chinese government has engaged in anti-Japanese propaganda for decades to bolster their own legitimacy. President Sun will not only end that policy, he is also prepared to enter into a new and mutually beneficial relationship with us. He and President Lane believe that these new reforms and the resulting prosperity will better legitimize his regime."

Tanaka fell back in his chair, thinking. "It's hard to believe that so much has transpired in just two days."

"Yes, isn't it?"

Tanaka bolted back up, pointing his finger at Ito. "There's something else going on, isn't there?"

"What do you mean?"

"You've been planning this all along, haven't you?"

"What do you mean?"

Ito watched the wheels spinning in Tanaka's fevered eyes.

"This whole affair with the Wu-14 and the *Liaoning*. The Americans are the ones who sank the carrier, and you knew all about it!"

"Not exactly." Ito wondered how much he should tell his old friend. Decided it didn't really matter at this point. "President Lane, President Myers, and Troy Pearce put together a plan to steal the Wu-14 technology a few months ago, and they needed my help. President Myers was the one who actually stole it. The idea was to acquire the Wu-14 software and confirm its operability and then reverse-engineer it to discover the best countermeasures. Once those were found, the Americans would inform the Chinese that the Wu-14 was worthless, and thus force the PLAN back into a defensive posture. But Ji and Feng had other ideas."

"So when the Chinese launched the missile, the Americans took control of it?"

"Yes. And President Lane decided on his own to take out the *Liaoning*. If he would've asked me, I would've said no, but in hindsight it was a brilliant move."

Tanaka nodded. "Yes, it was. We should be as bold."

"How so?"

"Once we acquire the nuclear missiles, we should inform the Chinese that the Americans are the ones who sank their carrier. We can still force them into a war against each other."

Ito sighed, shaking his head.

"Why not?" Tanaka asked. "You said yourself the Americans will do what's best for them. So should we."

"Yes, I agree. We should."

"Then you do agree with my plan."

"I don't, but I do agree we must do what is best for our country. We disagree on what's best for Japan."

Tanaka frowned. "What do you think is best?"

"I agree with President Lane that Japan needs nuclear

weapons immediately, but as I said before, there are conditions."

"What conditions?"

"First, that we announce a unilateral nonaggression pact with China and any other nation that wants us to sign it. We will pledge never to use nuclear weapons in a first-strike capacity."

"I don't completely agree with that policy, but I understand it. If that's what it takes to acquire nuclear weapons, we should agree to it. What are the other conditions?"

"Only one, really. Neither the United States nor China want to start World War Three. They believe there are certain elements in our government that want the two of them to go to war against each other. And they won't allow us to have nuclear weapons unless they're sure that those elements are silenced."

Tanaka stiffened. "I'll never speak again about the American strike on the *Liaoning*."

"You have people throughout the government and the JSDF who share your extremist views."

"I can keep them quiet."

"That's not good enough."

"You have my word, Ito-*san*."

"I want their names."

"No."

"I wonder which you love more? Your conspiracy or your country?"

Tanaka darkened, torn. Finally, he said, "I'll send you the list as soon as I get back to my office."

"No need, because we already have the names. The Naicho and the NSA have been running a joint intelligence operation tracking you and your co-conspirators for months now. I was briefed just this morning on your role in the death of the American scientist Yamada, as well as your other crimes. I should have you arrested."

Tanaka laughed. "You wouldn't dare."

Ito leaned back in his chair, planting his shoes on his desk. "No, I wouldn't. Your arrest would severely cripple the legitimate cause we've both been fighting for all these years. And yet, you remain a serious problem for the Americans and the Chinese, and a grave threat to our nation and our people."

"A threat? That's ridiculous."

"I must provide a guarantee to the Americans and Chinese that you will remain silent on all these matters even as I clean house and root out the ultranationalists who threaten all of us."

"I'll retire. You'll never hear from me again."

"That's not good enough for them, I'm afraid." Ito stood up. "Nor for me."

"What do you propose?"

Ito crossed around his desk and laid a hand on Tanaka's firm shoulder. "There is an honorable solution, old friend."

Tanaka's eyes hardened, fixing on a distant unseen place. "I understand."

Ito smiled faintly. "I knew you would."

"I'll make all of the necessary arrangements. It will take a few days."

"Of course. I'm sorry."

Tanaka shook his head. "There's nothing to be sorry for. I've been preparing for this moment all my life."

SEVENTY-THREE

The sun knelt beneath the far horizon, bathing the blue ocean in its sweet last orange light. Myers felt the warm waters brush past her knees and the gentle breeze in her hair was heavy with tuberose.

Pearce lit the candle inside the rice-paper bag covered in prayers for Kenji Yamada, written in kanji by the local Shinto priest. Troy even wrote one himself in English.

He set the float carrying the paper lantern down on the water, and the tide began pulling it away toward the bay beyond the cove. Within moments, the flickering lantern raft was beating its way toward the last rays of the setting sun.

"Two years ago, Kenji took me to the Lantern Floating Hawaii ceremony in Oahu," Pearce said. "It was Memorial Day."

Myers was startled to hear his voice. Pearce hadn't said a word since Kenji's interment next to his parents in the small Japanese graveyard up the road a few hours earlier. Besides the priest, they were the only two in attendance. She knew he'd been to a lot of funerals in his time. He was no stranger to death or to the loss of close friends.

Neither was she. But even she was particularly moved by the lonely finality of the small, sad service today. It only added to Pearce's dark mood that began when he loaded Kenji's casket into the plane in Japan.

"That ceremony meant a lot to me at the time. Wrote a lot of names down on that lantern that night. Kenji floated one for his parents, too."

The beach was deserted. She watched Kenji's flickering light trudge bravely on toward the far horizon. Something in her stirred. The vastness of the ocean, the inevitable night. Even the rhythm of the tide as it whispered on the sand called to her. "It's all so lovely and forlorn. I feel as if I'm watching a good friend leaving on a journey who knows he's never coming back."

"He believed that the spirit always returns to the ocean from which it came."

"There's something eternal about it, isn't there?" She watched Pearce's weary eyes scanning the far horizon.

He nodded. Held out his hand. She took it. His small, still smile in the dimming light surprised her. "Let me show you something."

Pearce led her out of the water onto the fine white sand, leading her carefully off the beach onto a trail cutting up the mountain. The sand beneath her bare feet soon fell away to grass and soft roots as the air thickened with the sweet fragrance of the flowering plants and trees that enclosed the trail. The climb was steep and the light all but gone, but Pearce clearly knew his way and took his time. She was neither tired nor afraid but her heart was racing. She felt like a little girl again, heading out for a grand adventure, hunting for secrets and ghosts in a mysterious garden on the far side of a forbidden wall.

They finally passed out of the canopy of trees back into the open air. They stood in a small clearing on a cliff overlooking the bay, surrounded by a wall of jasmine and gardenia plants, the world and its worries a distant memory. The sky was a deepening purple and the first bright stars shone above. The gently surging ocean murmured far below. The sights and sounds and aromas swept through her like a cleansing breeze. She felt like they were the only two people in the whole wide universe.

"Look," Pearce said, pointing at the water.

Myers saw the flickering lantern down below. The light seemed so fragile and small against the vast expanse of darkening ocean beyond and the endless starry sky above.

They stood in silence watching Kenji's lantern. Pearce's strong, rough hand still held hers. Their arms touched. She felt the heat of his body, the rise and fall of his breathing. She glanced up at the sky. The moon was a great round shadow, new and unlit. She could stand here forever.

She looked back down at the lantern bobbing in the gentle waves. It flickered again, then disappeared. Pearce's grip tightened. Kenji's light was gone.

"I'm sorry," Myers said.

"For what?"

"The candle went out."

"Maybe he's already home."

In the dark, she felt his towering frame turn toward her.

"He's lucky, then," she said.

Pearce's other hand brushed gently against her cheek. "He always was lucky."

The back of her neck tingled. Her mind clouded. "Really?"

Pearce's mouth edged close to hers. "Really."

His mouth was softer than she'd imagined, his body harder than she thought possible. The heat in his kiss rose, a devouring hunger that swallowed her up. He swept her up in his arms and gently laid her down in a bed of flowers, bathing her in kisses until she was ready to take all of him into her heart.

His power was like a storm breaking inside of her—thrilling and frightening in its strength. She felt the tears on his face mingle with hers as he thrust deeper and harder, igniting a fire that consumed her until they both shuddered with explosive release.

She held him close as he finally relaxed into her, burying his face in her neck. She stared at the canopy of lights shimmering over his broad shoulder, feeling him breathe against her chest, a falling star a silent witness to her boundless joy.

SEVENTY-FOUR

The Japanese solution to Tokyo's high land prices, crowded streets, and insatiable demand for golf were multistoried driving ranges like Tip-Top Golf World, one of more than eighty such facilities across the city, several of which were owned by yakuza bosses like Oshiro. Like his fellow countrymen, the sumo-size gang boss was a golf nut and shut the place down after ten p.m. every night so that he and his crew could practice their swings in private. It was not uncommon for his boys to celebrate birthdays, weddings, and even new criminal enterprises at the three-story range. Oshiro had even settled a few gangland truces at the Tip-Top after hours, where invitees could hit an endless bucket of balls into the lush natural turf ringed on three sides by steel netting.

Tonight Oshiro was celebrating his win of the Golden Sword tournament on Kobayashi-*san*'s fighting freighter. He cleared more than a half million dollars in betting that night, but the golden sword was worth many times that in honor alone.

Not bad for a fat Okinawan boy, he thought.

The top deck was everybody's favorite because the

balls flew farther. It was also satisfying to watch the white spheres sail high into the air and drop majestically onto the closely manicured greens or explode like grenades in the fine-grained sand traps scattered across the three-hundred-yard range. Even poorly hit balls skittering off the deck appeared more formidable when they began their journeys thirty feet in the air.

Oshiro smacked away with his titanium driver, dressed in his uniform of black silk overshirt and baggy silk pants, worn to hide his girth. His brand-new pair of custom-fitted black-and-white alligator golf shoes creaked beneath his weight with each powerful swing.

Three of his newest men, all fresh off the boat from Okinawa, swung frantically with their oversize drivers at the balls perched on the rubber tees, trying to impress their *oyabun* with their still imperfect strokes. Oshiro's older *kobun* laughed hilariously at them, shouting instructions, encouragement, or insults, cigarettes clenched in their crooked teeth. The seasoned killers were swinging their drivers as hard and as fast as they could, too. The fat Okinawan crime boss promised a hundred thousand yen for the farthest drive in the next ten minutes. So far, that honor belonged to Oshiro-*san*.

The constant ping of metal drivers was a barrage of noise, almost like gunfire. When Troy Pearce emerged from the third-story stairwell, no one noticed him or the suppressed .40 caliber pistol in his hand. They certainly hadn't heard him dispatch the two guards on the first deck. Finally, one of the yakuza saw him and shouted, pointing a finger. Oshiro's number-two man dropped his driver and reached for a pistol tucked in the small of his back, but his forehead caved in with a bullet strike before his hand touched the grip.

Pearce marched forward, gun raised. The other yakuza pulled their weapons, some expertly, some clumsily. All died before they got a shot off. Seven corpses lay on the Astroturf range mats, bleeding out into the plastic grass.

Oshiro's titanium driver clattered on the cement as it fell from his thick gloved hand. Pearce pressed the barrel of the pistol's suppressor against the Okinawan's broad forehead. Oshiro raised his hands. The silken shirtsleeves fell back. A colorful carp slithered up one beefy forearm, a raging tiger on the other.

"Who sent you?" Oshiro's thickly accented English was calm, collected. He was genuinely curious.

"You did. Karma's a bitch."

Not the answer the yakuza boss was expecting. "Dude, you know I have powerful friends."

"You mean Kobayashi? He's the asshole who gave me your address."

The Okinawan swore bitterly.

"Don't take it personally. He was in a lot of pain at the time."

Oshiro's eyes narrowed, calculating. "So why am I still alive?"

"You give me what I want, I give you a break."

"What do you want?"

"Did Tanaka put you up to killing the American, Kenji Yamada?"

"Who?"

"Wrong answer." Pearce slipped his index finger from the trigger guard to the trigger. Oshiro's eyes followed it.

"You mean on the boat?"

"Yes."

"Tanaka ordered the hit."

"Why?"

"He didn't say. Paid well. Said to keep one alive for a witness. Wanted everyone to think the Chinese had done it." His fat lips curled into a grin. "Start a war between you and China."

"Will you swear to that in open court?"

The smile disappeared. The Okinawan shook his massive head. "I can't, man."

"Why not?"

He shrugged, almost apologetic. "Honor. *Bushido*."

"I respect that." Pearce lowered his weapon.

Oshiro's broad shoulders slumped with relief. He lowered his arms. "What else do you want to know?"

"The men on your ship who killed the American."

Oshiro motioned to the corpses scattered on the deck.

"That's all of them?"

He nodded grimly. "My best men."

"That's not saying much."

Oshiro stood there, breathing heavily, stung by Pearce's insult. Sweat beaded up on his face. "What else do you need to know?"

"Nothing."

Oshiro blinked, confused. "So, I can go now?"

Pearce nodded.

The big man wiped the sweat out of his eyes with one of his massive paws. Started to walk past Pearce.

Pearce stabbed the pistol against his chest. "Wrong way."

The Okinawan frowned. He didn't understand.

Pearce threw a thumb toward the driving range. "That way."

"What?"

"I promised you I'd give you a break if you told me what I needed to know."

"And I did."

"And I appreciate that." Pearce jerked his head toward the floodlit grass three stories down. "So there's your break."

The fat man glanced over the side. A long way down. His cheeks wobbled as he shook his head.

"I'll die."

"Maybe not. That's grass down there. I've seen guys survive worse falls."

"Hell no, man. I'm not doing it."

"Have it your way." Pearce raised the pistol to Oshiro's face.

The yakuza saw the cold hatred in Pearce's eyes. "Okay. Okay!"

The cleats in the Okinawan's golf shoes scratched on the cement as he stepped gingerly toward the edge. He gulped.

"Dude, I can pay you, big-time."

"Last chance, fat man. So help me God, I'll put a bullet in your throat and watch you drown in your own blood."

The Okinawan whispered a prayer to an ancestor. His face darkened with resolve. He opened his eyes, glaring at Pearce.

"Fuck you, *gaijin*!"

Oshiro turned and leaped over the side, shouting a war cry.

Pearce leaned over the side to watch.

The corpulent body thudded into the turf. Even this high up, Pearce heard bones cracking in the soft grass. Oshiro screamed in agony. A three-hundred-pound worm in bloody black silk.

"There's your break," Pearce said, watching the fat man writhing in the grass.

Pearce knew that Kenji wouldn't have approved. But at least he would've understood.

Pearce lifted his pistol, put three rounds into Oshiro's head. The screaming stopped, a mercy.

Better than he deserved.

SEVENTY-FIVE

Tanaka knelt on the polished hardwood floor, his *kei-kogi* pulled down around his waist, exposing his muscular torso. The family's Shinto shrine loomed in front of him, its unvarnished shelves laden with offerings of rice wine, fish, and fruit. Candles and incense burned near the amulets representing the Tanaka household gods. A simple plaited rope hung slack above it all.

Tanaka whispered a prayer to his ancestors, fearsome samurai who loyally served the shogunate for centuries. Satisfied, he reached for the most cherished family heirloom, a short-bladed *tanto* belonging to his most ancient ancestor. He unsheathed it and set the scabbard down with ceremonial precision, placing the tip of the razor-sharp sword against his stomach, preparing for *seppuku*, the ritual self-disembowelment of a samurai who failed his mission.

Tanaka's powerful hands grasped the hilt and the blade as he prepared to open up his stomach and remove his own intestines, but a heavy thump outside his door broke his concentration. He opened his eyes but didn't move. Heard the *shoji* door behind him slide open.

"Pearce," he said, without looking back.

"Afraid I was going to be late." Pearce stepped over a body in the hallway into the room, sliding the door behind him shut. He gripped a familiar pistol shape in one hand.

Tanaka twisted around, still clutching the *tanto*. "You're just in time to watch how an honorable man behaves."

"How is suicide honorable?"

"I failed my mission. I must show the way."

"To whom?"

"My people."

"By killing yourself?"

"Life is not so important as integrity."

"I've read the *Hagakure*, too."

Tanaka nodded. "Yes, it makes sense that you would have. But to have read it and to have lived it all of one's life are two different things."

"Funny, I don't remember you putting on a uniform."

"Sadly, asthma prevented me from entering military service. And even if I had, what would I have done but take orders from you *gaijin* taskmasters? The gods smiled on me when they took my breath away. In my weakness, they showed me a better path to strength. But I failed in that mission."

"So now you seek a heroic death, an inspiration to your followers."

Tanaka smiled. "So you do understand. My death will be my greatest victory."

"You tried to drag my country into a war with China."

"To save my country, yes. I'm a patriot, the same as you."

"You're neither a hero nor a patriot. You're a murderous bastard."

"Japan can never prosper so long as your two countries keep feeding on her flesh."

"You had my friend Kenji Yamada killed. He was try-ing to save your country, too."

"Save us? How? By robbing us of our only source of energy? By keeping us slaves to American oil companies?"

"He was a good man. Better than you. You deserve to die."

"So let me die." Tanaka turned back around and faced his family altar. Tightened his grip on the sword—

Pearce raised his pistol. "That's the general idea."

Fired.

Two needle-shaped probes embedded in Tanaka's back. Pearce pulled the trigger and sent five thousand volts of electricity coursing into Tanaka's body, disrupting the neural signals between his brain and muscles. The blade dropped from his hand as his entire body contorted in a violent spasm, writhing on the polished wooden floor in searing pain. Tanaka hissed at Pearce through gritted teeth, eyes raging.

Pearce knelt down next to him, close to his contorted face. "No worries, Tanaka. Your gods will be smiling again, very soon."

Pearce's cell phone vibrated. A text message from Ian. His face blanched.

He texted Myers, now back in Denver. Told her where to meet him.

He glanced back down at Tanaka, passed out from the pain. "Enjoy it while it lasts, asshole," Pearce grunted.

His plans for Kenji's killer would have to wait a few days.

SEVENTY-SIX

The self-possessed young woman behind the desk wore a nurse's white coat over a black shirt, and a simple black nun's veil draped behind her back. A gold-winged caduceus was pinned to one lapel; a humble silver crucifix was pinned to the other. "Only family. He left strict orders. I'm sorry."

"He doesn't have any family." Pearce towered over the diminutive nun.

"He knows that and so do I. Since you do as well, then you must know that he's a very private man and doesn't want any visitors." She was stopping Pearce cold with a disarming smile.

"We go a long way back. We used to work together." She raised an eyebrow.

"We used to work for the same . . . company."

"You mean the CIA?" Another smile. A smirk, really. "Then you understand his need for security as well."

Pearce chuckled. "I'm surprised he told you."

"Confession is good for the soul."

Pearce took a deep breath. Never realized that stubbornness was a religious virtue. "I've brought him something."

She held out a delicate hand. "I'm happy to take it to him for you."

"It would be better if I delivered it in person."

"It would be better for me to give it to him than his not getting it at all, wouldn't you agree?"

Pearce glanced around. No security. Hardly surprising. Who'd want to break into a hospice? She was all of a hundred pounds soaking wet. He could just walk past her. Decided against it. Played his trump card. Pointed a thumb at the woman standing next to him.

"Do you know who this is?"

The nun shook her head. "Should I?"

"She's the godda—"

Myers quieted Pearce with a hand on his arm. "We're friends, and we've come a very long way. Perhaps you can tell Will that Troy Pearce needs to see him? There can't be any harm in that." She flashed her own charming smile, but the commanding tone in her voice struck home.

"Perhaps not. Please wait here a moment." She stepped away from the desk.

"Thank you, Sister." After the nun disappeared around the corner, Myers shot Pearce a withering look. "Seriously? You were going to cuss out a nun?"

The nun led them down the quiet hallway past a number of patients' doors, some of them open. The suites were furnished like living rooms rather than hospital rooms. Most of the patients they saw were alone or with medical staff. A priest was praying last rites over one.

They arrived at the end of the hall and stopped at the last closed door.

"He's expecting you," the nun said. "He has only twenty percent lung capacity. Please don't be long. He's very tired." She instructed them to use the antibacterial hand sanitizer as often as possible to help avoid infection, nodded her condolences, and left.

Pearce laid his hand on the door. "Thanks again for doing this with me."

Myers smiled. "Of course. But maybe you should go in by yourself."

"No. I want you to meet him. He's like a second dad to me."

"Okay."

Troy gently opened the door. He nearly lost it.

He'd been around death for most of his adult life, but seeing the shell of a man he'd once known as larger than life was harder than he thought possible. The adjustable bed was upright. Will was nearly skeletal, his flesh translucent and gray. His mouth was wide open, taking in short, shallow breaths. The skin around his mouth was nearly white. A hissing oxygen tube snaked from the wall behind his bed to his nose. Will's thick silver hair was now blindingly white and wispy thin. The flesh around his eyes had shrunk, making the orbs appear huge in the sockets, but the green irises still radiated his penetrating intellect.

"How . . . the hell . . . are you . . . kid?" He clumped his words together, exhaling them out between breaths. He held up a large but emaciated hand. Pearce touched it gently, afraid to hurt him.

"Doing good. But look at you laying out. Isn't there a junta you should be organizing somewhere?"

"Working . . . on . . . one . . . now. Gonna . . . take over . . . this place. More booze . . . less bingo." He turned his head with effort. "Who's . . . the pretty . . . lady?"

She laid a hand on his. "Margaret. It's an honor to meet you."

"You . . . with . . . him? Or does . . . a fella . . . like me . . . still have . . . a chance?"

"Soon as you're out of here, call me." She winked and mimed a phone receiver to her ear.

A croak escaped Will's throat, a laugh. And then a long bout of coughing, phlegmy and painful. He leaned forward, face reddened, choking.

"Oh, my God, I'm so sorry." Myers snatched up a plastic sputum tray and held it beneath Will's mouth. He coughed up yellow mucus tinged with blood, his eyes tearing from the effort. It dribbled on his lip and he spit, trying to clear it out of his mouth, and swatted at it clumsily with his hand. Will was a lifelong smoker and the cigarettes were finally killing him in the worst way. COPD was a bitch, like drowning in slow motion in a puddle of his own mucus.

Troy reached for a sanitary wipe and cleaned away the string hanging between his mouth and the tray. When he got it, Myers pulled the tray away and dumped it in the wastebasket, then pulled the basket over for Troy to toss the wipe. Myers grabbed two more wipes and cleaned off Will's face and hands. Troy had only known a proud man, strong as an ox, but Will was beyond shame at this point. His eyes were grateful for the care.

"Never thought . . . I'd have . . . a president . . . wipe . . . my ass . . . for me."

Myers squirted antibacterial into her hands from a bottle on the table. "So you knew who I was, did you?"

"I'm . . . a spook . . . I'm . . . supposed . . . to know . . . these things."

Myers beamed. "Our country owes you a lot, Will. Thank you for your service." Pearce had told her some of his storied exploits. Will was an old-school cold warrior and a fierce patriot. She fought back tears as Pearce squirted sanitizer into his hands.

"Just . . . keep . . . an eye . . . on this . . . guy . . . and . . . we'll . . . call it . . . even."

"That's a deal."

Will's eyes turned toward the far wall, focusing on the large crucifix in front of him. Pearce watched him labor to catch his breath, finally calming down. A few minutes later, he turned back to Pearce.

"How . . . was . . . China?"

"How did you know?"

Myers swatted Pearce playfully. "He's a spy, remember?"

"Everything worked out fine."

"Then why . . . do you . . . look like . . . shit?" Pearce's face still hadn't fully healed from the beatings he'd received.

"You should've seen the other guy."

Will nodded. "That's . . . my boy." His eyes searched Pearce's face. He gathered his strength. "So why . . . the visit? Come . . . to see . . . an old man . . . die?"

"Yeah. You know any?" Pearce said.

Will's eyes misted. "I . . . missed you . . . sport."

"Me, too. Sorry I haven't been around."

Will smiled. He lifted his hand, made a weak sign of the cross in Pearce's direction. "*Te . . . absolvo . . .* the priest . . . says that . . . a lot. I think . . . it means . . . dinner's . . . at five."

"I brought you something." Pearce reached carefully into his shirt pocket.

"A new . . . pair of . . . lungs . . . I hope."

Pearce held out a black-and-white photo, wallet-size and worn. A pretty young Vietnamese woman. ALL MY LOVE, 1965 written in a lovely feminine hand on the back.

Will's big hands trembled as he took the photo. Brought it close to his face. His eyes widened. Stared at it as if he were looking into the face of God.

"How?"

"I'm a spook, too. Remember?"

Will's face beamed as if he were a monk witnessing a miracle.

Maybe it was a miracle, Pearce thought. He couldn't believe it when a package from Hanoi arrived at the embassy just hours before he left for Hawaii. Dr. Pham had promised Pearce she'd pull a few strings to honor his request back on that helicopter. She said it was the least she could do for the man who had saved her brother's life, as well as her own.

Pearce knew that when Will and his dad were captured by the Viet Cong they would've been stripped of all of their personal effects for intel, and then those items would've been shipped off to central headquarters for analysis and, later, storage. Communists were mostly evil shits, but they were fanatical about storing and organizing the things they stole from other people. Knowing Will was with the CIA probably gave his Hanoi case file even greater importance. Pearce hoped Dr. Pham could find Will's case file, along with his dad's. Apparently, she had.

"Your wife?" Myers asked.

Will smiled with his eyes. Nodded.

"And then there's this." Pearce unfolded a piece of tissue paper. A small silver crucifix was inside, heavily tarnished. Will reached for it. Took it in his long fingers. Tried to open the delicate clasp.

"Here." Myers took the chain and opened it as Pearce helped Will lean forward. She draped it around his withered neck and fastened the clasp. Pearce helped him lie back down. Will fingered the Christ, hardly believing his good fortune.

"Still fits," Myers said, patting his other hand.

"I . . . converted . . . to marry . . . her. She . . . insisted. Her father . . . too."

Will shut his eyes, mouth open in a loose smile, lost in a memory.

"God bless you," Myers said. She stroked his weary head and whispered a prayer. She hadn't been to confession since she was a child or Mass since high school. But old habits die hard.

Moments later, his smile disappeared and his mouth opened wider. His breaths were short and shallow.

"I think he's asleep. We should go," Myers said.

"Yeah. We'll come back tomorrow." He took her hand in his, and they slipped quietly out of the room.

They returned the next day. Will had died during the night, taking last rites with a priest, clutching his wife's photo and the crucifix as he prayed. The nun said he went peacefully.

They drove back to the hotel in silence.

At his suggestion, Myers picked up the phone to order room service while Pearce headed for the shower. She worried about him. A lot had happened in the last few days. He'd lost people he'd loved and took the lives of many more. Not many men could handle that.

She wasn't sure how he liked his steak, so she hung up the phone and stepped into the steaming granite-and-glass bathroom to ask. He was curled up on the shower floor, weeping like a child, scalding water blistering his skin. She rushed in, slammed the shower off, gathered him up in her arms, and lay on the wet stone floor with him, holding him until his sobs gave way to a fitful, trembling sleep.

SEVENTY-SEVEN

Pearce and Myers flew a JAL Sky Suite 777 nonstop from San Francisco to Tokyo to meet up with President Lane and his mission to Beijing. But when they touched down, Pearce informed her that he wouldn't be attending the summit. "I'm no politician" was his excuse, and when that failed, "I've got some Pearce Systems business to attend to." Myers was clearly disappointed but said she understood and flew to Beijing on Air Force One without him later that afternoon.

Pearce called August Mann from the airport and confirmed that he had landed. Mann reported that everything was still running smoothly at the site and that everything was on schedule. Pearce arrived the next day.

The giant tsunami that struck the facilities at Fukushima had slammed the Unit 4 building particularly hard. The reactor had already been shut down for repairs before the deadly tidal wave hit, but it was still a nuclear catastrophe waiting to happen. The American-designed facility was particularly problematic for an area of the world prone to both earthquakes and tsunamis. One of its most distressing features was an elevated cooling pool storing more than fourteen hundred spent nuclear fuel rods that contained nearly forty million curies of deadly radiation. Exposing those fuel rods to the air, some scientists argued, would be an environmental holocaust. Now, several years after the tsunami, Unit 4 was sinking into the ground, threatening to collapse the building and destroy the pool.

August Mann ran the nuclear-deconstruction division of Pearce Systems, and he and his unmanned ground vehicles had been contracted to help remove the contaminated debris that humans couldn't touch. But once his automated systems were in place, TEPCO found other useful work for them to carry out, including tackling the Unit 4 building problem. Because of the hazardous radiation in and around Unit 4, it was impossible for anything but remotely controlled robots to work in the area for any length of time. Mann and his drone team were attempting to stabilize the foundation of the Unit 4 structure to keep it from sinking farther into the water-soaked soil in order to avoid the building's collapse and the resulting catastrophe.

Mann's remotely piloted tracked vehicles had carried hundreds of heavy steel rods and large metal cylinders across the irradiated mudscape over the last few weeks. There were so many problems at the Fukushima facility and its other reactors that Mann and his team were left largely unsupervised by the overworked, understaffed TEPCO managers.

Pearce and Mann were in one of Pearce Systems' off-site control stations a safe distance from the radiation poisoning the air, soil, and water in and around Unit 4. Pearce sat at the control station running one of the Pearce Systems tracked robots that was carrying yet another metal cylinder in its hydraulic claws as it lumbered toward the sinking foundation.

Pearce's cell phone rang. He tapped his Bluetooth. It was Myers.

"How'd it go?" he asked.

"Better than expected. President Sun was surprisingly compliant."

"Why are you surprised?" Pearce knew the Chinese respected force, and the sinking of the *Liaoning* alone would have been more than enough to convince Sun it was time to deal honestly with the Americans, for whom they'd lost respect over the last two decades.

"He not only agreed to the new security arrangements we've been discussing, but he's eager to reassess his country's predatory trade and currency practices."

"Uh-huh."

"You sound like you're busy. Did I call at a bad time?"

"No. I'm almost through here. Go on."

"Sun said that fair and balanced trade benefited everybody, his country most of all. He even acknowledged China's role in helping to create the imbalances that currently exist, especially the trade deficits. He clearly understands that stability means security in both economic and military matters, for his country as well as ours."

"Sounds like a home run. Congratulations."

"It's not a home run yet." She explained that Lane was going to have hell to pay as he tried to rein in the legions of former congressmen and generals who staffed the big lobbying firms swarming all over Capitol Hill. They were the ones perpetuating the current crony-capitalist system beggaring the country and profiting most from China's rapacious trade policies.

"That's why I don't do politics," Pearce said. His construction drone was nearly in position.

"Do you have any more thoughts about the president's offer?" Myers asked.

"What offer?"

"Drone Command. He still hopes you'll take it."

"Jury's still out on that one. Can't imagine myself setting up another government bureaucracy."

"I'd hope not. New wineskins and all of that."

"Look, I'm sorry to cut you off, but I've got to go."

"Sure. I'll be at the hotel by six o'clock tonight. Can you meet me there?"

"Try and keep me away." Pearce could feel her smiling on the other end of the phone.

She rang off.

Instantly, Pearce's face hardened with resolve.

Mann stepped closer. The lanky German fingered his beard, worried. "You sure about this?"

"Never more sure of anything."

"*Ja*. I believe you."

"Do me a favor and go grab yourself a cup of coffee. I don't want you in here." August was one of Pearce's oldest friends and the first man he hired into Pearce Systems. Pearce wouldn't allow his loyal friend to bear witness to an event that could land the German in prison if things went sideways, especially with a wife and two young kids at home.

"You're the boss."

"Maybe get a donut, too. Take your time."

Mann sighed with relief. "Thanks."

The trailer door shut behind Mann. Pearce gripped the joysticks and maneuvered the drone into its final position over the deep hole, then activated another set of controls and lowered the cylinder into the contaminated water. Once it was fully submerged, he turned on another monitor and punched a few keys. An LED light popped on inside the cylinder.

Tanaka's panicked, hyperventilating face filled the fish-eye camera. His desperate breathing rasped on the monitor speakers.

"Your breath-stealing gods must be smiling now," Pearce whispered. He punched another key, snapping off the LED light, throwing Tanaka into soul-crushing darkness. Frantic screams poured out of the monitor speakers.

Pearce punched another button and silenced the speaker, leaving Tanaka to his fate, buried alive beneath a nuclear shroud. In a few minutes, the remote-controlled cement truck would appear and seal him in his tomb forever.

His phone buzzed. A text message from Myers. "Forgot to tell you. Lane has another job for us."

"What job?" he texted back.

"We can talk about it later. Stay safe."

"Okay."

She sent another. "Can't wait to see you tonight."

"Same here."

And then she sent one more. "You okay?"

Pearce stared at the text. He wasn't sure.

He wondered what she'd think of him if she knew what he was doing. She deserved better.

He stared at the blacked-out monitor. Imagined Tanaka's breathless hell. Felt his own claustrophobia closing in. A nightmare. Guilt whispered somewhere deep inside but Yamada's mangled corpse shouted it away.

He needed a drink. Reached for Mann's pack of smokes instead but held off, remembering how Will had died. He settled for a stick of gum. Texted Myers.

"Yeah. Doing okay."

And he was.

ACKNOWLEDGMENTS

First and foremost, thanks to my new editor, Sara Minnich. You couldn't have made the transition any easier and your notes were spot-on. I'm thoroughly indebted to the entire team at G. P. Putnam's Sons for their invaluable support, particularly Ivan Held's steadfast commitment to the series.

My literary superagent, David Hale Smith at InkWell Management, is still on point, cutting fresh trails and kicking down doors for me and the Pearce Systems crew. It doesn't get any better than that. Stay tuned.

One of the joys of writing novels is the opportunity to meet the hardworking bookstore owners, managers, and staff around the country who sell them. I was particularly well cared for by Barbara Peters (The Poisoned Pen, Scottsdale), McKenna Jordan (Murder by the Book, Houston), Bob White (Sundog Books, Seaside), Amy Harper (Barnes & Noble, Lewisville), Michelle Abele (Barnes & Noble, Knoxville), and Gordon Brugman (Books-A-Million, Sevierville). Thanks again to you all—hope to see you soon.

I rely on the keen insight of friends and family on the first drafts of every novel, including this one. My first and best reader is always my remarkable wife, Angela, who apparently missed her calling in the literary world. I am especially grateful this go-around to Robbie D. Scruggs, U.S. Navy Captain (Retired) for our *Drone Command* correspondence and distant friendship. Martin Hironaga, as always, gave me a close and insightful reading. Of course, mistakes in the manuscript, fictional or otherwise, are entirely my own.

I also owe a special debt of gratitude to the amazing Nita Taublib, who first saw the potential in Troy Pearce, Margaret Myers, and a certain unpublished author. Blessings on your head.

Finally, thanks to all of you who support Troy & Co. in print, digital, and audio formats. It's been a privilege to connect with readers and fans through social media. If you haven't already done so, please join us in the conversation on Facebook and Twitter.

TURN THE PAGE FOR AN EXCERPT

Troy Pearce and his team of drone experts are called to action when ISIS launches a series of attacks on U.S. soil. The mastermind proves more elusive and vindictive than any opponent Pearce has faced before . . . and if Pearce fails, the nation will suffer an unimaginable catastrophe on its soil or be forced into war.

ONE

The sun's bloodred halo framed the Christ hanging from his towering crucifix.

Or so it seemed to Ahmed. He cupped his hands around his eyes to get a better look, his spent RPG launcher heavy on one shoulder and his battered AK-47 on the other.

Not a Christ. A Christian, and a Kurd.

It was a *kafir* they had crucified, he reminded himself. His limp body hung from a utility pole on top of the hill, his arms tied at the elbows to the crossbar with baling wire and duct tape. The *kafir* wouldn't submit, wouldn't renounce his infidel faith.

He crucified himself, Ahmed thought. He spat in the dust at his aching feet. The boots he wore were too small, taken from a dead Iraqi weeks ago.

He glanced back up. The blowflies swarmed around the moist tissues of the pastor's mouth and nose, laying their eggs. The orifices were caked with black blood. The eyes would be next, Ahmed knew. He'd seen it before, in the last village. And in the one before. The hatched larvae would begin their grim feast and in a week the pastor's skull would be picked clean. Disgusting. Ahmed spat again.

Brave, this one. Not like the Iraqi soldiers who fled like women when his convoy of pickups arrived in a cloud of dust yesterday, black ISIS flags flapping in the wind, each vehicle crowded with fighters like him. The Iraqis just dropped their gear and ran.

Well, not all of them.

Was it the flags that scared the cowards? Or the head of an Iraqi colonel hanging like a lantern on a pole on the lead truck? The Iraqis were probably Shia. Worse than infidels. Cleansing the Caliphate of all such non-believers was their sacred duty. Only through such cleansing and blood sacrifice would the *Mahdi* come with the prophet Isa and defeat the Antichrist. Had the Caliph not rightly taught that all of the signs are pointing toward the Day of Judgment? And was it not their duty to bring this about, one infidel corpse at a time?

Ahmed turned around. A line of utility poles marched down the long sloping hill. He counted ten more bodies hanging on them, including three children.

The pastor's children. Children of iniquity.

Dirty work, that, Ahmed thought. Glad he wasn't asked to do it. He would have, of course. Allah commands it. And if not, Kamal al-Medina ordered it, and he was more afraid of his commander here on earth than he was of the Exceedingly Merciful on his heavenly throne. He'd never seen Allah behead a screaming *kafir* with a serrated combat knife nor listened to him sing while he did it.

Such zeal. *It is to be admired*, he thought.

A Dodge Ram pickup honked behind him. He turned around as the truck skidded to a halt in the dust. A sharp-faced brother called out from the cab. He was a twenty-five-year-old Tunisian from Marseille. A French national like Ahmed, though Ahmed was a lily-white redhead of Norman stock and only nineteen.

"The commander has called for you," the Tunisian said in French. He threw a thumb at the truck bed. "Hop in."

Ahmed felt his stomach drop and the back of his neck tingle.

"But I'm on guard duty."

"I'll take your place after I drop you off."

"Why does he want me?"

The Tunisian lowered his voice. "Does the Black Prince consult with lowly commoners like us?" He flashed a crooked smile.

The pejorative reference to Kamal al-Medina's royal bloodline would have earned the Tunisian ten lashes with a whip if Ahmed reported the slur. He wouldn't, of course. Ahmed used it, too. They all did. And they all admired Kamal al-Medina as much as they feared him. The Saudi had given up everything—palaces, gold, power—to fight for the Caliphate and the *ummah*.

"No, he doesn't." Ahmed unslung his RPG launcher and rifle and clambered into the back of the Dodge. He slapped the cab roof and the truck whipped around, speeding toward the center of the small village of squat cinder-block houses, well kept and brightly painted in hues of red, blue, and yellow. Most doors were defaced with a spray-painted red Arabic *N. Nasrane*. A slur for Jesus the Nazarene and his followers.

It was also a mark for death.

Their truck sped past still more utility poles with a Christian corpse hanging from each, their sightless, downcast eyes keeping silent vigil over their lost village. The long shadows they cast were quickly fading in the dimming light. It would soon be time for the brothers to wash for evening prayers.

If only these Christians had submitted, Ahmed thought.

Submitted to the will of Allah and signed the *dhimma* contract and paid the *jizya*—perhaps that would have kept them from death. Easier still, they could have just lied to save their lives and fight another day. Was *taqiyya* not permitted in their book as well?

He liked this village. It was neat and well organized and surrounded by fertile fields. A village not much different from the one he came from in Normandy. He wondered how soon before those utility poles back home would be filled with Crusader corpses, too. He hoped he would live long enough to see it and to see even the whole world under the great Caliphate of God.

Inshallah.

The pickup skidded to a stop in front of the church guarded by two jihadis, an almond-eyed Kazakh and a graying Uzbek. Both good fighters, Ahmed knew. And zealous.

Ahmed leaped out of the truck bed and the Dodge sped off. Ahmed stood a moment, unsure of his situation. Had he sinned? The commander's zeal for God knew no bounds. Just last week he punished a brother who kept smoking cigarettes in secret. Sharia forbade it. Smoking was *haram*. "There are no secrets here. God knows all and he will not honor us if we don't keep his law," al-Medina proclaimed before personally delivering the forty lashes to the brother's back with a thick leather whip.

Ahmed weighed his chances against the two guards. There were no bullets in his battered rifle and his RPG had no grenade—not that he could've used either in close-quarters combat. He had his grandfather's old folding knife in his pocket, but that wasn't much of a weapon, either. Both guards were well armed and could kill with their hands. He'd seen it himself. Perhaps he could run, but then they would shoot him in the back like a dog.

The Uzbek nodded a dour greeting and pushed open one of the two front doors and signaled him to follow.

Ahmed hesitated before the open door. He hadn't stood in a Christian church since he was a child—his first communion. The small stone church in his village had long since been abandoned by the last Catholic faithful and converted into a bike shop. Still, he wondered what judgment might be waiting for him inside this holy place after a day of slaughter. The sun had fallen beneath the hills and the long shadows had given way to a general gloom.

"He's waiting for you," the Uzbek said. "Follow me."

Inshallah, Ahmed said to himself again with a shrug. He followed the Uzbek in. The old fighter limped heavily on his left foot into the broad expanse of the sanctuary and down the rows of mostly empty pews. The aisles were littered with chunks of broken plaster, half-melted candles, torn hymnals, and spent cartridges. A few of the brothers were passed out on the long benches, snoring from exhaustion. Three unit subcommanders stood on the raised platform and used a communion table to study a map they had laid upon it. A few dim bulbs in a chandelier overhead threw a sickly yellow light around them. A black ISIS flag hung from the rafters.

Ahmed's eyes drifted to the smashed ceramic Christ crunching beneath their feet, broken into a dozen pieces and tossed like garbage around the floor. This pleased him. A false Christ these *kafir* worship, and an idol at that.

The Uzbek led Ahmed to another door to the side of the sanctuary. He knocked on it. "Enter!" boomed from the other side. Ahmed recognized al-Medina's commanding voice.

The Uzbek nodded curtly to Ahmed, then hobbled away.

Ahmed took a deep breath, then pushed open the door.

Kamal al-Medina sat behind a small wooden desk, and his two senior commanders sat in a worn leather couch against one wall near him. The room was spacious and lined with crowded bookshelves. A small side table was dedicated to framed photographs of the pastor, his wife, and three children. The wife was stunning. This must have been the pastor's office, Ahmed concluded.

"Brother Ahmed!" Al-Medina stood. A wide grin spread beneath his dark, wooly beard. His lieutenants rose as well, also smiling.

Al-Medina came around from behind the desk and wrapped Ahmed in a bear hug. The other two commanders did likewise.

"Emir?" was all Ahmed could muster in his confusion.

Al-Medina laughed and spoke to him in French. "No need for the formalities. We're all brothers here, yes?"

Ahmed nodded, tried to answer him in faltering Arabic. Al-Medina held up a hand.

"I attended a private school in Switzerland, so French is no problem for me. But we can speak English or German if you prefer."

"I like, eh, want the language of the Prophet, peace be upon him," Ahmed insisted in broken Arabic.

"But I prefer to practice my French if you don't mind," al-Medina insisted.

"*Ça va*," Ahmed said.

"Excellent! Can I get you something to drink? Water, coffee?"

"No, sir. I'm fine. How can I be of service?"

Al-Medina clapped him hard on the shoulder. "You already have, my young lion. I heard what you did yesterday." Al-Medina pantomimed holding an RPG on his shoulder and firing it. "You killed those three Iraqis barricaded in the house firing their machine gun. They had the front echelon pinned down with their murderous weapon. But you jumped into the street and put a HEAT round right into their window. BOOM!"

Al-Medina clapped his hands when he said the word and laughed. The others laughed, too.

Al-Medina switched back to Arabic. "You saved many brothers that day. I just wanted to take the time now to properly thank you, and to reward you. Do you understand?"

"Yes, a little," Ahmed said, embarrassed by his poor Arabic skills.

Al-Medina signaled with his hand. "Follow me."

Al-Medina led Ahmed and the other commanders to an adjoining room. Stacks of American rifles, grenade launchers, ammo boxes, and even fresh Iraqi uniforms still in their plastic bags lined the walls.

"Take your pick. All courtesy of the United States government," al-Medina said with another laugh.

"For me? Anything? Truly?" In his excitement, Ahmed fell back into his French. He snatched up a brand-new M-4 carbine still glistening with lubricant.

"Anything you need or want." Al-Medina opened up a box. "Here, brand-new boots if you need them."

"Boots!" Ahmed set his new weapon down and raced over to the box of boots and began sifting through them, looking for his size.

"But there's something more for our young hero," one of the commanders said, chuckling.

"Ah, yes. I almost forgot," al-Medina said through a wide grin.

Ahmed looked up.

"Come, boy. Something better indeed."

The other men laughed.

Al-Medina led the nineteen-year-old to yet another door that opened to a great room. A dozen women sat cowering on the floor, their faces covered by hijabs. But their downcast eyes told all, dazed and red with tears. Some were even blackened.

"Take one."

"Sir?"

Al-Medina shouted an order. The women all jumped to their feet as one, startled by the harshness of his voice. They immediately pulled off their hijabs. Some were younger than Ahmed. Two were blond. Al-Medina saw Ahmed's gaze fall on one particular girl a few years older than he. Her dark blue eyes were wide with terror. She covered her bruised mouth with one trembling hand.

"That one is an American. An aid worker. The trucks are coming first thing in the morning to pick them all up and take them to market. But you can have her until then." He nudged Ahmed. "She's good, I can tell you."

"And it is not *haram*?" Ahmed had been taught that sex outside of marriage was forbidden by the Koran.

"It is *mut'ah*. A temporary marriage for your pleasure," al-Medina assured him. "The imam will bless it."

Ahmed's face flushed crimson, matching his thin beard. He couldn't believe his good fortune. He'd never been with a woman before.

The three older jihadis laughed at the boy's innocence.

"That one, then," Ahmed said, pointing at a dark-eyed beauty in the back, trying to hide her face.

Al-Medina pounded Ahmed's shoulder. "The pastor's wife! Excellent choice."

He prayed to God before he raped her. They all did. So did she.

Not the same prayer.

Not the same God.

The red-haired boy lay next to her, sleeping. He looked more child than man in the light of the single bulb when he first took her. But he was no child. More like a rutting pig. He stank of his own urine and sweat after days in the field. Too eager to care to bathe before the filthy act.

She had wiped herself clean of him with the sheets after he had finished but otherwise didn't move. He passed out soon afterward. She lay in the dark with her eyes fixed on the invisible ceiling, praying for the strength she'd need in the coming hours. She counted his breaths again, deep and long. Satisfied he was fast asleep, she reached for the razor blade she'd hidden in her garment folded neatly on the floor next to the mattress. Everything in her wanted to slit his throat and let him bleed out in his "marriage" bed. But there was too much at stake, and too many other lives hung in the balance. Her husband, she knew, was watching, too. He wouldn't have approved of her killing him even though the boy had raped her in his own bed. Her husband was a true Christian.

Certain the pig was out for the night, she carefully extricated herself from the tangled sheets. She stood slowly, then bent over to fetch her garment.

Suddenly he stirred.

No! She caught her breath. But he just rolled over and fell back into the deep rhythms of exhausted sleep.

She uttered silent thanks and dressed quickly. It was pitch black, but this was her bedroom and she knew every square inch of it, so there was no need to turn the lamp back on. She stepped blindly but carefully toward the small nightstand and reached behind it. Her groping fingers found the hidden cell phone. She listened again for the jihadi's breathing. He was still asleep. She opened the phone. One thirty-five. She panicked. Was there still enough time? The signal showed only one bar and less than 10 percent of charge left on the battery. She prayed it would be enough.

She prayed she wasn't too late.

She texted her message, hit SEND, and prayed again. She touched the blade in her garment, a small comfort. She would use it on herself if tonight failed.

God forgive me.

TWO

Troy Pearce stood in the dark on the gravel mountain road marking the border between southern Turkey and northern Iraq. He reminded himself that not too long ago he was in the East China Sea.

Literally.

President Lane called him a hero for stopping a war with China. But, standing here on the edge of another killing ground, it didn't seem to matter much. He didn't feel like a hero. He was just doing his job. And the cost he paid was high. Too high. He pushed the thought away.

Pearce wore black tactical gear with an olive-drab *shemagh* wrapped around his neck. His dark hair was flecked with silver and his pale blue eyes were tired. He rubbed his beardless face to push away the fatigue.

The tablet in his hand read 03:48:21 in the top right-hand corner but his eyes were fixated on the strand of ghostly white shapes on the black screen meandering steadily in his direction. The lead figure was a burly Kurdish guide and the thirteen others were the women he was helping escape on foot through the moonless night up the steep, grassy hills that lay between them and freedom. The image on his tablet was broadcast from a Heron TP medium-altitude long-endurance (MALE) UAV. It was being piloted remotely via satellite by his number-two man in the company, Ian McTavish.

"Got a visual?" Pearce asked Ian in his comms.

"Not yet. They're still on the other side of that ridge." Tariq Barzani had a pair of night-vision goggles pressed against his worried face. A woolen cap covered his bald head. Pearce noticed that his bushy mustache had grayed considerably since he had last seen him years before, but he looked tough as ever.

"Just five kilometers. They've still got time," Pearce said. "But they need to hurry." He handed Tariq the tablet. The Kurd studied it closely.

Pearce worried about the Turkish border guards. The gendarmerie was heavily gunned and as brutally efficient as the rest of Turkey's armed forces. They patrolled this area regularly with armed vehicles and overhead drone surveillance, but a ten-figure baksheesh placed in the hands of the regional commander bought Pearce a non-negotiable four-hour window. That window would slam shut in just seventy-two minutes. The women were making good time, but if the Turk border patrol suddenly decided to show up early, the whole operation would be blown.

Or worse.

"They know the danger, trust me," Tariq said. His sister's text earlier confirmed their departure from the village, but nothing more. His cousin leading the way confirmed their arrival at the rendezvous point, but for security reasons they all agreed beforehand to maintain communication silence until the group arrived at the border.

Five pickups were parked on the gravel road, a Kurdish driver and gunner in each. Plenty of room for the women and two friendlies who tagged along, Carl Luckett and Steve Rowley. They were ex-Rangers who had served under Mike Early, Pearce's closest friend during the War on Terror, now dead. Early had brought the two of them along on a mission he and Pearce had run a long time ago in Iraq—the same mission where he had first met Tariq, their translator. When Pearce picked up the phone twenty-four hours ago, the only thing he had to say was "Tariq needs us." The Kurdish peshmerga fighter had saved all of their asses and never asked for so much as a thank-you at the time. So when Tariq came hat in hand to Pearce's place and begged for help, Pearce dropped everything and pulled together a plan. They had a very narrow window, and this was the best Pearce could do on short notice. But, all things considered, it was a better play than others he'd made in the past, and he was still vertical and breathing after those. Besides, he hated ISIS, and anything he could do to frustrate them was a good day's work as far as he was concerned.

Pearce checked the screen again. With any luck, they'd be loaded up and rolling out of here with the women in the next forty minutes and be landing in Beirut within three hours at the latest.

God, how he missed Mikey. There was no safer place on the planet than standing next to the big hulking Ranger when the bullets started to fly. He hoped it wouldn't come to that tonight.

Pearce's private Bombardier Global 5000 corporate jet was waiting on the tarmac at an airfield nearby in Cizre. A few more well-placed bribes and a couple of hard-pulled strings generated all the necessary paperwork and travel permits they needed to fly unmolested in and out of Turkish airspace on a supposed business trip. Pearce Systems was an international security company, but much of Pearce's drone-based business was connected to commercial enterprises, so his cover wasn't too much of a stretch, especially with former president Margaret Myers working the phones on his behalf. Fortunately, the military-contracting side of his business was running the Canadian army's Heron TP operations in Afghanistan. With the Heron's range and endurance, it wasn't any trouble to reroute one for tonight's mission, and Ian had become a crack UAV pilot. Pearce couldn't imagine running any kind of mission anymore without eyes in the sky.

Tariq handed him back the tablet. Pearce resized the image.

"Shit!" Pearce tapped his earpiece. "Ian, we've got Deltas coming in hot."

A speeding convoy of trucks was racing toward the women.

"I see them," Ian said. "But—"

"No time to talk!" Pearce shouted at the others. "Saddle up!"

Luckett and Rowley leaped into their pickup as Tariq barked orders in Kurdish. He hardly needed to. Truck engines fired up and machine guns were racked.

"You've got company!" Ian shouted.

Pearce was already in the bed of his truck and pounding the roof to take off when the roaring *whomp-whomp-whomp* of helicopter blades came thundering over the hill behind them. The sound was deafening as two T-70 Black Hawks swept overhead. One hovered directly above them and poured a blinding searchlight on the convoy. Grit and dust from the rotor wash stung Pearce's face. The other chopper dropped thirty yards on the Iraqi side of the border, blocking the way forward with its heavily armed fuselage and another blinding searchlight.

"Stay or go?" Luckett shouted in Pearce's earpiece. Tariq's anxious eyes asked the same thing.

Pearce checked his tablet. The ISIS convoy was less than a mile from the women, who hadn't changed course or speed. They clearly didn't know that they were being hunted. It was now or never but—

The other chopper landed just a few yards behind them, the blades dangerously close. A squad of Turkish special forces leaped to the ground and charged toward them, weapons forward, shouting. Pearce's instinct was to turn the machine gun around and open up but his mind checked his gut—they'd be cut to pieces in a flash.

The Turks surrounded the trucks just as a middle-aged American woman in civilian clothes and a Kevlar vest jogged up. Her name was Hyssop, the embassy trade attachée. The slowing rotor wash fanned her short, thinning hair.

"What the hell is going on, Pearce?" Hyssop demanded. "I didn't authorize any of this!"

"I don't have time to explain. Call your dogs off and let us through—"

"Not going to happen! You're supposed to be on a trade mission, not an armed incursion!"

"We've got lives on the line out there!" Pearce said. "You've got to let us go. Now!"

The Turkish army commander, a captain, shouted orders to his men. They raised their weapons to fire.

"Troy! The women!" Ian's Scottish brogue shouted in Pearce's ear.

Hyssop grabbed Pearce's sleeve. "These guys aren't screwing around. Stand down now and I can still get you out of this—"

A truck engine gunned. Tariq's pickup leaped forward, scattering the two Turkish soldiers standing in front of it. Before the others could open fire, the captain shouted another order and the squad lowered its weapons.

"Tariq!" Pearce screamed.

Pearce watched as Tariq's pickup made a suicidal

charge straight at the other helicopter. The chopper lifted off before the truck reached it but as soon as it passed underneath, the Black Hawk's door gunner opened up with a salvo from its Vulcan machine gun, shredding the Toyota's thin steel and erupting the gas tank in a fiery explosion.

The Turks gathered around Pearce's vehicle howled with laughter.

Pearce shouted as he swung his size-fourteen combat boot. It cracked into the braying face of the soldier standing closest to him with a sickening thud. Pearce leaped down and crashed into the next Turk, driving the surprised trooper into the ground. Pearce lifted a fist to smash the second soldier's face when a pistol exploded just behind his head. Pearce's ears rang with the shot as red-hot ice picks stabbed his eardrums.

Pearce's fist froze in midair. He turned around. The captain's pistol was six inches from his face.

"Pearce, you asshole!" Hyssop sped over to him, throwing herself between him and the captain as she hauled Pearce up to his feet.

The Turkish soldiers manhandled the Kurds, seizing their weapons and cuffing them with PlastiCuffs. Two more soldiers dragged Luckett and Rowley out of their truck and hauled them roughly over to Pearce.

"You are in violation of Turkish law and Turkish national sovereignty. I have every legal right to execute the three of you right here as foreign invaders," the captain said. He glanced with disgust at his two fallen men, one still clutching his broken jaw and moaning through bloody fingers. "And for assaulting my men."

"Give me ten more minutes and I'll finish the job," Pearce said.

The captain held out a gloved hand. "Your comms."

"I'm sorry, I can't hear a word you're saying—"

The captain's face hardened as he raised his pistol again.

"Idiot!" Hyssop snatched the earpiece out Pearce's ear and tossed it to the captain. He pocketed it, then pulled out a pair of PlastiCuffs.

"Just try," Pearce said.

"Pearce, it's not just your ass on the line. You're about to make this into an international incident. There's a lot more in the wind than you're aware of here."

"Those shit bags just killed my friend—"

She got in his face. "And a lot more people will die if you don't shut this down right now."

Pearce glanced at Luckett and Rowley. The Turks were cuffing them behind their backs. But the ex-Rangers were still dangerous men, even tied up.

Luckett read Pearce's mind. He grinned.

"You call it, boss. We're with you all the way."

It would be a stupid move, Pearce decided. Gotta get back to the plane. He held out his wrists. The captain zipped the cuffs tight, then yanked the tablet out of Pearce's pants pocket and the pistol out of its holster.

"Let's get out of here. Now," Hyssop said, pulling him toward the first chopper.

"What about them?" Pearce nodded in the direction of the Kurds already being marched toward the other chopper.

"That's none of your affair," the captain said. He barked an order to the sergeant standing nearby who signaled two others. The three armed Turks prodded the four Americans back toward the first helicopter.

A minute later, Pearce, Hyssop, Luckett, and Rowley were airborne. Pearce watched the Kurds get thrown into the other Black Hawk, their hands bound behind their backs. Pearce knew the bloody history between the genocidal Turks and the hapless Kurds. He assumed the Turks would toss them out of the chopper like sacks of garbage as soon as they reached altitude.

Maybe the four of them, too.

As they pulled away, Pearce's eyes fixed on Tariq's truck down below, still burning in the dark. He swore.

Jesus, what a goat fuck.

As soon as they were airborne, the Turk captain opened up Pearce's tablet. He pressed buttons until an image pulled up. He stared at it. A feral grin spread beneath across his face in the red cabin light. He turned the tablet around and held it close to Pearce's face.

Pearce's heart sank. The ISIS trucks and men were on the women like a pack of wolves. But instead of rounding them up, they were killing them. A half dozen bodies already lay scattered on the ground as the rest fell in a dead run, one by one.

The captain's grin grew wider.

Pearce grunted with rage and launched at the captain, aiming his skull at the Turk's jaw. But the captain saw it coming and clocked Pearce across his ear with the butt of his pistol and Pearce crumbled to the steel floor, knocked out cold.